THE
SUPERYOGI
SCENARIO

THE
SUPERYOGI
SCENARIO

JAMES CONNOR

SKY GROVE

Sky Grove
www.skygrove.com

Eighteen verses from *The Yoga Sutra* are reprinted by permission of Geshe Michael Roach © The Yoga Studies Institute, 2004.

FIRST EDITION

Printed in the U.S.A., 2015

Cover artwork and character illustrations by Jeff Chapman

ISBN 978-0-9861469-0-9

For all yogis—
May the powers you develop
From asana and meditation
Bring happiness to countless worlds.

जन्मौषधिमन्त्रतपःसमाधिजाः सिद्धयः ॥ १ ॥

janmaushadhi mantra tapah samadhija siddhayah

POWERS CAN BE ATTAINED EITHER AT BIRTH,
THROUGH HERBS, SPELLS, EXTREME PRACTICES,
OR THROUGH DEEP MEDITATION.

CHAPTER IV, VERSE 1:
THE YOGA SUTRA OF MASTER PATANJALI,
WRITTEN APPROXIMATELY 200 A.D.

FACT: Instructions for developing superpowers such as flying, invisibility, reading minds, changing size, and walking on water are contained in ancient Buddhist and yoga texts. For example, 11% of the verses in Master Patanjali's *The Yoga Sutra* explicitly cover the development of yogic supernormal abilities.

FACT: Written accounts exist of historic lineage holders displaying supernormal abilities to thousands of witnesses. These masters include the eighty *Mahasiddhas*; Milarepa, the most famous yogi of Tibet; and Master Shantideva, the author of the renowned Buddhist work *The Guide to the Bodhisattva's Way of Life*.

FACT: In the last few decades, for the first time in history, many of the ancient texts written by miracle-wielding masters—texts locked within the walls of monasteries and ashrams for over a thousand years—have been translated into English, Spanish, and other European languages for dissemination around the world.

FACT: All the scriptural quotes in this book are accurate and have been checked against several scholarly sources.

FACT: Over twenty million people in America practice yoga, an increase of 29% in the past four years. Many millions more practice throughout the world.

FACT: Historically, when yogic superpowers develop, they have been utilized for good and destructive purposes.

1. THE SECRET WEAPON

Tina Tinsdale was a weapon that no one expected.

Her lithe yogi's body gave a hidden thrill to the bored TSA officer operating a full-body scanner—but she didn't care. Men and women often stared at her. Besides, she carried nothing more threatening than a yoga mat.

At the gate, waiting for her flight to be called, she amused gawkers by doing yoga *asana*. Like a trained acrobat, she moved through sequences more likely found in a circus than a typical yoga class. In rhythm with her inhale, Tina leapt from Downward Dog directly into Crow, or *bakasana* as she would say in Sanskrit. She balanced perfectly on her hands while keeping her knees close to her ears. Kicking out into Plank Pose, she steeled her mind for all she would do in the coming hours.

On the plane, Tina found her cramped seat near the center, just behind the wings. When the seatbelt light finally dimmed at cruising altitude, she fetched her backpack from a beige overhead bin and then disappeared into a tiny bathroom. Quickly, in a feat that required more pretzel-like contortions, she changed out of her yoga clothes into another skin-tight outfit: this time, a white latex- and neoprene-based bodysuit with a shadowy black S-curve running down one side. She zipped it low enough to flaunt her enticing cleavage. Calf-high boots and long fingerless gloves completed the outrageous outfit.

Tina activated her global positioning locator before strapping the watch-like device to her wrist.

I have time, but not much.

Sauntering down the airplane's blue-carpeted aisle, she looked like a punk-style Goth-chic who just stepped off a ski lift on a planet where couture came out of comic books. Men leaned into the aisle to follow her long legs and sexy boots. Atlanta-based stewardesses rolled their eyes at her strange fashion statement. But they were flying to New York, after all.

"I get cold on planes," Tina Tinsdale said, sitting down. This time, she left her seatbelt unbuckled. The portly man in the next seat tried to hide his copy of *Winning at Checkers*. She hoped he wouldn't try to talk to her as she needed time to concentrate. Closing her eyes, she focused inside.

I have to make them feel fear. They won't stop hurting others until they understand how it feels. Convoys of military machinery invaded her mind. Images of civilian lives that had been lost across the world in wars on terror flashed like fireworks—and then she saw the bombing that had taken the person she loved most.

Her heart clenched. If she could hold her heart like a hammer, she could shatter marble.

Tina pictured the atoms of her body becoming heavier and heavier… the mass, more and more dense. *I'm as heavy*

as a building. I'm as sharp as a giant drill bit. I'm Physique. The
physical laws of the universe no longer apply to me.

Due to her remarkable powers of concentration, Tina felt her mind shift. The peaceful woman she had been for so long vanished like gauzy cotton consumed by fire. She became her alter ego, Physique. Now her body would obey her command.

When her eyes popped wide-open, her hair changed from sandy blond to brunette. She watched her unpainted fingernails change from pink to coal black. Even her naturally hazel eyes turned a tarry-pitch as density changes moved down her body.

Already, plane seats in her row started to quake. She hadn't done anything of this magnitude before, but she believed she could. She squeezed the silver armrests of her seat, feeling the density of her body increasing.

Metal legs on her chair compacted before collapsing, spilling her and her seat into the aisle. Nearby passengers gasped in shock, clutching magazines or each other, as they leaned away from the spectacle. Her heavy neighbor's eyes bulged like a pond frog's first encounter with the ocean.

In the next moment, as if in a seizure, the whole plane trembled. The floor below her canyoned. Then the aisle literally gave way, splitting—swallowing the now raven-haired woman in a bizarre body suit.

Physique and her chair clanged hard in the underbelly of the plane, denting the outer hull. She heard screams from passengers above.

As the tail of the plane sagged, her stomach felt the plane dropping in altitude. She could hear the engines revving to counteract what pilots must have believed was a heavy downdraft. But this plane would rebel as if it were suddenly made of stone.

Now in cargo, Physique punched the sides with her bare fists, hating the awful flying bombing machines that took her love's life. Sound clanged louder than a blacksmith's hammer. Her flurries scored perforations in the dense wall as if it were made of cardboard. When she smashed through some wire bundles, systems failed, including the plane's flight controls.

Finally, one mighty blow pierced the plane's hull. As the aircraft lost pressure, oxygen masks dropped to terrified passengers. Sucked toward the hole, everything in cargo shifted. But not Physique: she felt heavy as a glacier and icy in her revenge.

When enough suitcases blocked the hull rupture, pressure stabilized.

Physique's work was almost done.

Now Physique visualized her body as light as an eagle. Cascading from the crown of her head like an avalanche over a dark ravine, her hair turned snowy white. Her eyes turned to pearl and her fingernails looked like bone. Pushing off the cargo belly floor, she floated toward the ceiling, raising her arms and knees like wings of an agitated swan.

But suddenly her nails, eyes, and hair went boot black. Physique straightened her athletic body into the shape of a dagger, stretching her arms to the hilt. She plunged down with more force than she had ever wielded. Striking near her perforated hammerings, she pierced the plane. Passing through like a bullet, her outstretched arms tore away a section of hull.

Plummeting, Physique reversed her mass. Wind pressed against her now feathery-light body till she floated gently on thermals.

Above her, she watched the plane's badly damaged tail section tremble before ripping away. The guillotined sections—and all aboard—plunged mercilessly into the ocean below.

But heart hardened by revenge, Physique felt nothing.

In her costume, she vaguely resembled a white seagull with black tipped wings gliding on winds, searching for safe haven. She checked the homing signal on her wrist.

As planned, Physique spotted a cruising yacht moving her way. The mid-sized ship with a broad back deck looked as if it might be headed toward the plane crash to search for improbable survivors, but Physique knew differently. To manage her descent, she continued to adjust her weight.

Physique landed smoothly on the stern with the grace of a ballerina. She felt proud of what she had done. *That will make them shake.*

Returning to her normal weight brought back her sandy hair and hazel eyes. She wasn't particular about her hair color these days: her natural look just took less concentration. And after performing this thunderous strike, Physique needed to rest.

A blind man emerged from the galley to meet her, tapping a dragon-headed silver cane across the deck. He wore a dark bodysuit, made of fabric similar to Physique's, under a long black coat that flapped in the ocean breeze like a fluttering sail. His dark hair matched the briefcase he carried.

Physique scuffed her boots across the deck to let him know she was close. She saw his nostrils flare at the scent of her adrenaline-soaked sweat.

"The money is compliments of our mutual friend," said the blind man.

Crouching down on the boat deck, she popped open the case. Coldly, she viewed thick stacks of hundred dollar bills, guessing there must be more than $200,000. "Tell your boss, I didn't do it for the money." Still, she took it. "But you can thank him for his boat."

"It's not his yacht," the man replied. "He doesn't work that way. He calls in favors."

Physique re-secured the briefcase and then avoided staring at the blind man's milky eyes. She wasn't much for small talk, but fortunately, neither was he. Tapping his cane, the man asked, "Where to?"

Without hesitation Physique answered, "Take me to Washington, D.C."

2. AN UNUSUAL MEETING

PRESENTING HIS FBI BADGE AT A CAST IRON GATE, Special Agent Kevin Kirby hoped he wouldn't regret his next words. Through the open window of his car, he said to a sun-glassed Secret Service man: "I believe I've been invited to a meeting with the vice president—but there may have been a mistake."

The dark-suited guard showed no emotion. Instead, he took Kirby's badge as another agent with a wanding mirror checked the bottom of his car for explosives.

In his mind, Agent Kirby replayed the unexpected call that brought him to this gate. A woman had identified herself as an aide to the vice president. She had given him this private address for an urgent meeting. Still, Kirby had reason to believe the call was a hoax—and not just because people liked to poke fun at him.

Not long ago, Agent Kirby had been an admired wunderkind credited with cracking insights in tough cases. But his status had taken a nosedive. If only he hadn't blundered with his last two high-profile assignments.

Wherever he walked at the bureau, everyone knew the reasons for his demotion. Despite his considerable intellect, he'd made no progress leading an expensive investigation involving two missing yogis—a case so bizarre, it had media and career criminologists drooling.

True, to save face, the bureau had skillfully exited Kirby from center stage. But in his reassignment to a counter-terrorism think tank, Kirby further sank his career with a fantastical report entitled *Dangerous Yogis*. The report had been perceived as so spectacularly comical that he'd become the bureau's geeky poster child for career suicide. Like a scandal-prone pop celebrity, Kirby had gone from rising star to public embarrassment.

Now banished to the lowest rung of Bureau investigations, Agent Kirby searched for fraud in college loans—something the government cared even less about than getting to the bottom of the last mortgage crisis.

So with all of Kirby's misfortune of late, he assumed that the invitation to the vice president's residence in Fairfield County, Virginia—for an urgent private meeting—was a joke by another equally bored desk jockey.

But apparently, he was wrong.

When the Secret Service agent returned his badge, the gate opened. A surprised Kirby traveled the long driveway, suddenly uncomfortable that his best JC Penney suit wasn't good enough for such a prestigious meeting.

Two dusky brown horses galloped in the long stretches of sloping, manicured lawn. It was like stepping back into the era of gentleman farmers. Nervous, Kirby pulled a Listerine breath tab from the glove compartment and dropped it on his tongue.

Kirby could barely believe he was about to meet with the vice president. He hadn't shaken an important person's hand in some time. Instead, he'd been desk-bound in a gray sea of cubicles, toiling under the glare of a full spectrum lamp—the type prescribed by doctors for seasonal affective disorder. Next to his desk lamp, a framed postcard of a giant Maui wave collected dust. Kirby had never surfed or been to Maui; he just didn't have family or romantic vacations of his own to remember.

The only positive Kirby imagined might come from his now boring nine-to-five pathetic excuse for a career was that he'd finally have time for romance. But even his love life issued perennial demotions and constant slaps to his face. A female colleague attempting to set up Kevin on a date had described his looks as: "Harry Potter grows up to be an accountant, gets contacts, and carries a gun." Apparently that description wasn't enticing enough, even with the well-meaning friend's addendum: "He's really sweet." At thirty-one years old, he was still perpetually single and, worse, getting most of his thrills from playing online strategy games like *Civilization*. He simply couldn't imagine why the vice president would want to see him.

Inside a dome-ceiling foyer, a relaxed contingent of the Secret Service greeted Agent Kirby. More Will Smith than Tommy Lee Jones, the Men in Black wanded and patted him down while discussing fantasy football. Though regulation, Kirby had stopped carrying his gun. No one at the bureau even seemed to care—further sign that he had been effectively neutered.

Kirby was shown into the vice president's grand office and told to wait. To calm his nerves, Kirby studied a collector's item on the wall: an old hand-drawn map of the United States. A thin red line traced a route from St. Louis, up the Missouri river, across the Rocky Mountains, and all the way to the Pacific.

Unexpectedly, the lanky vice president entered the room alone before the appointed time. Vice President Alan Lausunu had strawberry blond hair a little longer than you might expect for a politician. He wasn't the youngest VP ever or the most ambitious; instead, both parties respected this man's ability to soothe giant egos and end political stalemates.

As the vice president joined Kirby in front of the map, he said, "It shows the route that Lewis and Clark traveled to explore the land west of the Mississippi."

"The Louisiana Purchase, 1803," Kirby added. At least he had some American history chops.

"It was more than just a land purchase," the vice president responded. "Someone had to venture into unknown territory, to tell others about that untapped potential."

Kirby's investigative ears perked to the pattern in the vice president's words. *Unknown* and *unchartered territory....* Suddenly, he felt prickly under his navy blue suit.

"Thank you for coming on such short notice." Like many politicians skilled in communicating warmth and trust, Lausunu shook with both hands. "Please, have a seat." The vice president gestured to an ornate, antique chair in the style of Louis XIV.

Lausunu sat across from Kirby with crossed legs, leaning back comfortably. Massaging his chin, Lausunu measured Kirby like a scout observing an odd baseball prospect. Turning away from the vice president's intense gaze, Kirby scanned the room.

In a corner, worn yoga mats leaned in a woven basket.

The vice president followed Kirby's eyes. "I used to jog, but it's too hard on the knees. Do you do yoga?"

Kirby had endured enough yoga jokes since writing his *Dangerous Yogis* report. Thinking it best to avoid the subject altogether, he responded with a brief shake of the head that said, *no*. To change the subject quickly, Kirby decided to test the agenda. "You wanted to see me?"

The vice president cleared his throat. "Yes, about that report you wrote on dangerous yogis. Tell me about it."

The heat in Kirby's face suddenly rose. Still, he answered with surprising candor. "I'm not sorry I wrote it. I know everybody thinks it's silly, but that was the exercise: to think of threats we're not thinking of—before they happen." Kirby leaned forward, resting his elbows on his knees. "I was assigned to a think tank for several weeks to write a report outlining an unforeseen threat. Dangerous yogis are an unforeseen threat I know a little about, but I didn't think it would cost me my career."

"Why do you think your career is over?"

"I don't get invited to meetings any more. They call me 'Agent Could Be' or 'the guy that wrote a comic book report.' They moved my cubicle. Take your pick."

Vice President Lausunu listened closely. Then with a twinkle in his eye—as if he were giving an orphaned child a present—he said, "Then I'm sure you wouldn't be missed if the president and I had you work on a special project."

Just the words "special project"—the prospect of being back in the game—kicked Kirby's adrenalin into gear. "No, Mr. Vice President, I wouldn't be missed," Kirby blurted, perhaps a bit too eagerly.

After strolling to his stately mahogany desk, the vice president pressed the button to speak to his assistant: "We're ready for the briefing. You can send Sujata in with

Agent Rollins."

Sensing the game was starting *now*, Kirby tugged on his suit jacket to make it straight, and then wiped his hands on his legs when the vice president wasn't looking. More handshakes were coming—handshakes with important people.

"This is a joint operation of highest priority," said Vice President Lausunu. "Top Secret. We're partnering you with a senior operative from the CIA for international work— and in case things get messy."

When the door to the study opened, Kirby spied his new partner. He felt as if the vice president just slid an ice-cube down the back of his shirt.

Casually the vice president made introductions. "This is your new partner, Agent Marcus Rollins from the CIA. He can share his credentials as he sees fit. Most of them, to be frank, I don't even want to know."

Agent Rollins was a tall wiry man—six-one to Kirby's five-eight—with skin as black as midnight. The first thing Kirby noticed about him was the jagged scar across his left cheek, likely from a knife wound. Instead of shaking Agent Kirby's hand, Agent Rollins simply nodded without showing any trace of emotion.

Walking behind Rollins, Agent Kirby already recognized Sujata Bansal, the beautiful and brainy assistant to the president for national security affairs. From within the executive office of the president, she advised on domestic, foreign, and military policies related to national security. Lausunu said, "When you need anything or want to reach me, communicate through Sujata."

Agent Kirby recalled two interesting facts about Sujata Bansal that she repeatedly downplayed in the press in an effort to appear more accessible. A genius in math, Sujata entered university at fifteen. After deciding international politics "offered more interesting equations," she switched majors.

Dressed like a polished politician, Sujata wore a cream-colored office suit and modest pearl necklace. But her lustrous hair and glamorous smile gave her the appeal of a Bollywood star. Agent Kirby instantly found her attractive, but there were too many reasons to count why this woman was out of his league.

"Nice to meet you, Agent Kirby," Sujata said. "I confess I found your *Dangerous Yogis* report outlandish until this video showed up." She held a silver flash drive. "It was mailed to the White House, both democratic and republican party whips, and the chairman of defense appropriations before the crash of Flight 1632. As you watch this, I want you to be aware that what our suspect claims is consistent with the evidence from the plane wreckage and black box readings." Sujata studied Vice President Lausunu's face before speaking further. "As implausible as the woman in the video sounds, we have no other explanation for the downing."

Agent Kirby understood he was about to see something that only a select few had been shown. But he didn't understand why. He knew nothing more about the crash of Flight 1632 than what could be picked up by overhearing conversations in the bureau's cafeteria or by watching dramatic reports on CNN. The little he had deduced was that no one felt comfortable with the preliminary FAA report; instead, its release, by all involved, seemed to have been actively delayed.

Kirby leaned forward and placed his elbows on his knees.

Sujata opened a wooden cabinet to reveal a flat panel

LCD. On the video screen, Agent Kirby saw a Barbie-like blond woman, probably in her late twenties, standing in the bed of a large red Ford truck—an expensive F-250, the kind you could put a dune buggy into and still have room for motorcycles. The new truck was parked in what appeared to be a junkyard.

But that wasn't the unusual part. The truck's tailgate was down, giving a full view of this woman—wearing what could best be described as a superhero costume. White and skin-tight, with a black stripe in the shape of an S-curve running down the left side, it must have been custom made for her body. The outfit's sophistication suggested design by someone who understood high-performance fabrics and had little concern for budget.

Vinyl boots covered her calves and long fingerless gloves shielded her forearms. But the signature piece was what's known in comic books as a "domino mask": two diamond shapes hid her cheek bones and forehead, while holes allowed her eyes to peek through, like dots on a domino. Mirroring the shadow curve on the suit, one side of the mask was white and the other, black.

"By the time you get this video," she declared in a strong brassy voice, "I will have brought down Flight 1632 en route from Miami to New York. I've done this because you're making the whole world afraid. You've been bullying the world and ignoring good people who've tried every civilized method to get you to listen. I'm going to stop you, by making you understand how bad it feels."

She pointed at the camera as she said this. Her left hand rested on her jutted-out hip like a demanding diva.

"My demands are simple. America is practically spending more money on military than the rest of the world combined. This must end. You have till the end of the month. If you cut military spending in half, I'll stop. If you stand down, I'll stand down. Otherwise, I'm coming next for the congressmen and senators who keep overfeeding the war machine.

"You may believe that you're the only superpower—that you can do whatever you want—but I can bring the weight of a mountain down on anyone I choose.

"You will wonder how Flight 1632 was brought down and if this video is for real. I'm going to FedEx this video before I bring down that plane. I'll mail a second copy from the Congressional Post Office, a few days after the crash. Why? Because I want you to know I'm still alive and I can get to you at any time.

"Who am I? You can call me Physique. The physical laws of the universe no longer apply to me; I can do amazing things with my body. To show you, think of this truck as a plane or a building. Right now I'm in a junkyard outside of Macon called Pearl's."

In the next moment, her blond hair became white as she floated off the truck bed, defying gravity. When her hair turned dark—no, more than just her hair; her nails, and her eyes too—she came crashing down, buckling the truck bed like a beer can. Tires exploded instantly. She was a giant trash compactor grinding the vehicle into a twisted pancake.

When she leapt off the crushed truck, she *flew* through the air toward the camera. The presumed tripod trembled on impact as if hit by a small earthquake. Next, her hands—nails normal color again—held up a FedEx envelope. A finger pointed to the tracking number on the air bill. Then the screen went black.

The video chilled the room to frozen silence. Kirby deduced that the tracking number must have confirmed that the video was sent *before* the plane's demise—or he wouldn't have been invited here. The hairs on his arm stood like a spooked deer. Even if the video was an elaborate special effects hoax, this costumed woman Physique knew Flight 1632 was going down. But if her powers were for real, then she was virtually undetectable. If she could take a plane down in this manner, the damage she could do elsewhere was incalculable.

Vice President Lausunu broke the silence. "No one else knows about this, other than the few people who got the package. We think it's in the country's best interests to keep this bottled up until we can get a handle on it."

"Not even other congressmen or senators?" Kirby asked.

"They're a tough bunch. They understand the risks of public office. None of them would be pushed around by an act of terror anyway." The corners of Lausunu's mouth tensed.

Lausunu knew that Physique's calculations were close to right. Even the Pentagon's own data showed the U.S. outspending the top nine countries in the world combined. And when you added up the numbers for the past decade… well, it was pretty close. But this was an issue for the nation to debate and decide—not Physique.

"What do you want us to do?" Agent Kirby asked, motioning to the still silent Agent Rollins.

"Two things." The vice president leaned forward in his chair, clasping his hands. "Find her, before she hurts anyone else. And assemble our own team of *siddhas*." *Siddhas*, noted Kirby: the Sanskrit word for people with superpowers, contained within so many ancient yogic and Buddhist texts. Not only did the ancient texts describe a range of abilities like flying, reading minds, and walking through walls, they described the methods for how advanced practitioners could attain them.

Vice President Lausunu added, "If this is the new world we're operating in, and there are more supernatural threats on the horizon, I want you to find our own superpowered team to stop them."

Agent Kirby wasn't sure he'd heard correctly. "You want me to put together a team of superyogis? You're taking my report and this costumed-threat seriously?"

"I do," answered the VP. "Because you do." All of Kirby's "Agent Could Be" defensiveness melted away. Lausunu was the first to take his theories seriously.

"I'll give you the resources to find out if you're right," the vice president said. "Again, if there are bad yogis out there, the president and I want our own team of good yogis to take them down."

As Lausunu rose, everyone stood. Shaking Kirby's hand one more time, he said, "Your mission into uncharted territory starts now." He delivered a "go get 'em" slap to Kirby's shoulder.

Sujata Bansal showed out Agent Kirby and Agent Rollins while giving them airstrip information. She explained that she'd chartered a private plane to take them to the site of Physique's video in Georgia. Somehow, Kirby managed to stay cool when Sujata gave him her secure phone number. Although this was professional, no woman so attractive had ever given Kirby her private number.

Agent Kirby had often assumed a secret branch of the government dealt with the really weird stuff. He just never thought it would be him. Hoping his new partner had more insight into this strange world, he turned to Rollins when they got to the car. "What did you think of what just happened in there?"

Agent Rollins' answer told Kirby that only the vice president believed in him. "In my experience, there are two ways to advance in the CIA. Do something important, or get assigned to something so stupid that the powers-that-be have to promote you to keep you quiet. I'm finally covered on both fronts. They'll need to make me assistant deputy director after a year of this charade."

However, Rollins had yet to see the boot prints near the smashed truck.

3. PEARL'S JUNKYARD

DUE TO PHYSIQUE'S BRAZEN MESSAGE, IT DIDN'T TAKE Agent Kirby and a team of local field agents long to locate Pearl's junkyard outside of Macon, Georgia—or the red truck that resembled a squashed beer can. It was exactly as the video depicted. The two main foot indentations that crushed the truck stared back at Kirby like ghost eyes.

Keeping his own suspicions about the supernatural in check, Kirby investigated the site methodically. The scent of burnt rubber and rust seared his nostrils. He ordered every forensic test imaginable. Kirby didn't have to fill out requisition forms for as little as a stapler now.

That night, Kirby barely slept in a nearby cheap motel with thin walls. He wasn't bold enough to ask Rollins to turn down his blaring TV—especially after Rollins had refused earlier to talk over ribs and biscuits. "I'm trying to eat here," Rollins had said to shut him up. Kirby was, admittedly, over-stimulated from finally being out in the field again.

The next day, the un-dynamic duo returned to the sprawling junkyard. Ever the stickler for detail, Kirby circumambulated the crushed vehicle for a full thirty minutes. Nothing could be overlooked.

Kirby didn't think it possible, but Agent Rollins seemed even more moody than he'd been the previous day.

While Rollins hung back a few feet, cracking and eating pistachio nuts, Agent Cecil—the man heading the local investigation—briefed Kirby about their latest findings. "We've been over the truck again, just like you asked." Agent Cecil spoke with a slow, southern drawl. A heavyset man, he looked like he played lineman in high school football. (Though Kirby wouldn't admit it to anyone now, he played trombone in his high school marching band.) Cecil continued, "We even brought in two Hollywood effects people to look at it as you suggested. The vehicle shows no signs of pneumatics or even metal-on-metal compression. Nope, it wasn't smashed by machine or mechanical device."

"Did you find out who the vehicle belongs to?" Kirby asked.

"A respectable insurance executive. He reported it stolen. He'd left the keys tucked in the sun visor at his country club while he played a round of golf. Surprised folks it was stolen from in front of the club. Faraday's very exclusive, you know. But no one seems to have seen anything. We've been over the vehicle for prints again, but it's clean."

"So our suspect just walked into a country club lot and picked that truck? Is that what we're supposed to believe?" Agent Kirby felt twitchy, his investigative senses... tingly. "I want you and your team to scrub everything about that man's personal life. Find anything that could link him to our suspect. Does he do yoga?"

"Yoga?" Cecil looked confused. "He's a golfer. He really didn't look like the yoga type."

Finally back in the game after having been publicly spanked and grounded, Kirby felt pressure to move the case forward. "Then go through his financials; see if there have been any unusual transactions lately. This may be a random theft. But if it isn't, he's our best lead."

Agent Cecil sighed. Kirby wasn't the kind of man that other men liked taking orders from. Already, Cecil and his team had jumped through many hoops for this strange investigation; further, Cecil didn't like being pushed around by this younger northern hotshot. Particularly when Kirby had shared so little as to why one smashed truck was so damned important. To Cecil, Kirby appeared to be an over-ambitious Ivy League kid who had more authority than he deserved.

Ignoring Cecil's reluctance, Kirby continued pressing: "Did anyone in the nearby towns see her?"

Cecil smirked. "My men felt a little silly running all over Macon asking people if they'd seen someone resembling the person in the superhero shot we showed them." Indeed, some townspeople thought it was a street promotion effort for a new superhero movie—or that they were on the reboot of *Candid Camera*. "But there were several sightings of someone who could have been her, dressed in gym clothes… or I guess those are yoga clothes. Apparently, she's quite the looker. People thought she was a beauty queen or model or something. She wasn't seen with anyone, but she did make a fuss at a local diner that there was no vegan food on the menu."

Kirby caught Rollins, still at a distance, chucking pistachio shells on the ground, mucking up his crime scene.

Did Rollins prefer to get his information by eavesdropping?

"Anything else? Anything more promising?" Kirby asked Cecil. He felt the weight of Physique's threat on his shoulders—and felt annoyed that his partner appeared indifferent.

Cecil was prepared. "We know what motel she stayed at. She paid cash and made no phone calls from her room. The ID she registered with turned out to be a fake."

Kirby's intuition burned. *We need to catch her soon.*

"What did the boot prints show?" Kirby asked, stretching his trombone muscles to point at a set of prints in the clayey ground. Small posts and string surrounded the prints—like an archeological dig site—to keep agents like Rollins from trampling the evidence.

Agent Cecil shuffled his feet. "Those are mysterious too. They're a size nine boot with a sole exclusive to Steve Madden. They seem to match the boots she's wearing in the video-still you gave us. We might be able to track Internet sales of size nine black vinyl Steve Madden boots, but store sales…. Afraid that dawg won't hunt."

Cecil looked away. Kirby sensed Agent Cecil was holding something back. "What's the mysterious part, Agent Cecil?"

Cecil shook his head. "From the video-still and the size of the truck, our computer modeling puts her around 5'9" and 135 pounds. We checked with two soil experts, but the impact weight of the boot prints don't make sense. They're not even consistent."

Throwing up his hands, Cecil said, "Maybe it's better to show you." They walked to the boot prints a firehouse ladder's length from the smashed truck. Rollins didn't follow the two men, but stayed within earshot.

Agent Kirby already knew the boot prints were in the

same direction as Physique's leap off the truck. But Kirby had held the video back from the other agents—and in fact, he had only given them the most innocuous frame—to prevent leaks in such a sensational case. No one in the higher echelons of government wanted the public to know that the crash of Flight 1632 might have been an act of terrorism… especially one committed by someone with supernormal powers.

The first set of boot prints looked more like an impact crater than footsteps. As Agent Cecil pointed to them, he said, "The soil guys tell me those first prints could only be made by dropping 'bout ten thousand pounds. Then each step gets lighter. Next, they are down to 'bout two thousand pounds. Then six hundred. Last, all the way down to something closer to the 135 pounds we would expect. We just don't have an explanation for what we're looking at. Other than scrub the owner of the truck more thoroughly, I'm afraid there's not much more me or my team can do for you."

"It's important we find her soon," said Agent Kirby. The thought repeated in his mind.

CIA Agent Rollins had already returned to the car and started the engine, signaling in his own passive-aggressive way for Agent Kirby to hurry.

The leather seat burned Kirby's skin. Even before the car door completely closed, the wheels were spitting junkyard clay. "If I may say," Kirby said, "you don't seem much for investigating."

"You're really buying into this superpowered villain thing, aren't you?" Rollins said, speeding on.

The inexplicably-crushed truck and weight-varying boot prints impressed Kirby. "I'm just collecting the facts right now." Irritated, stressed, and sleep deprived, Kirby confronted Rollins—at least in a mild way. "What's really bothering you?"

"I'll show you," answered Rollins. After the black Ford Taurus exited the junkyard, Rollins pulled over abruptly. "Get out."

"Why?"

"Get out!" Rollins yelled, waving his hands in the air. This was the most energy he'd shown in the two days they'd been stuck together.

Kirby stepped out of the car annoyed. He looked around, but saw only Georgia red clay and pine trees.

"Start walking," Rollins barked through his open window.

Scowling, Agent Kirby reluctantly followed his partner's instruction. Kirby could hear the car slowly idling behind him like a turtle meandering down a tar road.

After about forty feet of walking and still seeing nothing, Kirby shrugged.

"Keep walking!" Rollins yelled, clearly enjoying being in command.

Kirby trekked on with Rollins following behind in the cool, air-conditioned car. The Georgia heat was as wet as a gym sauna. Wavy heat lines rose from the asphalt. Tar tainted the air. Mosquitoes buzzed toward him from the pine forest. Kirby thought, *It could be hours back to town, and more difficult if you were carrying a camera and a tripod....*

Kirby turned back. Rollins stopped the car and got out. Agent Kirby said, "She may have driven that red truck in, but someone else drove her out. That's what you wanted me to see."

"Yeah. But it's more than that," Rollins answered. "In

my experience, when someone films a terrorist threat, someone else is holding the camera. And if she did take that plane out, then who fished her out of the water? And how did they find her?" Agent Rollins eyes flashed with anger. "Then there's the phony ID that slipped past TSA computers. This is bigger than one girl with a political agenda. She's getting help from some serious players with resources and reach."

Agent Kirby returned to his seat. When the doors closed, Kirby said, "It's good to know I'm not the only paranoid conspiracy nut." Agent Rollins finally laughed. It was the first time the two men had genuinely connected.

Kirby wiped sweat from his brow. "You could have told me all that without making me walk."

"No, you're like me. You need to see things for yourself." Kirby took this as an unexpected compliment.

Kirby took out his phone. "I've seen enough to know she's dangerous and not some sort of diversion. We need to go through the airport video again. I'm guessing she didn't get on the plane in that outfit." After staring out the window imagining their next moves, he added, "If we're going to go public with a wider search, it's probably best to show her in something less ostentatious than her Physique costume."

But before he could dial, Kirby's phone rang, playing the *James Bond* theme. In the presence of Rollins, he immediately regretted his ringtone. "Agent Kirby," he answered in a lower voice than usual. He listened patiently to the entire explanation for the call. "And all this is on video?" he asked. "No, hold him. Definitely hold him. We can be there in six hours."

Leaning back with one hand on the wheel, Agent Rollins glanced at Kirby with a raised eyebrow. Rollins was used to not knowing where he'd be in six hours—and even enjoyed it.

"We need to get to New York," Kirby explained. "The NYPD have Eric Adams—the guy who inspired me to write the *Dangerous Yogi* paper. But this time, he might be on our side."

4. THE INTERROGATION OF ERIC ADAMS

IN A GRIMY INTERROGATION ROOM, ERIC ADAMS TUGGED at the cuffs locked around his hands. He knew the other hostages had been released the day before, but... he was something different. Any account about what he had done to foil the bank robbery wouldn't help him. And if a security camera had caught the end of the nineteen-hour ordeal? Well, so much for pleading hysterical group delusion.

Eric was in a headstand when the interrogation room door opened. Still upside down, Eric said to NYPD Detective Brennan, "If you're going to keep holding me, do you think you can send in my yoga mat? It doesn't seem like anyone's too big on sweeping around here." He came down from the pose. Then he flashed her a warm smile while trying to flip his blond hair from his eyes. The unwieldy cuffs kept him from using his hands.

To Detective Brennan—an attractive but hardened

woman with wavy, dark hair—Eric's manners and handsome golden-boy looks made him extremely likeable. He even smelled nice, like sandalwood, after three days without a shower. According to his records, he was thirty-three years old and unmarried. While an interrogation room wasn't the kind of place to meet a good man, she couldn't help occasionally flirting with Eric.

But this time—with the clock running down before the feds' arrival—Detective Brennan stayed strictly professional. "Eric, it's time you explained what happened at the bank Sunday morning."

She offered him a cup of coffee, but Eric declined. He didn't drink caffeine.

"I didn't try to rob the bank," Eric answered, as he had many times before. Unlike every other human who'd been held in a small, fluorescently lit interrogation room for days, Eric showed no anxiety. "And I'm not sure you can charge me for protecting people's lives." Eric brought his feet up by his thighs to sit in the interrogation room chair in a meditation pose.

Facing Eric across the table, Detective Brennan leaned back in her chair before crossing her arms. "That's not what we're talking about. And you know it. We need to understand how you did... what you did."

In truth, Eric wondered the same thing. Apparently, the effects of his long yoga and meditation retreat—even though cut a year short of his one thousand-day goal—were more powerful than he had ever imagined.

Eric sighed. A few weeks ago, he had been alone in an isolated mountain cabin in the Colorado Rockies. Now he was thrust once again in the middle of mayhem. Smack in another episode of his eternal question: *Why do bad things happen to good people?*

Detective Brennan pressed further, "Eric, I've seen the bank surveillance video...."

He would have to tell them something, but how could he possibly explain? Closing his eyes, he retraced his last steps.

Inhale... he had been teaching a breezy Saturday afternoon yoga class in Brooklyn. *Exhale...* trying to get his feet under him once again. *Inhale...* he'd stopped in a bank to cash his first paycheck since returning to the world. *Exhale...* thugs came in waving—of all things—guns.

At the time, Eric could hardly process what was happening. To Eric's mind—mostly peaceful and still from retreat—the world looked like a slow-motion dream. But he also still suffered from occasional episodes of post-traumatic stress disorder from his time in Afghanistan. Flashbacks had made his transition to civilian life difficult. Thank goodness he had learned how to breathe through them with meditation. But staring at a semi-automatic assault rifle—like the one he had once handled on desert missions—Eric wondered if he might be hallucinating.

Eric watched in disbelief as the goonish gunmen rounded up bank employees and customers. They were wasting too much time asserting their control over the situation. They should have focused on the cash and dashed instead of bumbling with extravagant shows of authority.

From the gunmen's griping, Eric had discerned that the cops had come quickly—so quickly that their already nervous wheelman, no doubt another amateur, had driven off. Now these desperate gunmen were trapped in a Brooklyn bank without a get-away vehicle.

"I only demanded an armored car and an open

highway!" shouted the main gunman, towering over his hostages. The man's hulking size intimidated most, but Eric had no fear of a big, unskilled man who hid behind a wrestling villain's red and black mask.

Cold marble pressed against his legs. Eric and the other hostages sat along a wall of teller windows like prisoners before a firing squad. A pistol and a flashy semi-automatic assault rifle wielded by two other men held them at bay.

In spite of the drama, Eric remained as cool as a retired gunslinger. He stayed quiet, noticing everything—particularly how the main gunman waved his large 45 caliber handgun erratically like he might actually pull the trigger. "They aren't taking me seriously," the man howled. "Someone has to die. Then, they'll know I mean business."

"Eric," said Detective Brennan, interrupting Eric's silent mental replay. "At least tell me why you volunteered to die."

Eric opened his steely eyes. He spoke from a deep well of pain inside. "I couldn't bear someone else getting hurt. Better me than anyone else."

Detective Brennan smiled. Finally, the oyster had cracked. She just had to keep him talking. She leaned forward on the interrogation table. "How did you know so much about the lead gunman's life?" She batted her eyelashes and gave her best *I find you fascinating* expression. Truth was, she really wanted to know.

Eric felt trapped by her question. He could have told her, "It was just strong intuition." But that wasn't quite the truth. Yet to be completely honest in this moment might create a whole new set of problems—the least of which was being confined in a mental institution for further evaluation.

You can see the world without walls between yourself

and others, once you get your sense of self out of the way. He would explain this to a close student who really wanted to help others, but Detective Brennan wasn't a close student or someone who understood anything about yoga beyond just exercise. So he couldn't tell her that the deeper states of meditation naturally lead to supernormal abilities, or that clairvoyance—the ability to read people's minds—was frequently described in spiritual texts such as *The Yoga Sutra*:

प्रत्ययस्य परचित्तज्ञानम् ॥ १९ ॥

pratyayasya para chitta jnyanam

III.19 WITH THE NECESSARY CAUSE,
ONE CAN READ THE MINDS OF OTHERS.

Instead, Eric chose something skillful he could say that was both true and would resonate at a level Detective Brennan could understand. "Somehow, he seemed like a part of me. I could feel what he was going through."

"Who is the unlucky victim?" the black- and red-masked villain had asked. His droopy, dark eyes scanned the line of hostages.

Looking at a freckled, red-haired girl in glasses, the lead gunman declared, "It's going to be you." He reached down and grabbed her by her curly locks. She gave a few terrified shrieks, protesting no. Tears poured from her eyes. But when the gunman shook her, saying in an eerie voice, "Be quiet," she obeyed.

Most of the hostages hid their weepy heads in their hands; few dared to see what happened next. But not Eric. He looked straight ahead, deciding what to do.

The masked gunman moved the large, silver pistol to her head. Only the shaking of the unlucky girl's body echoed in the room.

Why her? Eric wondered. *Of all the people to choose… why her?* Eric had to do something.

The masked man readjusted his grip on his gun.

In this tense moment, Eric called on his secret yogic ability, developed from years of focused meditation. Eric's eyes rolled back in his head, exposing only white. He gathered his concentration an inch-and-a-half inside the center of his forehead, at the tiny point of diamond light he knew in Sanskrit as the *ajna chakra*, the third eye. Focusing hard, a faint glow of white streamed through the skin between his eyebrows, though this was mostly masked by his floppy hair.

Next, Eric scanned the gunman's mind. It was like opening the door to a basement. Stepping into dank, dark cold told him he was inside the gunman's depressed mind. A stream of images flowed. Out of work, drinking beer, watching daytime television for several seasons, making angry posts on Facebook. The gunman's red-haired wife leaving him for another man and taking their little boy. Rage. *He's angry with his wife.*

Then Eric realized, of all the hostages, the bank teller with freckles and red hair looked most like the man's wife. Wanting to hurt his wife, the gunman was trying to do it through the girl. Not thinking rationally anymore, the man prepared to pull the trigger. This wasn't a bluff. One tiny twitch and he'd kill her.

Eric couldn't let that happen; he couldn't bear another person dying in front of him.

"Kill me, instead," Eric said suddenly, pulling his concentration from his *ajna chakra*.

Hands fell from covered eyes; all heads in the bank turned to the tall, blue-eyed man in faded jeans and a blue T-shirt who had just volunteered to die.

"What?" responded the masked gunman. "You don't think I'll do it?"

Eric slowly rose from the floor. A few years ago, Eric was confined to a wheelchair, an honorably discharged vet, paralyzed from the waist down; now he was walking toward a gun.

"No, I know you're going to do it. And I know why," Eric said. "You've been out of work for almost two years. Your wife left you and took your son. He's about three, isn't he? She ran off with another man who could provide for them. You want to show you can provide. You're angry. This woman looks the closest to your wife."

Eric's words mesmerized the gunman.

"She took your pride," Eric said. "You want to show her you're still strong. But it won't work by killing this innocent woman. If you want to show you're strong, you need to take down someone bigger, like me." Eric stood before him: once he had been a powerful swimmer and endurance athlete who had become a Navy SEAL—but that was before his career-ending combat wounds. Still, his athletic build made him a substantial target.

Bewildered by the details that a stranger had revealed about him, the gunman stammered, "How do you know all this?"

Eric pulled up his own secret shame. "I've been abandoned too. I know how much that hurts." Then Eric spoke words that connected on an even more profound level: "I am you."

Detective Brennan sipped her coffee. She had viewed the

video many times—everyone had. Now she asked about the unexplainable. "Nearly all the witnesses described seeing red and white light coming out of your chest. It's clear on the video as well. Eric, we need to understand how you did… what you did…."

"So we can understand what you are," said a male voice familiar to Eric as the interrogation room door swung open.

Eric recognized FBI Special Agent Kirby in his usual, cheap, navy blue suit. An African-American man in a darker suit with a suspicious demeanor followed Kirby.

"Agent Could-be," Eric said, "I should have known you'd be brought in."

Getting up from the interrogation table and straightening her jacket, Detective Brennan looked almost embarrassed, as if caught making out. She asked Agent Kirby, "You two know each other?"

Agent Kirby showed her his FBI credentials. "Yes, but we're not the best of friends." The men were approximately the same age, but couldn't look more different. Eric Adams was golden-haired, blue-eyed, tall, and unbearably handsome. And Agent Kirby… wasn't.

Detective Brennan looked at Eric for further information; this time he volunteered without hesitation. "Agent Kirby has been trying to pin a double-murder on me for two missing yogis, without even being certain that those two people are dead."

With the entry of Agent Kirby, Eric shifted from relaxed surfer dude to guard dog. All the work Detective Brennan had done to win Eric's trust and get him to open up was in vain. Eric said, "Detective Brennan, I think it's time you gave me my phone call to bring in an attorney before my civil rights get further violated."

Agent Rollins perched himself on the edge of the table

with one leg up before delivering his threat. "The Patriot Act allows us all kinds of latitude to hold and export people without having to worry about civil liberties."

"Wasn't the Patriot Act meant for illegal aliens?" Eric responded, looking Rollins directly in the eye.

Rollins answered, "I've seen the bank tape. You're looking pretty alien to me."

Eric went silent, closing his eyes to meditate. Given his previous entanglement with Agent Kirby from months ago, Eric sensed things could get ugly. Fortunately, he had been trained to patiently endure.

Undeterred, Agent Kirby requested that Detective Brennan bring in a video cart. "He's really good at being silent, unless we show him something he has to respond to."

Eric's gut clenched. He felt certain about what they would show him on the video.

Looking at the gunman, Eric had spoken words that connected on a profound level: "I am you."

What happened next had never happened before. Perhaps it was due to Eric's willingness to sacrifice himself... or perhaps it was due to his ability to finally feel empathy and love for someone so undeserving, someone holding a gun to an innocent person's head.

All that great compassion stuff he had studied and meditated on for so long no longer felt theoretical. This test was real. Eric surrendered control of his final moments to whatever the universe wanted.

What happened? An opening erupted at the center of his chest, a feeling greater than anything he had experienced before. The Gordian Knot of separation between himself and others severed, allowing his heart *chakra* to open fully.

Eric then saw directly into the gunman's heart. Angry energetic winds, *pranic* winds, stirred the man's thoughts to murder. Eric could see the disease as clearly as cancer. He could even see how to remove it.

Spontaneously, a glowing red light shined from the center of Eric's chest, reaching toward the gunman like fingers. The light closed around the disorder, pulling away anger from the gunman in the form of balled black smoke.

The stunned gunman released the girl.

Without hesitation, Eric inhaled the disease into himself. The black ball of venomous smoke touched what looked like a diamond at his heart's center. A flash of white light incinerated the darkness. Eric's back straightened and his chest flared forward.

Now, white light bolted forth, entering the gunman. "You're still a good man," Eric said. "You don't want to hurt anyone. Give me the gun."

The masked man passed the gun to Eric, then took off his ski mask. His eyes softened. He felt peaceful for the first time in years. All his thoughts and identification with his tortured self vanished like a cloud dissipating in the blue sky. The second of three gunmen lowered his weapon as well. His older brother had given up, and he followed his brother.

Eric might have been able to walk out of this police station with the other hostages—along with pats on the back—if it weren't for the third gunman. What happened in subduing that man made Agent Rollins suspect Eric wasn't human.

5. THE DIAMOND BODY

THE ROBBER BEHIND ERIC HAD SHOUTED, "DROP THE GUN, or I'll shoot!"

Back still turned, Eric slowly placed the surrendered weapon on the floor, and then kicked it away. The familiar feeling of a cold, metal pistol in his hand once again repulsed him.

"I'm not going back!" The final gunman declared.

Turning around, Eric saw the gunman flanking with a semi-automatic assault rifle that could easily take him and the other hostages down.

"Stay where you are," the gunman said.

"Stay cool," Eric responded. Eric rolled his eyes back into his head again. This time, Eric's forehead glowed more obviously.

What did Eric see? Bars, beatings, and worse. This man had been traumatized by the hellish experience of prison. Fear was the real motivator of men. Sending red light out,

Eric tried to pull away some of the disease.

Streams of red light like alien tentacles moved toward the bank robber. When the light entered him, he stammered, "Wh... What... are you doing to me?" He felt frightened, overwhelmed. Eric saw the man's mind pull the trigger on the assault rifle just before his finger complied.

In that instant, Eric's last wish was that the large caliber bullets wouldn't pass through his body to strike other people. But something else happened instead. For the first time in the world off his meditation cushion, his whole body turned crystal as if made of diamond. Simply, his visualized diamond body from meditation became his physical form.

The gunshots rang. Several women screamed. Hostages dove to get out of the line of fire. The first spray of bullets cut through Eric's shirt, but *bounced off* his stomach.

Eric stood with skin replaced by a crystalline outline.... *How is this possible?* The gun muzzle continued to flash, but the bullets kept bouncing like flicked cigarettes.

Closing the distance, Eric strode toward the blazing gun barrel. At point blank range, Eric tore the gun away before knocking the man to the floor with a diamond fist to the head.

Eric's shirt looked liked Swiss cheese. But there wasn't any blood. Any one bullet should have taken him down.

Color quickly returned Eric's face and body to normal. With skilled hands, he separated the clip of remaining bullets from the assault rifle before tossing them both in different directions.

Eric smiled at the frightened hostages. Their faces tumbled through emotions: shock, elation, relief, terror, but mostly... bewilderment. To try to ease the tension, Eric said, "This was my favorite shirt." Yet awkwardness remained between him and the others. They looked at him as if meeting an unknown species.

Breaking the uncomfortable silence, crashes thundered through the bank. Two SWAT team members on rappelling lines smashed through bank windows; a fuller team behind battering rams and shields crashed through doors. The go order had been given in response to shots fired inside. But now, realizing the danger had already been diffused, SWAT personnel refrained from throwing tear gas.

Eric no longer displayed his diamond body, but he was the only one still standing in the bank. Thinking that Eric must be one of the bank robbers, a SWAT man smacked him on the back of his head with a rifle butt, knocking Eric to the floor. Nearly unconscious, Eric lay face down as the police cuffed him.

The police rounded up bank employees, customers, and would-be robbers. Everybody, including the hostages, would be questioned at precinct headquarters to determine exactly what had happened.

Detective Brennan returned with the AV equipment. But before pushing Play, she walked around Kirby and Rollins to face Eric. She lifted up his bullet-riddled shirt, revealing a pattern of small bruises on his chest and stomach where bullets allegedly had struck.

"Those are some abs you have," she said, teasing him.

"Yoga isn't really about using the muscles, it's more about using the *bundhas*," Eric replied, never losing an opportunity to teach.

Looking closely into his deep blue eyes, she shook her head. "I have no idea what you're saying."

Agent Kirby played the video file of Eric disarming the bank robbers. It was a full-color, bird's eye view of the main bank floor, from a secret pinhole camera. He paused at key frames to zoom in. As Eric had suspected, the video resolution was surprisingly high and the frame didn't pixelate much even as Agent Kirby zoomed in to tighten the view on Eric and the lead gunman.

When red light took black smoke out of the gunman's heart, Agent Kirby paused the frame. "That's *tonglen*, isn't it? You're taking his obstacles away before giving him happiness."

Eric simply answered, "Could be," to Agent Kirby's assertion that he had managed to physicalize an ancient Buddhist meditation practice to remove afflictions.

When Eric went crystal right before the gun fired repeatedly into his body, Agent Kirby paused the frame again. "That's your diamond body, generated by wisdom and *bodhichitta*, isn't it?"

Eric just answered, "Could be."

"What's *bodhichitta*?" asked Detective Brennan.

Eric responded before Agent Kirby could. Finally there was one question he felt happy to answer. Giving the practical version, Eric said, "It's the wish to end suffering for everyone."

Not to be one-upped, Agent Kirby gave the technical version. "It's the wish to achieve enlightenment for the benefit of others." Even on this most virtuous point, tension stewed due to their adversarial history.

"Good to know you're studying the texts you took from me," Eric said. "Is it helping to make your case or undermining it?"

Eric really wanted to know the answer, but Agent Rollins interrupted. "When did you know you were bulletproof?"

Eric pushed on his rock-hard abs. "How would you figure out a thing like that?"

Agent Rollins pulled his gun and aimed at Eric's head. "Maybe we should test you again to find out?" Sick of the strange yogi stuff, Rollins wanted real-world answers.

Without flinching, Eric lifted his hands, showing his cuffs. "I'm chained to the floor. How are you going to explain your actions if you shoot and I'm not bulletproof?"

"Detective Brennan," said Agent Rollins, still pointing his gun at Eric, "Would you mind giving us the room?"

Detective Brennan crossed her arms. "Are you kidding? I'm staying. This is just getting good."

After Agent Rollins holstered his gun, he took out his CIA badge. He showed it to Eric and then Detective Brennan. "Actually, you have to leave," he said to Detective Brennan. "This is now a matter of national security."

Brennan snatched her coffee mug, then sighed, "Should have talked to me, Eric." As she left the room, she added, "Send me a postcard from Guantanamo or wherever it is that they send people they don't like these days."

Eric sensed he was going to miss Detective Brennan. He had no idea what Agent Kirby and Agent Rollins would do next.

6. AN UNUSUAL REQUEST

WHEN THE DOOR TO THE INTERROGATION ROOM CLOSED—slamming harder than the last time—Eric said, "People will be looking for me."

A smug grin came over Agent Kirby's face. For the first time, Eric looked worried. Finally, Kirby had leverage over him.

"That's not entirely true, is it?" said Kirby, as he walked behind Eric. "Between the bank and this precinct house, you've been off the grid for three days, but no one has filed a missing person's report on you yet. In fact, whatever friends you may still have in the world think that you're in retreat for another year."

Seeing that Eric provided no resistance to these points, Agent Kirby didn't press on Eric's deeper emotional weakness: Eric had been abandoned as a child in an orphanage. Instead, Kirby asked, "Why did you leave retreat early?"

Eric looked at his chained feet. "You know why. The retreat center didn't particularly like all those federal agents tromping in and out of the *tsam*. Management asked me to leave for everyone's benefit, thanks to you."

"What's a *tsam*?" Agent Rollins asked, leaning against a wall with his arms folded, now stuck in the role of Detective Brennan.

"It's a sacred retreat border to keep out malevolent spirits; but it's not exactly diplomatic immunity," answered Agent Kirby. He felt pleased that he knew more about this subject than his worldly, experienced partner.

"Now you've really attracted some attention," Kirby added. He played the video again—the part when Eric Adams had taken twelve rounds to the torso without being harmed. He sat on a corner of the interrogation table, running the video forward and backward, again and again.

"What is it you and Agent Rollins want?" Eric said, looking to cut to the chase.

"Odd as it may seem, we're here to ask for your help," answered Agent Kirby.

"What?" Eric was used to patiently enduring an adversarial relationship with Agent Could Be. Now he felt caught off-guard.

Rollins moved toward Eric, bristling. "Agent Kirby may be asking, but I'm not." He wasn't used to asking politely for anyone's help. "I'm sure I could find some government scientists who would love a new lab rat while we try to figure out what you are exactly and what kind of a threat you pose to national security."

The men loomed over Eric with two bad choices. Eric didn't want to be a prisoner in a secret government lab. But he also didn't want to assist Agent Kirby, the man most responsible for his removal from retreat.

Considering Rollins' words, Eric answered, "I understand your threat. I just don't know what you want."

"Eric," Agent Kirby said, "we know you're not normal… that you've developed some sort of yogic superpowers. The thing is, you're not the only one. And some of your 'colleagues,' shall we say, have become even more dangerous."

Agent Kirby took a flash drive from his pocket, but before he could show a single frame of the woman who called herself Physique standing in a red truck, Eric interrupted, "So you're not here to further your double-murder investigation?"

"From what I just saw of your selfless actions in the bank," Agent Kirby said, trying to turn a suspect into a friend, "I have reason to believe you didn't kill those two yogis. They are missing however, and you're the only one with a clear motive. You understand why I had to focus on you first, don't you?"

Eric's cheek twitched as he tugged at his chains.

Still, Kirby couldn't let their past go completely. "Make no mistake," continued Kirby, "If you did do it, and I find a way to prove it, I will take you down. But right now, I'm here to ask for help with something bigger. A lot of innocent people already have died. Many more are in danger."

Rollins pressed in like a government scientist studying Eric. At any moment, Eric expected Rollins to produce needles and start taking blood.

"Give me a moment," Eric said. He deepened his breath while thinking, *There's no longer any point in hiding something less spectacular than what they've already seen on the video.*

Eric's eyes rolled back in his head, glowing white before Agent Kirby and Agent Rollins. Focusing on his *ajna*, he entered Agent Kirby's mind.

When Eric opened his eyes, a nervous Agent Kirby went to play the video of Physique, but Eric stopped him again. "You don't have to play it for me. I could see it through your mind. I don't recognize that woman who calls herself Physique. But the powers she has are *garima* and *laghima*. She can adjust her weight at will to make herself as heavy as a mountain or as light as a feather. With those powers, she could bring down a plane, a building, a bridge, or heaven knows what else."

Agent Rollins backed away from Eric. The chained man's glowing eyes and words had just snow-globed his world.

Ignoring Rollins' visceral reaction, Eric thought about cause and effect. From all he had seen, using fear and violence to get one's way was as ineffective as spraying gasoline to extinguish a fire.

Eric said, "I understand what she's trying to achieve, but she's twisted in how she's using her powers. Those kinds of yogis should be stopped for their own good— before they hurt anyone else or give something sacred a bad name."

"So you'll help us?" Kirby asked.

Eric sighed. "If it's appearing in my world, I have a responsibility to clean it up." The last thing he wanted was another battle. And yet, his *bodhisattva* vows required Eric to help others no matter how uncomfortable the situation was.

Always the professional, Rollins put aside his discomfort and dizzying questions to focus on the immediate threat. "If we caught up to Physique, do you think you could stop her?"

"I don't know… but I would try."

Kirby and Rollins glanced at each other. They had

hoped for a more confident answer.

Eric spoke softly. "You both should understand more about what happened in the bank before you put your faith in me." Eric closed his eyes, visualizing the being he will become with a diamond body, the one named *Diamond Mind*. "I have this image from meditation of who I'm going to become in my next life. My body is pure like a diamond. It helped me let go of many obstacles and even get out of my wheelchair...." Eric remembered those very difficult years and the first miracle he had performed: to walk again.

"It seems in this one extraordinary circumstance at the bank I was able to bring that body into this life." Eric tried to articulate what had happened. "When I thought my life was over, in the next instant my mind switched how I saw myself. I have some understanding of how I created that diamond body and even how I shifted the first gunman's mind, but I'm not in full control of my powers yet. Physique seems different to me. She seems very confident in her abilities. I'm not sure I could stop her on my own."

"So we need a team of superyogis," Agent Kirby said, actually excited that the key recommendation from his *Dangerous Yogi* report seemed viable. "But we don't know of others like you. It's not exactly the kind of thing the bureau can put a recruiting ad for in the back of *Yoga Journal* and comic books."

"I know teachers who can read minds like I can," Eric answered. "It's really the most useful power for guiding students. But we're going to need something more to corner Physique."

"What do you have in mind?" asked Agent Kirby, finally sitting in the chair across from the superyogi.

Eric considered their options. "We could wait for more incidents to occur where yogis are forced to out themselves to protect others. Something is ripening now, first with Physique and now with me. With the unprecedented explosion of yoga and meditation in the world, I think we might be on the cusp of the first generation of western *mahasiddhas*."

Kirby recognized the word *mahasiddhas*: that term referred to the greatest yogis of ancient India, who in addition to transcending ordinary, dualistic views of reality, displayed many miracle powers.

"You think there's going to be a bunch more like Physique and you?" Agent Rollins asked. This made him nervous, but he hid it to the best of his ability by taking a large swig of coffee.

"Could be," Eric answered, smiling for the first time at Agent Kirby. With a snap of his head, Eric flipped his blond hair back from his eyes.

Agent Kirby folded his hands on the table. "Could you train people to develop superpowers?"

Eric knew real superpowers didn't come from radioactive spider bites or freak laboratory experiments. Real superpowers were developed through yoga and meditation. He answered without hesitation, "Yes, but it would take time and a lot of effort. The training may not even ripen in this life. I was at it for many years before truly amazing things started to happen, and I didn't get this way in just one lifetime."

"Stop," said Agent Rollins, raising his hand. He was increasingly uncomfortable with this whole situation, and didn't like the growing coziness between Kirby and Adams. "I don't know how you did what you did, but I'm not buying any past life mumbo-jumbo."

"But that's the thing," Eric answered. "The people in the West who are now interested in yoga, meditation, and studying ancient texts—they're not normal. They have major seeds from past lives that drive them into yoga studios. Any one of those seeds could ripen into something supernatural with the smallest nudge."

Standing abruptly, Agent Kirby clapped his hands. Under incredible time pressure, he had to keep the conversation on track. "We have two weeks left on Physique's deadline before she acts again."

Eric considered the situation. Physique was a significant threat. Perhaps he could train a team in two years, but not two weeks. Not from scratch at least.

His eyes drifted to the closed interrogation door. Part of him wanted to find a way to get out of here, back into daylight where the sun could warm his tensing shoulders.

Suddenly, an idea popped. Eric had learned to pay attention to the wacky ideas that seemed to drop into his lap like a telegram when he was in a crunch. "Then I'd recommend focusing on one person who is truly exceptional and has clear seeds that are currently ripening." He remembered one particular yogi from his past. "I think I know someone. You'll like her, Agent Rollins. She's practically one of yours already."

Rollins folded his arms again. "Who?"

7. THE DANGEROUS YOGIS REPORT

ALONE WITH ERIC ADAMS, AGENT ROLLINS RELUCTANTLY boarded a chartered jet. Climbing the swanky GV's foldout stairs, his feet felt heavy as bricks. For the first time, the experienced CIA operative was taking this half-baked assignment seriously.

The jet's luxurious interior failed to comfort Rollins. Sitting across the aisle and behind Eric Adams in the eight-seater, Rollins kept his white leather recliner in the upright position and his eyes pinned on Eric.

This superyogi thing might be real. Bank surveillance and squashed bullet rounds that NYPD detectives had recovered from the bank floor told him so. No stranger to war zones, Rollins had stepped on compacted slugs in both Afghanistan and Iraq. But that was after bullets smashed into the side of an armored vehicle—never from bouncing off someone's stomach. Further, how had Adams named

Physique or her powers without seeing the video?

Agent Rollins' stomach ulcer burned in a *this-could-go-really-badly* kind of way. Rollins had operated for nearly twenty-five years in all sorts of hostile environments; he even had made deals with the worst kinds of murderous thugs one could imagine. One of them had jabbed a knife in his cheek when a deal went bad, and still he worked that warlord. But Rollins always understood who he was dealing with and what motivated them: that worldly trinity of money, power, and respect.

But Eric Adams was a wild card. *Why did I get on a private jet with such an unknown quantity?* Rollins had seen double agents; in his line of work, too many played both sides.

Do I have training to deal with Adams? No one does. No one knew exactly what Eric Adams was capable of or his motivation. Eric wasn't an ordinary human being, and maybe worse, he was exceedingly nice. Rollins couldn't understand why that grated on him so much.

Rollins had spent his life around killers; his takes-one-to-know-one sense said Eric was like him in that way. There was a certain detached beadiness to his eyes. But something had shifted Eric into someone that Rollins had never encountered before.

Rollins already had reviewed Eric's service record in Afghanistan. The circumstances surrounding Eric's paralyzing injury and honorable discharge had been fudged. Something had happened before the military covered it up. The brass weren't talking, but Rollins would track down members of Adam's SEAL team to get the full story. Someone would eventually talk. They always did.

What was Eric exactly? *Could he be reading my mind right now?* Sitting across the narrow aisle, in a plush recliner,

Eric looked like he was asleep or meditating. Most soldiers learned to catch sleep whenever they could. But Rollins couldn't really say which made his side ache worse. In this business, you'd better be certain or you ended up dead.

Everything about Eric and Physique bugged him.

Questions... more questions than answers. *Even if we catch up with Physique, what if she turns out to be as bulletproof as Eric Adams? How will I put her down then? What prison wall could hold her weight-shifting antics if we brought her to justice through the courts anyway?*

Feeling uncertain, in the strangest of ways Rollins missed the Cold War. Then, it was just about containment—people with certain political views had to stay on their side of the curtain. Even the wars in Afghanistan and Iraq and Syria, to a certain extent, had been about containment. We just wanted to make sure the *jihadists* stayed at home. But this recent development... people to whom the natural laws of the universe no longer applied... what was the containment strategy for them? After all, any person sitting next to you could have secret yogic powers.

Rollins pulled some pistachios from his pocket and the *Dangerous Yogis* report from his briefcase. Keeping Eric in his peripheral sight, he opened the report for the first time.

Rollins hated not knowing as much as the younger Agent Kirby, who had been immersed in this spiritual wonderland for a year. He also wondered if Vice President Lausunu knew more about the superyogi threat than he was letting on.

Rollins cracked a pistachio. Eric didn't move. He cracked another. No response. At least he wouldn't have to offer Eric any of his nuts as he studied up on Eric's kind.

From Agent Kirby's report on Dangerous Yogis, written for the Counter-Terrorism Think Tank at Langley, Virginia:

DANGEROUS YOGIS

Advances in technology are always a double-edged sword. It seems any object can be used for good or evil. Even the most helpful advances, such as passenger airplanes or simple fertilizer, have been turned against innocent people as weapons in recent years.

Much of our job in law enforcement and the intelligence community is to keep technology from being weaponized by people who want to harm others to further their personal agendas. We've made significant advances to secure the obvious things, but there is a different kind of technology entering our culture that may have unforeseen consequences in the near future.

Yogic practices and Buddhist analytical meditation are spiritual technologies with a depth and power that are generally not widely understood. While these spiritual systems, knowledge, and processes are generally aimed for the beneficial purposes of making people kinder and more compassionate, the technology is allegedly capable of so radically transforming a person's consciousness that it can endow them with what can most clearly be labeled as superpowers.

While this may seem outlandish at first, one must consider that the yogic and Buddhist lineages are filled with historic accounts of *Mahasiddhas*, people who displayed miracle powers that would rival any comic book character. And sometimes, these *siddhas* acted in ways radically disruptive to the authority of the land.

Further, specific instructions fill yogic and Buddhist

texts for how to develop powers such as flying, invisibility, clairvoyance, and dramatically changing size, weight, or shape, etc. Often, warnings accompany these instructions stating that these powers may become distractions to reaching more ultimate spiritual goals. Thus, in many traditions they are actively discouraged. However, many of these texts have been recently translated into English, Spanish, and other European languages and are increasingly being explored in yoga studios and private homes around the world. More texts are certain to come.

While in the past an oral lineage in which a master could evaluate the worthiness of a student largely protected these secrets, now even the most esoteric teachings are available at bookstores and through the Internet. There are currently over twenty million practitioners of yoga and meditation in America alone, an increase of 29% in the past four years. Even if only the tiniest fraction of practitioners were to reach the highest levels of transformation, as the technology they are using claims is possible, there could be many unforeseen consequences. If these powers do start to emerge again, as they apparently have in the past, can we be certain that they will be wielded for the benefit of others? Or will these yogic powers be used selfishly? Simply, will dangerous yogis start to emerge?

This report examines: (1) Scriptural and historic evidence for *siddhis,* or superpowers, (2) How an ordinary person could achieve supernormal abilities, (3) What could happen if this technology was used for the wrong purposes, (4) Recommendations for how the U.S. government and other governments should prepare for this unforeseen threat.

Reclining a few feet away from Agent Rollins, Eric Adams had not been sleeping. He'd been resting in his image of his diamond body, while periodically observing the *Dangerous Yogis* report from the mind of Agent Rollins. Understanding the value of intel just as much as Rollins, Eric wanted to know what the government's intention was for yogis like him.

8. CAPTAIN ARIAL DAVIS

CAPTAIN ARIAL DAVIS PULLED HER F-15 JET FIGHTER out of a fifteen thousand-foot escape dive, then pushed the plane's throttles forward to accelerate to 450 knots. Her stomach moved to her throat, but she loved the sensation. This roller coaster dive was within the rules of engagement for dogfight training, but one false twitch of the stick could dip her out of the Military Operations Area (MOA).

The seasoned pilot trailing her, Captain Fulmer, struggled to follow. He gave up speed in a more cautious dive—loosing smash as the pilots say—while Captain Davis hurtled beyond his F-15's gun range. Still, he felt determined to stay on her six—her tail—and close the distance to take the winning shot.

They settled at five hundred feet. At her speed, it would take less than half a second to hit the ground: just slightly more time than dropping a glass from your hand. Still, Fulmer's macho bravado wouldn't let him be outdone by a woman pilot, no matter how many other pilots she had already bested that week.

With his big hands, Fulmer threw both throttles forward to full military power. The desert floor outside Nellis Air Force Base—the famed home of the Air Force's leading Fighter Weapons School for F-15s—blurred into a tapestry of browns and greens.

The air was so thick at this altitude, the plane shook. The stick vibrated as if in seizure. Energy poured under the wings. The ride became as bumpy as a shopping cart bouncing down a mountain. The plane begged to rise, dive, or bank—anything but fly straight.

As Fulmer's speed crossed 600 knots, he would have Captain Davis' jet in gun range in seconds. He licked his lips. The F-15 can climb sixty thousand feet in a minute, and this was the move he anticipated next from his prey.

But Captain Arial Davis had other ideas. Unexpectedly, she pulled back both throttles to idle while popping the speed brakes. Then she yanked hard on the stick, raising the nose, trading airspeed for altitude.

Her jet slowed like a train whose emergency break had been pulled, only magnitudes harder. *Bet he wasn't expecting this*, she thought.

Captain Fulmer spotted her jet pivoting up, but hesitated to reduce his speed. By the time he'd realized what she'd done, he'd lost the chance to take a shot. He hadn't lowered his throttles and pulled back on his stick hard enough to mimic her climb.

Engines cut to idle, with the jet's nose straight up, Arial Davis viewed only blue sky. She deliberately stalled the wings. Soon the jet's airspeed would drag to zero. For a precious moment, she floated in zero gravity. Even desert dust from her boots and the cockpit floor floated in the fighter—sparkling in the canopy like pixie dust. *Had time stopped?* Captain Davis closed her eyes and smiled, completely weightless.

Soon her jet slipped into a tail slide, while Fulmer sailed by underneath. Simply, he didn't think to stall his plane.

To stop the tail slide, Captain Davis kicked in the F-15's afterburners. She banged against the back of her seat as if she'd been strapped to a launching missile. But she remained fully in control. In seconds, she zoomed in on the other pilot's tail. "Guns. Guns. Guns," she called over the radio. She was well within the one-mile range to use her 20-mil cannons. Fulmer also heard a high pitch beeping in his ears, confirming that indeed, he had just been shot down.

Arial Davis dispatched the cocky Captain Fulmer just as easily as the others. "You lasted five minutes. Is that your best?" she taunted.

"You gave up smash," the excuse-seeking Fulmer retorted. He couldn't stand being beaten by a woman. Further, he knew she had pulled several unorthodox maneuvers.

"I'm not afraid to bend the rules," Captain Davis answered.

On the tarmac, Captain Davis' wiry main mechanic gleefully took more money from other pilots training at the school. Even giving two-to-one odds, he still won piles off Arial's skills.

CIA Agent Rollins and Eric Adams waited patiently in the main hangar's shade for Davis. Rollins felt ridiculous standing in his black suit next to a man with surfer hair in a T-shirt holding a blue yoga mat.

Eric could remember only that the Air Force pilot's first name had been Arial. It hadn't taken Rollins long to find her, as she was one of the few women currently flying fighters in the Air Force. For Rollins, it had been as easy as spotting a red umbrella in a sea of black. But Arial wasn't just flying jets, she was an instructor at Fighter Weapons School. This meant she had been the best pilot in her class and chosen the assignment cherished by all flight jockeys: *the* red umbrella standing in a sea of black.

Captain Davis taxied her F-15 to the front of the line before confidently climbing down from the jet. The patch on her shoulder had a target with a dart in it, giving the school its more common name, Targetarm. After taking off her flight helmet, she shook out long, wavy, blond hair. It bounced like some of her aerial circus twirls. She tossed the helmet to her mechanic, saying: "I rode him a little hard. But I didn't bend the spars. How'd you do today?"

"Thanks to you, I'm almost making as much as the officers," the young mechanic answered, referring to his betting pool.

As she strode into the open hangar filled with other planes, she recognized the tall, blond man with a yoga mat.

But one thing was different about him.

"Eric?" she asked, "You're out of your wheelchair!" She distinctly remembered Eric: as unusual as it was to see someone in a wheelchair at a yoga studio, it had felt more tragic to see someone with the body of Adonis confined to a chair. "What are you doing here?"

Eric just smiled. He was happy to see her living her dream. "That was some flying."

"I was born to fly," Arial answered, still puzzled by Eric's presence here along with the surly government suit next to him.

"I hope so," Eric answered.

CIA Agent Rollins showed Captain Davis his badge,

then tried his best to explain the situation. But the words stuck in his throat like hard candy. "Eric Adams is a yoga teacher with... special skills. We want him to train you... for a special project. I'm here to observe your progress."

"A CIA yoga project?" Captain Davis asked.

To Rollins, it sounded even more ridiculous when someone else said it. "Maybe it's best if Eric explains."

"I'm here to further your yoga training." Eric felt that was about all that needed to be said right now. But then he added, "And to watch its effects on your flying."

"There's no change in your official assignment. You'll still be an instructor here," added Rollins, returning to his sober tone.

Arial thought, *Eric must have special skills if yoga helped him get out of a wheelchair.* "OK" shrugged Arial, a little amused and curious about the situation. "If the government wants to pay for me to have a private yoga instructor, I'm in." She loosened the harness drawn tightly over her hips before unzipping her flight suit. Then she stepped out in a spaghetti strap tank top and form-fitting yoga pants—her usual outfit. She looked like a model from the cover of *Yoga Journal*. "I'm ready if you are. Let me just grab my mat."

Arial entered a changing room. Inside her locker door on a small piece of paper that no one else saw was her favorite verse from *The Yoga Sutra*:

कायाकाशयोः संबन्धसंयमाल्
लघुतूलसमापत्तेश्चाकाशगमनम् ॥ ४२ ॥

kaya-akashayoh sambandha sanyamal
laghu tula samapattesh cha-akasha gamanam

III.42 WHEN YOU TURN THIS EFFORT
UPON THE RELATIONSHIP BETWEEN
THE BODY AND SPACE, YOU GAIN
A POWER OF MEDITATION WHERE YOU BECOME
LIGHT AS A WISP OF COTTON,
AND CAN THUS FLY THROUGH THE SKY.

9. REUNION

Arial Davis took Eric to the quietest room the small complex had to offer: a small uninspired space she used as her private office. Closing the door behind her, she said, "We'll have to do it in here." Immediate regret followed her choice of words. "You know—whatever we're going to do."

She slipped off her boots and socks to walk barefoot on the scuffed white linoleum floor as if in a yoga studio. As Arial swept paper cups and used napkins off her clunky industrial desk, Eric peeked out a window at a tire-streaked runway. Soon fighters would be taking off like wasps scouting their territory, but for now, it was as quiet as a deserted highway.

Eric and Arial silently rolled out their yoga mats. "Don't mind the dust bunnies," Arial said, forcing a nervous laugh.

Eric spotted a burgundy-colored meditation cushion in

the corner, the kind filled with barley husks that sounded like a bean-bag when touched. Trying to break the ice, he asked, "You've been meditating regularly?"

"I have." She practically clicked her heels. "That *Yoga Sutra* course in New York changed my life. Otherwise, I wouldn't have known that yoga was originally a path of meditation."

Already reminiscing in his mind, Eric nodded. It had been a difficult time in his life: his SEAL career had ended, he had been bound to a wheelchair, and his fiancée had left him. Even the *pop* of a car backfiring in the street had triggered flashbacks.

Like most students at that teaching, Eric and Arial had been *asana* practitioners looking to go deeper. They'd wanted the deepest questions about life and reality answered—but Eric, perhaps more so than any others in the room, had really needed it.

When Eric rolled his wheelchair into the crowded, posh yoga studio just south of bustling Union Square in Manhattan, he wasn't sure what to expect. The course he had traveled across the country to attend wasn't just an ordinary teaching, but an historic event. It was probably the first time—maybe in a thousand years—when heavyweight Buddhist lamas and hardcore yogis had gone through Master Patanjali's *Yoga Sutra* together using recently recovered texts (long preserved in Tibet) to clarify how someone like Eric could travel the yogic path to enlightenment.

Feeling nervous and out of place, Eric even bumped his wheels into a wooden stand, knocking over yoga mats with a loud *thwack*. Arial was the first to help him. Restacking mats, she introduced herself.

Before this teaching, Eric and Arial had known some Sanskrit philosophy words like *purusha* and *prakirti*, and like good yogis, they knew how to make traditional *chai* and how to use a *neti* pot for cleansing the nose. And of course, Arial could stand on her head. But they had little idea how to practice the higher stages of Master Patanjali's famous eight limbs of yoga beyond the third limb of *asana*, the physical exercises.

Arial never forgot the biggest surprise from the first night of teachings: traditionally, yoga was more about *meditation* than the physical exercises. To Arial, this revelation felt like learning that raspberries, blackberries, and strawberries were not true berries, but aggregate fruits. Yet, Arial found ample proof once she actually started studying *The Yoga Sutra*.

When she counted the 195 verses in *The Yoga Sutra*, only three verses dealt with *asana*—less than 2%.

She also saw that all the key realizations necessary to reach enlightenment—outlined in at the start of *The Yoga Sutra* in *The Chapter on Meditative Absorption*—had to occur in deep meditation.

Both Arial and Eric quickly realized that taking physical poses to be a complete yogic path—while ignoring the seven additional limbs of yoga—was a great distortion. It was like taking bar stretching to be ballet.

This was a welcomed relief to Eric. He could adapt many yoga poses to help him maintain flexibility in his upper body. He could even feel how the poses made his heart "smile," as his physical therapist used to say. But there were too many poses that he would never be able to do from his wheelchair. And if that was what it took to reach enlightenment, then Eric Adams had already been ruled out.

Fortunately, as Eric and Arial had learned, the full teachings of yoga could still be transmitted.

"That course changed my life too," Eric said, smiling.

"I can see that!" Arial looked him up and down to communicate that she was talking about his healed body—but once again, she wished she could take it back.

"Once I started seriously meditating and studying more root texts...." Eric hesitated. "Well, let's just say there's a lot for us to talk about."

Eric's studies had taken him on a most unexpected journey. *The Yoga Sutra* was a curious mix of Buddhist thought, *proto-samkhya* Hindu philosophy, and the general meditation culture of India. Profoundly cryptic, *The Yoga Sutra* was impossible to understand without a commentary or supporting texts. Parts were like trying to decipher Egyptian hieroglyphics without a Rosetta Stone.

To really understand Master Patanjali, Eric and more serious scholars had found there was tremendous value in looking at the philosophical thought of Patanjali's time—before the commentarial tradition that came two hundred to three hundred years later slanted Patanjali's text in sectarian ways (something Patanjali did not do).

Comparing Master Patanjali's words to the instructions of his peers and predecessors gave Eric insight. It hadn't been just an academic exercise. Eric had wanted to experience something deeper. To someone in a wheelchair... someone who had recently lost everything that was important to him... someone suffering from deep traumas... only advices for true transformation could hold his attention. He believed the transformations Master Patanjali outlined in *The Yoga Sutra* almost two millennia ago were still achievable for an ordinary westerner like himself. And long retreat had proved him right.

The roar of an F-22 Raptor taking off the runway pulled Arial's attention. On tiptoes, she leaned against the window ledge, watching the plane bank. Her fingernails clicked in excitement against the glass. She never tired of watching anything that flew.

"Concentration is my edge in the sky," Arial said, starting to open up. "Everyone here has great reflexes and the balls to really push the envelope. You need a three hundred-knot mind to fly jets. But meditation gives me an advantage. On my best days, I've got a six hundred-knot mind."

"That's cool," Eric answered.

They fell into another awkward silence. Eric still hadn't explained what they were supposed to be doing and why. Eric cleared his throat. "So, we're going to focus mainly on meditation to push your wisdom."

Arial turned around. Her hands leaned against the windowsill. "I've been working for years on the emptiness meditations we got from those lamas. But they're really difficult."

These were the toughest meditations in all of Buddhist and yogic thought, used to discover the true nature of reality. In yogic terms, this involved separating *purusha* from *prakirti*—separating ultimate reality from deceptive reality to reach a non-dual state. Sliding into her Texas drawl, Arial said, "Every time I think I've got it, it just slips away like a greased pig."

Eric smiled. Meditating on the illusory nature of reality was difficult for anyone accustomed to thinking things are as they appear. It was harder than learning piano. But with continued exposure and effort, the occasional Mozart emerged—particularly if they wanted to find the cure to suffering as badly as Eric.

Arial wanted to ask him about his remarkable recovery, but other questions came first. "Eric, I'm just going to say it: this is weird. What's this all about? And why me?"

Eric stiffened, wondering how to explain. *What's the warm-up for "I'm here to teach you how to fly without a machine?"*

10. FLIGHT TRAINING BEGINS

ARIAL WONDERED ABOUT THIS CIA YOGA PROJECT AND Eric's remarkable recovery—but agreed to his suggestion to meditate before they talked further.

Knowing the room well, Arial turned off the overhead lights that buzzed slightly in a way that only a meditator would notice. Sunlight streamed through the window.

They sat across from each other. Instinctively, Arial found herself inching her cushion closer to Eric, who already had his eyes closed.

After a few moments of silence, Eric started guiding the meditation. "Hollow out your entire body. Fill it with empty sky."

Arial knew this visualization from *The Yoga Sutra* and *The Hatha Yoga Pradipika*. She had been doing it for years. Mentally, she cleared out all her flesh and bones—from her ear lobes to her toes. This helped subtle energy, called *prana* in Sanskrit, to flow smoothly—and made Arial feel wonderful.

Arial became a patch of floating blue sky contained by a nearly invisible outline of her body.

After some additional preliminaries, including the nine-stage breathing practice from the *Hatha Yoga Pradipika*, Eric said, "Now I want you to recall a flying dream you've had recently, where you're flying high in the sky without a machine. Make it as vivid as possible."

Arial replayed a recent dream. It was easy to visualize: she often had dreams like this. She sat in full lotus, a meditation pose, with her hands on her knees. She wore her olive drab flight suit, except the patch on her arm had a lotus flower with a red, flaming sword above it instead of the usual target with a dart. By thinking where to go, she floated effortlessly through the sky.

Eric scanned Arial's mind as she meditated. What he saw made him smile. Her single-pointed concentration was superb. During *pranayama* she wasn't just watching the breath... she was breath. There wasn't subtle dullness like haze hanging over her visualized image or subtle agitation from other ideas in the background moving like water under ice. Instead, she was locked into the experience. Arial's mind saw herself flying as clearly as she would see Eric if she opened her eyes.

She'd been meditating regularly; in fact, she was rapidly approaching the meditative level known as stillness, or *shamatha*, where she could keep her mind single-pointed on one object for as long as she wished.

Eric said, "In your mind, ask why you can fly in a dream but need a machine to fly in waking life." Eric's body felt light; all of his anxiety about the national threat he was supposed to solve—gone. He was simply a different person when he meditated.

Arial didn't take long to answer silently in her mind: *One is an illusion; the other is real.*

"You've told me the difference between how you see a dream and how you see waking life. Now find what flying in a dream and flying in a machine have in common."

Arial didn't catch the first part of Eric's sentence, "You've told me...." Instead, she focused on his instruction. *Both have flying... both have me....* Then she pushed deeper, catching her mind create the images. An odd thought arose: *They're both mental images.* A flash of possibility shot into her central channel—the energetic, subtle body channel that runs up the spine—and her body quivered. She recognized this sensation as having glimpsed a little bit of truth.

Eric's voice sounded as smooth as a glider: "If both are mental images, flying in waking life without a machine should be just as possible as in a dream."

Arial followed the logic. Flying in waking life without a machine would be a mental image too. She held this concept for seconds, but the idea was too radical. Simply, she had a pre-conceived belief that it wasn't possible. The stillness of her mind faltered. Suddenly, she became self-conscious. *How did Eric know I saw they were both mental images?*

Her mind crashed out of meditation like a student blowing a maneuver in a flight simulator. She deepened her breath, wiggled her fingers, then opened her almond-brown eyes. At nearly the same time, Eric opened his. His blue eyes were nearly the same shade as the sky in her dream.

"The patch on your flight suit: the lotus and the flaming sword. Do you recognize those symbols?" Eric asked.

Arial stared back in disbelief, thinking, *How did you know?*

Eric explained, "The lotus is the symbol for renunciation,

moving away from an ordinary life of suffering. The flaming sword is the symbol for wisdom that cuts through all illusions."

Arial's six-hundred knot mind raced. She went all the way back to Eric's introduction today. "When Agent Rollins said you had special skills, what did he mean… exactly?"

Eric's eyes were unwavering. Finally, he spoke: "Do you remember the verse in *The Yoga Sutra* about where yogic supernormal powers come from?"

"Eric… I didn't memorize the whole thing." Arial felt like she was failing a test that she wanted to pass.

Eric smiled at her with his kind eyes, waiting for Arial to remember. "Think about the four immeasurables…."

This was a powerful clue. The four immeasurables meant wishing love, compassion, joy, and equanimity for every living being. Finally, the short verse came to her:

मैत्र्यादिषु बलानि ॥ २३ ॥

maitryadishu balani

III.23 THE POWERS ARE TO BE FOUND
IN LOVE AND THE REST.

To her own surprise, Arial quoted these words. In response, Eric quoted another verse from *The Yoga Sutra*.

प्रत्ययस्य परचित्तज्ञानम् ॥ १९ ॥

pratyayasya para chitta jnyanam

III.19 WITH THE NECESSARY CAUSE,
ONE CAN READ THE MINDS OF OTHERS.

With this, Arial finally understood. *Eric can read my mind.* Looking down, Eric explained, "I've had many difficult things happen to me over this life. They succeeded in breaking my heart open to the pain everyone feels." Eric's mind lingered on some horrible trials. Loneliness in the orphanage… the blast that had ended… everything. "I wished for an antidote for suffering. My wish brought me to yoga and to teachers who had great wisdom. I even spent two years in solitary meditation retreat."

Eric paused, unable to reveal the extent of the changes within him. But in this context, alone with Arial—considering what they were here to achieve—there was a compelling reason to explain. "Something unexpected happened to me as a result of all that work… that changed me. I learned how to get out of the way. Now, when I want to help someone, I can see into that person's mind."

Eric closed his eyes again, but just before the lids fell, Arial witnessed his eyes rolling white—glowing more like moons than eyeballs.

Suddenly, the roaring jets were gone, the room was gone. For Arial, all that was left was a yogi before her, challenging her very concept of reality.

Arial was speechless.

She knew that instructions for developing special powers, called *siddhis,* and descriptions of miracle-wielding masters filled ancient texts. But at first glance, Eric looked like just another yoga teacher. Admittedly, a really handsome one who had managed to overcome paralysis and had glowing eyes. Still, he was just an ordinary westerner like her. *Wasn't he?*

"Arial, I don't think you're ordinary." Lids open, Eric's eyes still shined with a supernatural glow.

"The superpowers are real. In the same way I learned to walk again and read minds, I'm here to teach you how to fly without a machine."

11. AIRBREAKS

ARIAL SPRANG FROM HER CUSHION, RETREATING TO THE window. Eric's glowing eyes rattled her. Unable to control herself, she blurted: "Why are your eyes glowing?"

Sitting on his meditation cushion, Eric was as cool as a still lake. He innocently responded, "What color are they?" He actually didn't know.

"They're like moonlight."

"Are you afraid of moonlight?" Eric asked, remaining seated. Soon, his eyes returned to their normal steely blue.

People often wish to see angels or other supernatural beings. But when they finally do, it's simply terrifying. They know for certain—maybe for the first time—that they are not the most powerful thing in the universe.

Arial wasn't accustomed to having her power so obviously eclipsed. Despite feeling incredibly drawn to Eric—or maybe *because* she did—she considered bolting out of the room. She didn't know whom or what she was dealing with.

"You're going to teach me how to fly... without a jet," Arial stammered, restating Eric's proposition. "And the CIA bought into this?"

Eric grinned as if nothing strange had occurred at all. "Well, it was mainly an FBI agent's idea." Eric wanted to tell her more, but at this time he didn't have the authority. Rollins had made it clear that he couldn't tell anyone about Physique downing Flight 1632. But still, Eric needed to tell Arial something to calm her down—to keep her in the room. "Tell me what you remember about miracle powers."

Arial still stood by the window, arms crossed in front of her chest as if to contain the thumping of her heart. Her mind sprinted to a new thought. "People perform miracles in ancient scriptures. Buddhist, Hindu, Christian, Jewish... mostly, back when people were meditating really well and had the concentration to alter reality with their minds. But I'm not one of those people."

"Not yet." Eric smiled.

"Others learned some kind of black magic that allowed them to do unusual things. And I'm really not interested in being one of those people." Arial squeezed her arms tighter across her chest.

Following her words, Eric repeated the opening of the fourth chapter from *The Yoga Sutra*.

जन्मौषधिमन्त्रतपःसमाधिजाः सिद्धयः ॥ १ ॥

janmaushadhi mantra tapah samadhija siddhayah

IV.1 POWERS CAN BE ATTAINED EITHER AT BIRTH,
THROUGH HERBS, SPELLS, EXTREME PRACTICES,
OR THROUGH DEEP MEDITATION.

"What are you telling me?" Arial asked, adrenalized. Her voice trembled. "What are you exactly?"

This was not an easy question to answer... for many reasons. For one, Eric had learned that the main source of his power was not having to be anything at all. That way, he was free of limitations.

Real freedom is found by going beyond the self.

But how to explain? Eric no longer saw the world the way most people do. He no longer grasped to a strong sense of self. To him, life felt more like a dream, a cascade of cause and effect that was completely up for grabs—and he was no longer separate from any of it. Because of that, he could do amazing things.

"Come... sit." Eric motioned to the meditation cushion. Knowing that he had freaked her out, he wanted to ease Arial's mind. "Just hear me out; then you can decide what you want to do."

Arial didn't believe Eric intended to hurt her. Further, Eric exuded a confidence, fearlessness, and peacefulness that she couldn't resist. Reluctantly, she returned to her cushion. She found herself adjusting the straps on her yoga top, worried Eric could see through fabric.

Eric smiled kindly, keeping his body still and gentle. "There is something happening in the world. We're living in an extraordinary time of spiritual rediscovery. People are growing tired of the electronics race and all the questions our consumer culture can't answer. Many are looking deeper inside." Eric connected to things Arial already believed, before taking her further.

Arial slowly nodded. Wanting an inner spiritual practice was one of the things that had drawn her to yoga.

"All those miraculous things that used to occur fairly regularly will start to re-emerge again. But because we are importing a spiritual technology, there will be less understanding about where the powers come from. Some people who develop powers are going to be dangerous; others are going to be heroes."

"Villains versus heroes?" Arial repeated incredulously.

"Just consider what *The Yoga Sutra* tells us. Powers can emerge at birth or later in life, seemingly randomly, due to powerful practices performed in the past. Most likely this would manifest in people passionately attracted to yoga and meditation, but not exclusively. Everyone it happens to may not be prepared for the responsibility."

Thinking about the next words in the verse about powers, Eric said: "There could be people out there still using potions and spells, but I think those lineages are mostly dried up."

"That's *Harry Potter* fantasy stuff," said Arial.

"Maybe. But when an entire world, including adults, becomes fascinated with young wizards, fairy tales, and superhero movies, you have to wonder why those images are surfacing so strongly. What is manifesting psychologically for people? What are they being prepared for?"

Eric continued: "Then there are people doing extreme cleansing practices, fasting, and *asana* three-plus hours a day. That's not normal. Strange things are going to ripen." Indeed, Arial had seen enough of those hardcore yogis in the West to recognize something odd was happening. She knew *asana* junkies who scheduled their entire day around their fix.

"And finally, there are people who develop abilities as a result of years of deep meditation. You asked what I am." Eric paused. "I'm one of those people. That's how I could read your mind, and see the flaming sword and lotus patch on your arm."

Thoughts still racing, Arial decided that what Eric had told her was the best explanation for what he'd shown. However, meeting a person with yogic superpowers was a lot to process. Arial steadied her nerves. "Lots of people meditate and do yoga. Why me?"

"I volunteered you because you're the best candidate I know for the specific flying skills we're going to need."

"I fly jets!" Arial protested.

"Exactly," responded Eric. "I can't imagine how hard it was for you, as a woman, to fly fighters. And as I hear it, you're unrivaled in the sky. But still you used your vacation time to spend two weeks studying *The Yoga Sutra*. That's an unusual combination that can be further developed."

Eric's words resonated in Arial's heart. But did they make sense? Arial did have seeds for flying since birth. Even as a little girl she could remember explaining to her friends that her daddy and his daddy were pilots. And that's why she was named Arial.

Her granddaddy had not only flown crop dusters over cotton fields—since she was seven, he had taken Arial to the sky. She could barely see out of the cockpit, but still she'd hold the stick and fly by instruments. Like the men she looked up to, all her life Arial wanted to fly. Over Cheerios and a sippy cup, she'd tell her parents about her latest flying dream. As an adult, Arial Davis felt happiest pulling zero gravity maneuvers in the sky.

The tension in her jaw and hands released. Everything Eric had said was true. In flight school, Arial had to be the best to get her choice of plane. She hadn't wanted to be assigned to the heavies, cargo planes, or bombers. She wanted to break the mold and win an F-15. She wasn't interested in the F-16, which was more often used for ground bombing, or the ultra modern F-22, that would have given her such a tech advantage it wouldn't have been fun. She wanted to fly the last fighter where the pilot's skill—more than anything else—determined who would win the battle for air superiority.

Then there was her love of yoga. She sometimes felt almost weightless in her balancing poses. She even wondered if it was possible to float off the mat.

She leaned toward Eric. "What are you asking me to do?"

Eric answered, "I'm asking you to be a superhero."

A superhero, Arial thought. Something in her responded to that word more than the prospect of flying without a machine.

Arial searched for her real objection to this whole scheme. "When I said that flying in a dream and flying without a machine are both mental images... I meant they're mental images when you're in meditation! When you come out, there's a big difference between being in a dream and in the physical world."

"I understood what you meant." Eric touched the ground with his right hand, while his left stayed in his lap in meditation position. "Now we have a place to start. If I can prove to you that the outside physical world is a mental image too... if you can get used to that truth, I believe we can harness your seeds for flying to make a miracle."

Arial stretched her legs, leaning back. She tossed her long, wavy hair over one shoulder. "You really think you can teach me to fly without a machine?"

Eric was as confident as a carpenter pounding a nail. "I'll teach you by the book. But in the end, only you can get yourself off the ground."

12. JET ASANA

THE FOLLOWING MORNING, LIKE A CHIRPING SPARROW, Arial flitted into the spacious hangar at 7:00 A.M. Her blond hair pulled back into a ponytail revealed sparkly diamond studs that she normally didn't wear to work.

For most of the night, she'd been up studying *The Yoga Sutra*. Her main question: did any of what happened with Eric make sense? But she'd also found herself musing about how attractive Eric was... in spite of this being part of a CIA operation.

Reading the text from the in-depth course she took in New York, Arial had alternated between exhilaration and incredulity. Just the title of the third chapter kept her riveted: *vibhuti padah, The Chapter on Mystic Powers*.

As she read the tight verses, the exact methods for transformation eluded her. It felt like glimpsing blueprints for a grand cathedral. Sketchy lines could become vivid detail—if only explained by someone who truly knew.

Arial hadn't met anyone like Eric before. *Was there any body else like him?* To her, it appeared he had more in common with a *mahasiddha* than an ordinary human being.

Eric waited in the hangar in his usual faded jeans and baby-blue T-shirt along with Agent Rollins, who lurked in the same black suit as the day before. It hadn't been difficult for Eric to get Rollins to deliver him early from their government accommodations—apparently Agent Rollins didn't sleep much.

Eric had been up since 4:00 A.M. doing his own meditation and *asana* practice, thinking about what would help Arial most. His mind was clear as a diamond and sharpened like a dagger to strike at the crucial point. But his heart raced, pulsing with excitement to teach someone the deeper aspects of reality... someone who may actually understand.

Arial sauntered in with a sassy greeting: "You're not going to ask me to jump off a building, are you?" She hoped a little attitude might hide her fear and doubt about this secret endeavor to fly like a superhero.

Eric laughed, understanding her concern. "No, I won't ask you to jump off a building. You'd just get hurt. When you're ready to fly, it will happen on its own—and from flat ground."

Arial responded to his confident ease. "So what did you have in mind?" she asked. Moving closer, she offered him some of her bottled water.

Eric pointed to her jet. "I want you to do some *asana* on that airplane wing." He sipped her cool water, as if his suggestion was the most natural thing in the world.

I can do that, Arial thought.

As she climbed on the wing, the pit-a-pat of her bare

feet reverberated in the silent hangar. The wings of an F-15 could withstand one hundred tons of force: Arial's slender yogi's body wouldn't affect the steel spars.

Eric hadn't realized just how big an F-15 jet fighter was until he was standing next to one: it wouldn't fit on a tennis court.

From the ground, Eric called out standing poses from a traditional warm-up. "Start with Warrior One and Warrior Two, then move slowly into Triangle on both sides. I want you to stay in your hollow sky body the entire time. Watch your mind closely." His smooth voice echoed in the large open hangar.

Though pretending not to be interested, Agent Rollins heard and observed from a distance.

Arial followed Eric's lead, holding the simple poses each for five breaths. Her inhale matched her exhale like the length of perfectly mirrored phrases in a classical sonata. "Make the jet your focus," Eric instructed.

After she switched sides, Eric directed her to move into Side Crow, *parsva bakasana*. Arial's head looked toward the body of the jet while her legs tucked as high as possible toward her shoulder. She brought her feet off the ground— only her hands touched the wing. *This is easy*, she thought. *He doesn't know how good I am.*

Eric had prepared four questions to help Arial catch her mind constructing reality. Talking to her from below the wing, Eric started his lesson plan. "Do you see the whole jet at once or just parts?"

A silly question, Arial judged instinctively. *You only see parts. After all, you can't see the wheels when you look at the top or see the tail when you look at the nose.* The metal felt cold under her hands as her weight pressed heavily on her folded wrists. Still, she decided to indulge Eric, wondering why he would ask such an obvious thing.

But soon, watching her mind closely, Arial caught something odd. *How do I have a mental image of the whole jet, when I can see only a few parts at any one time?* Indeed, in each of those various poses, she saw the jet from a different angle—only part of the jet (sometimes wing, sometimes tail). And yet her mind had an image of the whole thing. She didn't know why Eric drew her attention to this phenomenon, but something felt fishy. Regardless, instinct pushed the question away. *What's the big deal?*

"Let's see if you can do a handstand up on that wing," Eric instructed.

Neither the height bothered Arial, nor the pose. To her, handstands were like jumping jacks to a first grader. She placed her hands down, straightened her arms without locking her elbows, tucked her stomach in, and then slowly lifted her legs. It wasn't as hard as it looked when you got the *bundhas*—the energetic locks— right. Her legs flexed like she was holding an orange between her knees, pulling her weight farther out of her hands. Her gaze stretched out over the wing. Now upside down, she only saw the tip of the wing. Nonetheless, her mind still had an image of the whole plane.

Eric posed his second question: "What part makes it a plane? Is it the wings, the engines, or the instruments?"

Not one piece of metal or wiring makes it a plane. It's the combination of them all, thought Arial. She repeated her answer out loud: "It's all the parts together that make it a plane."

She was still balancing in handstand when Eric climbed up on the wing and crouched close to her. "If I gave you all the parts in one big stack, would it be a plane?"

Upside down, Arial pictured a jumbled mess of parts.

That muddled stack would not be a plane, as it certainly couldn't fly. "No, it has to be in a certain order."

"Don't freak out. I'm just going to tweak something inside of you."

Arial expected Eric to give her a physical assist, just a small adjustment, like in a typical yoga class. Instead, his eyes began to glow before he spoke his final question: "How do you know what the order is?"

How do I know? I know what a plane looks like! It seemed simple, but for the first time, Arial realized something impossible about reality: whole and parts depended on each other in a way that couldn't be separated from her mind.

The implications felt dizzying. Her image of *jet* had come from viewing just a few parts that weren't the whole plane by themselves. And yet, if she didn't already have an image of the whole jet in the first place, how could she say that a part like a metal flap belonged to a jet? But when could her eyes ever see the whole plane at one time!?

Arial caught her mind in action. Best that she could determine, she had a tiny ideal image of *jet* in her mind that she overlaid on indications of parts suggesting *jet*.

A small bird flew through the hangar and perched on the tip of the wing. It cocked its head at the odd pair, Arial balancing upside down and Eric with glowing eyes, crouching next to her.

Still focused, Arial thought, *What is this hunk of metal to that little bird? I'll bet it doesn't see jet.* Suddenly, Arial realized seeing a jet depended more on her mind than on her eyes.

At that moment, Eric froze her thoughts. A beam of soft white light came from Eric's heart, entering her own.

Arial had been up most of the night; now she was upside

down and the early morning sun was entering the hanger. Arial wasn't sure what she saw coming from his chest. Still, the gleam felt good; she started to feel lighter.

Eric sent her a stream of wisdom from his mind to take her even further. Mentally, Eric asked another version of his first question: *Can you see all of a part at any one time?*

Arial realized that she couldn't even trace all the threads on the tiniest screw at once.

Finally for Arial, the most important point emerged: *How can I be certain it's really out there, if I'm the one laying a complete image on it?* She felt almost weightless, like she did just before reaching zero gravity.

Eric said, "Lift your right hand and go into one-arm handstand. Trust me, you can do this." Persuaded by Eric's confidence, without hesitation she released her right hand to balance just on her left.

"Push up on your fingers." Eric's voice was so gentle, it seemed possible.

For the first time, Arial somehow balanced on her fingertips. Imbued with wisdom, Arial felt altered. There were no further conscious thoughts; she witnessed her seemingly impossible pose without judgment.

Eric saw this was as far as she was ready to go. "Good. You can come down now."

Arial dropped down into Child's pose for a few breaths, before peeking out. "What did you do to me? What was that light coming from your chest?"

Eric avoided the question directly, but answered at a level that she could accept. "I only enhanced what you were already seeing." When he jumped down from the wing, he landed as softly as a cat. "The more you realize your outer world isn't as solid as it seems, the lighter you'll get."

Her fast start impressed Eric, but he had already noticed

another aspect of her personality that would hold her back: her ego. He'd have to devise a strategy for dealing with that fiend.

However, Eric stayed on his lesson plan. "What did you see about the plane?"

"Oddly, that seeing the plane depends more on my mind than on my eyes." Arial dangled her legs over the wing like a schoolgirl. "I don't even see all of the plane. It's more like I have an ideal image of a plane in my mind that I overlay on parts. But then... I'm not really seeing the parts either, am I?"

Eric smiled. "Good." He wanted to clue her into the mystery of wholes and parts today. "For the rest of the day, be as silent as you can. Try to catch your mind laying whole images over mere indications of parts."

Eric didn't tell her that this exercise was one of the most important preparations for seeing ultimate reality directly. It broke down how we construct our reality by imposing mental concepts.

Arial jumped from the wing to imitate Eric's cat-like move, but landed more like a show horse. "Got it," she said, quickly acknowledging Eric's assignment. She tossed her hair and flashed him a flirtatious smile before turning to leave the hangar.

She had to prepare for her own teaching day. After all, she had a handful of pilots to thrash this afternoon.

Eric returned to Agent Rollins who, with arms folded, leaned against a rolling mechanic's toolbox. "That balancing trick may be good for the circus," Rollins said, "but I'm not sure how it's going to help with our mission."

Eric tried to connect with Rollins. "I think you'll appreciate having air superiority when we encounter

Physique. I may be able to neutralize Physique's anger if I have enough time with her. If Arial can control the airspace—so Physique doesn't float away—we may have a better chance." Eric knew the importance of speaking another person's lingo: it broke down walls. Further, it wasn't so far from his own language of a few years back.

Rollins felt relieved to hear Eric talk SEAL again. He had worried that Eric had gone too New Agey to be of any use to them. Now Rollins started to talk tactics. "In the bank, you made the gunman drop his gun...."

"Only one of the gunmen," Eric corrected, remembering what had happened before he got 'shot.'

"Can't you just tweak her and get her to fly?" Rollins asked with the sarcasm of a schoolboy. Eric ignored Rollins' juvenile tone, recognizing that deep down, Rollins really wanted to know.

To Eric, it appeared Rollins was opening to the possibility of yogic superpowers, though the agent would deny it if asked directly. Eric could rescue Rollins from his materialist worldview—if only Rollins wasn't so wary of him.

Further, Eric could correct Agent Rollins' negative attitude, which came from a deeply ingrained *karmic* habit. From studying the agent's mind on the plane, Eric could see Rollins hadn't done much to make other people happy, so now Rollins wasn't happy. Simple cause and effect.

"I can't give something I can't do myself," Eric said. "And even if I could, Arial probably wouldn't be able to sustain it the way she is now. I wouldn't want her getting a hundred feet off the ground and then not understand how to stay there."

"So you're saying you can't fly, but you believe you can

teach her?"

Eric gestured to the jets all around them. "She's the one teaching people how to fly. I'm going to help her harness those seeds in an unexpected way. I can't promise you anything, but I could use your help."

Agent Rollins tilted his head to the side. "What kind of help?"

There was one thing Eric had seen clearly in meditation that would benefit both Captain Davis and Agent Rollins. "There's a physics professor out of the University of Virginia. He wears old-fashioned, black-rim glasses, and I think he's Thai-American. He participated in several *Mind and Life Conferences* with the Dalai Lama. You shouldn't have a hard time finding him: His first name is Elvis."

"The Dalai Lama is meeting with physics professors?" Somehow this was harder for Rollins to believe than any respectable Thai family naming their son Elvis.

"Sure. The truth will be the truth, no matter what method of inquiry you use."

"What do you want with this professor?" Rollins asked, willing to play along.

"I saw him speak before and was impressed. Arial is still an Air Force pilot. She believes in hard science. Hearing the latest findings from quantum physics should help her to let go of an objective, outside physical reality. That will help her fly faster. And I know the clock is ticking."

As Rollins' main task was to watch Eric, he decided on the spot to send Agent Kirby for this professor. It was Kirby's alma mater anyway.

Still, Rollins felt curious. *What is quantum physics saying that might support the development of superpowers?*

13. MUG SHOTS

In a dark mobile trailer filled with monitors, Agent Kirby applied drops to his dry, weary eyes. After watching hours of airport surveillance video, he felt jet-lagged. Shiny snack bags littered the gray console. Kirby reached for the nearest chip bag and turned it upside down above his opened mouth, but no crumbs came out.

Kirby felt grumpier than a Middle Earth dwarf. He and a boyish curly-haired colleague had identified several images of the woman who called herself Physique, but none had a good face angle. Sure, they could see the cotton baseball cap she had worn when entering the terminal and her blond hair that fell over her eyes as she had passed through security—but not her face. She even had practiced yoga in a corner near Flight 1632's gate—incredibly, with her back to the security camera the entire time.

As they watched her move from Downward Dog

directly into Crow, the junior agent working the video feed said, "We have great shots of her butt. It's definitely a yoga butt."

"I'm not sending agents to yoga studios to match a butt." *What would that line-up be like?* "You've got to give me something better."

"We know she's about 5'9", thin, blond, and buxom," said the operator.

Kirby sneered. "You want me to put out an APB for Barbie?"

Kirby had been on the Physique case for five days, but hadn't made any progress discovering her true identity or her location. If he didn't come up with something soon, he might get sent back to his cubicle.

"Well, there's this," said the video operator, jumping to the part on the video where she went into headstand. He ate some chips from his personal stash, and then licked his fingers before touching the already greasy controls.

Tilting his head to the side, Kirby tried to make out the features of the upside-down yogi. The video operator froze a frame, and then rotated the image 180°. Even though her elbows were close to her ears, they could see her determined green eyes, narrow nose, high cheekbones, and full lips.

"Now that's more promising," Kirby said. "We'll run with that."

Only a few miles away, Physique presented herself for a job interview using a new name, Delilah Spears. This time, her hair was brown.

After looking her up and down, the manager asked, "Wouldn't you prefer working as a hostess?" He had a pudgy face from spending too much time in the restaurant bar and short, brown hair with a cut from a barber who valued speed over style.

As in most restaurants, this manager's office was clearly an afterthought. It was barely bigger than a walk-in closet. Cases of booze occupied nearly every space.

Physique crossed her legs in the plastic foldout chair near the end of his desk, pretending to be a bubbly Delilah. Today, she sported a sexy emerald green dress that stopped mid-thigh; its scoop neck highlighted her ample cleavage. The dress was one of several things that she'd bought using money from the Bone Frightener. Delilah flashed her prettiest smile. "I prefer serving people more directly, rather than just escorting them to their seats. And in truth, if I'm waitressing, I think I can make more in tips. I still have student loans to pay."

The manager nodded, thinking, *We all have student loans to pay.* He pointed to a large photo album on his messy desk. "You'll have to learn the names and faces of all the congressmen and senators. Being so close to the Capitol, we're something of an informal clubhouse. They like to be recognized by name. Each one of them thinks they're going to be president some day."

"That shouldn't be hard for me." Delilah straightened herself in her chair like a beauty pageant contestant. "I'm something of a political science geek. Actually, I enjoy watching the House speeches on C-SPAN." In truth, she closely watched C-SPAN. *Why hadn't anyone in Congress introduced a bill to significantly cut military spending?* she thought. Her cheek started to twitch. *Were they trying to tick me off?*

She definitely wanted this job. Waitressing put her in proximity to dozens of senators and representatives, and provided the setting for the next step in her plan. "I like your office," she said. "It's... cozy."

The manager was easily taken in by Delilah. He couldn't imagine why any woman this pretty would be home watching C-SPAN, but he felt confident she'd be a winner with his high-profile clientele. "I have to run your name and social security number by Homeland Security before you can start. It takes about two weeks before they issue clearance. We're not a real high priority for them. Any problem with that?"

"None at all," she answered. Delilah Spears would certainly be clean thanks to some fancy work by the Bone Frightener.

The manager looked at the staff schedule on his white board. "I have two spots available: lunch and dinner. Which shift would you prefer?"

Delilah brushed her hair behind an ear. "I'd kinda like to meet some congressmen. When do you see more of them?"

"Lunch," answered the manager without hesitation.

"Then lunch it is in two weeks," answered Delilah, closing the deal that brought her one step closer to finalizing her sinister plan.

14. THE QUANTUM PROFESSOR

AGENT KIRBY FELT UNSURE ABOUT WHAT TO SAY TO ELVIS Jao, an eccentric physics professor from the University of Virginia. Named by his Thai parents after the famous American performer, Elvis Jao was a rock star in the physics community known for presenting with exuberance and expertise.

After students dispersed from a large lecture hall with fold-down seats, Agent Kirby made his way down the hall's stairs. While Professor Jao collected his papers, Kirby introduced himself and then delivered a few choice words: "Professor Jao, the FBI needs you to give an overview of the big ideas in quantum physics." Jao tilted his head to the side and pushed up his black, wire frame glasses. "The briefing will take place on an Air Force base. Afterwards, you'll be prohibited from revealing who you met in that room."

"Wonderful!" Professor Jao clicked shut his briefcase, excited to be picked by the FBI for an assignment. After all, it would earn him major coolness points with his grad students as well as enhance his mystique with the department chair. Professor Jao knew that all he needed to say was a few words to one particularly gossipy grad student: "Classes are cancelled tomorrow because the FBI needs me to assist with... well, it's classified." Then word would spread around the department like Greek fire.

Understanding that the briefing was on an Air Force base, Jao refused the offer of payment. His only request was that they consider taking one of the university's two atomic clocks up in a jet fighter at high speed. If Professor Jao could reproduce an experiment that validated Einstein's theory of time being elastic, he would score further cred. Then he'd have a real teaching gem to keep his students captivated.

Jao agreed to leave immediately with Agent Kirby. He could see himself saying to future students, "One time—when I was assisting the FBI with a classified investigation—I was able to offset time... and that's why the university's atomic clocks are out of sync to this day." With that bit, he'd have cachet for years.

Agent Kirby told Jao he'd see what he could do, but he couldn't promise anything with the clocks. Fortunately, this didn't dampen Professor Jao's enthusiasm in the slightest.

Elvis was used to speaking to large audiences of undergraduates, grad students, and peers at academic conferences. With his thick glasses, he looked more like a Thai Roy Orbison than an Elvis. Still, as he entered the classroom at Fighter Weapons Training School, the man had swagger. However, seeing only three people surprised him; further, as a scientist, Jao wasn't sure what to make of the composition.

An attractive woman in an olive green flight-suit—evidently an Air Force pilot—sat in the front row of desks. Next to her was a black man in a blacker suit with a menacing scar on his left cheek. There was no FBI flavor about the man; he seemed like something more covert. Two rows behind them sat a man with longish blond hair in faded jeans and a blue T-shirt, who looked like he'd be more at home playing volleyball on a California beach. Agent Kirby, in his navy-blue suit again, took a desk to the right of Rollins, one row back.

To not usurp Rollins' authority, Eric wrote two questions on a piece of paper and slid it to him. If all went well, this conversation with a respected physicist would loosen both Arial's and Agent Rollins' perceptions of a physical world that existed separate from the observer.

Agent Rollins cut right to the chase. He hoped they weren't wasting Professor Jao's time... or his. Rollins asked Eric's two questions: "To start, can you tell us... what has quantum physics discovered about the true nature of physical reality? And is this position supported by ancient wisdom from the East?"

After considering where to begin, Professor Jao launched, Elvis-style, with the most provocative opening he could muster. "Matter has lost its substance. There is no true physical reality or localized realism that can be discovered—only dependence on relationships to define existence in a perceived moment. The illusion of an objective physical universe that exists before observation, just waiting to be discovered, is continually shattered by further scientific investigation." Jao waited for the downbeat. He let this group absorb quantum physics' most significant discovery.

Professor Jao knew his audience would need more details to fully understand. But Jao had their attention. His talk would explain his opening summary. All of which could be further summed up with one word that he wrote on the white board behind him. Bending his left knee, he threw his full body weight behind an underlying stroke with dramatic flair:

Interdependence

With his back still turned to his audience, Professor Jao said, "Quantum mechanics is the physics of the infinitely small, and relativity... the physics of the infinitely large." His words bounced off the whiteboard. When he spun around, he unexpectedly karate-chopped the air. "Both of them say the same thing in different ways: the objective physical world doesn't exist the way we once thought it did."

Eric smiled in the back of the room. He sensed they were in for an exciting ride with Professor Jao.

"If you'd studied physics a hundred years ago," said Jao, "the professors would have convinced you that the physical laws of the universe were completely known, and all that was left for you to do with your scientific career was refine the decimal points. Since then, nearly everything in physics has been overturned. However, our culture still hasn't caught up.

"Let's consider three things most people believe to be true." Professor Elvis Jao snapped his wrist to count the points in a way that "The King" might have counted beats. "One, physical reality is made up of particles that exist without us observing them. Two, physical space can't be transcended. And three, time is a constant. Each of these has been proven false."

Arial's forehead wrinkled. She had heard bits about this stuff over the years, but never that quantum scientists had shown that there was no objective physical reality or that physical space could be transcended.

Professor Jao sensed her discomfort. But he had a quiver full of Nobel laureates to prove these points.

Jao continued, "One of the key findings of quantum physics is that we can't define what is there until we observe it. For example, all atomic and subatomic matter, not just light photons, can exist in more than one way. They can be waves or particles, depending on how you measure them. Thus, there is no objective reality. Rather, reality is fluid, depending on an interaction between the observer and the object under observation.

"As Heisenberg explained:

> Some physicists would prefer to come back to the idea of an objective real world whose smallest parts exist objectively in the same sense as stones or trees exist independently of whether we observe them. That, however, is impossible."

Jao laughed, "As if that weren't weird enough, consider the following: A wave is like the ripple after a pebble drops into a pond. It expands to many places at the same time. It's like energetic potential. When we look for a particle— the mass—the wave collapses and a particle can appear anywhere."

To illustrate his next point, Jao ran from one side of the room to the other, zigging and zagging. "However, there is no such thing as a trajectory in quantum mechanics. The particle just appears, by us looking for it.

"It's as Dr. Oppenheimer said:

> If we ask, for instance, whether the position of the electron remains the same, we must say 'no'; if we ask whether the electron is at rest, we must say 'no'; if we ask whether it is in motion, we must say 'no.'"

Like an Eskimo who had just described twenty different types of snow to Southern debutantes, Jao saw that most of the room wasn't catching the point: *there was no intrinsic reality at the atomic or subatomic level. And further, as micro-things aren't one way, how could the macro-things they create be one way? It would be as silly as saying if you drew enough pictures of cows, you could milk them for something to drink.*

"One of the founders of quantum mechanics, Heisenberg, puts it more directly," Professor Jao said. "In *Physics and Philosophy*, he wrote:

> Atoms are not things, [and that] materialism rested upon the illusion that the kind of existence, the direct 'actuality' of the world around us, can be extrapolated into the atomic range. This extrapolation is impossible, however."

Eric already knew that for people like Heisenberg and Bohr, atoms were a world of potentials and possibilities, rather than things or facts. This is exactly what he wanted Arial to hear.

But Jao wasn't done. He may have poked holes in the concept of an objective physical reality, but now he was about to reveal a shocking experiment that challenged the most basic beliefs about the nature of the physical world. Professor Jao said, "Now if the quantum wave can be at multiple places simultaneously, it also means that communication between correlated photons can transcend physical space."

Arial's ears perked to the idea of transcending physical space. She loved flying at supersonic speeds, but this was a different level of fast.

Jao considered the principal of non-local causation to be the single most important discovery in all of science. He decided to explain in layman's terms one dramatic EPR experiment verified by Swiss physicists in 1998.

Jao brought his index fingers together, and then separated them, while doing a few moves that Arial interpreted as those of a dancing robot. "After dividing a light photon, the law of symmetry says that the resulting smaller photons must remain perfectly correlated. Meaning, if one moves north down a chain of fiber optic cable, the other must go south. But if you present the smaller photons with branches that are six miles apart, how will they communicate to each other which route to take to stay correlated? Keep in mind these photons are traveling in opposite directions at the speed of light—and nothing is supposed to be faster than the speed of light."

Picturing the experiment, Arial imagined two jets speeding away from each other, communicating via radio commands. As the distance increased, so would the delay in signal. In the case of photons traveling at the speed of light, no communication signal could possibly reach the other photon in time for it to choose the same fork in the road.

Professor Jao saw that Arial understood the problem. "In the time their decision is captured, information could only have moved three and a half inches of the six miles separating those two photons. Would it surprise you to know that they *always* make the same spooky choice? If one takes the short route, they both do. And the same is true with the long route."

The odds were impossible. It was like tossing coins before two football games on opposite sides of a city at the same time and the tosses always resulting the same— no matter how many times the coins were tossed. Meaning, these split photons were still correlated regardless of physical space.

"But why?" Arial asked.

Jao adjusted his heavy glasses. "Because physical space and locality do not exist in quantum mechanics. The notions of 'here' and 'there' are meaningless, because 'here' is identical to 'there.' The relationship the photons share determines their reality, not any physical world."

In his mind, Eric repeated the essence of Jao's words: *The relationship they share determines their reality, not any physical world.*

Eric recalled a physics quote he'd once found which supported his own extraordinary experiences. In *Mind and Matter,* Erwin Schrödinger wrote:

Subject and object are only one. The barrier between them cannot be said to have been broken down as a result of recent experience in the physical sciences, for this barrier does not exist.

Eric understood that his unusual yogic ability to read minds, to transcend physical space like split photons in an EPR experiment, came from his ability to access the connection shared between him and someone else. In essence, the other person was a part of him, perfectly correlated through his image of that person's mind. And, like the surprising proof of wave-particle duality that won a Nobel Prize, in Eric's world there could be no other image of a person's mind except the one he measured.

A mischievous look came over Professor Jao's face. "Now to your second question: that no objective physical universe exists is something the Buddha taught twenty-five hundred years ago. Further, the Buddha described galaxies with many planets and even the existence of atoms that could be divided. We can see that the Buddha's key teaching—that everything exists through mutually dependent relationships, which the Buddha called *interdependence*—is surprisingly similar to the revelations that came from the two main theories of modern physics: relativity and quantum mechanics.

"Remarkably, ancient wisdom beat us to this position. I suppose it's a little humbling, but it appears we're rediscovering truths that someone before us already spoke."

Eric smiled again. He remembered having discovered similar correlations between quantum physics and ancient wisdom in his own research, which had given him more confidence to throw himself into inner contemplation to see the truth about reality for himself.

Eric hadn't always been a yogi—not even close. For most of his life, he had been an ordinary westerner with conviction in the superiority of science and a belief that a Google search could let someone else do the thinking for him. That was when he'd even cared about worldly knowledge. Other times, he hadn't asked questions deeper than "how do I keep my camo' dry?"

But once Eric became wheelchair bound, there was nothing to do but explore reality with his mind. Once he embraced sitting, his mind became as sharp as a sword.

Some days he imagined becoming like Stephen Hawking. Others days he felt like Chaurangi, a contemplative hermit forced to sit after losing his arms and legs. Eric found great inspiration in Chaurangi: after that *Mahasiddha* mastered the illusory nature of his body, he finally restored his limbs and flew in the sky.

When Eric first started reading teachings from the East, he was surprised by how the Buddha spoke of atoms and galaxies as casually as if he had an electron microscope and the Hubble telescope in his monk's bag. Eric recalled one example in the *Diamond Cutter Sutra*, where the Buddha said:

> Suppose some daughter or son of noble family were to take all the atoms of dust that made up all the planets in this great world system, a system with a thousand of a thousand of a thousand planets. And suppose for example that they were to crush each of these atoms into a pile of even tinier atoms that were equal in number to all these atoms of the planets. What do you think, Subhuti? Would the tiny atoms in these piles be very many?

Even skeptical Rollins, with an ear for data points, would have to consider these statements as way ahead of the curve. Somehow in 500 B.C.E., the Buddha already knew that Earth was part of a galaxy with over a trillion planets. He knew physical forms on those planets were made of atoms. And that atoms could be divided. And for the Buddha, these were just passing comments compared to the greater wisdom he'd sought to teach!

The fact that the Buddha could describe galaxies and divisible atoms approximately 2,400 years before Western science, had persuaded Eric to take more seriously the Buddha's cure for suffering.

Summing up his brief talk, Jao said, "What I want you to understand is that reality is always relative to the observer. Things cannot be defined in absolute terms, but only in relation to something else." Professor Jao karate-chopped the air again. It was his sign for cutting through confusion.

"Galileo said, 'Motion is as nothing.' You can understand this best when you fly your jet. Major Davis, is it?" Jao had read her name from her flight-suit and had tried to make out the rank from the insignia.

Arial folded her hands politely on her desk. "Captain Davis. But I appreciate your optimism."

"Why is motion as nothing?" Professor Jao asked her directly.

It didn't take Arial long to answer. She'd seen it many times in the sky. Flying past the speed of sound at thirty thousand feet in a cloudless sky was a non-event. But flying a fraction of that speed close to the ground felt exhilarating. "Motion can only be defined in relation to a second object."

"Good. The same thing applies to time. The faster you go, the more time slows down. This was one of the big surprises that Einstein introduced with his Special Theory of Relativity. He was certain because he saw it through thought experiments he conducted in his mind. It took years for people to prove it with technology, but we finally did."

"How, Professor Jao?" Arial asked, fascinated.

"Elvis. You can call me Elvis." He gave his body a little shimmy.

"OK Elvis," Arial smirked, "how can you prove that time doesn't exist truly?"

"I was hoping to show you, rather than just tell you." Elvis reached into his bag and took out the fanciest-looking atomic clocks Arial had ever seen. They were glass-encased steel, with a red quartz digital display. "These atomic clocks are precisely in sync down to a billionth of a second. If you could take one of these up in your jet and fly really fast, the motion would slow time down. In fact, if you could get these atomic clocks out of sync by even a nanosecond, I'd be quite the hero with my physics students."

Arial didn't want to stick her neck out further, so she didn't respond to Jao's request.

But Elvis prodded, "There's a big difference between talking about this stuff and seeing it for yourself."

Noticing Arial's discomfort, Agent Kirby changed the subject. He asked Professor Jao a question about mass and energy. As Jao answered, Eric used the opportunity to pass Arial a note. She unfolded the paper slowly. It read:

> Find a way to help Jao live his dream,
> and collect the merit to live yours. .

As Jao continued speaking, Arial wondered what Eric meant. Then she recalled that *The Yoga Sutra* explained how everything in your world depends on how you've treated others in the past. A key verse spelled out this first principle of *karma*:

ते ह्लादपरितापफलाः पुण्यापुण्यहेतुत्वात् ॥ १४ ॥

te hlada paritapa phalah punya-apunya hetutvat

II.14 THERE IS A CONNECTION OF CAUSE AND EFFECT:
THE SEEDS RIPEN INTO EXPERIENCES
REFRESHINGLY PLEASANT, OR PAINFUL IN THEIR TORMENT;
DEPENDING ON WHETHER
YOU HAVE DONE GOOD TO OTHERS,
OR DONE THEM WRONG INSTEAD.

The verse said that good results came from good causes, and bad results came from bad causes—always. This was how we created our experience of the world. She then remembered the second rule of *karma*: the result was always greater than the cause, just as a two thousand-ton oak tree was greater than the tiny acorn it sprouted from. Arial understood, just a little kindness could make beautiful things ripen.

In fact, making Professor Jao a hero with his students would plant powerful seeds—creating a relationship of interdependence to help her on her own journey to become a superhero. Then, they both would get what they wanted— and two people would be happy!

She had planned a simple, high-speed exercise for her own students to demonstrate fuel optimization using the afterburner and supersonic speeds to intercept a target. The closure rate of two supersonic fighters moving directly toward each other at supersonic speeds had to be experienced to be believed. Her plan might raise an eyebrow or two, but Arial could deal with that. It was actually a pretty safe exercise, compared to the dog-fighting and evasive maneuvers usually done around here. And after all, the two-seater training jet often had been used to give VIPs joyrides.

"I'll do you one better," said Arial to Professor Jao. "I'll take up your clock *and* you this afternoon."

Several hours later, Professor Elvis Jao strapped into the back of a dual-seater F-15. He cradled one of his atomic clocks like a baby as they flew through the sky at fifty thousand feet. After Captain Davis and the pilot a hundred yards away punched in their afterburners... crossing Mach 1... and reaching Mach 2... Elvis Jao shouted, "This is awesome!!!"

15. DEADLINES

BACK ON THE GROUND, AGENT KIRBY AND AGENT ROLLINS met with Eric to discuss his progress with Captain Davis. Eric didn't particularly care for a private meeting with both Kirby and Rollins. Sitting in the beige quarters reserved for government guests on the airbase felt too much like being back in the police interrogation room. They still had their guns and badges—all that was missing was the cuffs.

Eric had an uneasy feeling that Kirby and Rollins would, at any moment, turn him over to government men with lab coats. They seemed even more anxious than usual, like caged ferrets.

"How quickly can you get Captain Davis to fly like a superhero?" Agent Kirby asked in a hurried voice. He placed his cell phone down on the glass table between them, then scratched his forehead.

Rollins sat uncomfortably on the edge of a chair as if

ready to spring at any moment. "You better produce results soon, or we don't need you." He was used to speaking this way to CIA informants in hostile lands.

Rollins didn't even believe that flying results were possible. He was just looking for a reason to dispose of the enigmatic Eric so he could get back to the tough business of searching for Physique.

Listening to Agent Rollins and Agent Kirby press him, Eric thought, *This is part of a bigger karmic process. Be patient. Endure.* Just because Eric had cut the engines of suffering in deep retreat didn't mean all suffering immediately stopped. In fact, the opposite occurred for him. Eric had experienced ultimate reality so deeply that the effect was more like pulling up railroad tracks. Messy train wrecks followed as negative *karmic* deeds blew out for him.

You may have succeeded in getting your sense of self out of the way, but painful karmic habits and traumatic memories can still reassert themselves. Use your strength of wisdom, Eric. Hold yourself back from reacting negatively.

It was a kind of power to not be pushed around by one's own mind. But it was still a big-top wrestling match. For Eric, things would be this way until he reached nirvana, the complete end of mental afflictions, which in this moment felt like a long way off.

Agent Kirby and Agent Rollins were challenging tests for him. Agent Kirby had hurt him badly and Rollins... could.

Staying cool, Eric let his emotional stuff blow past him like a foul wind. "I hope Professor Jao's presentation loosened Captain Davis' grip on the physical world a bit." Indirectly, he was speaking to Agent Rollins, who was the toughest of nuts to crack. "But I need to shift Arial's belief level dramatically if we're going to get her to fly like a superhero any time soon."

Agent Kirby folded his arms across his chest, crumpling his blue JC Penney suit. "How do you propose to do that?"

"I'm asking for your permission to show her the Physique video."

Kirby tensed even more. The Physique video was, of course, highly classified. This wasn't a light request. Still, a phone call to NSA head Sujata Bansal could gain Captain Davis clearance.

Following a brief heated discussion, Agent Rollins and Agent Kirby agreed to try. The pressure was on and they were running out of time. In fact, only ten days remained on Physique's deadline before she threatened to strike next.

16. ARIAL'S RESPONSE

ARIAL WAS SILENT. SHE HAD JUST WATCHED THE truck-crushing video. To avoid being overheard, the fledgling team met in the small living room of Agent Rollins' and Eric's bleak government quarters. The two agents sat near Arial, while Eric stood behind by closed venetian blinds.

When Agent Kirby confirmed that data recovered from the plane's black box was consistent with Physique's wild claim, Arial's mind reeled. She stared at Kirby's black laptop on the coffee table as if viewing a portal to another dimension.

Arial imagined being the pilot of a plane that suddenly took on a massive imbalance of weight. *If Physique bent the tail out of alignment, the pilots never had a chance.* She pictured the innocent travelers on board—mothers, children, fathers, and young adults just starting their lives—and the people on the other side of the gate waiting to receive them. The urgency struck her.

Physique is a weapon that no one can detect.

Arial had glimpsed villains like Physique only in her younger brother's splashy comic books. But strangely, something felt familiar about Physique.

"I think I know her."

This was the response Agent Kirby and Agent Rollins had least expected from Arial.

"What?" stammered Kirby. His brown eyes blink-blinked as if Arial's recognition of this woman was more miraculous than the video of Physique crushing a flatbed with her feet.

Arial's conviction grew. "I've been doing yoga for a long time. I think I had a run-in with her a few years back. I went to a yoga workshop at an ashram in the Bahamas. Funny place. They have this very serious, sparse ashram on the beach. And their neighbor is an over-the-top resort and casino."

"The Santosha Center," Agent Kirby said. "It's very famous." Kirby recalled how the swami the center was named after had written an astounding eBook that described yogic superpowers. Widely circulated for free on the Internet, it was one of the books Kirby had referenced in his *Dangerous Yogis* report.

Arial's mind floated back to those days in the breezy Bahamas, trying to piece together the story. She remembered her strongest impression of the ashram. "It's funny because you can sit on the beach with sand between your toes and so easily see the difference between people who do yoga and people who don't. It's like all the grumpy hung-over people were staying at the resort where they had every materialistic comfort you can imagine, while the happy, energetic people were getting up before dawn to do their practice and community jobs to keep the ashram running. It was the most convincing ad for a yogic lifestyle I'd ever seen."

"That resort does have the best water slides though," Eric interjected, not wanting Arial to be down on something that made some people happy.

Eager for a good lead and less concerned about waterslides, Agent Kirby quickly brought the discussion back to the crucial issue: "Why do think you remember her?"

"That's the thing," answered Arial, "Yoga people are normally very happy and easy-going, but this girl wasn't. When she found out I was an Air Force pilot, she made a big fuss. Keep in mind, this was during the seventh year of the wars in Iraq and Afghanistan." Arial remembered how tired everyone had been of the war that was only supposed to last a hundred days.

"This girl kept jawing about how many civilians were killed in Iraq and Afghanistan. As well as the Predator drone program that had alarming ratios of civilians killed for every insurgent. I tried to explain to her that I flew F-15s that were mainly used to shoot down planes before they could bomb large groups of people, but it didn't matter. To her, I was a baby-killer, so I didn't belong at her guru's teachings."

Eric shifted uncomfortably in his chair. Twinges of guilt, which he had been running away from for years, gripped him. If only he could go back and speak with his younger self. He would do things… differently.

As Arial tried to remember what happened next, Agent Kirby leaned forward in the sofa chair. His first substantial lead felt just beyond his fingertips. He had to let her talk so she could pull up more memories. Recollections are like photos in old shoeboxes: you just have see a few before you remember what's in the entire box.

Arial's eyes brightened. "Apparently, her guru was heading to Afghanistan to teach yoga and meditation to promote peace in the region. He was raising money to support his foundation's efforts. I thought that was quite courageous."

"What else can you remember?" prodded Agent Kirby.

"I remember she went to her guru to try to get me expelled. I think she was involved with him. They seemed to have some sort of relationship, but I'm not sure. He said I could stay, that he felt happy I was there. After that, I remember he was extra kind to me and that was the end of it. Though every time he gave me special attention, it seemed to really tick her off. I don't remember her name. To me, she was just some tall, grumpy chick."

Agent Kirby took a color photo from his jacket pocket. It showed the woman he believed to be Physique, out of costume and doing a headstand in the airport—moments before she boarded Flight 1632.

Arial studied the photo. "It seems like her. She was prettier than nice. But I can't be certain."

Then another memory struck like a punch to the gut. "One time, when I was resting in Child's pose, the guru gave me an assist to help me relax deeper into the pose. I thought he was standing on my lower back... the weight was so much. But when I peeked out, he just had his hand resting on my back as he crouched next to me. That's a little unusual, right?"

Agent Kirby's eyebrows rose. Agent Rollins gave him a nod. Both felt the dominoes falling. "Do you remember his name?" Agent Kirby asked.

Arial tried to remember, but the foreign name hadn't

stuck. Plus, their encounter had been brief. "I'm afraid I don't. It was many years ago. I didn't really take to the style of yoga that guru was doing. Too much crazy *pranayama* and breath retentions. He wasn't a regular teacher at the center. Just a guest instructor and I happened to have leave then."

"Did you go to the Bahamas often?" Agent Rollins asked.

"No. Just that once."

Agent Kirby and Agent Rollins didn't ask any more questions—they didn't need to. Finally, they were back in the domain of simple detective work. In under an hour, the agents would be able to access the crucial records revealing when Arial Davis had flown to the Bahamas. With the exact date, it would be easy to then identify which guest instructor had taught at the Santosha Center. If they could find the teacher, they could find the student.

Eric had quietly observed the interview. The agents had an opportunity to do what they do best.

"I'd like to stay here and continue working with Captain Davis, if that's all right with you," Eric said. "You can send for me when I'm needed." Then looking at Rollins, Eric added, "I won't run off."

Rollins gave his no-frills nod to Kirby. More important things were surfacing than baby-sitting Eric Adams. Additionally, Rollins felt confident he'd be able to track Eric down (if he did run) just by checking cheap yoga studios. But closer to the truth, Rollins didn't like being cooped up in the same suite with someone—or something—he didn't understand.

Eric knew the deeper reason: people with unruly minds seldom liked to be around someone who could read theirs.

Agent Rollins said to Arial, "You don't mind watching over Eric for a few days while we go check this out?"

Arial smiled at Eric. Her eyes lingered… maybe a bit too long. "No, not at all."

After Agent Kirby and Agent Rollins stepped outside to make phone calls from their car, Eric flopped down on the tan sofa chair that Agent Kirby had occupied, and put his feet up on the glass coffee table. He didn't care that he could feel the springs through the cushions. He felt elated to be free of the agents for the first time in seven days.

Still, there was work to do with Arial. Unfortunately, even wearing comfy civilian clothes of blue jeans and a white T-shirt, she still looked rattled.

To break the sober mood, Eric asked a more innocuous question: "How much time did you roll off Professor Jao's atomic clock?"

Her mind concentrated on Physique, but Arial answered anyway: "Seven nanoseconds."

"What's a nanosecond?" Eric asked.

"It's like a billionth of a second… whatever that means." Then her face brightened. "But when Elvis got back to the hanger and compared the clocks, he said it was the coolest thing he'd ever seen. 'Definitive proof that time is an illusion!'" She mimicked Jao's karate chops in the sky. It brought a smile to both of them, but only for a moment. Her world was still sliding into unfamiliar, potentially hostile territory, and she couldn't unlock the brakes. Since Eric and the agents had shown up at her training facility, Arial had witnessed the most unusual things she'd ever seen in her life.

Eric understood her discomfort. When this new world started surfacing for him it had felt like he'd been crawling through mazes and mirages. But the best way out of confusion is through it. Fortunately, all these yogic superpowers shared one truth: everything is possible with an understanding of the true nature of reality.

Never wasting a moment to bring her understanding further, Eric asked, "Remembering that teacher in the Bahamas, did you notice that you now have a different perception of the experience?"

"You mean that guru probably taught that woman how to change her weight at will, like when he was giving me an assist?" As difficult as it was to believe, it was probably the truth.

"Exactly. But you didn't have that perception then." Eric pushed away a lock of golden hair that had fallen over an eye. "Since you only recall the past in the now—and each time the meaning may be different—can't you conclude there is no fixed, unchanging past? I think that's stronger proof for the illusion of time than out-of-sync nanoseconds."

Eric rose to get Arial a glass of water. She needed time to process all she'd seen.

Glazed over in deep thought, Arial was picking on some of the couch's stitching when Eric returned with a cool glass. Arial took a tentative sip before placing it down, uninterested in water. "Let's say I'm willing to accept that reality is an illusion, that everything is a mental image. Where do the mental images come from?" Among other things, she was thinking about how to fly.

Eric took his seat once again on the sofa chair and interlocked his fingers. "That's the best question you've asked me so far. Aristotle would have answered the question, 'why does it rain?' this way: 'Because plants, animals, and humans need water—that's why it rains.'"

"Meaning what?"

"Meaning you'll fly when a compelling need meets an intense desire to do so. I can show you the mechanism, and give you a good reason—but it has to be something you really need to do."

Arial considered what she had seen with Physique. More people would get hurt if she wasn't stopped.

Eric said, "Agent Kirby and Agent Rollins are good investigators. I think they'll find her. But I think Physique is going to be much harder to capture or kill then anyone can imagine." Eric leaned forward in his seat, while placing his elbows on his knees. He brushed the persistent lock of hair gently to the side once again. His blue eyes glistened like lapis stones.

"In the last few days, I've told and shown you things to change your belief level. Today, I've given you a compelling reason. I need your help to stop Physique. I want to bring her in alive."

Arial doubted she could help. Still she asked, "What do you need me to do?"

"Sleep on it tonight. Decide if you really want to be in this fight. You've seen who we'll be up against. She's deadly."

"And if I say yes?"

"Then your training really begins tomorrow."

17. ATTACKING THE EGO

THROUGHOUT THE LONG NIGHT, ARIAL TOSSED IN HER bed. Her pillows felt like coffin padding. She thought of the many people killed by Physique's actions, and then about the many more in danger should she strike again. In this light, she'd never had a choice. People like Arial and Eric were born to save others, no matter the risk to themselves.

After doing *asana* together in Arial's office overlooking a runway, Arial shared her resolve.

However, Arial was unprepared for Eric's first instruction for the real training. "Stop winning the dogfights with your students. You need to lose." His gaze was unflinching.

"You want me to what?!" Arial bolted up from her yoga mat to lean against her desk. She hovered over Eric, who still lounged on his own mat.

"Ego," responded Eric. "There's too much ego. There's too much sense of self. You're never going to be able to transform—to become a superhero—until you can get out of the way. Your concern for yourself and for preserving your image at all costs will block you."

Arial folded her arms across her chest. She protested, "I don't understand."

Eric quoted the great Buddhist master, Chandrakirti:

FIRST CONCEIVING AN "I,"
WE CLING TO AN EGO.
THEN CONCEIVING A "MINE,"
WE CLING TO A MATERIAL WORLD.
LIKE WATER IN A WATERWHEEL,
HELPLESSLY WE CIRCLE.

"Meaning what exactly?" Arial glanced at the round, clunky digital clock above the door. Things weren't going how she'd expected. She had looked forward to this, her first un-chaperoned day without gloomy Agent Rollins in the background. She had even worn an extra low-cut top during yoga. But now Eric was attacking her about her ego. *Doesn't he know how much confidence it takes to fly jets?*

Eric followed her jagged and uneven breath; too much inhale, not enough letting go. He considered what to say to help her. "When we first met in New York, I was still in a wheelchair."

"I remember," said Arial. She'd wanted to ask him about his remarkable recovery. It had just never seemed like the right time.

"I should tell you how I walked again when doctors didn't give me much chance." Eric stalled a bit, reluctant to speak of painful memories. Unconsciously, he rubbed his leg, feeling sensation where once he couldn't.

Eric replayed the moments in Afghanistan that had

ended his SEAL career… his fiancé leaving him… the years fighting depression… then he remembered the woman who for a short time had helped him put his life back together. She was the physical therapist who had made him do Tibetan Heart Yoga to keep his heart *chakra* open; she was the one who'd taken him to the spiritual center in California where he'd had his mind blown.

Finally, Eric explained, "I used to be an athlete. I know about competition. Even as a Navy SEAL I had pride in being among the best in the world. That was before a blast partially severed my spinal cord." Eric recalled how he'd had some sensation in only one leg, but couldn't control the muscles. The doctors felt he had little possibility of walking again without some breakthrough medical procedure that hadn't been discovered yet.

"After years of depression, I finally made it to a spiritual center and started learning about ultimate reality. I learned that because nothing has any nature of its own, anything is possible.

"Then one day, the lama changed my course. He said, 'Every single ailment you get is leading you in a certain direction. If you won't do what you're supposed to do, your body will force the issue. Since you can no longer define your meaning by accomplishments in the outside world, maybe you need to accept what your body is telling you—you need to look inwards.'"

Eric remembered his silver wheelchair. He'd refused an electric one. At least pumping the wheels had given his strong arms something to do. "I was this athletic hard-charging person being forced to sit—confined to a chair. But when I looked inside, I saw we are all confined in some way. Confined to a role, confined to an identity, confined to a body. In sum, confined by our ego. The real freedom is no longer being confined by your sense of self."

After years of study, Eric had seen how his ego kept him separate from others. Like some devious hoofed beast, Ego constantly kicked up dirt that had made him feel better or smaller than someone else. Any drama would do, as long as enough dirt had piled up for Ego to feel separate. That grotesque storm maintained the illusion of separation. Eric hadn't wanted to admit how dangerous division was, but finally he saw the truth. As long as there were walls between himself and others, he would never feel whole. But toppling the walls had buried the beast.

Eric's blue eyes gleamed from the place of peace he'd found. He'd learned how to get out of the way. He wanted to teach others how to do the same, because it ended so much suffering. He wasn't perfect yet, but he'd gone much further than he'd ever imagined possible after so many personal setbacks.

Arial saw how Eric's eyes sparkled. It felt comfortable and easy to be around someone who wasn't consumed by their ego. Eric felt almost transparent.

Hearing Eric's story prepared Arial for what she most needed to know. Eric outlined the key steps: "The fastest way to gain yogic superpowers is to no longer believe that anything in your world has a true, definitive nature. The best way to see that is to no longer believe in a truly existing self. And the best way to do that is to undermine the ego by serving others first. It's a chain of cause and effect."

Finally hearing Eric's instruction, Arial came down and sat once again on the yoga mat across from Eric. Still, she wanted to avoid further discussion about her ego. Her eyes looked down at the floor, unable to meet Eric's gaze. "You still haven't told me how you got out of the chair."

Eric followed the inhale and exhale of his breath before remembering the events that had led up to that important day. There'd been two parts. "First, I had to see in deep meditation that my body didn't exist the way I thought it did. Actually, that was easy for me. Once, I had the body of a very powerful athlete. A moment later, I couldn't move my legs. My body clearly didn't exist in any one way."

"What was the other part?"

"Interdependence. I had to learn how to change by taking care of others instead of worrying about myself."

For much of Eric's life, he had been using his body to win glory. When that ran out, no one cared about him—but worse, he saw that he'd gotten in a habit of not thinking much about others.

Eric remembered his life as a Navy SEAL. People used to step aside whenever he and his team entered a room. Everywhere he went, he felt respect and admiration. It was easy to think he was finally being rewarded after such a hard childhood. But how quickly that changed once Eric no longer walked tall.

Following his lama's instructions, Eric volunteered to help people who were like him. "I threw myself into helping other people—mostly other messed-up young vets coming back from the war. They were people like me who had lost limbs or become paralyzed. You can't imagine how hard it is to readjust to life when you can no longer walk."

Eric continued, "Here's the secret of interdependence. You take your good deeds and you map them to what you want. For me, it was seeing everyone walking again who wanted to. You consciously create your future reality." So Arial would remember, Eric repeated the process: "You take your good deeds to that place of pure potential in deep meditation—and create a new reality. If you keep at it, wonderful things start happening."

Eric recalled how happy he felt to see some vets get new prosthetics that helped them to function again with physical confidence. Some of the prosthetics were practically bionic. Then others received operations that had even reversed their paralysis.

"What happened to you?" Arial asked.

"In meditation, I kept seeing myself walk. My mind was so still and so concentrated—it was all I could believe. One day, I got up and walked."

Arial's eyes widened. "You just got up and walked! What did the doctors say?"

"No one was sure what to make of it. They did some studies, but couldn't explain what had occurred. But I understood. Using wisdom and good deeds, I changed my belief level to accept that new reality. In time, even miracles get forced upon you."

Arial picked at her yoga mat. She knew that much of her identity was wrapped up in her image as one of the world's best fighter pilots. She could protest; she could tell Eric that she was making the seasoned pilots better by consistently beating them. But the truth was, she'd often pulled aerial circus stunts to win—nothing that they were likely to run into in any combat situation with foreign pilots.

Eric said, "Here's the truth for you. As long as you identify with your small self, there will be no yogic superpowers. I think you're amazing. But to go beyond ordinary, you have to lose yourself in serving others. Then you can become what others truly need."

Eric pulled his faded jeans over his black cotton yoga trunks. He took a piece of paper from his pocket and gave it to Arial. "It's from *The Bhagavad Gita*, Gandhi's favorite book."

यस्त्वात्मरतिरेव स्यादात्मतृप्तश्च मानवः ।
आत्मन्येव च सन्तुष्टस्तस्य कार्यं न विद्यते ॥ ३-१७ ॥

yas tvatmaratir eva syad atmatirptash cha manavah
atmanyeva cha santushtas tasya karyam na vidyate

III.17 NO ACT IS DONE
BY A PERSON WHO DELIGHTS
IN THE SELF,
WHO IS SATISFIED
IN THE SELF,
WHO IS CONTENT
IN THE SELF.

Eric leaned on the windowsill looking out at the world. "It means you can't really help people, and do a truly good action, if you have attachment to your own ego."

He could feel Arial softening. "Other people came to me after my miraculous recovery," Eric said. "They wanted help overcoming their obstacles, in the way that I did." Eric remembered people who'd come to him for personal advice and guidance. They'd been of all ages and from different backgrounds. "Not very many made much progress I'm afraid."

"Why's that?" Arial asked, surprised.

Eric pulled out another piece of paper from his back pocket. It was another verse from Gandhi's favorite book:

यं संन्यासमिति प्राहुर्योगं तं विद्धि पाण्डव ।
न ह्यसंन्यस्तसङ्कल्पो योगी भवति कश्चन ॥ ६-२ ॥

yam sannyasam iti prahur yogam tam viddhi pandava
na hyasannyasta sankalpo yogi bhavati kashchana

VI.2 WHAT DO WE HAVE TO RENOUNCE,
FOR WHAT WE'RE DOING
TO BE CALLED "YOGA"?
NO ONE EVER BECAME A YOGI
WITHOUT FIRST GIVING UP
THE IDEAS THEY HAD ABOUT THINGS.

Arial laughed. "You got any more verses in your pockets?"

Eric smiled before walking to the door. "Not today. The next move is yours."

Later that day, Arial spoke to her favorite mechanic: "Let Captain Fulmer know he can have his rematch if he feels up for it." Zipping up her flight suit, she added, "But this time, don't place any bets."

18. MOVIE BREAK!

ONCE ARIAL PROVED HER WILLINGNESS TO PUT ASIDE her ego—by staying in the dogfights until her students discovered the winning maneuver—Eric ramped up the training. Over the course of three long days, he took Arial through his version of a mental decathlon.

For hurdles, there was a dizzying download of twelve different proofs of the truth of "emptiness"—meaning that nothing has any intrinsic nature of its own. For the high jump, they worked the accompanying analytical meditations. For the 100-metre dash, they memorized more *Yoga Sutra* verses.

Arial could finally explain how the last three limbs of yoga worked together: focus, fixation, and perfect meditation. Or as they are known in Sanskrit: *dharana*, *dhyana*, and *samadhi*, which together became *sanyama*, the combined effort.

Arial discovered the instructions for perfect meditation

had been hiding inside her favorite verse—the key to getting her to fly without a machine. It had just taken Eric to unlock what she'd already stared at so many times inside her locker.

कायाकाशयोः संबन्धसंयमाल्
लघुतूलसमापत्तेश्चाकाशगमनम् ॥ ४२ ॥

kaya-akashayoh sambandha sanyamal
laghu tula samapattesh cha-akasha gamanam

III.42 WHEN YOU TURN THIS EFFORT
UPON THE RELATIONSHIP BETWEEN
THE BODY AND SPACE, YOU GAIN
A POWER OF MEDITATION WHERE YOU BECOME
LIGHT AS A WISP OF COTTON,
AND CAN THUS FLY THROUGH THE SKY.

Using *this effort*, Arial examined four times per day the true nature of her body and space in meditation. Like a diligent scientist looking through a microscope, she stayed single-pointed in her analysis, performing many tests without being pulled away. Finally, when she had a "Eureka!" moment—when the true nature revealed itself— she held the realization, free of conceptualized thought.

During one of their long evening sessions, Eric explained, "Your body also depends on parts. That's easy to see. Now see that even empty space depends on parts, like up and down, or left and right. This means neither is self-existent. Parts depend on smaller parts to define their existence, right? When you can stay immersed in wisdom that sees both body and space as mental images, mere labeled projections, then you'll be able to fly."

Like throwing the javelin, Eric also gave Arial inner

body meditations to open her root *chakra*, the *muladhara*. This would allow her to reverse the downward energy running within her body, known as the *apana vayu* to yogis, and give her lift to get off the ground.

Eric was an endurance athlete of concentration. Sitting in Arial's office/meditation room, he was about to run the 1,500-meter dash—with more teachings on interdependence—when Arial popped. "Eric," she said rubbing her eyes, "I need a break. Can we have some fun?"

Eric laughed. He had stayed in solitary meditation for over 750 days and yet he hadn't done anything purely for fun since returning to the world. "What did you have in mind?"

Arial considered options. "Well, there's not much to do around here.... Take me to the movies!"

Eric laughed again. "I'm afraid I never got to deposit my first paycheck. I interrupted a bank robbery... it's a long story... but it has something to do with how I came to you."

"That's okay," Arial said. "I'll take you. Let's just get out of here before my head explodes!"

After a too-fast ride in Arial's electric blue Ford Mustang—which she had gunned out of every stoplight like a testosterone-pumped racecar driver—Arial and Eric stood in an Apple store. "How is this even possible?" Eric wondered. "The entire computer is in the screen?" Eric hadn't been in a mall or seen new technology in years.

"Eric, close your mouth. You're attracting attention," Arial joked.

Truly, Eric looked like a stunned toddler. After two years in an isolated mountain cabin, walking through the large glass doors of the mall felt like entering a magical realm. Any minute, he expected singing unicorns to fly down a shaft of rainbow light.

"The colors are... so beautiful." Eric pointed to the dazzling displays. "They're like candy. I feel like I could eat them."

"You need to get out more," Arial said, nudging him away from the goods. "Come on, we don't want to miss the movie."

More than two years had passed since Eric had left the world for deep retreat, and already so much had changed. Eric felt like he was in a new, sparkly world of design wizardry. Even a cell phone seemed more like an entertainment center than the wireless phone it had been just a few years back.

"Things change so fast," Eric said as Arial led him by the elbow to the cineplex. "Every moment is so beautiful and so amazing, you almost miss it."

"Miss what?"

"How much virtue it took to create a place of abundance like this—where so many wishes can be fulfilled in a few footsteps."

"Eric, this is just the mall."

"Not to me," Eric answered.

"And every town has several—"

"That's just it. When in history has it been so easy to have material wishes fulfilled? It's amazing." Eric turned to walk backwards, taking in the sights behind him. "It would be even more extraordinary if people could appreciate that it all comes from past acts of generosity." He turned forwards again just as they strolled past a lingerie shop.

"What do you see?" Arial asked.

Eric tried to find words to explain. His experience of reality had become so much richer since meditation altered his consciousness. "For me, the world is like walking through a living dream. It's magical, because I no longer see a separation between myself and the world being projected. We are part of the same moment. And each moment only comes once, never to be repeated."

For Eric, the world had become like starlight that had traveled for countless years to shine for just an instant. He experienced everything as a flash of lightning whose appearance had something to do with him. This was seeing the world without walls.

At the cineplex, a dozen flicks of every adventure imaginable—all in vivid digital and internal-organ-massaging surround sound—competed for their attention. But their decision was easy: a superhero movie. It featured a minor character they didn't recognize, but it didn't matter. The heart of these movies was always right: someone used whatever abilities they had to save the world.

Even in the afternoon, the theater was packed—not sold out, but filled with excitement. Arial leaned in close as they shared a helmet-sized tub of buttered popcorn. Eric also sipped a blue Slurpee whose electric color existed nowhere in nature. Even before the movie started, he wore his 3-D glasses, slouching low in his chair.

Eric looked at Arial with a goofy grin and stuffed popcorn in his mouth. For a moment, Arial felt like they were on a date.

"*Anima.*" Arial whispered Sanskrit to Eric, once it was revealed that the movie's hero could change his size at will: making himself as small as an ant or an atom, then as big as an NBA center to pummel the bad guys. Of course, the hero acquired his power from one of those typical freak laboratory accidents. But having studied this stuff, Arial recognized the power as *anima*—often the first in the list of eight classic yogic powers.

They both ducked when the little guy swooped through a keyhole to throw a 3-D punch.

Arial tried to see the world through Eric's eyes: as mental images coming from her past deeds. There was this little guy flying through the sky, beating up the bad guys, and somehow it was a part of her. Then a thought occurred: *I'm sitting next to someone who actually has superpowers. He's sitting here, enjoying himself—and no one else knows.* A more surprising thought followed. *How many other people in this theater might have powers that I don't know about?*

Immersed in 3-D, Eric enjoyed the experience. Even though he knew it wasn't real, he watched his mind revel in continuously being fooled. His body continued to duck slightly as objects appeared to sail past him. His heart raced and his emotions rose when someone was in danger.

In a quiet moment, Eric wondered, *What will happen when entertainment technology grows even more immersive? What will happen when people can no longer tell deceptive illusions from what we normally call reality?* Already the outside world was so like a 3-D movie. People were caught in the emotion of it. And when they didn't understand how the dream-like illusion functioned, it hurt them.

After the movie and some veggie burgers, Arial pulled into the driveway of Eric's little guest house before cutting the engine. Moonlight streamed through the windows. In the awkward silence, they both rested their heads back, looking straight forward.

Arial thought, *I wish he'd just kiss me.* She was enjoying her time with Eric. They had so much in common, and it was rare to be able to talk yoga philosophy with anyone. Yet Eric was immune to all her flirtatious tricks.

But Eric wasn't reading her mind this time. Instead of

being in the moment, Eric reflected on the day. How nice it had been to just relax and enjoy the pleasures of life. How wonderful it had been to spend the day in the company of a beautiful woman who smelled like roses.

In truth, he'd like to settle into a comfortable life. But he knew that illusion was so fragile. He'd been separated from women he loved before. He knew he was still vulnerable to how quickly things can change.

Those emotional scars still kept Eric distant, but there was more….

"Have you ever ridden in a jet fighter?" Arial broke the silence.

"Can't say I have," Eric answered.

Arial smiled. "I think I need one more day to recover before you can really push me further. So tomorrow after meditation, I'll take you up."

19. DEATH BY METADATA

SRI HARI DAS WAS DEAD. THIS MUCH AGENT KIRBY AND Agent Rollins had learned. But few would ever know the real reason why. It took an effort worthy of Sherlock Holmes to connect the dots, but Kirby and Rollins still didn't have enough information about the deceased yoga guru to lead them to Physique.

Kirby and Rollins sat across from the director of the National Security Agency (NSA), Army Gen. Robinson, who was willing to give them only a few minutes after being coerced by Sujata Bansal. He didn't even offer them coffee as he would most visitors to his office in Fort Meade, Maryland.

Sitting behind a pile of spiral-bound reports at his desk, he stuck to the official story told to the world. "Sri Hari Das and several of his yoga missionaries were murdered by machine gun-wielding Taliban in the Kunar province. As I understand it, he was trying to bring yoga to Afghanistan to promote peace, but the Taliban didn't want it." Gen. Robinson bristled at their naiveté.

Rollins knew the date and location of Sri Hari Das' death. He also carried a copy of a CIA surveillance photo showing a building that had been reduced to mud by more than just machine gun fire.

Cutting through the bull, Rollins slapped the photo down on the general's desk and said words that few wanted repeated publicly: "Triggered by SIGINT."

The general blinked, then looked out his window.

The drone program had many dark secrets, but the dirtiest of them involved signal intelligence. The NSA had figured out a way to track cell-phones via the SIM cards of Al-Qaeda and Taliban high-ranking targets—even when the phone was turned off. As long as a phone had battery life, the SIM card was a homing beacon. This meant that often the NSA had tracked bad guys by analyzing the activity of a SIM card rather than the content of a call. In short, the NSA had launched missiles at cell phones, presuming a bad guy would be on the other end.

Unfortunately, top Taliban leaders had deduced the NSA's targeting method and sometimes wielded it against them. Wanting Sri Hari Das out of Afghanistan, they had used Americans to do it by offering him a modern Trojan Horse: a cell phone containing the SIM card of a high-ranking Pakistani Taliban leader.

When Sri Hari Das recharged the phone and started making calls from the Kunar province, informally known as "Enemy Central" by Western armed forces, the NSA thought they had struck gold. When that SIM card made a phone call to the United States, the NSA had feared an action against the U.S. was in motion. Without further hesitation, they ordered a Predator drone strike, and that night leveled the small adobe home where Sri Hari Das was staying—believing they had killed a Taliban commander.

"What do you want?" asked Gen. Robinson. He already had too many leaks to deal with, and this particular unintended "death by metadata" plus the subsequent misinformation campaign could prove embarrassing for the NSA.

"I just want a phone number," Rollins answered.

A good general, Robinson knew when it was time to call for a retreat. "There was only one number in the States. We already checked her out. The number belonged to a yoga teacher named Tina Tinsdale, whom he was involved with. It took some time for us to calm her down, but I think she bought the story that her Hari had been killed by a Taliban RPG. Unfortunately, Ms. Tinsdale had been on the call when our missiles hit."

Within minutes following the hellfire missile blast in Afghanistan, a tactical team had kicked in Tina Tinsdale's apartment door in Baltimore, Maryland. Instead of finding Islamic jihadists, they'd found a blond women in tears collapsed on the floor. Still the assault rifle wielding team had taken her into custody and proceeded to question her for days—mostly until the NSA could figure out whom they'd actually killed in the drone attack.

After explaining the fuller story, Gen. Robinson cut a deal. "I'll give you a copy of the interview, if you go away."

Only days after her release, Tina Tinsdale had dropped off the map. Even her family had stopped hearing from her. She had been skillful enough to not let on during her interrogation, but she had never believed the official story. After all, she had heard Sri Hari Das' last words and the sound of the blast just before jackbooted agents kicked in her door. Those series of events and the grief that followed, more than anything, had pushed her mind toward her new persona as Physique.

Eventually a missing person's report had been filed for Tina, but there wasn't much follow-through on that. Her mother clung to some false hope that her impressionable daughter had disappeared somewhere in India and would surface again when she was ready.

Rollins and Kirby had uncovered Physique's true identity. And they understood her motive. Now back in the FBI building named after the bureau's first director, the more disturbing thing in the investigation was her bank account. Normally, following the money led to a suspect. But her account (which had $3,556) had *no activity* in it for fourteen months.

"Someone is helping her," Agent Rollins said. The bank account confirmed what he had suspected back in Pearl's Junkyard. "She can't have gone fourteen months without funds. Someone is bankrolling her whole damn program."

Agent Kirby and his team had already scrubbed all transactions on her account since her guru's death. None of the payments suggested she had set up a new account under a different identity.

Rollins said, "If there is one thing I can't stand it's a traitor. But it's worse when it's a conspiracy." Agent Rollins felt frustrated. He knew it was damn hard to set up a new identity in the U.S. But once it was done with no financial strings connecting the identities, detection was nearly impossible.

Physique was essentially off the grid until she chose to surface again.

Agent Kirby sensed what further worried Rollins. *What*

if more are being recruited like her? Now Kirby and Rollins were going to have to find Tina *and* the person or persons who had approached her to take advantage of her rage.

"We need to brief Sujata at the White House," said Agent Kirby. "We're going to have to scrub for more patterns—"

"To see if we can find who's behind her." Rollins finished Kirby's thought.

"It's going to be wildly unpopular with a whole bunch of people," Kirby added.

"You think I give a rat's ass about popularity? She's a killer. She needs to be taken down."

Both men were tense. Physique's deadline was four days away. And the agents knew they were a long way from finding her.

20. FLIGHT TIME

After morning meditation, Arial took Eric up in the two-seater F-15. Pilots referred to the two-seater as the family model, even though it was still a killing machine. The training jet had a full set of controls in front and back that were linked mechanically. This allowed an instructor to watch the controls move while a student performed maneuvers. When necessary, the instructor could take control by grabbing the stick.

After a roaring takeoff, Arial didn't go for speed as she had done with Professor Jao. For Eric, she pulled gentle maneuvers that gave him only a sense of what flying a jet fighter was really like.

Arial started with some lazy eights, reminiscent of ski-capped snowboarders cruising back and forth in a half-pipe. Corkscrew aileron rolls slightly increased the torque.

The cockpit felt cramped to Eric's long legs and broad shoulders, but he marveled at this strange new experience and Arial's confidence in the sky. One with the machine, she focused more on her thoughts than the controls. Anything she wanted to do, she simply thought and her body responded. Her fingers were like a concert soloist on violin, so swept up in the sound she wanted to create that she became the sound. Eric felt he was in the hands of a true virtuoso.

After big barrel rolls—wider than a carnival carousel and with parts upside down—Arial leveled out. At twenty thousand feet, Arial instructed Eric to take the stick and perform a gentle banking turn to the left, which brought them around in a wide U-turn. Eric had been in helicopters before, but not a jet. The most surprising thing to Eric was how nimble the jet felt—almost like a motorcycle. The slightest twitch on the stick and the plane responded instantly.

After Eric handled a few more gentle turns, Arial shook the stick, signaling that she was going to take over. This time she gave Eric a real taste of the machine's power. She arced back into a big circle loop that pulled more g-forces than the most aggressive roller coaster. The sustained five Gs were usually enough to make any beginning pilot puke. Fortunately, Eric hung in there, all the while clutching a vomit bag.

Seeing that Eric could use a break, Arial set the jet down on a small abandoned airstrip sometimes used for refueling. Dust kicked up from the tires.

As fun as it had been twirling somersaults, Eric was glad to be on the ground. Still feeling dizzy, he breathed deeply to settle himself.

Arial shed her flight suit for the more comfortable yoga clothes underneath. Planning something of a picnic, she'd brought a little lunch. There wasn't anything or anyone around for miles except for tumbleweeds and long shadows cast across the sand. Blue sky loomed large and dome-like showing the curvature of the earth.

Eric studied Arial. She didn't belong on the ground. She belonged in the sky.

"I'm going to fly you," Eric said.

"Excuse me?"

Eric flopped down on his back and took off his shoes. "Come over here." When Arial approached, he raised his legs. "Just lean into my feet and give me your hands. I'll take you up."

Arial finally understood. He was going to fly her like she was a little girl. She leaned into Eric's feet. Eric positioned them in the crease of her pelvis. As she leaned over, her lips came close enough to kiss Eric. She felt happy she wasn't wearing her lowest cut tank top, or certainly Eric would be staring at her naked chest.

"Ready?" Eric asked.

"Sure."

Eric straightened his long runner's legs, surprising Arial with how high off the ground she felt. Arial straightened her back, looked out, and pretended to fly like Superman.

Arial was imagining what it would be like, when she heard Eric's voice: "It's time. Time for you to fly."

Sensing something in this moment, Arial believed Eric's words. She recalled her best meditation on the lack of intrinsic existence to her body and space. They didn't have a nature separate from her mental image of them. But the emptiness side was only part of the flight equation. Consciously, she'd been mapping her good efforts to help her students become better pilots to create a new reality—one in which she could fly without a machine. With the things she'd seen Eric and Physique do—plus

understanding the hidden mechanics of cause and effect—
Arial finally believed a flying miracle was possible for her.

Eric closed his eyes. Rays of white light poured out of
his chest into her. Eric stacked images for flying and her
sky body together. Accessing subtle seeds in her mind, he
helped her to see everything was like a dream—appearance
arising, but with no true substance. Now, anything was
possible with the right causes.

Tingles rose up Arial's legs just below her skin.
Downward energy reversed itself to enter her lower *chakras*.
Then, the *pranic* energy shot up like a bolt of electricity,
lifting her like the Rapture.

Arial couldn't stay down. Soon, she floated away from
Eric's legs without effort.

Eric poured more light into her heart. Then he let go.
Arial continued to rise away like a helium balloon with a
message for the world: things are not how they seem.

Looking down, Arial saw the distance between herself
and Eric growing. But she was not herself in this moment.
She was a beam of energy, lighter than air; blissful and serene.

The height didn't scare her. She'd been in the sky so
many times. But finally, this time she'd become sky. She
lifted her head to look at the sun behind a cottony thick
cloud. Bands of light passed through like heaven's rays.
Wanting to go there, she lifted her arms above her head,
stretching her fingers. In an instant, she zoomed up. For the
first time, Arial Davis flew without a machine. It felt more
exhilarating than she'd ever imagined.

She moved through the air with speed. Arial banked
and looped easily. She didn't hesitate. She just thought and
did. At one point, she must have been a thousand feet off
the ground, feeling completely at home in the sky.

But then, thoughts of landing started to come. Feeling

unstable, Arial quickly moved into full lotus, bringing her legs up in a meditation posture. This forced the destabilizing, downward *pranic* energy back into her torso, which gave her lift. She'd been in this posture many times before in her dreams. Slowly, she descended, completely under her own control. She hovered in the air about eight feet off the ground in front of Eric.

"I feel like Wonder Woman without the invisible jet," Arial said.

Eric answered, "I knew you could do it. I always believed in you."

She looked at the desert dirt. The rocks and dust looked coarse and unappealing compared to the blue sky. "If I touch the ground, I'm afraid I won't get up again."

Standing beneath her, Eric said, "You have to think about how you created this. By understanding the nature of this appearance, you can keep your seeds going to allow you to fly again in the future."

But not wanting to come down, she extended her hand: "Join me…."

Eric smiled, "Maybe someday I'll be able to. But right now, this is your power."

Arial uncrossed her lotus legs before slowly coming to the ground. Even placing her feet on the earth felt different. Oddly, she had a sense of how unique a mental image it was to stand on two feet instead of four like most animals.

Eric offered her flight suit so Arial could prepare to take the jet back. Their lunch remained in her backpack. After what had just happened, neither of them felt like food.

As they walked toward the plane, Arial lifted off the ground again… just to be sure she could do it.

Eric said, "Keep it on the ground. There's still more for you to learn."

21. THE BALLOON LAKE

"Balloons?" Arial asked. "Why do we need balloons?"

"You can't imagine how difficult helium balloons are to find when you need them," Eric said, pushing a red balloon out of the driver's seat. He had trekked to a low-budget wedding supply store on the edge of town to find a multi-colored bouquet.

Eric drove today. He'd seen enough of Arial's weaving through traffic, scaring other drivers. He also wanted Arial to review this morning's meditation—where she replayed how she'd finally gotten off the ground.

Arial picked at her yoga pants and white tank top. She brought her feet and knees up on the seat, and then leaned against the door. "Where are you taking me... slowly?" She poked at one of the dozen helium balloons bobbing in the back seat.

"To a lake. For more training," Eric answered. He'd gotten directions to a man-made lake in a small state park that was usually deserted.

"Can I turn on the radio?" Arial asked.

"No, watch your thoughts."

After a few minutes, Arial said, "You drive slower than my grandma."

"Your grandma flies jets too?"

"Well, she was heavily influenced by my granddaddy. I guess we're a family of speedsters."

Eric raised an eyebrow. "You think?"

Arial looked at Eric. *Why is he so stoic today?* Just yesterday, he'd been so pleased with her.

After almost two hours of silence, they arrived at the small state park. The green sign for the turnoff wasn't much bigger than a mile marker.

Still the only one with a job, Arial paid the entrance fee and rented wooden paddles for a rowboat that was parked on a bank of the lake. The place felt so remote that she figured the park ranger was being punished. Or maybe, he just didn't like anyone interrupting his reading. She spotted a stack of comic books and enjoyed the incongruity of a man in a Smokey Bear hat sitting alone in a booth all day reading *Flash*.

The weekday meant they had the lake to themselves. They found an old-fashioned wooden rowboat that belonged in a French painting. Eric tied their dozen balloons around a rock before placing it in the middle of the boat. Arial sat in the back as Eric rowed them out to the middle of the lake.

The temperature felt comfortable. A light breeze gently stirred the lake; close to the shore, reeds rustled. Clouds reflected on the lake surface like pillows topping a dark bedspread. The sun shining through the multi-colored balloons cast rainbow hues on Arial's white tank top. Arial watched Eric throw his shoulders into each stroke. *Now this is romantic.*

However, Eric was thinking something completely different: *This is an ideal setting for flying drills.* Looking around the lake, Eric saw they were alone. Additionally, because the lake was the result of a man-made excavation, they were hidden from view by two large hills.

Eric spoke to Arial in the back of the rowboat: "Time to fly."

"I'm not sure how to get off the ground. Can you give me a lift?" Arial wanted him to do his heart-light thing again.

Eric just held the oars, ready for more rowing. "I already did. You have to be able to pull up the memory of that first experience. You have to replicate it—everything you were feeling, everything you were thinking. Those mental images will take you up."

Disappointed, Arial crossed her legs in meditation position. She closed her eyes and deepened her breath with a few rounds of *pranayama* before going back to the moment when she'd been suspended over Eric's body. His words replayed: "It's time for you to fly." His light entered her heart. She connected with the emptiness of this appearance and the emptiness of her own body. Suddenly, more quickly than she imagined possible, her root *chakra* opened again. Downward energy reversed, tingling up her legs. She felt the lifting energy intensify. Then her body rose out of the boat into the blue sky.

Today, she flew on her own.

Arial brought one knee up as she zoomed higher, arms stretched overhead. She was sky once again. She could travel anywhere she thought in an instant.

"Not too high today," called Eric from the boat. "We don't want anyone to see you."

Arial floated down roughly fifteen feet above the water. She could see her reflection on the surface of the lake. "Now are you going to tell me what the balloons are for?"

"This is a speed and focus drill. When I release a balloon, I want you to catch it by the string as quickly as possible."

"Piece of cake," Arial answered, oddly confident in her new flying ability.

Eric smiled up at her. As he started to row with powerful strokes, building up momentum, Arial lazily floated behind him. Eric's paddling was even slower than he drove. While the boat drifted under its own power, Eric untangled a single red balloon. Bobbing the string like he was counting one, two, three, he signaled Arial before releasing it.

Remarkably, Arial's eyes zoomed in on the string like a hawk's. She must have been thirty feet away—but she could count threads. This was certainly unexpected. Her eyesight was surprisingly enhanced. Her confidence swelled as she zeroed in on her prey. As the balloon rose, she sped forward, focusing solely on the rising string. She stretched out her hand and pinched down.

Touching the string—feeling a physical object between her fingers—tripped up her mind. Suddenly she couldn't stay all sky body. She fell fifteen feet like a flailing stone into the water. The cold water smacked her flesh. Wincing, she thought, *Did I just belly-flop from a high dive?*

As the balloon gently floated away, Arial slowly surfaced from the murky lake. Eric made her swim over to the rowboat. Accepting his help she climbed in, awkward and floppy as a drowned rat.

"You knew that was going to happen," Arial said.

"Let's just say I had a suspicion."

"And you didn't warn me?" The light breeze now felt cold on her skin.

"What do you think happened?" Eric asked.

"My sky body. I couldn't understand how sky could touch and hold something physical. It made me solid. I felt like Wile E. Coyote realizing he had run off a cliff."

"So you can transform into a sky body, but the string has to stay physical? Is that how it works?"

Teased, Arial caught his point—one he'd been telling her all along. None of the outside world is truly physical. Rather, labeling it *physical* makes it so.

Arial closed her eyes to visualize her sky body again. She felt the energy inside her rise before she floated out of the boat again.

Eric turned the boat the other direction as Arial trailed at treeline height. Once Eric built momentum, he released a purple balloon. Arial moved quickly. Maybe a little too quickly. She grabbed the string—thinking it wasn't physical—but she still fell. It was one thing to intellectually understand the world is made from changing mental images and another to actually experience it that way.

Three more attempts; three more falls. *Splash. Splash. Scadoosh!*

She heard Eric call out, "I wouldn't have guessed landing face first could make that big of a splash."

Arial sat in the back of the rowboat, dejected. Further, she realized her wet white tank top was completely see-through: *Yes Eric, these are my nipples and you'd still rather I chase balloons.*

"Let's try something else," Eric suggested.

"Please. Anything."

Eric took a box of pins from his pocket. They were the

kind with the round plastic ball on the end that her mom had used to hold hems when sewing. "Do you think you can pop a balloon?"

Do you think I can pop a balloon?! Arial glared back. Still, she took the stickpin. It wasn't much of a sword, yet in a few moments she returned to the sky holding the tiny pin for another attempt. Zeroing in on a balloon should be easy compared to catching a string.

When Eric released a red balloon, Arial raced toward it—no, through it. Wound up, she punched through it like Superman smashing through a brick wall. But the loud pop like a gunshot startled her. Losing her concentration, she fell. Uncontrollably, for some reason, she grabbed the string as if that would save her. *Sploosh!*

Arial paddled over to the rowboat; then hung on the side. She protested, "I'm not getting back in the boat until you let all the balloons go. I've had enough for today."

Eric shrugged. "Okay, but we'll just have to buy more balloons tomorrow."

"That's fine. I can't stand to look at another damn balloon."

Eric complied by letting the bunch go. They drifted up into the sky, celebrating their victory over Arial, seemingly mocking her. Eric said, "I had other drills planned for you."

"I'm sure you did. Just help me up."

This time when Eric leaned over, giving her his arm, Arial pressed her legs against the boat, pushing back. She pulled Eric headfirst into the water with her. *Splat!*

Eric came up slowly, moving the wet hair out of his eyes. "What did you do that for?"

"I don't want to be the only one in a wet T-shirt on the drive home."

When they got back to the car, Eric and Arial slopped

down all wet on the seats. In his booth, the park ranger scarcely looked up from Flash dodging Captain Cold's freeze ray while Eric returned the paddles.

As Eric drove slowly down the road, Arial asked, "Was this another ego-busting day?"

"Maybe. Was it for you?"

"I feel like I just spent the day in a carnival dunk tank. What went wrong?"

Eric kept his eyes on the road. "Mostly I just needed you to understand this isn't a game. There's more for you to work on. But not to worry. When there's a compelling need, you'll be able to do more with your abilities."

Dripping in her wet clothes, smelling vaguely of pond scum, Arial hoped he was right.

22. A COMPELLING REASON

As they drove over the sprawling Hoover Dam Bypass Bridge, Arial looked up at the endless blue Nevada sky. Only an hour ago she had felt confident about flying in that empty space. But now, in her dirty clothes—still uncomfortably wet in places where she touched the leather car seat—Arial didn't feel super.

She made the mistake of glancing at herself in the rearview mirror. Mascara—which she'd originally put on to look good for Eric—smudged her face, making her look almost criminal.

Arial tried to squelch feelings of shame as Eric explained her next step. "It's not enough to see the outside world as a mental image instead of physical—you have to go one step further to break down all walls."

Arial turned away from Eric to stare over the low concrete barrier that marked the bridge's edge, out toward Hoover Dam. The concave concrete dam was bigger than two football stadiums and held back enough water to cover a state like Connecticut, ten feet deep. *I hope that wall never breaks*, Arial thought.

Still, she listened to Eric's voice. "To stay in your sky body when you touch objects, you have to accept it's all your mind... consciousness taking form. Simply you're interacting with a part of you. All of it is you."

The immensity of that proposition felt too big for Arial. She started to feel annoyed, almost wishing that she had never bumped into such ideas.

Two buzzing Ducati motorcycles whizzed past their car like missiles. Leaning like racers, the reckless, youthful drivers in brightly-colored motorcycle gear weaved in and out of traffic as if the cars were standing still.

Ahead, Arial—with her sharp pilot's eyes—saw a navy-blue minivan vacate the speed lane while a station wagon was in its blind spot. At the same time, the station wagon's driver was pointing out the Hoover Dam for a child in the back seat.

"Eric, look out!"

Before pressing his brakes, Eric checked his rear-view mirror. A large trailer truck was following too close and wouldn't have braking room. Eric slammed his foot on the accelerator, diving the Mustang into the left lane as the minivan and the slate gray station wagon collided in front of them.

When the station wagon went up against the low concrete barrier, the whole world seemed to slow down. Eric threaded a path between the center guardrail and the crashing cars, but the trailer truck could not. Brakes locked, swerving into the left lane, the truck jackknifed at the worst possible place—the middle of the world's highest concrete arch bridge.

Striking the pinned station wagon, the skidding trailer shattered the concrete barrier. The collision catapulted the gray wagon across a narrow pedestrian walkway before it slammed through the last remaining guardrail.

The vehicle, with a mother and child inside, hung over the edge.

Eric and Arial sprinted from their car toward the crash site. Thrown glass, metal, and concrete crunched under their feet. They could see cars behind the mess coming safely to a stop and other drivers coming to the rescue as well. But when they reached the station wagon, it was worse than they'd feared.

The gray vehicle was badly smashed and teetering like a seesaw over the edge of an unsurvivable nine hundred-foot drop into the Colorado River.

When the young mother, bleeding from a head injury, tried to reach over the seat to unstrap her daughter from her car seat, the station wagon started to pitch back. Pressing his hands down on the hood Eric shouted, "Please, don't move!" The mother understood immediately: the balance was more precarious than a pencil balancing on fingertips.

Arial took Eric's place at the hood as he edged closer to the crumpled car door at the ledge. Arial looked around for more help, but pedestrians were filming on their smart phones, rather than getting close to the station wagon that appeared certain to topple at any second.

"What's your little girl's name?" Eric asked through the broken driver's side window.

"Lisa," the mother answered. She was afraid to move or take her eyes off her child.

"Lisa," Eric said, "I want you to unbuckle your harness and slowly climb over to Mommy. Can you do that?"

But Lisa didn't move. She was staring down at the

water nine hundred feet below, clutching her Raggedy Ann doll so tightly to her chest Eric thought the doll's button eyes would pop.

Eric placed his hands on the car door. He could feel the station wagon inching away from him. He pulled, but he didn't have the leverage or strength to hold three thousand pounds back.

"Lisa, honey," the mother said, "I want you to climb over to Mommy." But even stretching her arms out toward her child shifted the car's weight. The station wagon dipped and slid. This further scared the child.

Fortunately, two more courageous bystanders joined Arial at the car's hood. Others finally wanted to help, but there wasn't enough ledge space left to get more leverage.

Feeling the car sliding, little Lisa started whispering words only her doll could hear.

With some effort, Eric opened the car door, then slid his hand around the mother's arm. She said, "I'm not going without my child."

"I know," Eric answered calmly, "We'll go together." Both could hear the sound of metal sliding over concrete.

Eric shifted the grip of his free hand to the top of the car. He pulled with all his might as he still held the driver's arm loosely with his right. Eric wanted to use his heart trick, to go into little Lisa's mind to erase her fear... but there wasn't time. The mother stretched one arm to try to reach back and undo the harness, but the subtle shift in weight only made things worse.

Eric's worried eyes met Arial's. Straining with others at the hood of the sliding car, she knew what would happen in the next moment.

They felt more concrete crumble before they heard it. As the car fell, Eric yanked the woman out. At the same time,

Arial strode forward: "I won't let that child die." Then to everyone's shock, the blond-haired woman dove off the arched bridge.

As Arial accelerated past the falling vehicle, she saw the water coming up way too fast. She had only seconds. Reaching for the car door, Arial thought, *she is part of you. This is all part of you. And you have to save her!*

She ripped open the car door and unfastened the harness. Little Lisa leapt into her arms. Arial wasn't sure if she was flying or falling when she kicked off the station wagon just before it impacted with the Colorado River. The plume of water spewed like a hot geyser.

Moments later, Arial found herself slowly ascending with the child in her arms. Her awareness expanded beyond her body. This was a different world now; she would protect every being in it. Hair flowing in the wind, she flew to the top of the single-arched bridge.

She touched down at the bridge's center, then set Lisa down gently. She watched as Lisa threw her arms around her mother's legs. Now everyone was silent, staring back at her—a bizarre flying lady in stretchy yoga pants and a white tank top.

Arial saw shock and confusion in people's eyes. They weren't looking at her like a person who had just saved someone… more like she was some kind of strange, alien creature. When she backed away, people just let her pass.

Hearing the snapping of pictures from cell phones, Arial realized that people on the pedestrian walkway had gotten video of her leaping off the bridge and then ascending with the little girl. Nervous, Arial walked briskly toward her car. She heard Eric's footsteps behind her. Then panicking, Arial broke into a run. Eric, the much faster sprinter, easily caught her.

Arial shouted, "Give me the keys. I'm driving. We've got to get out of here." Now a mob of people started running after them, taking more photos and videos with their smart phones.

Arial slammed her foot on the pedal of her electric-blue Mustang as if initiating her jet's afterburner. After several minutes cruising over one hundred miles an hour, she finally heard Eric say, "You can slow down now. No one's following us."

Arial slowed the car, but her heart still raced. She couldn't fully believe what she had just done. *Did I really just dive off a bridge to save a child's life?*

"I wasn't thinking about me," Arial said. "Every thought was about saving that little girl."

"That's what it takes. You did it. I'm proud of you."

Arial was still stunned. "But when I got back to the ground... I don't know what I expected." Arial searched for the right word. "Everyone looked at me like I was... a freak."

Eric laughed. "We kind of are, you know." Then he asked, "Would that have stopped you from saving her?"

Without hesitation, Arial answered, "No." In this moment, she realized her old life was over. She wouldn't go back to just being a pilot.

Eric reached out to take hold of her hand. "Now you're a superyogi."

When they returned to the government quarters, Eric paused before getting out of the car. He said, "You need to stay here tonight. And maybe for a few days."

Arial didn't want to be alone right now, but she didn't know what Eric was suggesting.

Eric tried to reassure her. "I'll make a call to Agent Kirby to see if he can contain this thing. We don't want the media to find you."

"Wow, yeah. I'm really not ready for that."

"I know. No one is. But I'm sure Kirby and his men have a plan to keep this kind of thing quiet." He stepped out and came around to open her car door. Peeking in he said, "As much as everyone loves superhero movies and comic books, I'm not sure the modern world is ready for the real thing."

23. THE FADING PRESIDENT

Vice President Lausunu approached the president's bedroom in the White House with his hands dutifully clasped behind his back. Outside, two Secret Service agents let him pass. The doctor had already left.

President Eldridge rested in a canopy bed in his navy blue pajamas, eyes closed. On the bed, just out of reach, crisp copies of the *Washington Post* and the *New York Times* lay alongside a briefing book. On the nightstand, bottles of pills stood watch to help the president deal with pain from pancreatic cancer that had spread to his stomach. Once a strong robust man, President Eldridge had withered dramatically over the previous five months.

Vice President Lausunu brought the usual desk chair to the side of the bed. "It's me, Mr. President."

The president opened his eyes, prepared to speak with his vice president, a man he greatly respected and whose company he even enjoyed. "Help me up." He draped an arm around Lausunu's neck, so his VP could prop him up in bed.

"The doctors aren't telling me much, but I know I'm done when the Speaker of the House doesn't want to fight with me on issues." The president spoke of Speaker Drummond, the other party's likely next presidential candidate and a normally fierce opponent of the president. But in their last meeting, Drummond had stayed uncharacteristically tranquil.

The president gestured to the newspapers. "Not even the papers. No one wants to be the last person to say or write something mean."

"It's a wonder we don't live like that all the time. You may as well enjoy it." Lausunu tidied up the president's painkillers, putting them inside the nightstand.

The president observed his friend's cleaning. "Drummond's coming to check on me again?"

"Yes, this afternoon. He's just doing his job."

In times of a crisis to the president's health, the 25th Amendment made it the job of the vice president, the executive cabinet, and members of Congress to check on the president to ensure he's still mentally fit for the job. Vice President Lausunu was trying to be inclusive by reassuring the majority leader from the other party that President Eldridge was still capable.

"Alan," said the president weakly, "we should talk about transferring power."

Vice President Lausunu sighed. He didn't want President Eldridge, forced by health issues, to end up in a category with Nixon, the only president to have resigned, as Nixon had abused his power. This president deserved better, even if he couldn't finish the final year of his term. "Not just yet. Your body may be failing you, but your mind is still sharp. You can still make decisions; I can carry them through."

"The country needs a strong president. I can't be that man anymore."

"The people make this country strong," answered Vice President Lausunu. They'd talked about this view many times. Increasingly, the president had been moving toward his VP's position. Lausunu wanted a smaller less active government. Lausunu believed firmly that the less government did, the more people would step up themselves. To him, free markets and free people had a natural way of working things out, provided the rights of individuals were equally protected.

After a few moments, the president said, "Drummond's welcome to come, but tell that son of a bitch to stop quizzing me on current affairs. It's insulting. Tell him I want to talk about Unicore. And who the hell does he think he is to hold up the free market?"

Vice President Lausunu smiled. That was more like it. He surmised that if the president didn't have such drive to stop his rival from derailing his agenda, he probably would have died weeks ago. In his own strange way, Drummond was keeping the president alive—though Drummond would be mortified if he knew.

"We need the Unicore deal," said the president. "It's in everyone's interest that China and America work together on important projects."

Breaking down suspicion between countries had never been an easy process. It was harder than getting siblings to behave in the back seat of a long car trip. However, mutually beneficial trade had always proven among the best ways to do it.

President Eldridge and Vice President Lausunu took up this charge. In spite of its unpopularity, they were particularly focused on increasing America's involvement with China. They hoped to address diminishing resource issues before the two superpowers came into conflict. This was why the Unicore deal—bringing advanced oil shale technology to America—was so important to both men.

"I've gotten Drummond to agree to lunches with the business delegation from China," Vice President Lausunu said. "He won't come himself, but he's agreed not to use his power to stop other congressmen from deciding on their own."

"How many votes do we need?"

"We're a ways off. At least twenty-five from the other side."

President Eldridge shook his head. It was a tricky margin to overcome on such a politicized issue. They would have to try a new approach. "I don't want any of these lunches to be secret back-room stuff," said the president, affirming his previous strategy. "Let's get it out in the open. Just get those Chinese executives sitting at tables with different members of Congress. Get them talking about what the technology can do. Get them talking about their families. Get everyone to see that these Chinese executives are just as interested in making a buck and doing business the American way as the next guy." President Eldridge gestured for some water from the bedside table before adding, "And get some reporters from the *Wall Street Journal* and the *Economist*. I want this to be an open, honest, transparent discussion. Let's find a way to work it out."

"Yes, Mr. President. When Drummond comes to see you this afternoon," added Lausunu, "Just get him to reaffirm his promise not to use his power to block discussion. I'll do the rest."

The president smiled at his friend. Eldridge had enjoyed the visit—especially someone treating him like he was still the president.

24. CRASHING THE CONGRESSIONAL LUNCHEON

PHYSIQUE COULD HARDLY BELIEVE HER GOOD FORTUNE.

Her first week on the job as a waitress, and this rustic informal clubhouse had been chosen as the restaurant site to host a luncheon with members of Congress and a Chinese business delegation. Once again, the Bone Frightener's insider tips had proven advantageous.

For two days, Physique had watched stern Secret Service agents scout the restaurant. The old brick building from the late 1880s was the kind they preferred—solid, without many windows. Only small, hand-blown wavy glass high up allowed light to stream in like spotlights on the wooden tables and whitewashed roman pillar that held up the main floor ceiling.

As Physique approached the metal detector and the agents with wands, she thought, *They're worried about guns.*

But I'm no small weapon.

Wearing the standard white button-down shirt over black slacks, Physique looked every bit the waitress. An authentic Virginia driver's license, courtesy of the Bone Frightener, showed she was the same brunette with green eyes as the fake name on her ID. Delilah Spears was also on the approved staff list. Just as in the airport, Physique passed through the metal detector easily, and then raised no concern from a female Secret Service agent who wanded her once more for weapons. Underneath her waitress clothes, her skintight body suit went unnoticed.

While helping other servers set white-clothed tables, Physique counted the names on the seating cards. Spread across twenty tables and two floors, roughly forty-five representatives, including the chairman of the defense appropriations committee, were expected. Her anticipation grew. She was a coiled snake waiting for an unfortunate rabbit to return home.

Physique had mapped every inch of the two-story structure since the first day of her orientation. She recognized which beams held what part of the floor. She had counted her steps—she knew exactly where to stand to bring the ceiling down on particular tables.

The only thing Physique had not planned for was Samantha Morris.

Samantha Morris was a tall, athletic brunette with wavy, Botticelli-like curls. She accompanied the renowned Chinese CEO, Dr. Huang, as she had many times on his trips outside of China. Dr. Huang introduced her as his interpreter, but in truth, accent aside, Dr. Huang's English was as good as nearly anyone's. In actuality, Samantha was his personal security guard, heading a small detail to protect the Chinese delegation.

While she didn't expect trouble, Dr. Huang had made enemies around the world. Any time an invention threatens tens of billions of dollars, one couldn't underestimate the lengths the traditional powers-that-be would go in order to stop it.

Even hiding behind dark glasses, robotic Secret Service agents couldn't help but crane their necks. Samantha's height, beauty, and athletic build projected a commanding presence like a champion women's tennis player. She seemed to be a force of nature that nothing could get past.

This impression wasn't far from the truth. Samantha had previously been a champion in martial arts—and could be again, any time she wanted. A few years back, Samantha had created a stir in the *wushu* world. She'd knocked out two male champions who'd had longer reaches and outweighed her by forty to sixty pounds. Not only that, the knockouts had come *in spite* of them wearing sparring headgear. Each fallen champion reported that they hadn't fought anyone as strong or as fast as her. Further, neither wanted a rematch.

In truth, Samantha loved to fight. She was so good at it that she'd never really been tested. Still, as a woman, Samantha felt ambivalent about her abilities—she regarded them as so distinctly unfeminine that she hadn't fully embraced her warrior nature. Samantha was a tiger pretending to be a kitten.

Today, Samantha wore a simple black suit that came in at the waist, complementing her broad shoulders. Accentuating her voluptuous chest, she wore a delicate silver camisole. Her long, brown, wavy hair was partially pulled back, but she had foregone her favorite dangly earrings in case she had to get forceful with someone.

Further, Samantha wasn't carrying any weapons—not

that she needed to. She knew that once inside the restaurant, the Secret Service would have the venue covered. No one in the U.S. government wanted to have an international incident, particularly one involving a delegation from China.

Instead, Samantha simply enjoyed being the beautiful translator, and today that was an easy job. It mostly involved clarifying the occasional word for Dr. Huang if needed, usually from a Southern congressman whose accent Dr. Huang wasn't familiar with. She was polite enough to not pronounce the word again in clearer English. Rather, she spoke using her fluent Chinese, which she had honed through study and frequent trips to China. Indeed, her melodic Chinese tones were as perfect as her various *wushu* forms.

Sitting next to Samantha, Dr. Huang looked small. But when asked by several members of Congress, he confidently explained the essence of the technology that China proposed to bring to America. "My company has perfected a cleaner technology to turn oil shale into usable petroleum," Dr. Huang explained. "We have successfully implemented it in several of our provinces back home. So China has an advanced technology, but the U.S. sits on one of the largest deposits of oil shale in the world." He spoke of the unused land surrounding the Rockies.

Dr. Huang was reluctant to say the next words. He wanted to choose them carefully. "As research shows," he said, "U.S. companies have created a viable oil shale process, but it is not as clean as ours. Bottom line...." He looked at Samantha to make sure that phrase was correct.

She nodded, before repeating, "Bottom line...."

Dr. Huang continued playing off her rhythm, "... the cost per barrel of oil produced from the Chinese shale process is lower and cleaner for the environment than yours. What we can bring you, if you'll allow it, might end both America's and China's reliance on oil from the Arabian Peninsula—or at the very least, significantly reduce demand. I think that is good for both our countries."

Still playing the waitress, Physique took the order of Dr. Huang's table. When she stood near the chairman of the defense committe, a heavy-set man with a thick double chin, she nearly snapped her pen. But she smiled all the same. *Soon I won't have to play nice.*

Physique was buying time, waiting for more members of Congress to arrive. Eying the chairman's egg-shaped head, she held herself back. *I'm not going for just one.* The place was two-thirds full. Physique just had to be patient a little longer to make a bigger omelet.

Dr. Huang asked, "Can I have a hamburger and fries?"

"Of course you can," answered Physique, "This is America." Her line got a few chuckles from the congressmen at the table. They smiled at their pretty waitress. Dr. Huang knew ordering a hamburger and fries was good cultural relations, but as it happened, he actually liked the American standard, especially with lots of ketchup.

"Congressman Reynolds, you're from Texas aren't you? What will you be having?" Physique asked, putting on her wow-you're-so-important face.

"The great state of Texas will join Dr. Huang with a burger," said Congressman Reynolds, who always wore a cowboy hat even when in D.C. He planned to stay polite on this venture until he figured out which way the wind would blow for his financial backers.

Physique finally took Samantha's order. She didn't pay

Samantha much mind as she wasn't one of her targets. "What's the most popular vegetarian dish in the house?" Samantha asked.

"I usually have the Caesar Salad without the chicken," answered Physique, still watching the room.

"I'm not sure that's going to be enough for me," Samantha answered. They were both tall women, coming in around 5'9", but the waitress was certainly more skinny *vata* compared to Samantha's muscular *pitta-kapha* body. "You'd better bring me a side of fries with that," concluded Samantha.

Meanwhile outside, in a bulletproof limousine, the vice president prepared to make a surprise entrance. Wearing freshly shined shoes, he sat with his closest adviser, Sujata Bansal, to review the names of all who'd been expected at the luncheon. Looking at her clear plastic clipboard, Sujata offered her opinion on who was swayable. She asked him once more, "Are you certain you want to stick your neck out on this issue? It's complicated. And unlikely to be popular with voters."

"It's what the president wants," answered Vice President Lausunu, undeterred. "And if I don't stick my neck out first, how can I expect Congress to?" Vice President Lausunu hadn't been expected at this lunch. Following his instincts, he'd decided to drop by, shake people's hands, and thank everyone for meeting.

After the vice president stepped out of the limo in his navy pinstripe suit and sky blue tie, he waved to the TV cameras and reporters covering the event. Secret Service agents flanked him to the restaurant door, but Lausunu made efforts to stand clearly out-front. By associating himself first with any news stories, he provided cover for those members of Congress still on the deal fence.

When Vice President Lausunu entered the restaurant, no one quite knew what to do. Some felt the need to stand, as they saw him as a proxy for the ailing president. But Vice President Lausunu waved them off by signaling those at the the closest tables to stay seated. As planned, he walked around shaking a few hands while listening in on discussions.

Physique spotted Vice President Lausunu immediately. It was easy. The tall, charismatic man smiled like a lotto winner.

The snake had been delivered a bigger meal than she could have ever hoped for. Her blood boiled. It was time to strike.

25. PHYSIQUE STRIKES AGAIN

PHYSIQUE RECOUNTED THE ELEVEN SECRET SERVICE agents inside the restaurant. Armed, they presented the only threat to her plan. However, Physique knew none of these agents were trained to deal with her unique abilities.

Physique climbed the creaky wooden stairs to the second floor as she noted the various positions of the black coats.

She went through her motivation again. *I'll strike from the air like a missile. Then they'll know what it feels like. I'll make them feel fear. Only then will they stop.*

She marched across the second floor, toward the key floor beam above the entrance.

Concentrating, with each step her density increased.

Her fingernails turned inky black.

In a Secret Service agent's glasses, she could see the reflection of her hair changing color as she leapt into the air.

Physique shouted, "We're going down!"

Before he could even draw his gun, Physique smashed through the floor and the first beam of the restaurant.

A table with members of Congress fell fifteen feet through the gaping hole. The beam and debris smashed two agents below and blocked the entrance doors. Clanging, thunking, and screams filled the restaurant.

Springing from their tables, panic-stricken suits searched for an escape. Others buried their faces in their arms.

In the cloud of dust and debris, only Samantha Morris noticed Physique rising from the wreckage. Wonder widened her eyes. How could a waitress have survived uninjured from that fall?

But then Samantha saw something even more unexpected: her waitress leapt up, kicked off the walls, and glided back through the gaping hole to the second floor. The movement looked otherworldly—and, considering the circumstances, laced with creepy intent.

Samantha heard shouts from Secret Service agents. They huddled around the vice president, instinctively protecting his body. Soon they raced for the kitchen doors. Undulating black suits and shouts of "go, go, go" sounded like the ruffled feathers and the cawing of an agitated crow.

The survivors on the second floor were scampering toward the stairs in hysterics when Physique landed near the hole she had created. Leaping twenty feet at a time from table to table, she crossed the room in seconds. The lightest shade of blond hair streaked behind her like feathers on an arrow.

She shifted her weight to that of a massive wrecking

ball, and then smashed down on the staircase, tearing out an enormous chunk of floor and a set of stairs. Dozens of people, including the last agent on the second story, tumbled with the wreckage. Below, the second strike crashed into the cluster leading the vice president. He and a few remaining agents fell backward.

Inexplicably, the agents witnessed a dark-haired woman rising from the rubble. Impossibly, she lifted a huge wooden beam like a crane clearing wreckage. But instead of helping them escape, she wedged the beam firmly against a passable gap to the kitchen. Then she turned to glare at the vice president.

"Physique," the vice president uttered.

Hearing that word and understanding its meaning, one agent pulled his gun. He fired two quick shots before Physique knocked him across the floor unconscious. To everyone's shock, one bullet ricocheted off her forehead. Denser than iron, her mass had prevented the bullet from penetrating. Even Physique wasn't certain she could resist bullets, but not anymore. Now she felt truly emboldened.

Still the blow to the head stung Physique. She winced before leaping back through the new hole, escaping other agents firing their pistols. At the sound of semi-automatic gunfire, people in the room dove under the tables. For protection from further building collapse, this didn't make any more sense than grade schoolers hiding under desks when drilling for a nuclear attack. But instinctively, everyone in the room crouched down.

Everyone except Samantha.

On the second floor, Physique paced unhindered. Two bodyguards from the Chinese contingent rushed forward to subdue her, but swinging her arm like a sledgehammer, she launched them across the room. People cowered near walls. Physique tore off her waitress blouse and her charcoal-covered slacks. She wasn't serving anyone here any more.

Physique stood in a short white and black S-curve body suit that rose high on her thigh like a bathing suit. She unzipped her top enough to reach near her left breast and pull out her white and black domino mask. Only calf-high black boots remained from her waitress disguise. Feeling the part, she said, "Now this party really starts."

Physique reveled in her destructive splendor. Her eyes looked wild—she felt the power of a hydroelectric dam surging through her. Physique's hands shook from trying to contain such power, but she wouldn't have to hold back for much longer. In two decisive moves, as she had meticulously planned, she had everyone trapped; all the exits were sealed. She wanted them to feel fear, knowing that death could come from above whenever she chose. Before choosing her next place to strike, she scanned the second floor to see where the greatest number of congressmen huddled.

Samantha couldn't make sense of what she'd just seen. But she recognized everyone was trapped in a collapsing building with a strange, deadly attacker.

Dust thickened the air. Two Secret Service men struggled to move giant pieces of debris blocking the kitchen. Even if they had the strength, they wouldn't have enough time.

Grabbing Dr. Huang by the collar, she jerked him off the floor. After lifting the heavier Congressman Reynolds off the floor as well, she yelled, "Follow!" Without hesitation Samantha ran across the room toward the brick wall. With each step she focused on her target—a narrow strip of last-century bricks at the height of her heart. *What's the deal with brick walls? Three or four bricks thick? You can do it. You have to do it.*

Samantha launched herself into a flying sidekick, yelling "Kia!" She smashed through the bricks. Surprisingly, she hit so hard that she cleared through to the other side. Samantha even stayed on her feet when she landed in the alley. She brushed dust from her black jacket sleeve while noting the three-foot hole she had just created. She could hardly believe her success. *I knew I was strong, but not that strong.*

She was free, but other people in the building weren't. Without hesitation she moved toward the wall. Power surged in her arms, beyond anything she had ever felt before. She wouldn't hold back now.

Crouching as if riding a wild horse, knees bent, she focused on another set of bricks. This time, she smashed her fist through the wall, shattering bricks as easily as breaking boards.

Hearing the tumult inside, one ambitious cameraman, circling around back for a telling shot, caught Samantha smashing through the brick wall with her fists. "Go live! Go live now!" he called out. "You're not going to believe this!"

Samantha punched and kicked a refrigerator-sized hole to let people pass. Inside, Dr. Huang stepped aside to let Vice President Lausunu and Congressman Reynolds escape first with the remaining trio of Secret Service agents.

As Vice President Lausunu stepped through the brick wall into the alley, he looked at Samantha and her hands. The last thing he remembered thinking before the Secret Service agents whisked him away to the safety of his bulletproof limo: *There isn't a scratch on her.*

Samantha stepped through the hole quickly—back into the restaurant. She pushed Dr. Huang through, yelling, "This way!" As people pushed toward the improvised exit, another section of floor came crashing down. When Physique rose from the debris, she saw people escaping. And Samantha saw her.

Without hesitation, Samantha hurled two bricks at Physique. Samantha threw with the force of a major league pitcher, but her target didn't flinch. Instead, Physique smashed her hands into the incoming bricks, reducing them to powder.

To allow for faster movement, Samantha stripped off her blazer to just her silver camisole. Then she stepped between Physique and the pillar. When Samantha raised her arms into fighting stance, her womanly biceps bulged like a prizefighter's.

26. SMACKDOWN

"Looks like someone needs a smackdown," said Samantha, still holding her arms in fighting position.

"I'm feeling heavy today," answered Physique. "You don't want to piss me off."

Samantha scratched a line in the dust with her foot. "You're not getting past me."

"Please," scoffed Physique. "I'll go *through* you!" With that Physique rushed forward before launching a mighty right cross.

Physique telegraphed her punch like a beginning brawler. As Physique's right came toward Samantha's head, Samantha pivoted to catch Physique's arm as it moved forward.

The weight and force behind her punch left Physique off balance. Samantha used Physique's momentum to toss her like a shot put, away from the thick central pillar.

Thrown down, Physique became enraged. No one—no

one—had ever pushed her around. She rushed at Samantha to tackle her around the waist. Samantha stood coolly in front of this charging bull. Just before Physique made contact, Samantha dropped backward to the ground as she pressed her foot into Physique's stomach—propelling her overhead. Physique sailed head first in a dive roll before crashing loudly on a table.

Using a gymnastic martial arts maneuver, Samantha popped to her feet. Physique may have thought she was hot stuff with her supernatural power—but she had never fought someone with Samantha's skill.

Panicked, people escaped through the hole in the wall. Physique was an unnatural demon turning the room into some dreadful realm where mountains slammed together, smashing damned souls. No one could believe a person was standing to fight this she-devil and, for the moment, holding her own.

Above on the second story, remaining survivors jumped one at a time across the floor gap. They leapt for the remaining stairway to the roof, where a rickety fire escape promised safety.

Rising from being thrown a second time, Physique felt taken aback. This woman fighting her was fast and bizarrely fearless. Physique decided to show her something to instill fear. She visualized her density rapidly changing. Hair changing lighter, she glided up with a giant leap, then came crashing down toward Samantha's head.

Physique could bring maximum weight when crashing through something. Becoming immobile like a marble statue, she allowed gravity to do the damage. But in order to move her body farther, she couldn't go full heavy. Still, even moving, the power of one of her blows could crush anyone's skull.

Undaunted by the strange, harpie-like creature she had just witnessed, Samantha serenely timed Physique's landing strike. Stepping back, she delivered a looping ax kick to Physique's shoulder as she crashed into the floor. However, Samantha felt like she had just kicked an iron pillar. The blow had no effect on Physique. Samantha immediately delivered a spinning back-kick to Physique's solar plexus—but this actually knocked Samantha back.

"What are you?" Samantha said, stunned. She'd kicked brick more fragile than Physique.

"You'll never know," Physique answered. Like a catapult, she leapt over Samantha, sailing toward the pillar. Samantha tried to intercept her—but it was too late. Physique delivered an ax-like elbow to the tree trunk-sized pillar. The pillar cracked before shedding a huge chunk. Physique leaned her weight into the pillar, to crack it farther.

Samantha thought, *My God, everyone is going to die.* Too many people were still trapped in the building. Samantha grabbed Physique's arms, trying to pull her away.

Physique showed no fear of Samantha. Her hair was getting darker as she turned to scowl. "I told you I was feeling heavy today."

In a lightning fast move, Samantha squatted under Physique's body, grabbing one arm and one leg. "But I'm feeling strong," Samantha grunted as she hoisted Physique above her shoulders. Samantha spun away from the pillar, throwing the colossus above her head with all her might.

Physique changed her mass in midair, this time to glide down like a feather. Physique realized that fighting this martial arts wonder directly was pointless. But she had one last trick up her sleeve. Physique said, "You may be strong, but you can't fly." She kicked off a wall and escaped to the second floor.

Although Samantha had foiled much of Physique's

attack, her labor wasn't done. No—Samantha caught the sliding pillar with raised arms to delay the second floor from falling.

When Physique landed safely on the empty second floor, she realized her mistake. *They've made it to the roof... to the fire escape. I'm taking this building down now!* Physique sprinted to the roof, only to find it nearly empty too. She spotted the last evacuees clicking their way down the fire escape to the alley, almost out of her reach.

Pissed off, Physique tromped toward a corner ledge. Enraged, she thought really heavy.

Samantha strained. Exhausted and pushed beyond her known limits, she no longer had the strength to push the sliding pillar back. The far edge, bearing half the weight of the pillar, crumbled before her eyes. Now the weight of the ceiling plus the pillar dropped entirely on her arms. Her muscles shook. *Do I have any power left?* She yelled to the last people escaping the bottom floor, "Can't hold! Go!"

Struggling to support the pillar's weight, she watched a final person step out into daylight. *I've saved seventy people today. That's a good last deed.*

Through the hole in the restaurant wall, the camera feeding live footage to CNN showed an amazing image: an incredible woman with strong arms—who had saved so many lives—holding up the impossible.

The woman released the pillar, falling away for cover. The live camera showed the ceiling cave in on the entire room.

Whatever little hope remained for Samantha was sadly extinguished when every last red brick of the building came crashing down.

27. THE CAPITAL CHASE

As the old brick building crumbled like a sandcastle under a child's foot, Physique leapt off the toppling structure. She glided thirty feet to a neighboring roof. A plume of dust from the demolition wave spread throughout the block. Her attack was finished. Now she could focus on her escape.

Physique had hoped to slip away unnoticed in the confusion following the building collapse—literally just walk away from a cloud of dust—but her battle with that strong woman had cost too much time.

The thumping of helicopter blades and wailing of sirens from approaching police vehicles assaulted her ears. Lights flashed like fireworks off the dust clouds. *They're not coming to capture you. They're coming to kill you.* But that was just the part of her mind still associated with the meek Tina Tinsdale talking.

Physique answered, *Let them come. They still have no idea*

what I'm capable of.

When the dust settled enough to reveal the rooftop across the street, Physique sprinted toward the building ledge. It was a long jump for Physique—over sixty feet. Jumping high like a kangaroo, she let her momentum carry her as she shifted her density lighter. She sailed toward the opposite roof, laughing at the ring of police cars and SWAT vehicles preparing for a confrontation below.

Only a news chopper tracked her impossible rooftop leap. When the chopper swooped in low for a closer angle, Physique glided across their path at almost the same altitude. In midair, Physique saw the pilot's and the news reporter's jaws go slack.

One more avenue to go. The relentless wail of sirens quickly faded. For the moment, the police were blind. *They don't know where I am. I might have enough time. If I can only get to Memorial Bridge....*

When Physique reached her final building, she pulled her car keys and her geo-sync locator watch from a zippered pocket. She walked to the ledge. Below, she saw her white SUV. Now, she had a choice. Should she commit fully to the Bone Frightener's escape plan? Or should she choose her own route?

A black police helicopter swooping toward her like a hungry falcon pushed her decision. She activated her locator watch, and then stepped off the ledge.

Plummeting, Physique changed her weight to land as softly as a leaf. Wind rushed up against her bare thighs. Once again, she was in the Bone Frightener's cunning hands.

Landing, Physique stunned bystanders. A costumed woman dropping out of the sky onto a city sidewalk was too otherworldly to process.

Physique liked that they were afraid of her.

Her reflection looked like a cloud in the window of her SUV. She let her feather white hair quickly change back to sandy blond and her eyes return to their natural hazel color.

Exhausted from so much weight shifting, she climbed in her SUV. Her concentration was fading under so much fast movement. She wanted to sit still and focus on her breath, but she had to keep running.

Weaving through traffic, Physique saw flashing lights from police cars in her rear-view mirror—but she only had to be a few car lengths faster to get to Memorial Bridge first.

Upon turning onto the wide and long bridge that connected Washington, D.C. to Virginia by spanning the broad Potomac River, Physique saw what the Bone Frightener had predicted. On the far side, just before the white marble tombstones of Arlington National Cemetery, police had set up a roadblock. Further, they were taking up firing positions. As she drove forward, scrambling Virginia state troopers laid out road spikes. In her rear-view mirror, D.C. police blocked their end.

Authorities had picked a good location to make their stand against Physique. With both ends of the bridge cordoned off, and no innocent bystanders around, Memorial Bridge was a dead-end alley. Even Physique's powers were limited here. This stone bridge was too much like its 14th Street cousin—the one that had been struck by a crashing passenger plane decades ago. That collision had done little more than take out a few guardrail stones before the plane plummeted into the wide and dark Potomac. As exhausted as she was, Physique doubted she could take this bridge down.

Spying the flashing light on her locator watch, Physique

skidded the Ford Bronco to a stop—nearly rolling the vehicle. She jumped out of the driver's side. Then, to the astonishment of everyone watching, she leapt off Memorial Bridge.

At the same time, a powerful cigarette speedboat raced through one of the giant stone archways of Memorial Bridge that bowed like an undulating sea serpent.

Physique adjusted her weight for timing. Upon her firm landing, the driver gunned forward like a needle-nose drag racer.

The bucking speedboat looked like the kind that drug kingpins commonly used to outrun Coast Guard ships in the waters around Florida. But this wasn't the wide-open Atlantic—not yet.

Dizzied by all the commotion, Physique finally got a good look at her driver: an Asian woman with long black, red-streaked hair that flowed in the wind like a war banner. Her skin-tight black body suit with red trim looked similar to the one Physique had worn for her plane escapade. Physique clumsily made her way to the driver's side, ducking the driver's dark whipping hair. The driver also wore a black domino mask similar to Physique's. Blazing on the driver's abdomin like the hourglass warning of a black widow was a red flame icon.

"Who are you supposed to be?" asked Physique.

"I'm the woman saving your heavy ass," shouted the driver, "so don't piss me off."

Physique bristled at anyone taking jabs at her, but they had bigger problems. On the smooth Potomac, even though a speedboat could race as fast as a car on a highway, the police copter could fly faster. Physique could see the menacing bird moving into shooting position while a police sniper edged out on the helicopter's running board.

Physique said, "Well, I hope you're bulletproof."

Physique leaned her hand against the wheel just before seeing the first flash of muzzle fire. Bullets raised splashes in the water where the boat would have been. It looked like skipping stones on a lake, but these weren't pebbles prancing.

"Take the wheel and get me closer to the copter!" shouted the driver.

"You want to get closer?!"

"Yes, Miss I-can-change-my-hair-color. Don't go all blonde on me now," shouted the driver. "You're not the only one with superpowers."

Physique took the wheel while the mysterious ninja with attitude went to the back of the boat. Physique started to zig and zag to avoid gunfire, but each time, she banked the speedboat closer to the copter.

The next volley strafed the boat. Fiberglass went flying.

"Oh, now you've really ticked me off," said the woman in black. Closing her eyes, her mind focused on the object she disliked most—the police helicopter. She withdrew her breath into a tiny capsule at her navel. She could feel the heat sparking in her body. She just had to focus it at one tiny point…. "Agnite!!" she shouted, calling on the mystical power of her name, which rhymed with 'ignite.' Raising her hands, she launched a ball of fire like dragon's breath.

Hit directly through the open door, the engulfed helicopter swerved, but then flame caught fuel. The copter exploded above the Potomac.

Trailing at a safe distance, a news copter broadcasted the entire thing live to the world—including the masked woman who had just shot flames from her hands like a bazooka.

"You better keep driving until I cool off," said the flame-throwing woman to Physique. Her hands still glowed red like blacksmith's tongs just taken from a forge. "I'm Agnite," said the woman, moving to Physique's side. "I've got a bit of a combustible temper, so... consider yourself warned."

Physique recognized the Sanskrit word for fire, *agni*, signaled Agnite's power. "I've got weight issues," retorted Physique. "So don't test me either."

Just past the yacht club of Old Town Alexandria, Agnite told Physique to cut the engines. Agnite studied her geo-sync locator watch. "Blindside will meet us here."

Physique had met Blindside, the pilot of her last ocean voyage, and learned what he could do. Talking to a man without a face gave her the creeps.

After giving Physique a little shove, Agnite took the wheel. She maneuvered to a dead stop in the middle of the Potomac. An instant later, a small, black submarine — suitable for three to four people or drugs penetrating U.S. waters—surfaced.

When the hatch popped open, the chasing news copter witnessed Physique and Agnite escape below. Police speeding down the scenic parkway overlooking the Potomac also witnessed the event. But unfortunately, their cars weren't made for the sea.

"Honey, I'm home," called Agnite, stepping down the sub ladder.

Seconds later, Blindside partially materialized near the helm. Agnite leaned into him and embraced his clothed shape with a big hug.

"You're all hot," the faceless man said.

"We ran into trouble and... well, you know how I get."

Minutes later the vessel submerged—easily passing under the Coast Guard gunboats racing to intercept them.

These three dangerous yogis had carried out another

deadly strike, this time directly on American soil.

As they sped toward their rendezvous with the Bone Frightener, they recounted their exploits. They'd attacked from above, gone through authorities, and finally escaped below. Reveling in their abilities, the yogis reinforced each other's specialness. They felt separate from the rest of humanity. With their supernatural yogic powers, they deemed the world theirs to command.

28. BRICKS AND HEARTS

IMMEDIATELY FOLLOWING THE OLD BRICK BUILDING'S dramatic collapse—carried live across several news networks—local people living and working in the area rushed to the restaurant site.

A bucket brigade to move bricks quickly formed. Men and women, people of all ethnicities, nationalities, and religions, came together to rescue or recover whoever remained beneath the rubble. Debris was stacked like a burial mound, but brick by brick they worked to uncover the center of the restaurant. In their hearts, they hoped to find the courageous woman they had seen on TV: the dark-haired warrior who had saved so many lives by sacrificing her own.

After hours of relentless digging, Samantha's body was the first to be found. Showing no signs of life, her body reminded rescuers of the many who had fallen trying to protect others when even larger towers had collapsed.

Two paramedics rushed to her uncovered tomb. After placing the silver lens of a stethoscope to her chest and listening for a pulse, one paramedic called out, "Her heart's still beating!" Euphoria rolled among her rescuers—enough to keep weary arms lifting bricks and broken concrete in the quest to find other survivors.

Soon paramedics carried Samantha out on a stretcher, passing her overhead to clear the rubble. Her once strong hand dangled limply over the side.

Everyone close enough gently touched the stretcher: they longed to touch the body of someone who had saved so many, but that seemed close enough. An ambulance whisked Samantha away to Walter Reed, a military hospital with doctors best suited to treat the trauma and internal injuries that had sent her into a coma.

Safely back at the White House, with guards on full alert, the vice president briefed President Eldridge. The supernatural attack was too big to cover up. Too many eyewitness reports. Too many cell phone cameras. Too many news reports. "We're under attack by an enemy the world isn't ready for," concluded the president.

Despite his hesitation, President Eldridge decided to go public about the existence of rogue yogis wielding supernatural abilities—and what they intended to do about it. The ailing President decided to muster whatever energy he had left to deliver the message himself from the Oval Office.

After receiving a call directly from Vice President Lausunu with further instructions, Agent Kirby called Captain Arial Davis. "Physique's struck again."

Both she and Eric were unaware of the day's events. Instead, they had been hiding out in Eric's government quarters meditating and doing yoga.

"Turn on any news channel," Agent Kirby said. "The news footage is everywhere."

Eric and Arial saw footage of Samantha Morris bashing through a brick wall with her fist, saving the vice president and others. Then they saw the news video of Physique leaping from building to building, as well as coverage of a flame-throwing woman taking down a police helicopter. Kirby stayed silent while the pictures brought Eric and Arial up to speed. It was a dangerous new world; both Eric and Arial felt unprepared for the magnitude of the battle.

Finally, Kirby said, "You don't have to worry about the cover-up for that Nevada bridge thing—superpowered yogis are prime time now. The president is going to recognize your existence in an address to the nation this evening."

Arial couldn't find her next breath.

"Your own identities will be kept secret for the time being," added Kirby. "But you are needed for a briefing at the White House. Take a jet and get here immediately. The skies will be yours as all civilian aviation is grounded."

Eric watched the news images. People would be terrified—and worse, wanting revenge. He foresaw a whole new cycle of terror and violence with only a few, cool heads knowing how to stop it.

When the images of the boat chase played again, Eric couldn't help but notice something about the Asian flame-throwing woman: her sharp movements seemed surprisingly familiar. But he felt uncertain. Was he seeing an archetypal association or someone he actually knew—someone who had once been close to him?

After ending the call, Arial said, "Looks like Physique has some friends, and they want us to stop them."

Eric nodded, "Time to save the day."

29. THE PRESIDENT'S LAST ADDRESS

WITH THE HELP OF VICE PRESIDENT LAUSUNU, PRESIDENT Eldridge put on his best suit and tie before being wheeled into the Oval Office. There was no hiding how sick the president was: he'd lost too much weight since the public had last seen him. Still, President Eldridge knew it was his job to calm the nerves of the nation by steering a strong course through this tragedy. He and the vice president had personally written the tight speech.

He propped himself up in his desk chair for the live address. A camera crew gave him the count down. In spite of his illness, he radiated presidential authority. The power of the Oval Office gave him strength.

"My fellow Americans and friends around the world," began President Eldridge, "I want to speak to you about the events that occurred earlier in Washington today.

"I will speak frankly about what we know and what

we're doing. Mostly, I'm urging everyone to stay calm. America has faced threats before. By working together, we have always overcome them.

"It seems we live in unusual times: when ordinary people are developing what can be most simply described as superpowers. Throughout history there have been accounts of special beings who performed miracles, and of people who abused their power. I would urge everyone not to see this as a radical change in human evolution; rather, to recognize this as a continuation of our human ability to do extraordinary things beyond perceived limitations. As history shows, we can use our remarkable abilities to benefit others or we can use our abilities to harm."

Before reading the next line on the teleprompter, President Eldridge thought about the *Dangerous Yogi* report that Vice President Lausunu had shared with him following the downing of Flight 1632. President Eldridge continued, "Most people in history who have developed miracle powers have done so through spiritual practices which have altered their hearts and minds. I therefore must urge leaders and teachers in all spiritual traditions to emphasize the need to observe basic morality.

"A person may develop special abilities, but they are still subject to basic human morality and the laws of the land. Anyone stepping outside of this, particularly to pursue their own personal agendas at the expense of others, will be dealt with severely.

"At this point, the FBI has identified the lead assassin and her motive for orchestrating the building collapse that took the lives of fifteen people today, including five members of Congress, four members of a Chinese business delegation, Secret Service agents, and state police. From the information we've gained—which I've already shared with China's president—we have no reason to believe that this attack was aimed at disrupting business alliances with China.

"Sadly, I must report that based on our current findings, this is not an isolated attack. The lead assassin also appears responsible for the downing of Flight 1632, which took the lives of one hundred-sixty Americans and eleven foreign nationals.

"In short, these attacks appear to be the deeds of a few rogue individuals with supernormal abilities. However, their powers make them weapons of only limited destruction.

"Therefore, I urge you to remain calm. We've faced superpowered nations before that presented a far greater threat to our country. We've even faced rogue individuals pursuing their own agendas. Each time America and basic morality have prevailed."

President Eldridge paused. He felt his remaining strength slipping. Suddenly, new words came to him. His eyes left the teleprompter.

"America is strong and will overcome this challenge," he said. "But I may not be here to see that day. My own health is slipping as I'm in very advanced stages of cancer. Indeed, this may be my last opportunity to address you personally. My body may be failing, but it also brings a clarity to my mind."

President Eldridge then shared something that he and Vice President Lausunu had been discussing for several months. The president wanted to say it before he passed. "America has been the prevailing superpower for some time. Perhaps this is an opportunity for us to reflect on how we have wielded that power. Perhaps we have made many in the world afraid. And perhaps we need to change by exercising our own power more… gently."

President Eldridge continued, now returning to the teleprompter: "I may not be with you much longer, but new leaders and new heroes will step up. We all saw the images of Samantha Morris, the woman who with bare fists and broad shoulders, broke through a brick wall and held up a pillar to save others. Eyewitness accounts suggest she's responsible for saving the life of the vice president, forty members of Congress, and nearly the entire Chinese business delegation.

"Samantha is currently in a coma due to the injuries she sustained protecting others. I ask that the prayers of the nation be with her. She is proof that heroes will step forward in our time of need.

"Tomorrow morning, Vice President Lausunu and a special agent from the FBI will further brief the press with the details of our investigation. But tonight, I want you to know that Vice President Lausunu is way out in front of this superpowered villain threat. In fact, he's already assembled a team of our own superpowered yogis to assist law enforcement in bringing these villains to justice.

"Once again, our country is stronger than the small group of people perpetrating these attacks. We shall emerge victorious.

"Thank you, good night. And God bless America."

"We're clear," shouted the White House press secretary. Broadcast had already returned to the news networks.

Standing off to the side, Vice President Lausunu restrained tears as he looked at President Eldridge. Both men knew this was likely President Eldridge's last address to the nation.

As a doctor wheeled the president back to his room, he

stopped to speak to Lausunu. Putting his arm on Lausunu's sleeve, he said, "Good luck tomorrow. It's a new world. And no one is going to know how to deal with it."

30. PHYSIQUE MEETS THE BONE FRIGHTENER

"You're going to meet the Bone Frightener now," Agnite said as the small escape submarine headed toward the surface, somewhere in the middle of the South Atlantic. "Are you ready?"

Both Agnite and Physique held the sub ladder to brace themselves as if holding a pole in a jostling subway car. Chill shivered Physique's body. She tried to not touch anything metal with her bare legs.

"What's he like?" Physique asked. She had never met him in person—and understood that very, very few ever had. The butterflies in her stomach felt drunk as the sub rocked.

Agnite answered, "Very powerful. And very smart. He's some kind of a wizard."

"You mean like Merlin?" Physique asked, not sure what to make of that description.

"Sure," answered Agnite, smirking. She tugged at the red streak in in her hair.

Blindside's silver dragon-headed cane dangled from the crook of his arm. Only his coat appeared behind the helm of the sub. Physique heard Blindside's voice speaking from the hollow coat: "He can give you anything you want. But it usually has some kind of twist. So think carefully what you ask for."

Physique had wanted to know more about the Bone Frightener for over a year, yet so few had even said his name, let alone described him. Finally someone was talking. "What do you mean?" she asked.

Blindside offered only cryptic gestures. The sleeves of Blindside's long, dark jacket rose in the air. He seemed to be showing her his hands—that is, his invisible hands. Then suddenly, his ghostly eyes became visible, followed by his face. Physique studied his eyes. They were cloudy, staring off into nothing, dead as a doll's.

Fortunately, Agnite explained further: "Marc was a great painter before he went blind. No one could help him, till the Bone Frightener appeared to me one day. He said that he could restore Marc's sight. He put us through some weird trials to get to him. But eventually we earned a meeting."

Confused, Physique asked, "Wait… *appeared* to you?"

Agnite smirked again. "That's a longer story…. Soon, you'll see for yourself."

Blindside had one hand on the helm, but his head was turned away from the conversation. He seemed more distant than usual, as if remembering something from long ago. "When I finally met the Bone Frightener," he said, "I told him I wanted to see again, so I could paint. He taught me how to harness the power of my remaining eye consciousness. I take my conception that people can see me—that mental image, which in my case is only a one-way street—and reverse it. With the right amount of concentration I can see out... but then there's a catch."

Physique understood the twist. "Then people can't see you."

"It has its advantages," shrugged Blindside. Like steam vanishing off a mirror, he changed back to his invisible form. His eyes disappeared first.

It had taken much effort for Blindside to crack his master's specific instructions, so cryptically hidden in a *Yoga Sutra* verse, but he'd finally seen color again.

कायरूपसंयमात् तद्ग्राह्यशक्तिस्तम्भे
चक्षुःप्रकाशासंप्रयोगेऽन्तर्धानम् ॥ २१ ॥

*kaya rupa sanyamat tad grahya shakti stambhe
chakshuh prakasha asamprayogentardhanam*

III.21 If one turns the combined effort
upon the body's visible form,
then one can attain invisibility,
since the eye becomes disassociated
from the object appearing to it,
as the power to grasp unto
this object is suspended.

For over a year, the Bone Frightener's means of communication with Physique had been primitive. There had been no traceable phone calls, emails, or video chats. Just handwritten notes slid under the door of wherever she was staying. He described himself as an anonymous admirer... a man of great wealth and influence... someone who was like her, with special abilities... someone who would work behind the scenes to help her gain revenge for her beloved guru's killing.

How the Bone Frightener had identified Physique in the days immediately following her being snatched for questioning, she would never know. She certainly had not revealed her special abilities to the NSA. But the Bone Frightener always seemed to know what Physique needed next.

And always, the notes were signed in the same way:

Ox

It wasn't hugs and kisses. Only later had Physique understood the symbols as skull and bones of the Bone Frightener. She had learned his name from the phrase repeated at bag drops. The person giving her a package would say, "Compliments of the Bone Frightener." The brief meetings occurred in a movie theater, a park, and even a busy café. She rarely met the same person twice. Having no idea what was in a package, she couldn't wait to get to a private place to open it. As it turned out, each person had given her some new shard of information, money, fake ID, or costume piece she needed.

Eventually, Physique assembled the elaborate plans designed for her by the Bone Frightener. Part treasure hunt, part riddle-solving, the Bone Frightener never said exactly what to do, he just seemed to nudge her in a certain direction. To deduce the cryptic instructions required ingenuity. Sometimes, the clues were quite difficult. Then Physique had felt frustrated that her beloved guru wasn't there to guide her. She'd turn the messages over and over again as she held yoga poses. Finally, she decided the Bone Frightener was testing her intelligence and resolve—or maybe just amusing himself.

But this time, if she pulled off the capital caper, he promised they would meet face-to-face—or something cryptic to that effect.

The submarine surfaced like a killer whale to a moonlit night, then bobbed up and down as black eight-foot swells lapped at the hull. Physique and Agnite climbed out on the slippery deck. The sea breeze was cold, full of water vapor and the smell of brine. Both women clung tightly to the safety rail. One false move in the dark and no one would find them out here.

Physique never liked the sea. The ocean had a deep power far beyond her own.

Soon, Physique heard a motorboat's drone. Eventually, she saw something that looked smaller than a whaling skiff. *How did that little boat get so far out here?*

Two dark-skinned African men pulled their boat alongside the submarine. They looked like Ivory Coast pirates, only they weren't carrying machine guns. One of the men handed Physique a simple envelope. In the moonlight, Physique managed to read the warning.

In sunlight,
satellites will search
for a surfacing sub.
OX

"I knew I was going to get wet," said Physique, handing the note to Agnite. So far, she'd managed to avoid water, but not this time. If she was ever going to meet the Bone Frightener, she had to follow his cryptic instruction and sink the sub.

Fortunately, she looked like she was already in a bathing suit. Physique tossed her boots into the boat. "Tell Blindside to release the sub's ballasts. I'll do the rest."

After Blindside and Agnite boarded the little skiff, Physique straddled the open sub hatch. She focused deep within, refreshing her well-practiced analysis that her body wasn't one way, before pushing her mental image of herself really heavy.

Changing her density, Physique's hair, nails, and eyes turned as dark as the ocean. When the submarine started sinking, cold water rushed between her thighs. Determined to do the job completely, Physique stayed all the way to the end. It didn't take long before the sub and Physique disappeared beneath the dark waters: one headed for the ocean's bottom and the other soon bobbing up.

When she broke the surface, her white hair reflected moonlight. The African sailors quickly pulled a chilly Physique from the water into their little boat. Then the group sped off into the darkness.

Physique shivered. "I don't like water much."

"Neither do I," Agnite answered.

Agnite lit a fireball with her hands to warm Physique's gooseflesh. Heat felt good to Physique; she snuggled toward the flame. It had been a while since Physique had felt anything like kindness from a friend. Agnite may be irascible, but the fire was a nice gesture.

However, a big commotion burst from one of the African drivers. He shouted at the women in French while pointing at the sky.

"I guess they don't want any light," shrugged Agnite. She withdrew the flame, but shot her driver a menacing scowl.

Physique noticed how nonchalant the two Africans

were about witnessing actual miracle powers. Perhaps they had grown accustomed to seeing such displays. Or perhaps they had powers of their own.

Finally, Blindside spotted a large yacht in the distance. So large, in fact, that a helicopter relaxed on deck. The boat might as well have been a floating Swiss bank account.

Once aboard the yacht—to meet the Bone Frightener—Blindside and Agnite headed for the ship's kitchen, hungry for sustenance. Meanwhile, Physique entered the main hall of the magnificent vessel.

Physique had never seen a boat this big. Her legs felt strangely solid. Slowly, she realized the yacht's entire inner structure had been built on fulcrums allowing the inner chamber to swivel, to counter rocking waves. It felt almost like being on land again.

Moonlight streamed through windows of the empty, dark hall, illuminating expensive teak on the walls and the floor.

"If I tell you who I am, do you swear not to tell anyone?" a voice said.

Physique recognized the voice. Without further thought she answered, "I do."

"I'm a force within you that drives you to do things."

Physique kept moving forward toward the voice. Then in the moonlight, she saw her beloved guru sitting in meditation in the center of the room. His body was thin except for his familiar potbelly. However, he was dressed in a way that Physique had never seen him before. He looked like a yogi in ancient Indic ritual attire. Ash from cremated corpses smeared his body, while bone ornaments banded his biceps and ankles. Even his necklace appeared to be strung together from the bones of human fingers.

"Guru Sri, you're alive!" exclaimed Physique, kneeling

on the floor.

The Indian sage calmly answered, "I'm in the ground, only appearing to you now because that is what you wish."

Physique said, "You've been guiding me this whole time."

"Have I?"

Physique wasn't listening to his cryptic responses. She felt too overcome by the reunion. Physique crawled forward. "We can be together again?"

"Not as before. I've been taken from this world."

Physique stopped. His otherworldly appearance was almost transparent in the moonlight. Her heart ached.

"It has taken much for me to speak to you now in this way. We don't have much time," said the guru. "What is it you want?"

From Blindside's warning, Physique knew to be careful with her request. But her desire came quickly. She clasped her hands at her chest. "To make the mighty tremble, so they understand fear. Then they will stop abusing their power... stop making poorer and weaker people of the world afraid."

"Fear is my specialty," smiled the Indian man dressed in bone. "To instill fear, you have to hit with something bigger."

Bigger than what I've already done? I've taken out a plane and a building, she thought. "You mean like a bomb?"

"No," her guru answered firmly. "Something unexpected. What people don't see coming is what really makes them afraid."

Physique didn't know where to begin with this instruction. She pressed for clarity, "What do you want me to do?"

"In my presence, you've already made your wish. The

means will come to you. This boat is headed for an island off the coast of Africa. You will find your answer there."

Then he spoke his final words: "Search for how to strike from afar with something bigger… something unexpected."

His brown body shimmered in the moonlight like a mirage before vanishing too quickly before her aching eyes.

31. POWER EXAMINED

AFTER THE TENSE PRESS BRIEFING, AGENT KIRBY FOLLOWED Vice President Lausunu through the halls of the White House to the vice president's spacious office.

Once inside, Vice President Lausunu took off his shoes, coat, and tie—then rolled out a blue yoga mat. Like a tree resisting the wind, the vice president balanced on one leg raising his hands above his head. He centered himself on his breath.

Lausunu had previously told Agent Kirby that he did yoga regularly, so Agent Kirby wasn't overly surprised. Besides, Kirby's head still rung like a punch-drunk boxer's from the flurry of reporter questions: *How long have you known about the existence of yogis with superpowers? How many superpowered yogis do you believe exist? What is being done to monitor their activities? What powers do the yogis on our side have to counter these villains? With all due respect, when will you show the world our team to prove they exist?*

Following his own briefing, Vice President Lausunu had calmly stood by Agent Kirby's side the entire time, giving the young agent emotional support as Kirby had explained unusual facts.

Agent Kirby collapsed in a sofa chair. "Why do I feel like we just handed chimps grenades?"

Vice President Lausunu laughed, still maintaining his balance. "Just wait till they start throwing them back at you without the pins."

Agent Kirby looked dejected, so Lausunu consoled him. "We told as much as we know; we did the best we could. Now it's up to the press to decide what they'll do with the information."

The unprecedented nature of the attacks had whipped up a frenzy. Worse, most of the news media had no interest in calming people. After all, calamity caused folks to tune in for more information. The more sensational the story, the more viewers and readers a news outlet had—which was its own kind of power.

Vice President Lausunu knew America was in for another wave of fear mongering. Perhaps the American public had even become addicted to it. No matter how bad the news was for them, most nervous Americans switched it on every morning and night like addicts reaching for a fix. "You can count on the media to do what serves them best," Vice President Lausunu said to Agent Kirby. "But it's our job to best serve the country by preventing another attack."

At his mahogany desk, Lausunu called his aide to bring in National Security Adviser Sujata Bansal and Agent Rollins with the vice president's new duo of superyogis.

Neither Captain Arial Davis nor Eric Adams had been to the White House before—and certainly never for a private meeting. Captain Davis felt honored; her mom would be proud (if she could only tell her).

Unfortunately, Eric didn't like being in the White House. Everything radiated power. One or two bad decisions in here and tens of millions would get hurt.

In spite of the circumstances, Vice President Lausunu exuded a relaxed, casual charm. He rolled out two more yoga mats and angled them toward his like points on a star.

"As long as you're here, I thought you could help me with my seated spinal twists," said Vice President Lausunu. He gestured for Arial and Eric to join him on the mats. "Good for releasing tension I understand." Wearing her dress blues, Captain Davis looked every bit the Air Force officer. But when the easygoing vice president offered a yoga mat, she instinctively entered more comfortable territory. After unbuttoning her Air Force jacket, she quickly flopped down on the mat in her yoga top. Still wearing jeans and his usual blue T-shirt, Eric also felt more comfortable on the floor.

Seeing Agent Rollins' discomfort with this unorthodox meeting set-up, Lausunu reported, "Gandhi once said, 'I'm so busy today, I better do twice as much meditation.' And he defeated the British Empire without firing a shot."

Sitting on his mat, Vice President Lausunu brought the soles of his feet together and leaned forward in Cobbler's pose, *baddha konasana*. Eric and Arial mirrored him.

Eric had healthy reasons to mistrust government power. He had seen up close how brutally it could be wielded. Still, Eric liked Lausunu instantly. While this whole setting may have been contrived to make Eric and Arial feel more comfortable, Eric appreciated that the man who was about to become the Leader of the Free World chose to meet them on yoga mats.

Studying Lausunu, Eric saw a good man who wanted to

do good things. They existed in every field; not just spiritual, but in business and government as well. Meeting one often felt like finding a precious gem. So in this moment, Eric felt he needed to put aside his preconceived ideas and just help.

Agent Kirby, Agent Rollins, and Sujata pulled up chairs behind the yogis. Even they—after a few minutes of watching gentle long-hold restorative yoga—started to feel more relaxed.

The yogis stretched their hips to release tension by sitting in Cow Face pose, *gomukhasana*. Their crossed knees made their feet stick out like floppy cow ears.

Mid-stretch, Vice President Lausunu asked his first question to Eric. "I've seen the video from the bank robbery you stopped. Do you think you could stop Physique?"

Everyone wanted to know. "I'm not sure," answered Eric, before saying something more unexpected. "Given a little time, she may stop herself."

Lausunu hadn't considered this angle. "What do you mean?"

From years of study and meditation, Eric had gained deep insights into the inner workings of reality. He could explain the deeper causes for power: rules that stayed true whether discussing superyogic abilities, business leadership, or government authority. Eric began, "Power, like everything else, is a changing thing."

A student of power's ebb and flow, Lausunu nodded.

Eric switched legs to stretch his other hip while checking out the vice president's office. Sensing Lausunu's next office would be oval, Eric said, "Power is bestowed to test the degree the holder can handle."

Then speaking further like a Confucian scholar, Eric said, "When one doesn't wield power well to benefit others, it will be taken away. But like a river, there's a time lag between the flow downstream and the supply being shut off."

Vice President Lausunu reflected on Eric's words. Lausunu also believed this. In fact, he had seen it occur too many times on the political stage: after rising rapidly, someone with immense talent and charisma would conclude they were so special that the rules didn't apply to them. In quick order, entanglement in some self-inflicted scandal usually removed them from power—faster than they'd risen.

Lausunu appreciated Eric's ability to communicate in a way he could easily understand. He wanted to return that gesture with language specific to a yogi. "You're speaking of *karma*, the relationship of cause and effect—aren't you?"

"Yes," answered Eric, pleased the VP had some concept of the term. "The power someone has today comes from past acts of goodness. But it has nothing to do with the power they will have tomorrow."

Vice President Lausunu extended his leg in a type of runner's stretch, *janu sirsasana*. "What if Physique believes she's right: that we're the monster that has to be stopped?" Lausunu was aware of the many critics around the world and at home who feared the United States' unbalanced exercise of power.

Eric mirrored the vice president's pose. "Believing what she's doing is virtuous may help her to maintain her powers for longer, but eventually negative ripenings from her deeds will catch up to her."

"Why's that?" asked the VP.

"She's done something that she wouldn't want done to her. Physique wouldn't want the roof to crash in on her head, but by doing it to others, she's guaranteed it will eventually happen to her. *Karma*, while slow, is infallible."

Eric added, "If America's power shrinks, it has nothing to do with Physique, but with how well our country wielded power in the past."

The vice president considered Eric's deeper warnings. The lingering weakness in the economy, the over-reliance on the government sector, diminished respect around the globe: all signs that power had been abused.

"So you believe Physique's power will run out?" asked Lausunu, summing up Eric's message.

"I'm certain it will. But I can't tell you when. It could be this life, next life, or some life after that."

Lausunu switched legs. He was hoping to hear more immediate options. After all, he'd pledged to protect a country. "If it's the next life, that isn't going to end the current threat."

Still with one leg bent, the vice president leaned his body forward over the outstretched leg, nearly bringing his head to his knee. He enjoyed the *prana* moving from the deep stretch.

Eric was only slightly more flexible than this man who was much older than himself. Arial rested lightly on her leg, looking up, smiling at the vice president.

Unfortunately, Eric knew there was no short game with *karma*. No one—no matter how much they liked to pretend otherwise—was in control of the present moment. Instead, previous actions determined what came in the present. After all, as any scientist would agree, effects come from causes. Thus, trying to change the current moment was like trying to reshape dried concrete. The truly wise knew you could only shape better molds for the future while patiently enduring your current circumstances.

Eric continued, "Power must be used to benefit others. That's the message we should share to prevent other yogis from falling into Physique's trap." Indirectly, Eric was also speaking to the vice president, sensing that the power this man would soon wield would impact far more people than just one yogi with *siddhis*.

"Please understand," Eric said, "Physique is remarkable. And she didn't get that way overnight. At some point, she had many pure aspirations to help the world, combined with a deep practice... that's how these powers emerged."

Rollins sense of danger buzzed, fearing additional supervillains surfacing. He wasn't on the floor stretching. He preferred his stiff suit and solid chair.

Eric explained, "When the powers first emerge, it's a dangerous and confusing time for a yogi. Powers can accompany specific *chakras* opening, but also all kinds of repressed emotions can express themselves. Unfortunately, any window in which a yogi misuses his or her abilities could be long and cause considerable suffering for a lot of people. You have to understand, the emotional upheaval and temptations to misuse abilities are really challenging. Good yogis get through it only by serving others."

"OK," said the vice president. "So you're recommending a proactive approach. We educate yogis on how to wield power in a beneficial way, so they won't lose their abilities—"

"By not harming others," Eric summed up.

Lausunu considered the benefits of this long-term strategy. "It reminds me of something Confucius taught to help stabilize the warring kingdoms of ancient China." Expressing his core belief, Lausunu said, "'If the ruler is good, the kingdom will be good.'"

Eric smiled. "Confucious applied the principles of *karma* to help China become the most prosperous and advanced kingdom on the planet for centuries." Eric didn't tell the vice president the unspoken corollary to Confucius' teaching: if the people are good, the ruler will be good.

"In Beijing, they're replacing statues of Mao with Confucius," responded Lausunu. "Looks like China is gearing up for another run at prosperity."

Arial got off her yoga mat to help the VP keep his back straight during *ardha matsyendrasana*, seated spinal twist.

The VP leaned into her leg during her assist. "They tell me you can fly. Can you stop Physique?"

"She's a glider. I'm a jet," Arial answered, standing over him. "As long as I attack from above and from the opposite side of her motion, I can control the skies."

"And on the ground?" asked the VP.

Captain Davis gestured toward her jacket. "I'm Air Force. The ground isn't my domain."

Lausunu twisted to the other side. "I watched a bullet ricochet off Physique's head from point-blank range. We need a plan for what can stop her in the short term."

"I'd like to see Samantha Morris, the woman who fought Physique," replied Eric.

"I'm afraid she's still in a coma and the prognosis isn't good," Sujata interjected. She had already received the latest updates from doctors at Walter Reed.

Eric rose to his feet. "Then if it's all right with you, I'd like to go immediately. Samantha's the only one who has stood up to Physique directly; if I can help her heal, she might play a vital role in subduing Physique."

"You can heal her?" asked the vice president.

Eric smiled gently. He didn't know for certain. Instead, he answered as he always did. "I have to try."

32. ERIC MEETS SAMSA

AN EDITOR AT *USA TODAY* CRAFTED AN INFLUENTIAL headline: *Samsa Saves VP*. Although Samantha had held up a pillar instead of bringing down several like the Biblical Samson, the imperfect abbreviation conveyed her amazing strength.

The label spread quickly: in two days, nearly everyone referred to her as Samsa. For the first time in quite a while, America had a bona fide hero.

On their way to visit Samsa, Eric and Arial came upon a small prayer vigil outside sprawling Walter Reed hospital. Candles in jars, flowers, and crayoned pictures drawn by children surrounded an impromptu shrine built in the grass. In one drawing, Samsa held up a pillar while people escaped through a hole in the brick wall. In another, Samsa even had a red cape. Eric read words written on poster board: *You gave your strength when we needed it most. May our prayers now lift you up.*

Eric picked a white rose from a lovely bundle placed before a picture of Samsa and decided to take it to her.

On the third floor, where Samantha rested in a coma, a contingent of Marines and off-duty Secret Service agents stood guard. Reflections of their boots and uniforms in the dark, polished wooden floor, made it feel as if an entire platoon was present. Whatever the orders were, it was clear to Eric that they viewed Samsa as one of their own. They would stand guard until Samsa could stand with them again.

Sujata had placed the necessary phone calls while Eric and Arial were en route. Her authority allowed Eric and Arial to quickly enter Samantha's private room while everyone else remained outside.

Eric had seen soldiers in comas before and knew what to expect. Still the sight was a punch to the gut: a machine did the breathing for a woman who was once so strong.

Folded, a wheelchair leaned in a corner like a pair of roller skates: someone's bit of optimism that Samsa would wake up ready to wheel right out of here. Not fully understanding the subconscious thoughts that compelled him, Eric unfolded the chair. For the first time since his own miraculous recovery, he sat again in a wheelchair.

Eric rolled over to Samantha's bedside while Arial stood by the door. Eric's strong arms maneuvered the chair easily—well-practiced from too many years. To see Eric in a wheelchair again disturbed Arial. Instead of watching, her eyes traveled to flowers in the room.

Eric looked at the sleeping brunette in the hospital bed. A plastic mask covered most of her face. His heart made boxer's fists. Her hair was so dark; the hospital respirator, so raspy; the wheelchair metal, like a gun-barrel.... Unexpectedly, his mind started to slip away... a flashback was coming on. In the next instant, as if sucked through a time machine, he re-experienced the most damaging day of his life.

Eric laid flat on a hilltop in sandy, camouflage fatigues, looking through the holographic sight of his carbine assault rifle.

Since midnight, his small team of four Navy SEALs had been perched on this ridge above a small village. But he had long since shed his night vision goggles. Now the afternoon Afghan sun blazed overhead.

Local intelligence had provided a valuable tip: a high-ranking Al-Qaeda operative responsible for training in improvised explosives was going to meet with a Taliban field commander to coordinate strikes. Eric's team of SEALs had been sent deep into this unsecured area of Afghanistan to verify the meeting. Once confirmed, they'd call in an airstrike.

Eric's team would watch and wait. He didn't mind. *At least I'm not neck deep in frigid water*. Further, no one was shooting at him.

The remote Afghan town felt sleepy. Few people walked the streets, and when they did, they moved quickly inside. At the center of the town, a tall three-story building stood. If a meeting were to occur, it would happen there, in the most important building.

When a small caravan of dust-covered trucks pulled in front of the building, Eric clutched his radio: "We got movement." Eight machine-gun wielding, bearded Taliban jumped from the truck beds. Once the men from the passenger seats went inside the building, the others followed. The trucks quickly disappeared around the corner.

They were hostile Taliban combatants, but this was their territory, and by themselves, didn't merit an airstrike.

Eric searched for a particular operative. He had the man's face memorized from intelligence photos. Finally, the overweight man—known as the Toolmaker—showed up. He was easy to spot with an eye-patch covering his right eye.

Eric called in the air strike.

Eric and his SEAL team had performed this kind of operation before. Laser rangefinders allowed them to upload precise GPS coordinates for the strike, which could guide missiles within inches of their intended target.

But then something unexpected happened. A group of school-aged kids emerged from a nearby building and started playing soccer right in front of the very building that was about to be struck.

A wave of nausea swept Eric's body. He had just called in a strike that would level that building. In minutes, Predator drones would light that area up.

He didn't feel much toward the men with guns, but he couldn't watch a blast consume a dozen children playing soccer. He radioed again: "This is Mako 17, request immediate delay of air strike. There are now a dozen children playing in front of the building."

Eric started to hyperventilate. *Would his request be followed or ignored?* Command really wanted the Toolmaker—enough to send in SEALs. He radioed again, this time asking for confirmation that the airstrike had been aborted, insisting that he would initiate the airstrike again once the area was clear. But none of these decisions were up to him: he was a soldier whose mission had been completed once he spoke words into a metal box.

His other spotter radioed him. "Lieutenant, it was clear

when you made the call. What's done is done."

Dizziness swam through his head. The Predators hadn't reached the building yet, but the kids were still playing outside. It was possible Command might not strike once they had the same visual Eric had of ten-year old boys kicking a soccer ball. But if the drones approached from the blindside of the building... they would see only Eric's coordinates and certainly launch Hellfire missiles.

Minutes and seconds.... Suddenly, inexplicably, Eric found himself running down the hill toward the town.

One might have thought a camouflaged American soldier running toward the center of an Afghan town would have been enough to scare the children away from the doomed building—but they were so enthralled with their own game that the kids never looked up from the bouncing checkered ball.

They didn't even notice Eric until he charged right into the middle of the pack. He booted the soccer ball away with all his might.

More amused than startled, the pack of kids chased after their ball, away from the building, caught up in a new kind of game.

Just then the door to the three-story building opened.

Eric leveled his assault rifle on the doorway, expecting Taliban soldiers with machine guns to come pouring out. But instead it was a young Afghan woman. Relieved, Eric backed his finger off the trigger.

Although mostly concealed in baggy black cloth, a beautiful, bright blue scarf and strand of dark hair peeked out. Seeing Eric, she froze in the doorway. Her green eyes darted side to side.

Eric wanted to tell her the children were safe. But then he heard the buzzing sound of a Predator drone pass overhead.... They both did. Their eyes met. It was the very last thing Eric experienced before the blast consumed the building.

Eric's head slammed against the hospital wall. He had thrown himself away from the imagined blast by spinning the wheels of his rolling chair. The blow to the back of his head and loud clang against the wall returned Eric to the room.

"Eric! Are you okay?" exclaimed Arial, rushing to his side.

Scrunching his eyes, Eric deepened his breathing. Searing pain coursed through his skull.

Eric reminded himself of where he was: *You're not in Afghanistan any more. You don't have to go back into battle.*

He heard Arial's comforting voice. "What happened to you?"

Eric opened his eyes slowly. Unexpectedly, he felt tears spill down his cheeks. "Man… I really don't like hospitals."

"Eric, you went comatose for a few minutes. Your eyes were wide open…. You had a flashback, didn't you?"

Ashamed, Eric spoke softly. "Yeah… I haven't had an episode like that in years. I thought I was over them."

"Maybe we should just go." Arial tugged at Eric's sleeve.

But Eric shook her off. He had a new mission. Determined, he wheeled his chair back toward Samantha's bedside.

He had saved a dozen Afghan kids from certain death on that fateful day. But once again, as he had too many times before, he remembered the dark-haired woman in the doorway. He wished he could have saved her too.

Eric hadn't had enough power or wisdom then. But this time, personal traumas aside, Eric was blessed with a new ability to see on a deeper level. This time, Eric might be able to save the dark-haired woman in front of him.

33. SAMSA AND THE REALMS

LOOKING INTO SAMANTHA'S MIND, ERIC SAW WHAT HE had expected: at the initial layer of consciousness, her mind was completely shut down. Prairie-flat lines on the screen depicting the electro-magnetic output of her brain could have told any doctor the same thing—but Eric saw directly what Samantha was experiencing. She wasn't aware of sensory objects—or herself.

Eric deepened his ragged breathing and reset his motivation to try to help her. But his mind felt like frayed sackcloth. He had to settle before he could reach her on a subtler level.

Finally ready, Eric scanned for her consciousness. Her conceptions for hardness, wetness, warmth, and movement—the classical four elements of earth, water, fire, and air—had already dissolved. Now even her most subtle mind, the final conception of duality, was slowly dissolving into the clear light of death. If it weren't for the respirator, she'd have already passed. She'd been in this state for several hours. Eric knew then what no one else could be certain of: Samantha Morris would not make it through the night.

Eric slumped in the wheelchair, uncertain what to do next.

Arial noticed Eric's dejection. "What did you see?" she asked. She stood near the foot of the bed in her Air Force dress blues, watching Eric more than Samantha.

"She's dying. It won't be long before she's gone."

To bring her out of the coma, Eric had hoped to intervene by lining up images of outer objects and conceptions of herself in her mind. But she was past the point where people reported seeing white light when the gross mind collapses. She was about to reach where there was no color at all.

Arial took the blue Air Force cap off her head. Someone was about to die. "Can you stop it?"

Eric rocked the wheels on his chair gently. "I'm not sure how. This is beyond my training. It's in the realm of God stuff."

God stuff.... Eric believed in God more as the innate purity within everything—a synonym for ultimate reality— rather than a guy in the sky with a long beard who could intervene. But for Eric, Samantha's condition was beyond his capacity.

Still Eric looked further into Samantha's mindstream, searching for something he could do to help her.

Sadly, Eric saw Samantha would not experience her coming death as the dissolution of everything into total purity, known to completion stage masters as the clear light. Instead, the final moments would be like unconsciousness deepening. Then, her most subtle mind would stir, bringing her into the in-between state, called the *bardo*. When her consciousness fully arose again—as consciousness must through simple cause and effect—she would take a new rebirth.

As heroic as Samantha Morris may have been, she hadn't escaped the cycle of suffering, *samsara*. Such a feat would be truly heroic. Instead, Samantha was destined to be reborn in one of the six realms.

But would it be a good rebirth or bad? Eric looked deeper at her seeds of virtue nestled among the negative thorns that Samantha had collected across lifetimes. On the balance, she was ivy, climbing upward: her next life would likely be even more pleasurable.

In Samantha's case there was enough anger, violence, and disrespect for Eric to be concerned, yet as far as he could tell, the most powerful deeds suggested a rebirth in the human realm or as a demi-god in the form realm.

"What are you doing now?" Arial asked, unable to wait.

With his eyes still closed, Eric answered, "I'm looking at her past lives to predict where she's headed. Give me a moment. She's pretty entertaining."

With no other consciousness from Samantha in the way, Eric was surprised how easily he could see the flow of her mindstream. She had deep ties to China. Even in this life her strongest connections were to Chinese culture and helping Chinese people. To understand why, Eric changed directions, searching deeper into her past life.

In her previous form, Samantha had been the only child of a *wushu* and *chi gong* master who had lived in Southeastern China during the early part of the 20th century. The Asian family lived near the water, in Xiamen. With no sons, many of the *wushu* master's best disciples thought they would inherit the house if they married Samantha, then named Wu Mei. A clever girl, Wu Mei could see through their selfish intent. Knowing that she had developed better martial arts skills from studying so closely with her father, she challenged all suitors to fight in a *Lei Tai* contest. There, combatants fought to be the last person standing on a raised platform. She boasted she would only marry a man who could throw her. One by one she sent her would-be suitors toppling off the platform to the amusement of many in Xiamen.

Looking further, Eric saw Wu Mei had also learned acupuncture. With her mastery of the energetic body, she had become a well-regarded healer.

Unfortunately, most of the last century had been difficult for China. Foreign occupation forbade open training in martial arts, a civil war prevented training in meditation, and Mao's Communism brought disdain for the old ways, as well as suppressed teachers from gathering groups of students.

Throughout China's dark period, Wu Mei, an independent free thinker, continued to teach and cure people secretly, often at great risk to herself. This proved to be the main source for her tremendous strength in this life—as protecting life is the main *karmic* cause for strength and health. Still, she longed for freedom to openly pursue her training and teaching.

Combined with her virtue, this wish led to another human rebirth—this time in America, where she finally had freedom to pursue her deeper interests. She was born into a Western family that owned one of the first kung fu schools in San Francisco. But in her heart, she was still Chinese. As a little girl, she ate with chopsticks, expressed obsessive preferences for anything Chinese, and continued the habit of fighting and defeating bigger, stronger boys.

Eric was about to follow her *karmic* seeds further when an older woman with short gray hair came through the door. The woman's pained look announced that she was Samantha's mother.

Knowing from Eric that Samantha was about to die, Arial felt uncomfortable in the presence of Samantha's mom. "I'm so sorry," Arial said meekly. She held back tears before quickly exiting the room.

Samantha's mother shuffled slowly toward the bed. Before now, she had only seen her daughter in perfect health. Eric brought a chair over and helped her to sit by Samantha's side. Looking at her daughter on a respirator, the older woman showed obvious grief.

"I'll give you the room," Eric said gently.

"It's all right. You can stay. I always suspected Samantha had a boyfriend. She just didn't tell me."

Eric smiled. "I'm just a friend."

Her mom held her daughter's limp hand. Needing to talk to someone about her daughter, she said: "She didn't like to be the stronger one in a relationship. You look strong enough to handle her."

"I think Samantha's stronger than all of us put together. I'm pretty sure she could throw me."

"That's how she would say it," her mom laughed. "She didn't want a man that couldn't throw her."

"Is that right?" Eric said, knowing where this habit came from. He put his hand on the woman's shoulder. "I'll be back. Tell her how much you love her. I think she'll like that."

Out in the hall, Eric found Arial. "That was uncomfortable," said Arial.

Eric wanted to slump against the wall to think, but he didn't want to dash the hopes of Marines and Secret Service agents standing guard. He searched for an empty room on the same floor. Arial followed silently behind. Eric was so consumed in thought, he bumped into a burgundy couch in the hallway.

Eric knew Arial didn't understand how precarious Samantha's situation was. How could she? Most yoga training didn't explain the cycle of suffering, the six realms of existence, or how rare it was to gather enough merit to gain a human birth and even see the word *yoga*.

Eric marveled at how long he had been able to turn a blind-eye to tortured existence in the cycle of suffering. Anyone could see two of the six realms—human and animal. And if two realms were possible, one could easily understand that there might be more.

Arial was unable to contain her concern. "What's going on with you?"

Eric motioned for Arial to join him in a vacant room. "I'm thinking about all the places she might be reborn. I'm pretty sure she'll either come back as a human in China or as a demi-god in the form realm."

"Wow, a demi-god in the form realm," said Arial, "that sounds cool." Arial sat on the vacant hospital bed.

"It's still a mixed birth. Her virtue will result in a place where everyone is beautiful, lives long, and is surrounded by every pleasure they can imagine."

"Sounds like L.A."

But Eric started pacing again. "She'll join a group of demi-gods in the form realm who mostly experience pleasure. But out of jealousy, she'll fight beings above her— only to be continually trounced by the more powerful.

Then one day, her *karmic* credit card will max out and that life will come to an end."

Eric recalled how beings like that experienced extraordinary pain when they tumbled down, usually to the lower realms.

"So it's unfortunate to be born as a demi-god?" asked Arial, confused.

"Beings of wisdom have observed that of all the realms, the human realm is the best bad place to be. We have just enough pleasure to allow us to relax and think, but enough pain to drive us to find a solution."

After some moments of silence, Eric said, "I'll tell you something, Arial. If people truly understood how difficult it is to gain a human birth, they would be working like their hair was on fire to escape altogether." Now when Eric saw a person getting caught up in petty issues and smaller pursuits—instead of using their life to sever the root of suffering—sometimes, he just wanted to grab them by the shoulders and shake.

Eric continued pacing in the empty hospital room, considering Samantha's situation further. He felt caught between two bad choices. "If Samantha is reborn in the form realm, she'll be too blissed out or consumed with jealousy to study the antidote to suffering. Then, when her merit runs out, she'll eventually fall into a lower realm where she'll be engulfed in pain."

"And if she's reborn as a human?" asked Arial.

Eric knew China was rediscovering its Buddhist, Taoist, and Confucian roots to balance an inner void that capitalism couldn't fill. The mix would be a kind of Confectionism, but with as much virtue as Samantha had, she'd find teachings on ultimate reality and cause and effect. "She'll be all right."

"So what's your concern?" Arial hadn't seen Eric so wound up before.

"I'm not certain we can beat Physique without having Samsa on our team. When it was you and me against Physique, I felt more confident. But now we know she has some powerful friends."

Arial felt the same way. "That flame-throwing girl makes me nervous."

Eric then expressed what was really consuming him. "It's possible I can bring Samantha back even after she passes through the death state, by triggering certain *karmas*. But I don't know that I should." Instinctively, his hand covered his mouth.

Arial crossed her arms at her chest. "I don't understand."

"Her *karmic* destiny is much bigger than our current need. If she's going to be reborn in China, she may play a role in reviving martial arts or meet teachings on wisdom there. I shouldn't interfere.

"But if she's going to become a beautiful slugger in the form realm, perhaps it's best for her that I bring her back." Eric tried to weigh the decision as if he could hold those two different realms in his hands.

"Then isn't it clear what to do?" Arial asked.

Eric dropped his hands and stared at the closed door. "The thing is, she's done what she needed to do with this life. She's ready to move on to another form. I wouldn't be bringing a human back to this realm, I'd be bringing... a demi-god."

Arial wasn't sure she'd heard Eric correctly. And if she had, she didn't know what he'd meant. Her tone turned brazen: "What are you saying... exactly?"

Eric's steely blue eyes stared back at her. He spoke directly. "Samsa's going to be a lot stronger than she was before. And much harder to kill. She'll still look human, but she'll be more like a super-being from another planet."

It took some time for that idea to register with Arial. Finally she smiled. "That's good for us, right?"

Eric wasn't so sure. "I don't know what will happen if I bring someone here who doesn't belong in this world." He was wary about stepping further into acts of the *mahasiddhas*. As Eric hadn't achieved full enlightenment yet, he couldn't be certain about the outcome of this action on Samantha's spiritual development if he succeeded in preventing her from transitioning to the demi-god realm. "There's the opportunity for her to study deeper things here... but how much this world needs her now may tip the equation."

Eric paused before speaking his next words: "It may be best to bring Samsa back."

34. TO RESURRECT SAMSA

THE HOSPITAL ROOM WAS DARK. CLAWING LIGHT FROM under the door and glowing diodes from hospital equipment illuminated Samantha's body. The raspy sound of the respirator marked time, a sort of mechanical *ujjayi* breathing. Eric had convinced both Arial and Samatha's mother to get rest, and now, finally alone with her, the key moment had come.

Eric shut off the signal that monitored Samantha's vitals. He didn't want alarms sounding during this delicate procedure.

As the clock approached midnight, her death was imminent. Observing Samantha's dissolving subtle mind, Eric reviewed his course of action. *If she'll be reborn as a human, I'll do nothing. If she'll be reborn in a lower realm or as a demi-god, I'll intercede to the best of my ability.*

Next, Eric shut off the respirator, literally pulling the plug.

He wouldn't be able to defend his action to the nurses or doctors outside. But knowing that she was in fact dying now, it seemed to Eric the best way to facilitate a smooth return… if he could make it happen.

From studying closely with his teacher, Eric knew of a key moment that can come at death—after the entire world and sense of self dissolve from the dying person's perspective—which a fortunate few recognize as the *clear light*. In this doorway between worlds, a special wisdom can come that realizes nothing truly exists separate from deeds that project illusory worlds. As Eric's teacher had explained, it's like seeing the clear state behind the dream, before the next dream begins, and knowing there is no solid reality. Further, it's recognizing this clear purity as your fundamental, divine nature.

If one is well trained in how to perceive that moment for what it means, and if one has practiced years of meditation to give rise to a specific wisdom during this dissolution, one can sever the root of ignorance right then and there.

But for nearly everyone else, that final moment of dissolution is usually experienced as a deep moment of unconsciousness, often followed by intense fear due to feeling disoriented to a level beyond any reasonable use of the word "disoriented." When the next thought or subtle energy stirs, that movement projects the next life. Is it any wonder a human birth is so hard to attain if fear would prevent it?

Eric watched the last moment of Samantha's subtle consciousness flicker to an end. Like an abruptly ending dream, her mind slipped away from the human realm.

Eric wondered what he would see next. Fortunately, Samantha Morris wasn't prone to fear or anger or possessiveness. Her next thought, from force of habit, was to become someone even stronger to better protect others. This habit (or *throwing karma*) now sent her into the intermediate state, the *bardo*, destined for a birth in the form realm as a demi-god.

Seeing all this occurring through his yogic powers of perception, Eric resolved to try to interrupt the process and bring her back to the human realm. He believed it was possible, but he wasn't sure of the exact technique. He started by sending his own human seeds for this realm on rays of white light from his heart *chakra* to her freshly emerging state of mind. Eric was willing to shorten his own human life to restore hers.

"Samantha Morris," Eric said, now entering her newly forming mind, "there are many people here on Earth who need you to protect them. They need your strength. There is much more for you to do in the human realm. Samantha Morris, come back. Come back to Earth to protect all of us."

But her mind was still rapidly shifting toward a demi-god birth. She took on qualities of increased strength, no physical pain, and greater physical bliss. Even her *bardo* body was starting to glow as if lit from a radiance within. Simply, Eric was losing her to the form realm. Soon the course of her mind would be like too many dominoes falling to change directions. Still, he had to try one last time.

"Samantha, we need you. We need you to stop Physique."

Of all the words Eric had spoken, that last one triggered a visceral shift in Samantha. For many hours, her subconscious had still been working out ways to beat Physique. She remembered Physique vividly—and Samantha wanted a rematch. Samantha had some unfinished *karma* with that one.

Finally the mental images Eric had planted for the human realm started to ripen within Samantha. Eric witnessed her consciousness shift from a shiny, dream-like body to something far more physical.

Within moments, Samantha opened her eyes again, back in her body at Walter Reed Hospital in Washington, D.C.

Only it wasn't exactly Samantha. Now a soft glowing aura surrounded her: the shine of a demi-god from the form realm mixed with a human body. Samantha sat up in bed before delivering her first words in this new form. "I feel... good," she slowly intoned.

She pulled the taped electrodes off her body. Then she slid out of the hospital bed. Eric pushed back in his wheelchair, giving her room to walk around. Samantha was too captivated by the newfound bliss cascading through her body to notice him. With one quick tug, she ripped off her hospital gown to stand completely naked. Her skin glowed from head to toe; her body looked every bit like a demi-goddess.

Eric couldn't help but stare. She was radiant. It had been several years since he had been in the presence of a naked woman, so alone during his two years of silent retreat. But further, he had never seen a demi-goddess— not to mention a naked one. Her stomach was lean like an Olympic swimmer's; her energy radiated from her navel, the source of power in martial arts.

Samantha looked at her beautiful, glowing body while caressing her arms. Finally, she noticed Eric in the chair watching her. Vitality filled every pore of her body. Strong sexual urges and power came from her lower *chakra* energy.

"I feel really good," she cooed, walking toward Eric. "And you might be the most handsome man I've ever laid eyes on."

She grabbed Eric by the center of his shirt and pulled

him out of the chair to her body. Her skin smelled fresh like saffron. Without hesitation, she kissed him deeply. Sensual bliss from her new body poured into Eric. The connection grew passionate. Eric felt her strength pulling him farther toward her. Still Eric tried to regain some composure.

Eric broke off the kiss. "You think you're dreaming, Samantha. But we've never met before."

She looked at him, trying to decide if any of what he said mattered.

But then a more unexpected question came. "Who's Samantha?"

"You're Samantha Morris. Something happened a few days ago that brought you here."

She looked around the hospital room and back at her glowing raised hand. "I don't remember anything. Not even my name." After a moment of silence, she added, "And I don't recall feeling this good, or being... glowy." She reached for Eric again, but he'd already moved away.

From the private bathroom, Eric brought her a robe that she reluctantly put on. Light still radiated through the robe, though slightly diminished. The exposed skin of her neck, face, and hands still beamed.

"There's no easy way to tell you this, so I'll just say it plainly," Eric said. "There was an attack. You saved a lot of people, but in the process, you died. I brought you back."

"I died... and you brought me back," Samantha repeated slowly.

At that moment, the door burst open and two young nurses came charging in—no doubt, having just recognized from their monitoring station that the respirator had failed. Behind them, two Secret Service agents assessed the situation. When the first nurse saw Samantha glowing in the middle of the room, she dropped her clipboard and fell to her knees. "It's a miracle!" The second nurse held her hand to her mouth.

Samantha looked at the two women's bodies in front of her. They weren't glowing. In fact, she was the only one resembling a stoplight in the night. Trying to make sense of the situation, she looked toward her companion.

"She's come back to protect us," Eric said, standing by Samantha. "Everything's all right now. She just needs some time before she'll be ready to speak with you."

The second nurse didn't know what she was witnessing. She moved forward and touched Samantha's arm. A heightened heat radiated from Samantha's body, as if she were standing in front of a grow lamp. The nurse felt Samantha's forehead. Each touch sensation from the tender nurse's hand provoked waves of bliss through Samantha's body. Samantha gently took the nurse's hand: "I feel good...."

"I'll get the doctor," said the nurse.

"She's better now," said Eric. But seeing that no one was ready to leave them alone, Eric took a different tack. "Samantha, show them that you're strong again, so they'll leave us alone."

Samantha turned to look for something to lift. The first thing she saw was the big mechanical hospital bed. Unsure of her own strength, but feeling powerful, she grabbed the bottom of the bed with one hand to see what she could do. Slowly curling her arm, she lifted the entire three hundred pound bed as if it were a small log. She set it down with an enormous bang.

The nurses and agents backed away. She'd scared them, but she didn't fully understand why.

Eric spoke to one of the nurses: "I have to move her shortly, can you get her some clothes?"

"I have a locker," the nurse dressed in scrubs answered. "She can have mine."

"Thank you." Then to one of the Secret Service agents, Eric said, "Contact Sujata Bansal. Set up a private location where we can go. Tell her Samsa's back."

35. REVELATIONS FOR SAMSA

GLOWING LIKE A WARM STAR, SAMANTHA CROSSED HER legs in her bathrobe. Moments before, she had lifted this heavy hospital bed. Now she sat in the middle of it. In a moment of understatement, she asked Eric, "I'm not normal, am I?"

"You're unusual," Eric answered. He closed the hospital room door to give them some peace. "Normal depends on what realm you belong to."

"Why don't I remember anything?" Samantha wasn't scared, just without bearings.

Eric joined her in meditation position on the bed to console her. "This is a new life for you. You may never consciously remember much from your past life. But deep-seated habits will come to you naturally because of who you were."

"Who was I?"

"You were a really good person in your last life, which

has made you who you are now."

Samantha smiled, but her lip quivered. "Then why were those people afraid of me?"

"You're different than everyone else. You're stronger. There's a reason for that. You're here to protect people."

"But why am I different?"

Eric tried to explain. "When you belonged to this world, seeds of virtue ripened, which made you super strong. You were unusual even then…. When you died, I watched you about to be reborn in another realm. It may have seemed like a higher rebirth, but when your next life ran out you'd have fallen into a very bad place. So I brought you back—to protect you while you protect us."

Samantha's shining forehead crinkled.

Eric tried to be as clear as possible. "You're living in a human realm. But you're not fully of this world. You're a mix of human and demi-god. You may be different than the people here, but serving them will protect you."

"From what?"

"From abusing your power," Eric answered. Eric reached out and held her hand. "I'll help you through the confusion, until you find your way."

Samantha looked at her arm and felt overwhelmed. "But why am I glowing? I don't want to be different than everybody else."

"It's a form realm thing. But maybe I can help you blend in a bit more."

Eric's eyes glowed white. He meditated on subtle mental imprints that affected how she saw herself. Eric left his eyelids open to make Samantha feel she wasn't alone in her unusualness. Sending rays of white light from his heart *chakra,* he lined up more of her mind's human images. Soon, her skin stopped glowing; finally she looked more human.

"It's a temporary measure," he said. "In time, maybe I can teach you how to control it."

"You're like me!" She threw her arms around him. She felt excited that she wasn't the only one of her kind on this planet.

But Eric didn't want to give her a false impression— or say much more. "Not exactly."

"What are you then?" Samantha pointed to his chest. "And who are you? I saw the light coming from your chest. You said you brought me here. I think I have a right to know."

She did. More importantly, Eric had to help her. He would try to explain what he was... more clearly than he had ever spoken before to anyone.

Eric looked around. Once again, with the glow of Samantha's skin dialed down, only the light from underneath the door and a few nearby machines illuminated the room.

Still sitting in meditation posture, he spoke softly. "My name is Eric Adams. I am someone who cut the root of suffering by seeing ultimate reality directly. In some traditions, I'm what you call a *realized bodhisattva* or a stream-enterer. I'm not a fully enlightened being yet. But I've already seen that time coming in a future life."

"What does that mean for you now?" Samantha asked.

"Mostly, that I experience the world differently than I did before. I no longer believe that I exist truly in one way. And now, when I see other people, I understand how they're a part of me... and that I have to take care of them."

Eric reflected further on the past year—since that transformative day in meditation. "Strange things still happen in my world. I still feel pain, but I see it mainly as past bad deeds burning off. Now that I'm certain that actions create my experience of reality, I'm very careful with how I treat others."

Samantha paid close attention. Even though she didn't fully understand, she sensed Eric held a deep truth.

Eric continued, "The powers I have... they didn't happen for me when I reached meditative stillness or even immediately after I'd perceived ultimate reality. They came on later, unexpectedly, out of an intense wish to protect people. In that way, we're the same.

"I haven't told anyone this before," Eric said, shaking his head. "Mainly because the real freedom is in not needing to be anything. Not even in thinking of myself as a *bodhisattva*. Instead, I just try to be what the person across from me needs. Right now, you need me to be someone who understands reality. I promise to guide you out of the confusion, if you want me to."

Samantha nodded. Most of what Eric had shared was still beyond her comprehension, yet she felt safe with him. She believed he could answer her bewildering array of questions.

Eric smiled. "I can show you how to see the truth for yourself—to make the most of this new life. Given the changes you've already been through, it will be easier for you than most... that is, if you apply yourself. Then, when this new life ends, you'll be more in control of where you take your next rebirth, if you have to take one at all."

Exhausted, Eric lay down on the bed; Samantha curled up next to him. He put his arm around her, relieved to finally have shared his secret with someone. Eric's world had changed so radically since his transformation. As he shifted, so shifted his reality. In his spiritual practice, he had vowed to free everyone from whatever realm of suffering they were imprisoned in. Should it really be any surprise then that today he pulled his first demi-god from the form realm in order to teach her how to cut the root of suffering?

Samantha still felt adrift in this new world. She couldn't remember much from her previous life or even the realm that Eric had reported sparing her from. Still, Samantha was different. And somehow, she knew Eric was different from anyone she had ever met. Perhaps he could guide her out of confusion. She snuggled closer to his body, then laid her head on his chest. Bliss moved through her. She started to glow again—for now, feeling content.

36. CHECK OUT

THE MORNING WENT BADLY FOR SAMANTHA. HER MOM came back to the hospital just after sunrise. Instead of a glorious reunion, the visit unlocked a painful madhouse of confusion.

Samantha could only say, "I'm sorry. I just don't recognize you."

Her mom repeatedly told her stories about her childhood and their family, but it just made Samantha feel more like an alien in this world. And that was before more doctors got involved.

Of course her sudden recovery amazed doctors. It seemed like everyone with a stethoscope needed to poke and prod her. Only one sensitive doctor took time to comfort her mother: "The amnesia may last for only a few days. We'll keep her under close observation."

But Samantha's mom kept going into fits suitable for a daytime soap opera. "It feels like I lost my daughter a second time!"

When a nurse tried to take a blood sample from Samantha, the needle snapped without penetrating her skin. Eric had kept Samantha's glowing in check during the morning mayhem, but this new evidence that she obviously wasn't normal proved too much for Samantha. She started glowing again. Then everybody—the nurse, the doctors, and Samantha's mom—really freaked out.

"Enough!" shouted Eric. "She's a superhero. Not a science project!"

Eric found the eyes of the Secret Service agent who had brought him to the hospital. "Get the car. We're moving her now."

"We don't have a location yet," replied the agent.

Eric stood in the middle of mayhem. "It doesn't matter. She can't stay here. We'll just drive."

Mumbling something about "presidential authority," the agents got everyone, including Samantha's mom, out of the room.

Eager to leave the hospital too, Samantha changed into the clothes that the nurse had brought. The bra was too small for Samantha, so she discarded it. The white V-neck T-shirt and skin-tight jeans fit so snuggly across Samantha's strong shoulders and broad hips, they might as well have been a superhero bodysuit.

"How do I look?" Samantha asked, happy to be in street clothes, even if they were a little revealing.

"Like a teenage stoplight. I can't take you outside like that." Eric sent light from his heart to dial down her glow again and help her look more human. This time, the strangeness of the procedure only increased Samantha's insecurity. She tugged at her Botticelli curls. She worried she wouldn't be able to control her glowing for the rest of her life.

Samantha hesitated to follow Eric toward the door. So far this whole experience had been as confusing as being trapped in a room filled with funhouse mirrors. She wanted to cry like any newborn.

Seeing her on the verge of a meltdown, Eric said, "When I open this door, there are going to be many people looking at you, needing you to be something for them."

"What's that?"

"A hero," Eric answered. "You saved a lot of people at the risk of your own life. It's a very scary world out there— people need to see a hero walking away in triumph. Can you do that for them?"

Samantha took a moment to compose herself before answering, "I'll try."

Eric pulled the door back to allow Samantha to walk out alone. Marines and Secret Service agents immediately stood at attention out of respect. Everyone in the hall, including hospital staff, went silent. Patients who could, mostly military personnel, came to the doors of their rooms to watch her walk by. Samantha was awed by the deference everyone showed her. Responsibility weighed on her shoulders—though she didn't fully understand why.

"Good to have you back, Samsa," said a young Marine before she got in the elevator.

In the hospital lobby, the same scene replayed. Everyone recognized her: a tall, bosomy, athletic woman with wavy, dark hair and piercing blue eyes. They looked at her with admiration and hope, but she still felt confused.

Before they got into a black Secret Service limousine, Eric said, "You need to see something."

Eric led her across the grass to the impromptu shrine. At the shrine, nearly seventy people gathered in informal prayer. "Look, it's Samsa!" shouted one of them as she approached. Everyone stood. Some even seemed to bow.

When some people started to shed tears of joy, Samantha felt further disoriented. She looked at the pictures on the shrine. *It was all dedicated to her.* She read the collage of newspaper headlines looking for clues: *Samsa Saves VP, Woman Slows Building Collapse, America's Superhero in Coma.* She even saw a photograph of herself printed on the cover of *Time Magazine* holding up an impossibly large pillar. The cover headline read: *Who is Samsa?* Samantha wondered the same thing.

A little brown-haired girl, from among the people at the shrine, was the first to step forward and speak: "When I grow up, I want to be strong like you."

Samantha smiled, and then asked her genuinely, "What would you do if you were strong like me?"

The little girl pointed her finger at a comic book illustration taped on a wall of the shrine. The girl said, "I'd stop the mean people." The little girl's finger shook as she pointed at the rendering.

On the dramatic cover, a buxom brunette fought a terrifying woman with black nails and black hair dressed in a black and white bodysuit. The cover read: *Samsa vs. Physique.*

Samantha's mind flickered. She saw flashes of this woman like some strange beast charging her in slow motion. Suddenly, she recalled more details from that fateful day at the restaurant. Samantha remembered the demon flying away, leaving her to die under the strain of a giant pillar. "Physique..." Samantha uttered. Her hands clenched into fists, her eyes rolled back in her head, and then her body started to glow again.

A local news cameraman who'd been stationed outside

Walter Reed for shots of the prayer vigil, caught Samantha's whole transformation.

Eric rushed forward. The visit to the shrine hadn't turned out as he'd hoped. "Time to go," he said, gently taking Samantha's arm.

But Samsa was as solid as a stone pillar. Eric wasn't strong enough to move her. No one was. She snapped her head to the side, barking, "Where's Physique?!"

"It's our job to find her," Eric answered, in a softer voice. "You can deal with her then. Let's go."

In the limousine, Eric watched Samantha's mind: anger boiled as she replayed images of her battle with Physique. She didn't remember anything else from her life right now—just her final moments fighting a woman who seemed as strange as herself.

"I didn't know you would still have anger," Eric said. "Form realm beings don't have anger anymore."

Samantha snapped again, still wound up. "Well, I'm not in the form realm, am I?"

"We're going to try to bring Physique in without harming her," Eric said, still remaining calm, sitting by Samantha's side.

Samantha glared, "You may have brought me here, but don't think you can control me."

"Samantha—" Eric began, but she cut him off, raising her hand.

"I'm Samsa now. And Physique is going down."

37. SAMSA'S FIRST TANTRUM

A FEW HOURS AFTER THEIR ESCAPE FROM THE HOSPITAL, Samsa and Eric walked into the place from which Agent Kirby had begun his journey into unknown territory, the vice president's study. Lausunu had insisted on extending his private Charlottesville, Virginia home as a token of gratitude for Samantha saving his life.

Greeting them, Kirby, Rollins, and Arial gaped at Samsa as if viewing an unburied treasure. The well-lit study did nothing to diminish the obvious glow coming from Samsa's vibrant skin. In her tight clothes, she looked like a naughty angel. Arial, normally the center of attention, felt like the moon being blasted out by the sun.

"It's wonderful to meet you," Agent Kirby said, nervously stepping forward to shake Samsa's hand. "I'm Special Agent Kevin Kirby and this is my partner Agent Marcus Rollins."

Agent Rollins only gave his typical nod. Looking at

Samsa's glow, Rollins had the odd thought that she might be radioactive—but he quickly dismissed that as comic book kid stuff.

Samsa cut right to the chase. "You're going to help me find Physique?"

"Yes," Agent Kirby answered. "There are many people looking for her now."

Indeed, every agency and branch of military service was pulling out their best tricks to locate the sub from the attack on Washington.

"Good," said Samsa, curtly. "I'll be outside." With that she turned for the door.

Agent Kirby called after her, "We don't have any idea where she is right now."

Samsa snapped her head before briskly leaving: "Then you need to hurry."

Confounded, Agent Kirby and Arial looked to Eric for answers. She was glowing and attractive—but kind of mean. They had a more magnanimous image of the hero *Samsa* in their minds.

"It's been a rough morning for Samsa," Eric offered. "She doesn't remember anything from before the battle with Physique. She's only focused on taking Physique down."

"Oh, I like her," Agent Rollins said loudly. He'd finally met a superhero his speed.

Eric put his hands in his pockets. "Let's give her some time to cool off, then I'll go get her."

A moment later, the jarring sound of crashing metal and breaking glass thundered from the front of the house. Two Secret Service men burst into the study. "It's Samsa. She's going berserk."

The team rushed to the front yard. What they saw surprised them. Samsa had picked up the black Ford

SUV that Agent Kirby, Agent Rollins, and Arial had arrived in—and was tossing it twenty-yards at a time across the giant lawn. The SUV flew like a shot put from her hands. Catching up with the unfortunate vehicle again, Samsa pounded the hood with both fists. The hood collapsed as car tires exploded.

"Hulk smash…" said Arial dryly.

When Samsa crescent-kicked the vehicle like she was a giant trash compactor, Agent Rollins said, "I wouldn't want to be Physique."

Arial gave a sideways glance toward Eric. "Looks like your newborn is having quite a tantrum."

Arial had done her best to explain Samantha's rebirth and the six realms of existence to the agents during the two and a half hour car ride to Charlottesville. She thought she'd been torturing Agent Rollins, who kept making strange grunting noises.

"Everyone go back inside," Eric said, shaking his head. "I'll deal with this."

Disappointed, the team followed Eric's direction— though they of course watched from windows.

As Eric crossed the giant lawn, Samsa tore a door off the SUV like she was snapping someone's arm; then she bent it in half.

"What are you doing?" Eric asked. He was trying to decide if he was at a safe distance to avoid being creamed by flying debris.

Samsa shouted at Eric, "Don't try to control me!"

"I'm not trying to control you. You're going to have to learn to control yourself."

Samsa leapt up before dropping an elbow on the roof, crushing the vehicle farther.

"Look, you're scaring the horses," Eric said. He pointed

to the two brown horses who had bolted to the far end of the lawn, nostrils flared.

With one hand she flipped the car for several rolls. Then she continued after it like a crazed puma pouncing on its prey. "This is what you brought me back for, isn't it? Because I'm stronger than everyone else. Well, I had to see how strong." She punched and kicked the vehicle, making massive dents. Oil and fuel spilled onto the manicured lawn.

"Is that all?" Eric asked. He slowly followed after the glowing, wild woman.

Samsa continued taking out her rage on the twisted hunk of metal. "I didn't remember my mom..." *Thwack.* "I don't remember my life..." *Stomp.* "Physique did this to me...."

Eric moved within ten feet of her. Not wanting to be caught flat-footed, he stayed on the balls of his feet like a racquetball player. Then he gave it to Samsa straight. "It's more complicated than that. For starters, you were a bodyguard and a trained martial artist who liked to fight. You chose to fight Physique. And I'll bet partly because it never occurred to you that there might be someone stronger and badder than yourself. Physique isn't your enemy. Your sense of 'me' is."

Samsa's eyes narrowed. "What do you mean, Physique isn't my enemy...?"

"Look at you." Eric waved his hands, coming closer. "You're scaring the horses. That was Agent Kirby's car— someone on your own team. And now you're tearing up the vice president's beautiful lawn, when you're his guest. All because you're only thinking about yourself."

"But my mom..." stammered Samsa.

"You think you're the first to not remember your mom?"

Eric put his hands in his jeans pockets. "I was abandoned in an orphanage. I didn't even know mine." Eric still felt uncomfortable with this fact about his life. Perhaps it was one of the reasons he was so determined not to give up on anyone or leave anyone behind.

Samsa stopped her tantrum long enough to see Eric's point.

"I didn't bring you back just to fight Physique," Eric said. "I brought you here to learn how to destroy your grasping to a 'me'. That's the real fight. You'll find that's tougher than any adversary you can hit with your fists."

Samsa sighed. Her face was streaked with dirt and oil. She countered, "I have no idea who I am, and you think my problem is a sense of 'me.'"

"Let's get you cleaned up," offered Eric gently. "Then we'll talk about the real enemy."

38. THE REAL ENEMY

ERIC TOOK SAMSA UPSTAIRS TO FRESHEN UP, AND THEN he borrowed some yoga clothes from a vegetarian chef that the vice president employed. Once again, her voluptuous figure stretched the skimpy T-shirt for all it was worth, and the yoga pants pulled around her curves. Still, the outfit was better for sitting than skintight jeans. Fortunately, Samsa looked calmer after her shower and happy just to be alone with Eric again.

They sat on the floor in the spacious bedroom set aside for Samsa. A colonial four-post canopy bed marked the room's center. Fighting Samantha for attention, the afternoon sun granted a warm glow.

Given her memory loss, Eric intended to take things slowly. Looking for a starting point, he asked, "How much do you remember about yoga?"

Samsa did remember something. She answered, "It's great for flexibility. I think I used it in my martial arts training so I could get my kicks higher."

"Anything else?" Eric asked, hoping for more.

"It's good for the figure and helps you relax," Samsa shrugged.

Eric patiently counted his breath. That about summed up what most of the western world thought of yoga. *Good for flexibility... helps you relax... and can give you a firm yoga butt.* Secretly, he'd like to go to the front lawn and kick Samsa's compact car.

Eric brushed a golden, floppy lock of hair from his eyes. He said, "The yoga tradition is much older and much richer than most people doing yoga for exercise even realize. Yoga is a path to become whole with the true nature of reality."

"Enlightenment," Samsa said wistfully. She started twirling a curl in her hair. From talking with Eric, she'd gathered that this was his obsession.

Eric knew there were many vague ideas about what enlightenment meant. But when Samsa said this word, Eric thought of total, pure enlightenment—when one overcomes all forms of ignorance. This was Eric's wish for the world.

Eric sat still while Samsa shifted on her pillow. "The opposite of enlightenment is ignorance," he explained. "Ignorance stays in the conception of separation between self and others. All the pain in the world comes from protecting a small 'me' instead of connecting with the larger picture."

To help Samsa understand, Eric said, "You can think of the problem as your ego, if that's more helpful."

"Ego?" repeated Samsa. The word got her attention. It felt twisted and bent as Frankenstein's hunchbacked sidekick.

"Ego makes you feel separate. It makes you feel better or worse than other people. It makes you freak out when your identity is threatened—or, in your case, lost." Eric could see that this was why Samsa was acting so erratically: she felt groundless and wasn't used to it.

Returning to her personal obsession, Samsa protested, "But Physique is separate from me."

"It looks like that. But it's an illusion. The most important aspect of enlightenment is that you'll no longer feel separate." Eric closed his eyes, wishing he could stay in that conception.

Eric had seen the deeper truth in meditation; he could often reconnect with that experience off the cushion. Meditation told him that nothing existed without consciousness establishing it and that he only saw people as separate out of a mental habit. In time, he would overcome this innate habit. But routinely, he still saw people as separate from his mind—particularly when they pushed his buttons.

Samsa squirmed on her cushion, confused and impatient.

Eric had found a way out from all the pain of making things two when they really were one. He was the next guardian in a lineage of masters who had kept this path alive for centuries. He hoped his words could reach Samsa. "The entire path to enlightenment can be seen in the first four verses of *The Yoga Sutra*. They tell us what we have to do."

Samsa trusted Eric enough to keep listening.

Eric spoke the Sanskrit to Samsa before translating the verse into English. Words flowed like a song.

अथ योगानुशासनम् ॥ १ ॥

Atha yoga anushasanam

I.1 I WILL NOW REVIEW FOR YOU
HOW WE BECOME WHOLE.

"Notice, right from the start, he's stating the problem," Eric said. "We're not whole yet. We think we're some separate 'me' running around in a crazy world of less important 'others.'"

Samsa's cheek twitched. There was no way that she and Physique were one.

योगश्चित्तवृत्तिनिरोधः ॥ २ ॥

Yogash chitta virtti nirodhah

I.2 WE BECOME WHOLE BY STOPPING HOW THE MIND TURNS.

"Now he's stating the solution. We reach our goal by stopping how the mind twists things around." Eric brought Samsa's attention to one key word in an attempt to help her remember this most important verse. "*Virtti* means to twist or turn. It comes into English as *weird*.

"What is it that we have gotten weird and turned around?" Eric asked, looking deeply into Samsa's blue eyes. "We think the world is out there coming at us, instead of coming from us. With wisdom you'll see everything as a part of you."

तदा द्रष्टुः स्वरूपेऽवस्थानम् ॥ ३ ॥

Tada drashtuh svarupevasthanam

I.3 ON THAT DAY THE SEER COMES TO DWELL WITHIN THEIR OWN REAL NATURE.

"Now he's saying what specifically happens to stop our mind from being weird. By seeing that we don't truly exist in one way, we free ourselves from limitations. By seeing we depend on causes for every moment of appearance, we see our real nature."

"That doesn't seem that difficult," Samsa said, finally getting engaged. "Isn't it obvious that people change all the time?"

"Then why did you get upset that you couldn't remember your life or your mom?" Eric countered.

"Because those were things that belonged to me that I didn't want to lose."

Eric gazed at her intently. "If things come from changing causes, could anything belong to you permanently?"

Were this a martial arts contest, Eric Adams would have just performed a counter throw. Even though Samsa was much stronger than Eric, facing his mind intimidated her. He was too many steps ahead.

"You got upset because you were holding on to an impossible idea—that things belonged to you permanently. That caused you to suffer when things ran their normal course," Eric explained. "It's the same with your sense of a truly existing 'me.' It's an impossible idea, impossible to defend; in fact, it causes you nothing but suffering. So it's your real enemy."

My real enemy…. It felt strange to consider that the thing she grasped to most—her sense of me—was not her friend.

क्षीणवृत्तेरभिजातस्येव मणेर्ग्रहीतृग्रहणग्राह्येषु तत्स्थतदञ्जनतासमापत्तिः ॥ ४१ ॥

Kshina virtter abhijatasyeva maner grahitir grahana grahyeshu
tat stha tad anjanata samapattih

I.41 THOSE EXTRAORDINARY PEOPLE WHO SHATTER THE
WAY THE MIND TURNS THINGS AROUND
USE A BALANCED MEDITATION, WHICH IS FIXED AND CLEAR
ON ITS OBJECT. AND THIS OBJECT IS LIKE A CRYSTAL,
WITH THE ONE THAT HOLDS IT, AND WHAT IT HOLDS,
AND THE HOLDING ITSELF AS WELL.

"Finally, Master Patanjali shares the technique to shatter our ignorance. We have to use balanced meditation which sees no difference between our mind, outer objects, and the meditative experience itself."

Eric could see that Samsa had had enough for now. "The other verses explain the details, but if you just held these four verses of *The Yoga Sutra* in your heart, you would have a clearer picture of the path to enlightenment. You'd know what you have to do to overcome your small 'me.'"

Samsa smiled. She would at least consider it.

Eric explained, "It takes time to undo a mistake you've been making for countless lifetimes. To get at ultimate wisdom, we can use any ancient spiritual text—whether Hindu, Buddhist, Jewish, Christian, Muslim, Taoist, or Confucian—whatever you are attracted to. It doesn't matter to me. All the prophets were trying to take people to the same realization using different words and different techniques. All of them lead toward the same place. You'll understand that clearly once you've seen ultimate reality."

Eric paused. There was one more thing he needed to tell her. If Eric was going to train Samsa, she would have to meditate. "But to see ultimate reality directly, you have to learn how to step out of deceptive reality. To do that, there is no substitute for deep meditation."

It was the same for Samsa as everyone else: if she stayed at the level of a hectic, busy life—soon to be continually

overstimulated by every electronic gadget imaginable—
she would be blocked from deeper things.

Samsa heard Eric, but again returned to her fixation.
"And Physique, how are we going to stop her?"

"We'll change our world from within," Eric answered.
"But we'll also act in our outer world." Eric pressed his right
hand to the ground in a gesture the Buddha once used to
show that deceptive reality mattered. "Make no mistake,"
he said, "we have to stop Physique, but not for the reason
most would give."

"What's your reason?"

"We need to stop her because she's a part of us that's
become twisted and weird. By hurting others, she's hurting
herself." Then Eric said the unexpected: "We need to stop
Physique to protect her. I want to bring her in as peacefully
as possible, and then help her heal."

"You don't want me to kill her?" Disappointment
showed in Samsa's face.

"There is one more important verse in *The Yoga Sutra*
that you need to memorize."

Samsa rolled her eyes. "No more verses today, Eric."

"You musn't think like that." Eric grew as stern as
his lama who used to correct him when he was being
intellectually lazy. Suddenly, Eric seemed ten feet tall to
Samsa. "This wisdom is how you become a real superhero.
This wisdom is how you really protect all beings. The real
fight is in your mind, Samsa. You can't win that fight with
brawn."

Samsa felt her ego wanting to defend itself. And
it didn't feel good. Eric might be right after all. "OK,
what's the verse?"

अहिंसाप्रतिष्ठायां तत्सन्निधौ वैरत्यागः ॥ ३५ ॥

ahinsa pratishthayam tat sannidau vaira tyagah

II.35 IF YOU MAKE IT A WAY OF LIFE
NEVER TO HURT OTHERS,
THEN IN YOUR PRESENCE
ALL CONFLICT COMES TO AN END.

"Meaning what exactly?" Samsa asked.

Eric closed his eyes again, this time to envision pure wisdom spreading over the globe. "This is the real way to end war, by realizing that violence comes from within, then not continuing the cycle of violence when twisted, weird people act brutally. More than anything, I hope to end war on this planet. But it can't be done until ignorance is overcome."

Eric felt ashamed. There hadn't been a single day in Eric's whole life when a shooting war hadn't been taking place somewhere on the planet.

"But what about—" Samsa began to protest, but Eric cut her off, raising his hand.

"We can debate this many times in the future. For now, think of how many versions of 'thou shall not kill' and 'turn the other cheek' you've seen in religious teachings. Maybe those enlightened beings know something that this world has to learn."

Eric smiled at Samsa. He'd been both gentle and stern. And shared what was deepest in his heart. But her will was strong. It would take time to help her undo her old habits— and it would take a mixture of carrots and sticks. Eric said, "I appreciate you listening. Why don't you just relax. I'll bring you some dinner."

Eric returned downstairs and entered the spacious kitchen. The country estate had an old world feel, but all the appliances were shiny and modern.

Agent Kirby sat at the kitchen table waiting for Eric. The contrast between talking to Samsa about *The Yoga Sutra*, and then running into his FBI-nemesis, Kirby, narrowed Eric's eyes.

Even though Eric had had so little sleep in days, Kirby jumped right in with what he wanted. "I spoke with Sujata at the White House," reported Kirby. "The media's reporting that Samsa walked away from Walter Reed unscathed. She's a national hero. The vice president and his advisors feel it will calm the nation's nerves if people see her."

Eric's hands rested on the island counter in the center of the kitchen. "She's not ready."

"Can you get her ready?" Kirby pushed away a plate strewn with crusts from a ham sandwich.

Eric could already see how this superyogi thing was going to go. There were no "thanks for bringing her back, thanks for healing her;" just "can you get her ready" for the next thing. Nobody was asking, "How are you doing, Eric?" Still, Eric simply asked, "What do they have in mind?"

"Just to read a short, prepared statement at the Rose Garden and receive the Medal of Honor from the vice president. No questions. It's actually quite an honor. The medal has only been awarded once before to a civilian."

Eric sensed Kirby was holding something back, even without reading his mind. "There's something else you're not telling me."

Kirby invited Eric to take a seat at the kitchen table. "Well... because she's a superhero with strange powers, the president's cabinet thinks everyone would feel more comfortable if she were wearing… a uniform."

Eric pulled up a chair. "What kind of uniform?"

"A superhero uniform." Kirby tried to keep his face as straight as possible. "In fact, they're sending a team of comic book artists here tomorrow to design outfits for her and the rest of the team."

Willingly, perhaps for the first time, Eric sat silently with Agent Kirby. He tried to imagine an actual costumed superhero in the White House Rose Garden. Finally, Eric uttered, "Man, this is getting weird."

39. THE COSTUME DEBATE

DEBATE IN THE VICE PRESIDENT'S SPACIOUS STUDY OVER the merits of Samsa, Arial, and Eric becoming costumed superheroes filled the evening. In the beginning, no one had particularly strong opinions: after all, these issues had never been truly considered.

As the team took turns expressing concern over the White House's latest public relations maneuver, Samsa left the discussion early. The whole thing felt too overwhelming for a person still trying to find her way in a world she couldn't fully recall.

Uncharacteristically, Eric had more questions than recommendations. But as the unusual debate continued, positions hardened. Agent Rollins and Agent Kirby fired most of the verbal shots.

"They're weapons," Agent Rollins said. Standing, he pointed at Eric as if holding a gun. "And the most effective weapon is the one you don't see coming."

"Are they a strike force or a deterrent?" Agent Kirby asked, still seated in a sofa chair.

"They're a strike force," Rollins answered. "Our task is to take down dangerous yogis who have gotten out of line—and that's a strike force."

Eric winced. Before this conversation, Eric hadn't seen himself as a deployable weapon. From his Navy SEAL days, he'd had enough of being a strike force.

Revved up for a fight, Agent Rollins was unwilling to concede any ground. "Even as a deterrent, it's better that people don't know who or where they are."

Perched on the couch, Captain Arial Davis sipped calming chamomile tea scored from the vice president's extensive tea selection. She coyly countered, "But that's not really possible now with Samsa, is it, Agent Rollins?"

Indeed, Samantha Morris was the story. Media raptors had even interviewed male martial arts champions she'd defeated and Phys. Ed. teachers from her high school. They wanted to know if any signs of her supernormal abilities had appeared earlier.

Agent Kirby stood up, trying to command the room. "The world needs superheroes as examples. The bigger danger, beyond Physique, comes as more yogis develop supernatural powers. We don't want them running around as isolated individuals pursuing their own agendas, do we? We need to offer them a place where they can go for support and can use their powers for a greater purpose."

"But Physique thinks she's already using her powers for a greater purpose," Arial countered.

Agent Kirby pointed like he was playing trombone. "Exactly! But as a rogue individual. We need superyogis aligned with our national interests."

For all of Arial's intelligence, she couldn't express what

was really bothering her. She felt nervous about being raised up as some grand protector—after all, they were beginning superyogis and unproven as a team. Further, did one foiled bank robbery, saving one child, and slowing down Physique really make them superheroes?

As usual, Eric sat comfortably on the floor in meditation posture. He could sit for hours like that. "What about the interests of other nations?" Eric asked. "What if their superyogis don't match our national interests?" He didn't want yogic powers to become a new arms race.

Agent Kirby returned to the chair facing Eric. "Then maybe this goes international at some point, supporting international law. But for right now, we need a place for superyogis to go and stay on our side. Since the main problem is public fear, the White House needs to run the play outlined by my report. Main Street needs to see that Pennsylvania Avenue is capable of policing superyogis and can bring them to work in cooperation with the government."

Eric had too many concerns, starting with giving false impressions that this small team could protect people from all kinds of unforeseen attacks from yogis gone wild. Further, he knew they couldn't be everywhere, and that an attack could occur anywhere at any time. "Do you want to set up a Justice League of superyogi crime fighters?"

"Yes," answered Agent Kirby, unafraid of the comic book reference, "to support and train superyogis in alignment with our national interests."

Eric's neck stiffened. He didn't believe that government could secure morality. "Seems to me the government doesn't have a great track record for training super-talents to support our purposes. Anyone we train could flip at any time—even become a weapon against us. Weren't Manuel

Noriega, Saddam Hussein, and bin Laden all people the CIA trained?"

Agent Rollins smirked. He'd also seen blowback too many times from government interventions on behalf of national interests.

Agent Kirby finally put his heart on his sleeve. "Look, I know this is complicated. Maybe even too complicated for us to solve. But you don't want people like Agent Rollins and me being scared of you, do you? Help us to feel more comfortable around you."

Kirby had voiced his deepest fear and Eric understood. Eric had felt his unusual qualities create tension between him and the agents too many times. Eric asked, "And a superhero costume makes you feel more comfortable?"

"It's something we know and understand," answered Kirby.

Arial put her teacup down. "Maybe superhero costumes might help." She remembered how awkward she'd felt after saving the little girl. "You saw how people looked at me. I felt like an alien."

Eric had similar feelings after disarming bank robbers. And when Samsa had started glowing in the hospital, people didn't know what they were looking at. They were frightened.

Agent Rollins saw the discussion was heading further into Kirby's comic book land. He didn't have the power to overrule the White House anyway. Instead, Rollins offered a tactical solution. "Samsa's cover is blown. You may as well put her in a costume on the White House lawn. There are pictures of her everywhere and now she glows like a fricking lighthouse."

Rollins started cracking pistachios again without using his fingernails; instead, he used a half shell as a lever. "But you two are different," he said. "For as long as possible, we need to hide your identities. If hoods, masks, and code names are part of that diversion, so be it."

"So the costumes would have masks?" Arial asked. "I just need to know if I should call my mom before she sees her daughter flying on TV." Arial couldn't imagine how that conversation would go. *Mom, you know how superheroes fly in the movies? Well, your daughter just got boots and a cape.*

"We do the mask thing for you and Eric," Rollins answered.

At least she wouldn't have to call her mom. Arial looked at Eric, nodding her consent. "I always was a little jealous of Navy pilots with cool call signs. The Air Force doesn't do that. If I flew for the Navy I'd want to be called *Airspeed*."

Eric heard Arial's superhero name like trumpets calling for a charge. This moment marked a turning point in his own life. He could finally step out of the shadows of suspicion, firmly into the light of benefiting others.

On one transformative day during his two-year meditation retreat, his merit had blessed him with a vision of the enlightened being he would become. In meditation, he'd seen his future self directly. His teacher had already foreshadowed this event by giving him a secret name, *Diamond Mind*. This name reflected the clarity of wisdom he would one day possess.

Now, sitting in this room, discussing the more obvious mantles of a superhero, Eric realized what he had to do. He had to completely let go of Eric Adams. That fractured man still had too much baggage to allow the hero Diamond Mind to fully emerge.

The team waited for Eric's response. His eyes started to glow. "And you can call me Diamond Mind. If it's who I will become, I may as well start now."

40. COSTUME DESIGNS

SUNLIGHT GLISTENED OFF THE BLOND WOOD FLOORS LIKE arrows off a bronze shield as Eric, Arial, and Samantha meditated in a sparse room. Today marked the first time the team would present themselves to the world as the superyogis Diamond Mind, Airspeed, and Samsa.

Responsibility weighed on them as differently as gravity on separate planets. Eric saw this day as the next step in his evolution, the inevitable result of all his training. Arial felt a sense of duty: she was an Air Force pilot whose skills had been upgraded. But she also worried that her power wouldn't be enough for the task. Samsa's feelings were more mixed: she didn't understand the power she had gained, but she felt driven to stop Physique.

Eric didn't lead the meditation. Instead, he had encouraged the new superyogis to focus on the personal meaning this day had for each of them. But ten minutes in, Samsa interrupted, whispering, "Eric, I can barely concentrate. I have so much bliss in my body, I don't know what to do with it."

"I'll teach you how to use the bliss later," Eric answered. "But for now, send bliss on rays of light to everyone. Wish the whole world could feel that great. Imagine giving that sensation to everyone you meet today."

Arial was a naturally strong meditator, and even better from her years of training. But today (overhearing the conversation between Samsa and Eric) her mind experienced agitation and even jealousy—both over Samsa's body of bliss and Eric planning to pay special attention to Samsa later.

Arial acted out her jealousy by leading a post-meditation flow of yoga balancing poses best suited for her own cottony light body—poses which generated their own feelings of bliss in Arial. However, the series didn't have the desired effect of taking Samsa down a few notches. Simply too strong, Samsa powered through the tough poses.

"That felt great," Samsa said afterwards to Arial. "You really pushed my body. I love that."

The series was only physically hard on Eric, and disturbing because he could sense the emotional dynamic building between Airspeed and Samsa. Rather than paying attention to their *drishti*, the point of visual focus in each yoga pose, Airspeed and Samsa had eyed each other to see whose pose looked better. Still Eric said nothing. He didn't want to dampen spirits on a day like this.

The three superyogis were in deep conversation about how the wisdom in *The Yoga Sutra* corresponded to the wisdom in the Buddha's *Heart Sutra* when a knock rapped on the door. Agent Kirby excitedly entered like a comic book geek crossing the threshold into Comic-Con. "You won't believe who the White House has brought in to design your uniforms. Some of the greatest artists in comic book history are downstairs."

Seeing how revved up Agent Kirby was, Eric asked, "Who'd they bring in?"

"Well for starters they got Tim Yee. He may be the best pencil illustrator of all time. He practically reinvented how comics looked in the late 90s. I don't think anyone got the mix of superhero strength and gritty realism better."

"He's that big?" Arial asked, never having heard of him. But of course she wasn't a student of comic book art—or she'd know.

"Arial, he's so big, he owns his own jet," answered Kirby. The jet impressed Arial more than the man's penciling skills.

"They also brought in Eduardo Buenos, the famous Brazilian artist," Agent Kirby said. "No one has made female superheroes look sexier."

"That's a good thing, I think..." Arial said, suddenly feeling nervous in her slinky spaghetti-strap yoga top.

Kirby's enthusiasm overflowed like soda from a shaken can. "Wayne Marcus, one of the best comic writers of all time, is downstairs too. This guy knows what people want from superheroes. He used to own a comic book store before he turned pro."

"You seem to know a lot about comic books," Samsa said, grimacing on one side of her mouth while trying to smile on the other. She wondered if comics would help Agent Kirby find Physique.

"I do," answered Kirby unabashedly. "But the people downstairs *are* comic books. Everyone is represented—from DC to Marvel and even an independent like Boom!"

"I get it," Eric laughed. "This is a bi-partisan comic initiative. Very smart of Lausunu not to alienate the vocal comic book base." Between the two giants of DC and

Marvel, Eric tried to imagine which comic book company was favored by more Republicans and which one by more Democrats.

"The group downstairs knows how to make this real for the public," Kirby said, now standing like a frenetic, cartoon bunny with only one foot in the room. He clearly wanted to be back downstairs. "But they're also here to work with you—to design stuff you'll feel comfortable in. So let's get to work." Kirby actually clapped his hands as if breaking a team huddle.

On the way downstairs, Agent Kirby continued to explain the origin stories of the other participating illustrators. He also reported that each artist had been granted special security clearance for this endeavor—and they would keep anything they saw or heard in the room strictly confidential. "In short, these are people who honor the superheroes' code. They can be trusted." To someone like Kirby, being an avid reader of comic books was almost as good as swearing on the Bible.

When the superyogis entered the vice president's living room they saw illustrations mounted on posterboard of many of the greatest superhero icons of all time. Even Samsa could recall most of them.

The superyogis were about to join this pantheon.

Then there were the comic book experts. They were mostly middle-aged men in baseball caps, which matched their boyish big hearts. Two women with sass rounded out the group—one a noted illustrator in blue-framed glasses and the other, an award-winning costume designer, dressed in all black with severe black bangs. Upon seeing the superyogis, looks of wonder brightened the illustrators' faces. After all, heroes like the ones they had drawn, written about, and clothed for movies for so many years—keeping the heroes' code alive in the world—were now standing in front of them.

Although Agent Kirby had briefed the design team about each superyogis' code name and their powers, the designers had secretly hoped to learn more about their amazing abilities. Like a great orator, Wayne Marcus spoke first with clarity. His short-cropped beard evoked nobility. "It's an honor for all of us to meet you. We've dreamt of a day like this for most of our lives."

Plane-owning millionaire Tim Yee added, "Looks like all those years of art school are finally paying off."

Eduardo Buenos took a different tack. He patted the couch and said to Airspeed and Samsa, "Come over here, with me. I'm going to make you both look fabulous." This broke the ice and got the illustrators down to business.

To see what caught the girls' eyes, Eduardo showed comic book spreads of great female superheroes. The illustrators had been directed to design costumes that resembled superheroes that the public already liked. Amidst the great splashes of color and curves, the first thing the girls noticed was the amount of skin. "I can't believe how scantily clad they are," Arial said.

"Well, comic book readers are mostly male," Eduardo explained. "To teenage boys and middle-aged men, kick-ass women with sex appeal are big drivers for comic books."

Jane Diaz, the noted illustrator, sat casually on a second couch watching the superyogis. Fiddling with her glasses, she added, "Wonder Woman also has a huge fan base among lesbian readers."

"We all know that much of the power women wield over men comes from their sex appeal," Wayne Marcus explained. "So it's only natural when we want to convey a powerful woman in a comic book, we pump up her sexiness."

"We do the same with men's muscles to give them a statuesque... overabundance," added Tim Yee, famous for sculpting exaggerated muscles on his heroes.

"What I want to show you both," Eduardo said, "is that a women's superhero costume is basically a bathing suit with boots, then gloves or bracelets."

Airspeed and Samsa looked again at the spreads. They could see the one-piece bathing suit Wonder Woman wore... the bikini that Storm recently sported. Sure a tight fitting catsuit occasionally slinked on the scene, but mostly bathing suits and boots heated up the pages.

Eduardo imagined the women on a beach. "How comfortable are you both with living in a bathing suit?" He really wanted to know. "We'll do things as revealing as your tight yoga clothes... but just a little more provocative." He knew their designs would in fact be much more provocative—but he didn't want to scare them off in the first ten minutes.

Neither Airspeed nor Samsa felt particularly shy about their fabulous bodies. And it was true that some of their snug yoga clothing was just as revealing as a comic book costume. Unexpectedly, Samsa stripped off her T-shirt, revealing chisled abs and a red bra. "Let's go for it. I can beat Physique fighting naked. I don't care what you put me in."

The men stared at Samsa's glowing, barely contained breasts. Closing his eyes, Eric counted his breath. When he'd advised Samsa to see herself giving bliss to everyone she met today, this was *not* what he had in mind.

After a few moments—during which the universe seemed to stand still—Eduardo composed himself enough to speak to his fellow illustrators. "Well, seeing what we have to work with more closely... you know what to do."

Taking out sketchpads, the illustrators went to work. They didn't use pencil and paper anymore. Their tools were electronic Wacom pads and pressure sensitive styluses. They sketched directly on computer screens that laid flat in front of them, selecting any brush or color they desired.

The award-winning costume designer, Carol Burge, motioned for the girls and the female illustrator to join her in the other room. "I need to take your precise measurements. This is going to get a little intimate."

With the women gone, Tim Yee focused on Diamond Mind. "Did you read many comic books when you were growing up?"

"Still do," Diamond Mind answered. "I know who you are—your work on the Superman books was amazing. It's an honor to be working with you."

Tim Yee felt embarrassed. "This is a bigger deal for me... than you'll ever know."

Closing his eyes, Diamond Mind reached into Tim's mind. Tim Yee caught the light shining from Diamond Mind's eyes as they rolled back, along with a little hint of light from the forehead. In a flash, Eric could see years of Tim's comic book illustrations and the values embodied in those superheroes. *They protect life... they don't kill their enemies... and they don't stop, no matter how many times they get knocked down.* Eric and Tim both admired that last quality most.

Eyes now open, Diamond Mind smiled at Tim. Eric noticed how comfortable he felt around comic book people. Their enthusiasm for superhero stories—despite being sometimes ridiculed as juvenile by a jaded mainstream— revealed a personal aspiration to become something greater to better serve the world.

It occured to Eric that comic book artists, writers, and comic fans would likely make great *dharma* students. They were true believers that human beings could become something more. Further, they already had the aspiration to protect others. They just needed to be taught how— using deeper wisdom that went beyond the drama of a comic book page.

"That's quite a tell you have," Tim Yee said, referring to the way Eric's eyes changed as he read someone's mind. "Maybe we can hide the light with your mask." Tim studied Eric's lock of wavy blond hair that dangled from his forehead like Superman's S-curl. He'd hate to cover that with a Batman-like cowl. Tim thought, *Maybe a mask that rises to his hairline, but lets his friendly hair flop over?*

When the women returned to the room, including Samsa with her shirt on once again, Jane Diaz announced, "Airspeed's legs and bottom are to die for. We have to draw attention to them."

Everyone stared at the blushing Airspeed. Finally, she said, "I'm not taking my pants off, if that's what you're hoping for."

Wayne Marcus said to Diamond Mind, "I understand none of this team would be here now if it weren't for you." Eric didn't react one way or the other. "Have you thought about what you want to call the team?"

Now Eric looked surprised. "I hadn't given it any thought. Do we need a team name?"

Marcus and Yee responded in stereo: "Definitely."

Wayne Marcus explained, "DC Comics is famous for the Justice League, and Marvel has both the Avengers and the X-Men. It's a best practice really."

Diamond Mind didn't know where to begin with choosing a comic book name. He asked for recommendations.

Marcus felt pleased to be asked. Indeed, he did have an idea. "Well, I think it's interesting that we're at vice president Lausunu's private home and apparently he was the person who green-lighted Agent Kirby's superyogi program. It occurred to me that Lausunu spelled backwards is *Unusual*. Perhaps your team should be called *The Unusuals*."

The Unusuals. Airspeed nodded. Standing across the room trying to keep her bottom to the wall, she called out, "That says it, doesn't it?"

Diamond Mind looked to Agent Kirby. He leaned against the VP's desk and shrugged. "It fits well. You are unusual."

"I'm good with the Unusuals if everyone agrees," Diamond Mind said.

A quick, informal vote followed. Even Samsa agreed. Though Agent Rollins, lurking in the back of the room, abstained. He still maintained his sulky position that this whole showy masquerade was nonsense.

"For your costume," Tim Yee asked Diamond Mind, "I need to know where the light rays come out of your body. I heard you send lasers from your heart or something."

"It's not like that," Diamond Mind said. "It's more like light visualized from my meditations takes physical form." Diamond Mind pointed to the center of his chest. "The light comes from my heart *chakra*. It's not an organ, but a tiny energetic drop."

"What do the light rays look like?" Tim asked. "Can you show us?" The illustrators leaned forward in anticipation.

Diamond Mind didn't want to be rude, but he didn't feel a compelling need to display this ability for the sake of a costume. He looked to Airspeed for help. She understood Eric's hesitation.

"I've seen it," Arial said, gesturing with her hands. "It's like long sunbeams bouncing off a diamond." That was a good image—but the illustrators still wanted more.

"Wait," Agent Kirby said, eager to help. "I can show you. I have the bank video." Without further hesitation he attached his computer to the video display screen. He felt confident that viewing this video was covered by the illustrators' security clearance.

Neither Airspeed nor Samsa had seen the video that exposed Eric's abilities. Interested, they moved closer to the screen.

Red and white light gleamed from Eric's chest. Eric took half a dozen rounds to the chest while turning transparent like bulletproof glass. Samsa noticed Eric snapping a punch from his shoulder with the authority of a trained boxer. Her esteem for the contemplative philosopher grew.

"Wow," Tim Yee said. "You're like Professor Xavier meets Green Lantern meets Superman."

"I can't fly and don't have much strength," corrected Eric. "That's where Airspeed and Samsa come in."

"And for the sex appeal," Eduardo added, still singularly focused on his favorite task.

When everyone laughed, Agent Rollins grumpily stormed out. He'd had enough of playtime—actual lives were at stake. Agent Kirby started to go after him, but Eric stopped him. "He's gonna have to learn how to lighten up. Having a sense of humor is a big part in making any spiritual progress." Agent Rollins had of course shown no interest in making spiritual progress, but Diamond Mind wasn't giving up on him.

To refine their designs, each illustrator presented concepts to the group. Seeing themselves as comic book characters in action made Airspeed and Samsa giggle.

The illustrators stayed at it with relentless concentration, each in their own paradise, doing exactly what they were born to do—but this time, for real heroes.

41. DIAMOND MIND'S MEDITATION

Wɪᴛʜ ᴏɴʟʏ ʜᴏᴜʀs ᴛᴏ ɢᴏ ʙᴇꜰᴏʀᴇ ᴛʜᴇ ʙɪɢ ᴀᴡᴀʀᴅ ceremony, the costumes arrived in locked metal briefcases.

As only Samsa was going to the White House, there wasn't any real hurry for the other yogis to try on their costumes. Still, Samsa insisted, "I'm not putting on my costume unless we all put them on." She even extended the conditions: "You have to stay suited up the entire time I'm on the playing field. I mean it. I'd better see you in costume when I return or I'm going to start breaking things again. Okay?"

Clearly, Samsa couldn't take this next step without Diamond Mind and Airspeed, but in truth, stony reluctance slowed each of them from taking on their new identities. Before, with the comic book illustrators, they were still in the realm of make-believe. Now, the metal cases sitting in their rooms represented something more tangible for each of them: a kind of death and rebirth. Eric suggested they meditate separately before donning their uniforms. Hopefully, in two hours everyone would gather the nerve to see Samsa out, fully dressed.

Eric meditated with intensity. Each time, he put his ideas on trial. Any ignorant illusions would be shattered. For Eric Adams, meditation was a steel cage death match: many ideas might go in, but only the truth could exit the ring. Before transforming into the superyogi Diamond Mind, he had to witness the lack of a truly existing self. That way he could be free of any limiting identity, a sense of "me" that could hold him back.

To get to that, Eric didn't engage in common notions of meditation such as simply watching the breath or emptying the mind of thoughts. No—to get to that truth, Eric wielded the most powerful weapon championed by the Buddha and countless masters after him: logical analysis. This type of meditation shattered wrong views that created suffering. Eric had to be certain he had the proper wisdom to take on this role. Perhaps it could even overcome Eric's heebie-jeebies about publicly stepping out in superhero tights.

Like a detective with a suspect in a dark room, the interrogation began with a question. *Is there a "me" that truly exists?* The detective in Eric's head asked, *"How do you think of the 'me' now?"*

"I'm made of a body, mind, and feelings," Eric responded keeping his answers honest and immediate.

"Well, does your body change?" posed the voice, hidden in the dark.

"Yes."

"Do your feelings change?"

"Of course."

"*In fact, they don't ever stay just one way,*" the detective observed.

Eric conceded the point without considering the implications.

Then the detective added, "*So you're laying a sense of 'me' onto something that isn't as concrete and consistent as you imagine.*"

Stung, Eric admitted that because his body, mind, and feelings didn't stay one way, they weren't true and dependable. After all, his body in peak SEAL shape belonged to the past, and his feelings changed like the weather. He had seen his body become wheelchair bound. He had seen his swagger dissolve into months of depression. So how could he claim he had one truly existing body or set of feelings?

"*Well, maybe I'm my awareness,*" Eric conceded, trying to hold on to something solid that he could stick his label of "me" onto.

The detective made the next move: "*When your mind becomes aware of different things like a sound within a song, or the taste of a piece of fruit, or the smell of the rain, does your awareness change?*"

"*Sure, to different objects, but I'm always aware.*"

"*Are you?*" The detective reacted sternly, knowing Eric was lying.

Eric realized that he couldn't remember his SEAL team pulling his body out from under the demolished building in Afghanistan—or the days before he woke up in a hospital tent. If he was his awareness, he would have gone out of existence during his coma—and even every night during sleep. Awareness, too, came from changing causes.

The detective pressed, "*Look here. You claim there is something solid that proves there is a 'me': a body, a set of feelings,*" *and a mind. But on closer investigation, those things don't truly exist in one fixed way. So isn't it more like—out of habit—you're labeling a truly exising 'me' onto a few changing indications?"*

Eric waited for more clarity to come.

"For example, awareness of the past is no longer here. And awareness of the future has yet to come."

"Wait," Eric protested. *"I can think of the past. I can think of the future."*

"And when are you doing it?" asked the detective, springing the trap.

Eric's mind raced. He watched mental concepts form like drops from a dripping tap. *"In the now... I can only access past or future in the now."* This meant there was no way to know whether he was getting the past right, because it was never actually the past... instead, just a present-moment memory.

"And the awareness of now? Can you even find it?" the detective pressed.

Moments of now are like splitting tenths of a second in an Olympic track dash. Time could be incrementally divided until Eric could only say an instant was "now" by merely shouting that label. Suddenly, Eric caught that the label "now" only existed artificially in his mind. Witnessing how this worked, Eric realized time was a fabrication.

Further, he realized that even his sense of "me" was a fabrication. The habitual label arose over changing images like a persistent weed—but it didn't have to spoil the garden.

Now taking over the investigation, Eric asked himself, *"What's there before the label?"* Feeling brave and bold as his detective, Eric wanted to go beyond ordinary conceptual thought. *"Show me what truly exists."*

Investigating this bold question, Eric found nothing

that could withstand analysis. Everything rises and falls. Nothing stands on its own. Eric came up empty and understood the most profound wisdom: nothing could be established as being separate from his mind's labels. Instead, everything existed in relationships of dependence. Things appeared, but they were not self-existent. They were interconnected, depending on mind.

Suddenly, clutter and grasping to false delusions cleared away like clouds evaporating in a crystal sky. Corresponding surges of blissful *prana* entered Eric's central channel of wisdom—collapsing side channels of ignorance that could only exist while he believed in the separation of self from outer objects. A boom like the sound of Arial's jet going supersonic accompanied this rush of *prana*. Breath became perfectly even in both nostrils: so gentle, so fine, it was hardly there.

Eric's analytical meditation had produced a genuine realization—an approximation of the absence of self-existence. Now Eric switched to fixed meditation by holding the realization like one might gaze at a precious jewel. For some time, Eric stayed single-pointed on his realization with intensity and clarity.

The winds of his inner body settled until single-pointed stillness became perfect. Eric's body felt lighter and more blissful than florets of dandelions floating on a warm breeze.

But he didn't settle for this peaceful experience. From this platform of stillness, Eric felt ready to go for the kill—to destroy innate seeds of grasping to a "me."

Eric had seen that his mind, body, and feelings kept changing. He'd recognized that insisting on the label "me" was merely an ignorant habit.

Eric took a giant step into the unknown. *"What's there without fabricating this concept of 'me'?"*

The sound of something like a flute trilled in Eric's inner body. Breath stopped without any effort. His mind became incapable of producing any thought that mistook true existence. In the next instant, *prana* in the central channel dissolved at a specific point in his heart *chakra*. Subject consciousness dissolved. Then there was only the clear light of a diamond.

No one to think. No thing to think about. No separation. Just an experience of the absence of self-existence, while understanding this too was an illusion. This experience was beyond words. It felt closest to being the clear light of a diamond. But this was just the closest image his mind could produce when he later recalled the experience.

Staying in this direct experience, time stopped for Eric. It would seem like only minutes to an outside observer in the conventional world. But for Eric, the veil of ignorance that had covered the entire universe, every realm, and his sense of self pulled back, revealing the most startling truth anyone could ever imagine: there wasn't one reality… there wasn't separation… whatever appeared, he was responsible for… and that's why actions mattered.

What stirred his mind again? Feelings of compassion. You see nothing; then love everything. *I don't want anyone to suffer. I don't want anyone to feel limited.*

"Good. You see the truth," the detective said, returning this time to play the good cop. *"If you try, you could develop the habit of taking care of everyone as you. You could go beyond the ego. That would be a miraculous thing. That would bring an end to all suffering."*

Reflecting on the beauty he had witnessed in his analytical meditation, Eric knew the wisdom side of his mind had spoken truly. If he could see further in the darkness, Eric would see the voice of wisdom as the enlightened being he would become—moving beyond the constraints of time to guide him in the illusory now.

Eric's wisdom was strong. He just had to improve his method, his interaction with the world. Eric asked for blessings to overcome his innate, but changeable habits, to go beyond his small self. Now, his main practice required breaking down the walls between himself and others.

Eric knew this was the true source of power—but not just any kind of power. Lots of people had power: incredible wealth, superior abilities, and lofty positions that gave them influence over the lives of others. Then there were those, like Eric, who had superyogic abilities. Inevitably, more of both would emerge. But power didn't make someone super. In the end, putting others' needs before your own made someone super.

Eric opened his eyes. Diamond Mind's suit symbolized what he vowed to do: *I will protect everyone as myself.*

Rising, Eric went to the metal case placed on the end of his bed. He entered the combination he'd been given. For the first time, he would dress as Diamond Mind.

42. DONNING THE ARMOR

ERIC UNLATCHED THE METAL CASE IN HIS ROOM AS IF HE was opening a door to a new world.

On a field of steel-blue fabric, the insignia for Diamond Mind blazed: a white diamond outlined by red. The emblem was more stylized than an ordinary diamond on a deck of playing cards. In fact, the lines of the four walls curved toward the center. This made the diamond shine like a four-pointed star.

The insignia reflected how much the costume designers had gathered from their until-the-sun-rose discussions with Eric. Naturally, the comic book illustrators had wanted to know where real superpowers came from, beyond the bungled lab experiments described in comic books.

Electronic sketch pads tossed aside, Eric had offered half a dozen proofs for the diamond-like nature of things and described how everyone's world was a projection coming from past deeds. "True yogis learn to immerse themselves in wisdom that liberates everyone from thinking that things are one way. They also immerse themselves in compassion to save all beings from suffering. This is the double-diamond of wisdom and method. Then, out of sheer willingness to do whatever is necessary to protect others—the essence of the hero's code—yogic superpowers can appear."

They also discussed supervillains. Eric explained, "Just as it takes years for a young tree to bear good fruit, sometimes virtuous intentions ripen as powers at moments when intentions aren't completely pure. A villain could take a good apple that took them long to grow and selfishly poison it in a moment." This was how someone like Physique could arise.

The comic bookers received the teachings as enthusiastically as any yogis. Perhaps it was inevitable that these groups would meet. Eric knew the *karma* was rare to perform the deep mental work required to understand reality. Too many dismissed the process. But Eric understood the stakes were higher than a no-limit poker game. To not ask hard questions about the true nature of reality was to be wrong about everything. Further, not knowing the truth about how reality works led people to spend their whole lives defending a small self at the expense of others—and that created all the suffering in the world.

Downstairs, waiting for Samsa and Airspeed to appear, Diamond Mind studied his costumed image in the foyer mirror. The steel blue and white full body suit matched his new blue boots. To his relief, the designers had avoided the dreaded grandpa's underpants on the outside, common

DIAMOND MIND
AKA ERIC ADAMS

**WITH THE NECESSARY CAUSE,
ONE CAN READ THE MINDS OF OTHERS.**

Yoga Sutra, III.19

AIRSPEED
AKA ARIAL DAVIS

WHEN YOU TURN
THIS EFFORT UPON THE
RELATIONSHIP BETWEEN
THE BODY AND SPACE, YOU GAIN
A POWER OF MEDITATION WHERE YOU
BECOME LIGHT AS A WISP OF COTTON,
AND CAN THUS FLY THROUGH THE SKY.

Yoga Sutra, III.42

SAMSA
AKA
SAMANTHA MORRIS

**AND IN THESE POWERS
LIE THE POWERS OF THE WAR-ELEPHANT.**

Yoga Sutra, III.24

FATHER AGUA

AKA FATHER DIEGO MARTINEZ

TURN THE COMBINED EFFORT UPON THE FACT THAT THIS GROSS BODY IS AN OBJECT WHICH COMES FROM THAT SUBTLE NATURE, AND YOU'LL GAIN MASTERY OVER THE ELEMENTS.

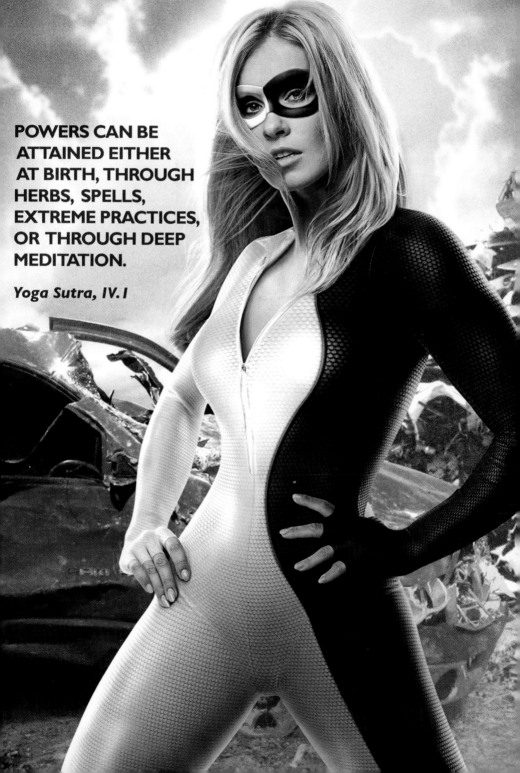

PHYSIQUE *AKA TINA TINSDALE*

POWERS CAN BE ATTAINED EITHER AT BIRTH, THROUGH HERBS, SPELLS, EXTREME PRACTICES, OR THROUGH DEEP MEDITATION.

Yoga Sutra, IV.1

BLINDSIDE

AKA MARC VINCENT

IF ONE TURNS THE
COMBINED EFFORT UPON
THE BODY'S VISIBLE
FORM, THEN ONE CAN
ATTAIN INVISIBILITY...

Yoga Sutra, III.21

AGNITE

AKA ANGIE KIM

WHEN THE CAPSULE IS HELD,
THE INNER FIRE IS AWAKENED.

Hatha Yoga Pradipika II.75

to older superhero costumes. Instead, the blue color at the chest area narrowed like a fencing vest to a point just below the navel. There, another band of blue belted around the torso. Below, the trunks ran white like a football player's. Across the shoulders and down the white sleeves, a thick blue stripe conveyed speed. *Perhaps a bit optimistic*, Eric thought.

Metallic blue over white with one red highlight at the heart gave the costume an international futuristic touch. *That's good.* Eric's intentions reached beyond borders.

The cool functionality of the mask was the most surprising feature—it rolled up from the neck! Eric understood the main benefit of this design: he could change quickly into his superhero uniform just by stripping off clothing over the body suit and by unrolling the mask. The unrolled blue fabric with eyeholes reached to his hairline, like a hood without a top. The bottom of his nose, mouth, and square chin also were left exposed. A smaller curved white diamond echoing the diamond at his heart *chakra* marked the center of his forehead.

Eric scanned a note that detailed additional features of the suit. Courtesy of innovations mainly developed by NASA, the suit was self-regulating for body temperature, fireproof, and even sewn with high tensile-strength Kevlar in case his bulletproof self-image failed.

Eric studied the mirror once again. He appeared every bit the superhero: his athletic muscles bulged through the suit and the mask gave him an air of mystery. Further, the double-diamonds perfectly positioned at key *chakras* conveyed his yogic abilities. Diamond Mind was a commanding force to be reckoned with.

Standing in the foyer, Diamond Mind was the only witness to Samsa's stunning entrance as she came down the wide staircase. She was a ruby shining on golden skin.

Her shoulders were bare—in fact, most of her was bare. Her fire engine-red costume appeared superheated by the glow of her skin.

Wrapped was the word that came to Eric's mind. All her essential parts were wrapped to convey taut strength. Thin straps held up her red top, barely covering her substantial cleavage. The straps were no doubt sewn with tensile strength Kevlar, five times stronger than steel. The top also wrapped around her back and then her navel, forming an "X" across her firm abs.

Her powerful legs rose from red calf-high boots all the way up to the tiniest, red wrapped mini skirt anyone could imagine. As Samsa sauntered down the stairs, a hint of red flashed from beneath her skirt, like a cheerleader's undergarment.

Long, red sheath-like fabric bracelets that buckled underneath also wrapped Samsa's wrists and forearms— instantly signaling strength. The only common element that Samsa's and Eric's costumes shared was the white, curved diamond emblem. That insignia ornamented the center of her bracelets and her power source—her navel— where the red bands around her abdomen crossed. A single band of white near the top of her boots pointed down like an arrowhead, echoing the diamond shape. The overall statement was red, hot, and powerful.

Reaching the bottom of the stairs, Samsa asked, "How do I look?"

"Powerful," Eric answered. His mind could barely muster more words.

Samsa spun around to show Eric the full costume, especially how it wrapped around her neck and waist as if it was the most stable halter-top Houdini could have conceived. Overall, her back and shoulders were even more exposed than the front—that is, if her long brown hair was pulled up. With radiance pouring from her bare skin, the designers had clearly wanted to communicate *she's not from this world.*

Samsa said, "It took me a while to figure out how to get into this thing, but I feel even stronger in it."

A moment later, Airspeed entered with style. Unlike Diamond Mind and Samsa, she didn't take the stairs. Airspeed glided through the air, gracefully hovering with one knee bent, descending slowly to the ground floor without landing. *Sleek* was the word that came to Eric's mind.

"Whoa, check out those kinky boots," Samsa said, as impressed by the thigh-high boots as Airspeed's flying.

Airspeed's midnight blue costume looked like the uptown version of Diamond Mind's blue steel. Of the two women's costumes, Airspeed's most resembled the traditional female superhero's suit. The body was cut high up on her hip like a bathing suit, drawing attention exactly where the Brazilian Eduardo had intended. The top—exposing only her shoulders—ran high up her neck, leaving ample room for the large double-diamond emblem in the center of her chest.

Midnight blue boots reached to her thighs, while matching gloves stretched up her arms. The dark boots sported a white stripe near the center of her thighs. Her blue gloves were marked in the same way as Samsa's, with white, curved diamonds.

Practical, large diamond-shaped glasses, like traditional aviation goggles, evoked a mysterious domino mask and hid her identity. The sides of the glasses disappeared behind her flowing blond locks.

Instead of a cape to signal her flying ability, Airspeed

sported a red sash. She'd tied it high around her waist on one side, allowing the fabric to drape around her exposed hip. The two sash ends floated gently behind her like the tail of a kite.

"Are we going to have to make a no-flying-in-the-house rule?" Diamond Mind asked.

Airspeed answered, "I can't help it. This costume just wants to fly." But taking the hint, she modestly let herself glide to the ground. Both women studied each other in their new superhero outfits. Finally, both conceded at nearly the same time, "You look great."

In the next moment, two Secret Service agents coming through the front door froze in their tracks. Slowly, both heads swiveled, staring at Samsa and then Airspeed and then back to Samsa, unable to think further.

"I think I just gained the power of invisibility," whispered Diamond Mind.

"Well, at least we know our costumes are set to stun any male villain we come across," Airspeed said. Indeed, the ladies' costumes seemed to have given the agents the power of perfect, single-pointed concentration.

As both agents were still unable to speak, Samsa offered, "You're here to take me to the White House." Samsa received a dazed nod in return.

But before Samsa departed, the three diamond yogis posed for one picture in the vice president's study. Diamond Mind stood in the middle. None of them slipped back into the "say cheese!" wide grins of their previous lives. Instead, having donned their armor they stood strong and proud. Their intensity said one thing: "Evil's going down."

With the click of the camera, the Unusuals were born.

43. PHYSIQUE GOES TO THE MOUNTAIN

MEANWHILE, AS THE DIAMOND YOGIS STEPPED OUT IN costume, Physique went further undercover. A continent away from the superyogis, pebbles crunched beneath her feet as she trekked up a steep ocean-side mountain. She followed Lorenzo, her young exuberant guide from the Canary Islands' La Palma seismology team. Lorenzo's legs were strong and his body trim from frequent exploration of the volcanic Old Ridge, known to locals as *Cumbre Vieja*. In the blazing sun, he looked like a soccer-playing Javier Bardem, who was also born in the Canary Islands.

African safari-style clothing, a brimmed hat, and large, expensive sunglasses shaded Physique's fair complexion. Her safari garb also reinforced her new persona as a South African socialite.

In spite of the stunning tropical vistas that would thrill any nature-lover, the hike up the mountain with

Lorenzo grew tedious for Physique. Focused on her mission, her mind reflected on how she came to this dagger-shaped island.

Only just days ago, the surprisingly luxurious rendezvous yacht had coasted into the main harbor of La Palma, one of seven islands that comprised the Canary Islands off the northwestern coast of Africa. Temperatures in the mid-70s felt comfortably subtropical to Physique... the breeze, moist with the briny smell of ocean. Physique had learned from Blindside that these islands weren't named for exotic species of birds, but from the Latin *Canaria Insula*, meaning *Island of Dogs*. During Roman times one of the islands had been noted for large, dangerous dogs; but these beasts had long since been removed. Now, the islands sported ports and resorts, sprinkled between nature preserves and banana farms in an autonomous region still vaguely associated with Spain.

With its sizable influx of wealthy European tourists, the Canary Islands, the Hawaii of the Atlantic, was an ideal place for her—a beautiful blond woman—to hide out. She could easily blend in, sporting her sunglasses, jet-setting vacation garb, and entitled attitude. Her standoffish moxie probably disguised her best. Few would feel worthy to socialize with her.

It also helped that the Canary Islands wasn't the kind of place that asked many questions.

When the luxury yacht moored in the resort harbor, the Harbor Master didn't come out personally to check passports as she and Agnite relaxed in bikinis on deck. Instead, the Captain had cleared customs for everyone by politely flashing passports and tipping a little extra for an easy moor. This meant that they could come and go as they pleased. The truly wealthy didn't have time for conventional bureaucracy and of course, certain courtesies were often extended for big money tourism.

It also helped that few in the Canary Islands cared for the news events of the United States—any more than someone in the States cared about happenings in the Canary Islands. And here, off the coasts of Morocco and Western Sahara, even if someone had been aware of her attack on the American capital, odds were they would be quietly rooting for the underdog.

In Physique's spacious cabin on the ship, she had found the beginnings of her new quest to *"search for how to strike from afar with something bigger... something unexpected,"* as the Bone Frightener had put it. Somehow—as she had hoped—her guru wanted his death avenged. He was even guiding her from beyond the grave using powers she couldn't imagine.

Physique had found a manila envelope with a South African passport and unusual backstory for her new identity as Kia Devree, the distant niece of a wealthy Dutch South African mining magnate. Physique was learning to play these alter-identities with growing skill. She marveled at the degree to which the Bone Frightener had gone to set up her cover.

For years, for some unknown reason, the Devree family's foundation had donated money to a team of seismology researchers in La Palma. This small team monitored a fault line that stretched across the steepest island in the world. Physique's mission as Kia involved inspecting how the family's grant money was being spent—but she actually would be watching for whatever the Bone Frightener wanted her to see. He seemed to revel in these kinds of vision quests.

In the envelope she'd found in her cabin on the yacht, she also discovered headphones and a gold-colored iTouch with a single song on it: Jimi Hendrix's *Voodoo Child*. She'd heard the song before, so she didn't give it much mind.

The envelope had also contained the mailing address of a trusted associate of the Bone Frightener in Washington, D.C., should she want to send another video to the powers-that-be.

Inside her cabin's closet, Physique had also found safari-type hiking clothes amidst the occasional evening dress and bikini sarong. Whatever the Bone Frightener had in mind, she had everything a South African socialite would need in the Canary Islands.

Now, after several tedious hours of hiking over hard, rocky ground, Physique—AKA Kia Devree—stood in front of a six-foot wide indentation in the mountainside. Her guide Lorenzo, who had been talking incessantly, finally fell silent, as if the mossy indentation that traveled on like an overgrown creek bed spoke for itself. They'd trekked so high above the sea that now tall pine trees, rustling in the wind, provided a shady canopy.

Physique took off her hat, letting her blond hair catch the cooler mountain breeze. "So *this* is the fault line," concluded Physique, speaking as Kia Devree.

"Of course," Lorenzo answered.

"I just didn't think it would be so… obvious." A coffin-length trough ran between the two plates. "You can see the mountain splitting in two." Physique didn't know anything about geology, but she imagined Kia Devree wouldn't either.

Lorenzo straddled the trough at a narrow point, jutting

his hips forward as he explained, "In 1949, volcanic eruptions caused this long fissure to open. The side of the mountain you're standing on moved downwards and westwards by two meters."

Physique attempted to appear interested, but she felt thoroughly bored. "Has there been any further movement?"

Lorenzo pointed toward the southern end of the island. "There was another eruption near here in 1971 that spilled hectares of lava."

I hope he isn't going to march me there next, Physique thought. *One side of a mountain moved six feet, sixty years ago… this isn't earth-shattering stuff.* She flicked her nails, and then she tried to smile. "Why do you think it's so important to monitor this fault line?" she asked, putting on her best Kia. "Aren't there more active fault lines in far more populated areas?"

"Well, this isn't just a fault line. This may be *the* fault line," Lorenzo answered. "Because what happens here could affect so many along the coast of the Atlantic."

A puzzled look came over the South African socialite's face.

"Well, have you ever heard how Atlantis fell into the sea?" Lorenzo looked like he might break into an excited gallop.

Finding a cushy patch of moss, Physique sat to give her legs a rest. "I thought Atlantis was a myth."

"Not among archeologists," Lorenzo insisted, still standing on his strong mountain legs. "Recently, an entire ancient city has been found submerged in the mud flats north of Cadiz, Spain. Many believe that was Atlantis." Lorenzo was about to share further details about how the new location corresponded more closely to Plato's description of Atlantis—the ill-fated, continent-sized

Atlantic sea-going superpower—but he was interrupted.

"And…" said Physique, not much for speculation.

"Well, then there's the Greek Island of Santorini. It has no beach."

Physique thought, *This had better get interesting quick or I'm going to push him off this cliff.* Instead she tilted her head to the side. "What do you mean?"

"Well, you just walk off the end of the island and quickly fall into water that's hundreds of feet deep." After seeing that Kia Devree still wasn't putting two and two together, Lorenzo explained further. "In ancient times, the island was called Thera. Looking at the geological evidence, it's clear that one of the most violent volcanic eruptions in history caused the mountain on Thera to tumble into the sea. It's unmistakable. There's a crater thirty-seven miles in circumference. Geologists call it a *caldera*." Lorenzo trilled the "R" and held his arms out like he was holding a round laundry basket. "Any time that much land mass falls into the ocean, it creates a massive tsunami. That tsunami probably swallowed all of Atlantis in minutes."

Lorenzo knew archeologists' recent discovery of a buried city sixty miles inland suggested how powerful that tsunami had been. Lorenzo also knew that even countries beyond the Aegean Sea had recorded that great wave. He wanted to impress Kia with his knowledge, but again he was interrupted.

"So you think you're preventing the next Atlantis from happening?" asked Kia, summing up Lorenzo's point.

Lorenzo placed one foot high on a rock while resting his hands on his hips like a bullfighter. Lorenzo had been parading his body in front of Kia for hours, wondering when she would show some interest. "This volcanic island is nearly one hundred times bigger than Thera. If this mountain falls into the sea, the seismic shock wave could cross the Atlantic faster than a jet plane. Entire cities on the Atlantic coastline, like New York, could be swallowed by a tsunami."

Physique hung on his words. Finally, the amorous Lorenzo had said something that interested her. She pictured a tsunami crossing the Atlantic, striking seaboard cities like New York, Boston, and Miami. "You don't say...." Her enthusiasm for the hike suddenly grew. "This is important work, perhaps we should hike the entire fault line."

Lorenzo felt pleased that their sponsor's attractive niece seemed approving, but he didn't want to totally exhaust her. "That would take some time. Are you sure you're up for it?"

Physique jumped to her feet, enthralled with her new devious idea.

"I'm not saying there is any eminent danger of this mountain collapsing," Lorenzo added, not wanting to sound alarmist. Lorenzo had been carefully coached by his superiors on what to say and what not to.

Lorenzo summed up the research team's official position: "It's just that if cities have been wiped out by a tsunami before, it can happen again." He looked out over the Atlantic, imagining a wave of catastrophic proportions. "So, by studying the depth of this fissure—which no one really knows at this point—we can better understand the risks. That's a big reason we started drilling projects at key venting points, so we could see what's happening underneath the island."

"Drilling projects at key venting points...," repeated Physique. A smile came to her face like a fox finding a nest of baby birds. "Let's start there."

Later, happily alone in her cabin on the yacht—having briskly refused Lorenzo's invitation to take her out on the town with the words, "I don't date seismologists"— Physique listened intently to the *Voodoo Child* song. It contained her final clue. Fixating on the opening lines about chopping down a mountain, she felt certain about her next move.

44. SAMSA AT THE WHITE HOUSE

TV NETWORKS INTERRUPTED THEIR REGULAR programming to broadcast the Rose Garden ceremony. Millions stopped what they were doing to watch the national event—or, more precisely, to witness the crowning of America's first actual superhero.

Samsa didn't disappoint. As she walked out into the Rose Garden, the afternoon sun could barely compete with her radiance. A regal cloak, heavier and fuller than a cape, added to her nobility—and covered up much of her raw, unclothed skin. Like her main uniform, the cloak was red with blue and white trim at the bottom. It was also lined with white, curved diamond stars. Still, her strong body and shining light peeked through. Awed by her beauty, few noticed the faint scent of garden roses in the air.

With Samsa standing next to him, Vice President Lausunu kept his remarks brief: "America has always had heroes. People who stepped forward in times of crisis to do what was right and what was necessary. Today, we honor one of those heroes, who in the face of terrible violence, showed incredible courage to save others."

Turning to Samsa, Vice President Lausunu said, "How you did all you did, and your apparent transformation after the event, remains a mystery to us. But we are happy you are still with us. We ask you to continue to serve as America's hero.

"Samantha Morris, affectionately known as Samsa, on behalf of a grateful nation, it is my pleasure to present you with the Congressional Medal of Honor."

Cameras clicked as the vice president draped the medal around Samsa's neck. The press knew that the Congressional Medal of Honor had been awarded to a civilian once before... as well as to a woman... but certainly never to a glowing superhero in red boots and a bustier. This was a moment for history.

The press also understood that although there would be no questions, Samsa would give a brief statement. There had been much speculation about what she would say.

"Thank you for this honor," Samsa began. Her strong braceleted arms gripped the edge of the podium. She would certainly rather fight a garden full of opponents than have to speak publicly to this many people. However, her poise hid her bounding butterflies. "I want you to know that I'm just like everyone else. I'm not really sure how I got here, or why I have the abilities that I do. But while I'm here, I promise to use whatever powers I do have to the best of my ability, to protect others.

Samsa's voice sounded even more strong echoing through speakers. "I also want you to know that I'm working with a team of superyogis, individuals who have exceptional abilities like mine, to prevent attacks like the one that just occurred from happening again. I can't promise that we can stop everyone and everything. But as long as I have strength in these arms, you can count on me. Thank you again."

Applause broke out as everyone stood, lifted by their hearts. America had its first real superhero.

But elsewhere in the world, questions arose as to when other countries' superyogis would step forward. And in India, where they had seen their share of *siddhas*, there was mostly indifference. They knew that a few superyogis seldom created much peace.

Diamond Mind and Airspeed watched Samsa's historic unveiling from the couch in the vice president's study. As Airspeed rested her head on Diamond Mind's strong shoulder, she said, "She did good, didn't she?"

"Yeah, she did good," answered Diamond Mind.

"I was thinking," began Airspeed, "If we do meet up with Physique again, and I have to fight her, I need something more than just the ability to fly. I don't want my bones to shatter if I hit her when she's turning heavy."

Switching off the TV, Diamond Mind asked, "What did you have in mind?"

"Well, I was wondering if you could do your light-thing and inject me with some of your diamond stuff... I mean, um...." Airspeed felt embarrassed. Her request hadn't quite come out right. "To make my bones strong like a diamond." She said this firmly, but blushed even more.

Trying a different tact, Airspeed said, "I found the verses in *The Yoga Sutra* that explained what you did at the bank."

"Which verses?" Diamond Mind pretended not to notice her awkwardness.

"Well, it's four verses really. They come right after my favorite one about flying. I wrote them down." From inside the long glove on her left arm she pulled out a small piece of paper, and then unrolled it like a scroll. Although she had written down the Sanskrit, she just read the English:

बहिरकल्पिता वृत्तिर्महाविदेहा ततः प्रकाशावरणक्षयः ॥ ४३ ॥

bahir akalpita virtti mahavideha tatah
prakasha-avarana kshayah

III.43 THOSE WHO NO LONGER PERCEIVE ANYTHING
AS BEING OUTSIDE
EXPERIENCE THE TRANSFORMATION
INTO THE ULTIMATE BODY.
WITH THIS, EVERY VEIL WHICH COVERS THE LIGHT
IS DESTROYED.

स्थूलस्वरूपसूक्ष्मान्वयार्थवत्त्वसंयमाद्भूतजयः ॥ ४४ ॥

sthula svarupa sukshma-anvaya-arthavattva
sanyamad bhuta jayah

III.44 TURN THE COMBINED EFFORT
UPON THE FACT THAT THIS GROSS BODY IS AN OBJECT
WHICH COMES FROM THAT SUBTLE NATURE,
AND YOU'LL GAIN MASTERY OVER THE ELEMENTS.

ततोऽणिमादिप्रादुर्भावः कायसंपत् तद्धर्मानभिघातश्च ॥ ४५ ॥

*tatonima-adi pradurbhavah kaya sampat tad
dharma-anabhighatash cha*

III.45 WITH THIS YOU ATTAIN
POWER AT MICROSCOPIC LEVELS
AND ALL THE REST.
YOU ACHIEVE A PERFECT BODY,
WHICH CANNOT BE HURT
BY ANY EXISTING THING.

रूपलावण्यबलवज्रसंहननत्वानि कायसंपत् ॥ ४६ ॥

rupa lavanya bala vajra sanhananatvani kaya sampat

III.46 YOU GAIN THE BODY OF PERFECTION:
EXQUISITE IN ITS APPEARANCE,
STRONG, SOLID AS DIAMOND ITSELF.

Diamond Mind smiled. Airspeed was rapidly becoming
his best student. He said, "Nothing truly outside, nothing
truly inside... that could take a while."

At once, they both looked at the clock.

45. TO MOVE A MOUNTAIN

Physique had walked nearly every foot of the fault line on the mountain with her goatish guide Lorenzo. He had even taken her to see a waterfall dropping into a deep ravine in the mistaken hope that it might spur some romance.

This time she came alone.

It was a clear day with vibrant blue skies. Even though she was approximately six thousand feet above the all-encompassing Atlantic, Physique didn't notice the incredible view or people parasailing on the beaches below. She ignored how densely wooded the well-watered mountain slopes had become. She didn't even notice a mineral water stream that flowed with bright oranges and greens. Instead, she focused on only one thing: she wanted to know if she could, in fact, move this mountain.

Standing on the lower side of the fault line, at a high point on the Old Ridge, she went through her motivation.

I'll create such a catastrophe that the powerful will have to stay at home to rebuild. Then the world will be free of their meddling.

Her concentration tightened like tuning a guitar string. She planned to go heavier than she had ever gone before. Her hair, nails, and eyes quickly went pitch black. The ground compacted beneath her feet. Soon the earth trembled around her. Birds scattered, taking to the sky. She collapsed rock beneath her, but... the mountain didn't move.

She tried again. And again. Eventually, she was forced to admit that she couldn't take down this entire mountain on her own. She stamped her feet and kicked volcanic dirt in a temper tantrum. When that didn't work either, dejected, she made the trek back to the boat.

In the yacht's galley, she found a handsome, well-dressed man seated in a grand swivel chair sipping cognac from a large glass. His slicked back hair signaled wealthy European. Behind him stood three men in dark suits and dark glasses—clearly private security. Physique clenched her fists, preparing for a fight.

"Who are you?" Physique demanded.

"Oh, ma chérie, relax," said the man. "Our mutual friend, the Bone Frightener, sent me to help you. I'm Max Devereaux. Perhaps you've heard of me?" He rose from his chair and walked toward her.

Physique shook her head a defiant no.

Max Devereaux kissed her hand between the base of her fingers. "I've heard of you," he said. "You've been a very bad girl."

Physique pulled her hand away. "Do you have powers to help me?" she asked bluntly.

Devereaux walked toward a window of the galley, looking out on La Palma from the water. "I have lots of power. But mine is the kind you can buy and trade. And what I deliver… usually goes to the highest bidder."

Tonight Physique wasn't in the mood for riddles. "What kind of power is that?"

"Tsk tsk. Let's not discuss this in such an uncivilized manner. You've been hiking all day. You must be famished. Why don't you wash up and slip into one of your evening dresses. Think about what you need. Perhaps I can get it for you."

"Why do you think I have an evening dress?" Physique asked, still put off by this unexpected intruder.

"This is my boat," Devereaux answered, "and I put the dresses in your closest personally. The blue one suits your mood, tonight. Oui?"

Physique sulked off to wash the mountain dust out of her hair. As the shower massaged her tired body, she pondered who this Max Devereaux could possibly be. *Who would own a boat like this? What kind of power could be bought and traded?* But no answers came—at least nothing definitive. She brooded on what she needed to take down the mountain.

She'd read contradictory scientific studies on the La Palma mega-tsunami scenario. However, they all agreed on one thing: a volcanic blast of magma, or superheated water, had to come from deep within the volcano to move the mountaintop. Simply, lubrication was necessary.

Suddenly, she realized what Max Devereaux was. He could, in fact, assist her.

Physique slipped into the silky blue cocktail dress. Her mood brightened to something resembling charming. She let her blond hair fall long as she dolled herself up. Her lips tingled under the pleasing pressure of lipstick. She even found a long, diamond necklace in a drawer—no doubt another gift from her mysterious visitor. The center jewel felt cold on her chest.

Devereaux had brought a personal chef with him to prepare a five-course meal—French, of course. He rose from the candle-lit table as she walked into the dining room. "That's better," he said. "You look radiant. Shall we?" He motioned to the white-clothed table. Rows of heavy, ornate, antique silverware reflected the gently rising moon.

As Devereaux poured some champagne, he said, "You must understand. I'm quite used to dealing with people who want to change the balance of power—but rarely with such a dangerous beauty as yourself. This is quite a treat for me. I hope we can enjoy the evening."

Devereaux had skillfully ensured that all the appetizers and entries were vegetarian. Physique was hungry from all her activity. Looking over the menu choices, her mouth watered. The almond chèvre, a delightful vegan alternative to soft spreadable goat cheese, tomato and basil tartlets, and chocolate mousse with strawberries particularly caught her eye.

After the roasted butternut squash in a warm cider vinaigrette, Devereaux asked, "Now, ma chérie, what is it that you need?"

Physique answered without hesitation. "I need to take down a mountain. But not in tiny pieces. I need something that will make the mountain fall in a certain way."

Devereaux thought before answering. "That sounds very destructive. Are you certain you want to go that big?"

"Yes," answered Physique, again without hesitation.

Devereaux felt oddly attracted to her unbridled, destructive power and even her passionate mean streak. He had collected many things in this world, but never anyone like Physique. He watched toned muscles move like marble under her velvety skin. She could punish him... in beautiful ways.

Devereaux said, "I can get what you need. But I'm afraid it's a little beyond the budget the Bone Frightener set aside for me. Our mutual friend has been one of my best customers for some time so I wouldn't want to refuse him. Perhaps we can work something out... between us."

Physique considered the luxurious setting and his sly eyes. "Perhaps," she answered.

"I don't mind putting in myself for the top, provided I can be on top," Devereaux said pointedly. "I think that would be safer for me. Agreed?"

Physique paused, considering her limited options. "Agreed. But only after you deliver."

After topping off her champagne to propose a toast, Devereaux said, "Make your preparations, my dangerous beauty. In two weeks, I shall return with something that gives quite a bang."

46. KIRBY'S
PHYSIQUE THEORY

A WEEK LATER, AGENT KIRBY, AGENT ROLLINS, AND Diamond Mind were summoned to a tense National Security Council meeting at the White House. No pastries or jellybeans graced the table. Instead, eight of the most powerful and stressed-out people in America sat with folded hands around the hardwood table in a dimly lit room.

Vice President Lausunu had personally invited Diamond Mind, as head of the Unusuals, to this gathering. Eric entered the White House in civilian clothes, but quickly shed his tan pants and blue button-down shirt to reveal Diamond Mind's costume. Eric figured if the chairman of the joint chiefs was in his Marine uniform, he should wear his dress blues as well.

At the meeting, the restless security council reviewed a new threat from Physique. This video was shot close.

Physique's menacing eyes pierced from behind her black and white domino mask. A burgundy sheet hung as a backdrop, giving no indication of where she was. Physique threatened, "I will strike again if the White House doesn't take action by Ash Wednesday to cut military spending in half."

Then Physique turned catty: "I've seen the unveiling of your hero, Samsa. I'm not afraid of her. I'm the real superyogi." She flicked her nails and gnashed her teeth. Her sign-off felt ominous. "Bow to my demands… or I will see you soon."

Sujata Bansal's midnight blue suit with brass buttons signaled she was all business today. Addressing the secretaries of state and defense, and other agency bosses, she said, "Physique's given us ten days to declare a major policy change. But we're not taking directions from a terrorist. She's clearly not afraid of us or our team of superyogis. So we need to find her." Bansal's voice was stern and commanding. "Where do you think she is?"

Speaking for the other department heads, the secretary of homeland security reported. In spite of his serious position, he wore an olive green suit with a baby-blue shirt and striped tie. This bit of strategy made him seem as congenial as a community college president. "None of us believe she is currently in the United States. Her out-of-costume picture is everywhere. And all our resources are working overtime running down every tall, blond yogi tip that could be her. Simply, we believe it's too hot for her to still be in the States. Someone may be hiding her now, but if we increase resources at our borders, someone will see her if she tries to return for another strike."

"And if you're wrong, what then?" Bansal asked, pointing her finger.

The chairman of the joint chiefs of staff, himself the commander of the Marine Corps, answered, "Then madam, it's time to deploy the Marines with some heavy weapons to defend the capital."

Vice President Lausunu sighed. He didn't want to instill more fear in the country by bringing out tanks and armed soldiers. And he didn't like bickering among the security department heads. Seeing that no one had any further recommendations, Lausunu tried a change of tactics. "Agent Kirby, back when you were invited to that strategic think tank to anticipate unforeseen threats… if you hadn't written about dangerous yogis, what would you have written about?"

Remembering the think tank that had started this whole adventure, Agent Kirby answered. His voice nearly cracked. "I would have written about environmental terrorism. Big acts of sabotage that turn nature into a weapon." Nods in the room signaled that some knew what he was talking about.

"Avalanches were used as a strategic weapon in World War I to wipe out whole brigades," offered the joint chief. He was an older man with strong eyes that would never need glasses, and was well studied in the art of war.

Kirby nodded. "I was thinking about someone trying to trigger an earthquake in a populated area, but I decided that was too far fetched."

"So you wrote about dangerous yogis instead?" Agent Rollins sniped, wishing his partner would just keep his mouth shut in this assembly of heavyweights. The group laughed, finally bringing a little levity. None of them were used to a world with superyogis gone bad or sitting at a White House conference table with someone dressed like Captain America. Even Diamond Mind couldn't believe he was in a conference room with the presidential seal on the wall. He'd come a long way from his SEAL training on the Silver Strand sandbar of Coronado.

"You had an intuition about dangerous yogis then; it proved to be correct," continued Lausunu to Kirby. "If you had to guess, where do you think Physique is?"

Kirby thought this was probably another one of those career-altering moments in which it would probably be best to say nothing. But he was in the White House… being asked his opinion…. How could he restrain himself? Kirby tried to hedge. "I do have a theory, but it's based on so little evidence, I'm reluctant to share it."

Lausunu poured a glass of water from a tall silver pitcher. "I'd like to hear your theory." He knew that they had no other viable leads.

Kirby shrugged. Both his FBI boss and Agent Rollins looked nervous. Kirby took out his fake rabbit-fur flash disk and connected it to the room's projector. He stood near the projection screen at the front of the room and cleared his throat. After some awkward silence, Kirby began: "Agent Rollins had the satellite analysts at the CIA scrub the ocean photos one more time for anything—even the smallest thing—that they couldn't explain in the days after the sub escape. They came back with this."

Instead of something remarkable, a highly pixelated photo of what looked like a small campfire in the middle of darkness blackened the screen. Even when enhanced, the distant satellite image didn't show anything surrounding the flame. Further, no running lights appeared to indicate a vessel at sea. Agent Kirby's FBI boss instinctively brought his hand up to cover his mouth, but Kirby continued: "This light or fire appeared for twenty seconds and then disappeared in the middle of the Atlantic Ocean, with no apparent cause. On its own, it's nothing. But considering that Physique's accomplice produced flames from her hands, this could be a signal fire to summon another vessel."

"Then what?" asked Bansal, unimpressed.

"Well, Physique's timetable for her next strike seems odd to me," Kirby answered. "By Ash Wednesday? Is that of religious significance to her, symbolic, or influenced by her current surroundings? I suspect as some sort of Hindu yogi, albeit with Christian roots, the beginning of Lent— forty days marking Jesus' fasting in the wilderness—isn't her message to us. Further, fire and ash don't seem to be her thing either. She's more about throwing her weight around, isn't she?"

"So what are you suggesting?" asked Bansal.

"I believe Physique's in a predominately Roman Catholic country that celebrates Carnival, the time when people are encouraged to go wild before buckling down for the forty days before Easter."

"That could be any one of a number of countries on several continents," interjected the director of the CIA. "Brazil and Spain come to mind first." He had a bent nose and the face of bulldog.

"True," said Agent Kirby. "But then I was thinking about the location of the possible signal fire. That small escape sub is unlikely to have that much air or fuel on board. Plus, Physique had to know we'd mobilize the Navy to search for her. So, wouldn't it be in her best interests to get as far away from the U.S. as fast as possible?"

Sujata Bansal and other quick-minded security professionals could see what Kirby was suggesting. Sujata voiced it first: "So if you draw a line from Washington, D.C. to your proposed signal fire, you get a heading. Where does it lead?"

Kirby showed the next slide with the ship's presumed navigation heading. "I think Physique is in the Canary Islands—and La Palma, to be precise."

"La Palma?" asked Vice President Lausunu, surprised. He stroked his red power tie. "Why there?"

"This is where it starts to get a little scary," Kirby answered. "I think Physique may be trying to strike the U.S. by creating a mega-tsunami."

The room fell quiet. Over 150,000 were killed in a day when the worst tsunami on record had swept Indonesia. And the recent devastation to Japan looked like Godzilla had stomped ashore.

"But tsunamis are primarily Pacific Ocean threats," reminded Lausunu.

"Have you ever heard of the La Palma Mega-Tsunami Theory?" Agent Kirby asked. He cued a video from a BBC Horizon program that modeled a computer simulation of a landslide-generated mega-tsunami. As the video played, Kirby narrated.

"The La Palma Mega-Tsunami Theory goes like this... In 1949, a series of volcanic eruptions opened a visible fissure at the top of what is known as the steepest island in the world relative to height and size. From the surface, it appears that this volcanic island is literally splitting apart. Some scientists believe it is only a matter of time before a further eruption occurs, and when it does, that eruption could hurl up to one and a half trillion metric tons of rock down on the Atlantic. The splash would generate a mega-tsunami with an initial height of a terrifying two thousand feet. That wave would race across the Atlantic so fast that the North African coast would be hit within an hour, the English coast within three and a half hours, and the eastern seaboard of the United States within six hours. By the time the mega-tsunami hits the eastern seaboard, the waves would be between one hundred and two hundred feet." The BBC video showed huge waves destroying coastal cities, with buildings toppling like dominoes. Kirby concluded, "The waves would travel fifteen miles inland... inundating Boston, Miami, New York, and many more cities and towns."

Vice President Lausunu leaned forward on the table. "Is that really possible?"

"No!" Sujata interjected, annoyed with Agent Kirby's presentation. She knew that this was bad science supported by glitzy Hollywood graphics. "I looked into the La Palma scenario myself, after the first scientific report was published making these over-hyped claims. The set of conditions under which La Palma falls into the sea are so exaggerated and so unlikely that most experts conclude it isn't going to happen. Further, even if La Palma were to somehow fall into the Atlantic Ocean, it's of no threat to the United States or our allies in Europe."

Immediately, in a flat, expressionless voice, CIA Director Reynolds concurred: "La Palma is no threat to the United States or Europe."

"Why is that?" Vice President Lausunu asked. He wanted to be certain.

"The algorithm used in that first scientific report made a critical mistake," Sujata Bansal said. "They calculated the mega-tsunami based on the water displacement from an *underground* seaquake. We all know how devastating those can be. La Palma is different: it would be a landslide. A big splash would occur on the surface of the water, but the wave would dissipate before crossing the Atlantic."

"Are you sure?" the vice president asked.

"Certain. You can see the effect at any swimming pool. When a kid does a cannonball off a diving board, it creates a vertical splash several times his size. But the wave quickly dissipates on the surface as it spreads out in all directions; it doesn't even reach the end of the pool.

"However, as we've also seen, an underground seaquake is very different. It sends shock waves underwater that can go unnoticed by ships on the surface. The waves don't amplify in height until they reach shallow coastal waters. A La Palma landslide, cataclysmic as it would be for the Canary Islands, would scarcely make ships rock in an American marina."

Agent Kirby returned to his seat. But he wasn't feeling sheepish. "I agree with everything Sujata Bansal and Director Reynolds just said. A La Palma collapse presents no danger to the United States or Europe. And under normal conditions, La Palma can't collapse. But the question is, what do Physique and her cohorts believe?"

Agent Rollins fiddled with the pistachios in his right pocket, but didn't dare crack shells. He recalled how in 1993, Sheikh Omar Abdel-Rahman and nine other terrorist conspirators thought they could take down the World Trade Center with just a truck bomb parked next to a concrete underground support. They'd failed to achieve their goals, but injured many. It hadn't taken long for a more scheming supervillain to mastermind a far more devious method.

Agent Kirby added, "And we don't fully know what Physique or her cohorts are capable of under supernormal circumstances."

For several moments, the room remained silent. Sujata Bansal recalled that the La Palma mega-tsunami scenario aired on the Discovery Channel and the BBC. Even though the BBC later issued a partial retraction, the story continued to spread on the Internet by people without the math skills to see flaws in the algorithm. Further, she knew people would believe what they wanted to believe. Sujata understood Kirby's unusual logic: Physique could have learned about La Palma like anyone else who watched YouTube or basic cable, so she may believe that she could destroy the American east coast by bringing that mountain down.

Sujata fingered the pearls on her necklace as if they were abacus beads. She asked CIA Director Reynolds, "Do we have any operatives in the Canary Islands?"

The wrinkles on Director Reynolds' forehead deepened. "None. The Canary Islands are of no threat to the United States."

Sujata Bansal tossed her hands. The logic may be there, but she couldn't recommend taking action on something this outlandish—particularly something that didn't threaten the United States. She looked at Vice President Lausunu, silently asking, *"What do you want done?"*

"Well, we can't very well have Navy SEALs storm the beaches of a resort island in the middle of Carnival," said Vice President Lausunu, picturing such an incursion. "That would be an international fiasco. And the evidence we do have is so flimsy, we'd look like fools."

Sitting at the furthest corner, Diamond Mind sensed Vice President Lausunu was about to take the Canary Islands off the table. Instead of letting it go, he gently interjected. "May I ask a question?"

"Of course," Vice President Lausunu answered, addressing the masked man as he would any department head.

"How many people live in the Canary Islands?"

No one had the answer until Agent Kirby spoke up.

"Over two million. And there will be another half million tourists over seven islands, as Carnival in the Canaries is second only to Rio."

Diamond Mind folded his hands neatly on the table like the CIA Director, trying to fit in. "Is it reasonable to assume a Physique-engineered landslide on La Palma would be catastrophic to the Canaries?" Diamond Mind asked.

"Quite," answered Kirby. He sat directly across from the costumed hero. "Anyone caught at low elevations, including the coastline of nearby Morocco, would likely be swept out to sea. It would simply be the worst tsunami in history."

Diamond Mind made his point: "So millions of people could get hurt because of Physique's gripe with the U.S.?"

Agent Kirby didn't need to reply. Everyone knew the answer.

Rollins seethed. Because of Diamond Mind's earnestness, something would have to be done. Rollins couldn't stop himself from thinking, *I really hate that guy.* Rollins looked toward CIA Director Reynolds as if to say, *I can't believe you have me baby-sitting this Boy Scout.*

Sensing Rollins' discomfort, Vice President Lausunu asked for his point of view. "Agent Rollins, you've been quiet. What's your recommendation?"

In a politically tense room such as this, Rollins had to choose his words carefully. "I don't know if Physique and her co-conspirators are on La Palma or not. But if she is, she probably isn't expecting us to seek her there. She's likely to make mistakes; then we'd have a chance to take her down."

With that, Lausunu came to a decision. He stroked his tie again. "All right. I don't see the harm in putting some feet in the Canaries to investigate. But this stays a highly covert operation until your team has some hard evidence.

Rollins, you take lead on this exploration. I'll give you seven days. Then I want the Unusuals back to help protect the capital."

After the meeting broke up, as a sign of respect Diamond Mind and the agents stood to allow the powerful people in the room to leave first.

Agent Kirby spoke to Rollins and Diamond Mind. "Thanks for backing me in there. It's just an intuition, but I've been wrong before."

"Don't I know it," Diamond Mind answered. As forgiving as Eric was, strain still lingered due to how relentlessly Kirby had pursued him over the disappearance of two yogis who were Eric's students.

Diamond Mind poured himself a glass of water. His diamond emblem reflected in the pitcher's silver. Watching the water tumble, he imagined a manufactured tsunami hitting the Canary Islands and the destruction that would follow. He knew no one on his team had any powers to stop a mega-tsunami.

"Before we go to the Canaries," Diamond Mind said, "I think we should try to recruit someone else... someone who knows about water."

"You know someone like that?" Kirby asked.

Diamond Mind put the silver pitcher down. "Maybe. Right now, it's just an intuition."

47. FATHER AGUA

HOPING TO FIND A WAY TO THWART PHYSIQUE'S tsunami, the Unusuals, dressed in civilian clothes, found Father Diego Martinez in the Gila River Valley of Arizona near the Mexican border.

Father Diego Martinez wasn't in church today, but in a desert field supervising construction of an aqueduct that would bring water to dry land that no one wanted. Pick axes and shovels clinked. Dust floated in the air from a group of Mexican men cutting ditches to create a watercourse. Squat prickly pear cactus and parched brown earth stretched toward the craggy, Gila Mountains.

Though it was surprisingly cool on this Arizona early-spring day, the charismatic Father Diego stood with one leg bent on a small hill, wearing only his uniform of black pants, black shirt, and white priest's collar. His rolled-up sleeves exposed strong forearms. He was young, in his early thirties. He possessed a magnetism that made people want to help him with whatever he was doing.

Approaching the priest, Arial couldn't help herself; she whispered to Eric, "He's unusually handsome for a priest, wouldn't you say?"

Samsa overheard and gave Arial an approving thumbs-up. But Eric shushed Arial, as he had great respect for the man. In fact, Eric had studied the priest's essays in retreat. In Eric's lonely hours on a desolate mountain, the writings of Father Diego and other Christian mystics from throughout the centuries had spoken directly to his experience.

In 1950, a small group of Benedictine monks had traveled to India for a remarkable experiment. Instead of trying to convert the Hindu yogis to Christianity as one might have expected, they decided to practice as yogis—to experience for themselves everything they could of the yogic path. These middle-aged Benedictine monks founded an *ashram*, invited accomplished Indian yoga teachers, and soon started doing *asana* and meditation. After many years, several monks began to experience the fruits of yogic practice; then they reconciled non-dualism— the lack of true separation between self and others—with the teachings of Jesus.

Just out of Divinity School, a restless Father Diego Martinez had chosen to go to India "to discover the other half of my soul." Father Diego practiced in the ashram for eight years before returning to America. From his essays, Eric concluded that Father Diego had experienced a similar kind of transformation as Eric had experienced in retreat— and likely would have similar powers.

The Unusuals approached Father Diego. "We heard about the good works you were doing and wanted to bring some bags of concrete to help," Eric said.

"That's a very good offering." Father Diego wiped his hand on his leg before extending it to Eric.

Keeping the swirling wind in check, Arial brushed away hair that had stuck to her lips. "We also brought some extra lunch for your workers."

Contrasting with his raven-colored hair, Father Diego's big smile beamed like the Arizona sun. He called out to his team in Spanish, "These nice people have brought concrete and food to help. Take it from the back of their truck."

Inside the rented silver pickup truck, workers found two full palettes of sixty-pound sacks and two coolers with Subway sandwiches and Gatorade. The smaller Mexican men wouldn't let Samsa carry any of the heavy concrete sacks, shooing her away from the manly task. She shrugged and smiled at Eric, knowing she could lift the whole truck with one hand.

Samsa was happy to be incognito with her glow under control. She wore large sunglasses and a ball cap to hide her now famous face. Rollins had threatened to leave her behind if she couldn't appear normal, but she wouldn't have it. Stubbornly, she meditated until she could display her softer, human side. Ironically, more than Diamond Mind, it was Rollins who got her to meditate.

"I haven't seen you before," Father Diego said. "Which Mormon church do you belong to?"

Arial stated flatly, "We aren't Mormon."

"Really? Usually, it's the Mormons who come to help without wanting anything in return. Nice people. So service-oriented."

"But you're out here helping," Arial said, starting to play the inquisitor as she and Eric had planned. "What makes you think you can get water to flow on this land? It's dry as hell here." Arial immediately regretted her choice of words.

"Hell" sounded like a curse word.

Eric put on sunglasses to hide his glowing eyes from Father Diego before beginning his mind-reading trick.

"Some might call it faith," Father Diego answered. "But I see it more as devotion." He looked out on the workers creating the aqueduct. "These people deserve a better life: a chance to grow their own crops instead of always working someone else's fields. It's what they really pray for. This is barren land no one wants. But if water comes here, it will deepen their faith in God."

Arial found herself swept up by the sincerity of his words. She moved closer to the priest. "I heard that people around here call you Father Agua. That you walk in the desert until God gives you a vision of water underground. Is that true?"

Father Diego slowly chose his next words. It was unusual for a stranger to speak so directly to him. "I think God gives us all visions from time to time, maybe in the form of strong intuition... when we are really thinking about helping other people." He looked down at the ground, then scratched his nose. "Maybe the name 'Father Agua' is more a term of affection."

Standing safely in Father Agua's peripheral view, Eric followed Father Agua's mind. He saw the priest doing yoga balancing poses in the desert... feeling the subtle pull of the water element in his body attract other water molecules. He was a human divining rod. With his arms outstretched in poses like a tree or a warrior throwing a spear, his limbs mysteriously started to drift toward water.

Arial continued with her line of provocative questions. "But even if you believed water was somewhere underground, how could you get it out without expensive drilling and pumping systems?"

Father Diego thumbed the silver cross around his neck and scratched the dirt with the tip of his boot, almost as if starting to draw a line. Rather than explaining his process precisely, he answered indirectly. "Jesus said, 'If you had faith the size of a mustard seed, you could move mountains.' All things are possible with faith."

However, Eric caught unusual images in Father Agua's mind. He saw Father Agua drawing a circle in the desert… then sitting in meditation until water from an undiscovered underground river pushed its way to the surface like *kundalini* rising. Eric realized that Father Agua had gained the miracle power to literally pull water toward him.

"Is that what you're seeking?" Father Diego asked. "You need to find water for some land?"

Eric took off his glasses. Father Diego saw only the white of Eric's eyes shining light. Quickly Eric's blue eyes rolled back into place. Eric answered, "No. We need to stop water. I'm interested in speaking with you about your yoga practice and meditation in the desert."

Instantly, Father Diego understood the blond man in front of him wasn't normal. He glanced sideways toward his church members building the aqueduct. Father Diego said succinctly, "Not here."

Walking to their vehicles, Father Diego added, "I have the feeling I'd be better off if you were Mormons."

The Unusuals followed Father Diego to his small adobe church on a hill in the desert. It being Thursday, no one was inside. On the right, beyond the dark wooden pews, a large shrine to Our Lady of Guadalupe watched over the chapel. A few red votive candles burned in front of the Virgin Mary in the miraculous form of her appearance to a Mexican peasant. An uneasy Father Diego said, "I often hear prayers and confessions in this place. Which one did you come for?"

"Maybe a little of both," Eric answered, sensing Father Diego's discomfort. "It's probably better to show you." Eric turned toward Arial. She closed her eyes to concentrate; then she floated like the angel in the nearby stained glass window. Light from the window streamed behind her. Father Diego's eyes grew wide. He smiled at the wondrous sight.

"Airspeed, as we call her, has command over the air element," Eric said. "And Samsa has command over things with the earth element."

Samsa took off her sunglasses, ball cap, and denim jacket. As she shook out her hair, the glow came on. With one hand, she lifted the large marble altar above her head. After gently putting it back down, she brushed the brocade to make sure no wrinkles were there: her way of saying she meant no disrespect.

"Samsa..." Father Diego whispered. "Even here, in this remote desert, children tell me about you." Father Diego looked at Eric. "And you? What element do you have command over?"

"My powers are just beginning," Eric answered modestly. "But it seems to have to do with the space element. For instance, I moved my awareness into your mind to know your water secret."

Looking around, Father Diego noticed someone was missing. "And the fire element? Who has power over that?"

"We were kinda hoping to leave that to the other team," Eric answered.

Father Diego sat on the steps to the altar. "That's probably wise."

Walking up the aisle, closer to the *siddha*-wielding priest, Eric said, "I've seen you pull water toward you with force strong enough to move rock. If you knew there was a tsunami coming and millions of people would die, could you stop it?"

"I don't know." Father Aqua no longer felt any need to hide his abilities from yogis who were like him. "I don't have much experience with oceans. We're fairly land-locked here."

Eric tried a different tack. "You've been in deep states of meditation. What do you know about angels and demons?"

"I know a little something, but Saint Anthony knows more. I often think of him when I'm meditating." Father Diego closed his eyes to envision Saint Anthony alone on a silent retreat.

Father Diego said, "In the desert, Saint Anthony was assaulted by visions of angels and demons. Sometimes the angels looked like hideous demons while the evil spirits looked like beautiful angels. He asked, when the enticing and dreadful mix so freely, how do you tell the difference?"

"What did he conclude?" Diamond Mind asked.

Father Diego answered for himself: "I've found that if the appearance offers what others want, at the expense of myself, it's an angel. If the appearance offers what I want, at the expense of others, it's a demon. I know of no better test to keep my angels and demons straight, than to place the needs of others above my own."

For the first time since this whole superyogi thing started, Eric's eyes teared. He knew he was in the presence of another realized yogi—someone who could overcome innate self-concern to put others before himself. Eric said, "I'm afraid the demons are on the march, and we're the closest thing to angels this world has to stop them. If we don't act immediately, a terrible day of death could visit the planet. We need you to come with us. And do all you can."

"Where are we going?" Father Diego asked. This was a strange request indeed.

This time Arial answered. She mirrored Father Diego's earlier words. "To Africa—the Canary Islands—where a very dangerous yogi with twisted faith is about to move a mountain."

Sharp of mind, Father Diego quickly put these superyogis' questions together. "And you're afraid this mountain could cause a tsunami. I see...." He closed his eyes to pray, thumbing the silver cross around his neck. *Angels or demons?* A few moments later he answered their request. "I will go with you, but before we leave, there's one more thing I must do here."

"What's that?" Arial asked.

Rising in his chapel, Father Agua answered, "The people here need water. They deserve to have their faith rewarded."

That night, the fully assembled team of superyogis trekked into the desert—to the place Father Agua had felt a hidden, underground river. So deep, the slender vein, it was no surprise it hadn't been found earlier.

Bright and full, the moon allowed Father Agua to navigate without flashlight or headlamp. He was accustomed to peaceful nighttime strolls in the desert. His skilled feet danced around lance-like bases of agave plants and scraggly mesquite bushes.

In spite of his SEAL training, Diamond Mind wasn't as graceful. After several spearing stabs to his shins, the beach boy considered changing into his diamond body. Airspeed opted to fly behind them while Samsa—skin impervious to needles—bulled right through.

When they came to a clear spot near the buried treasure, Father Agua drew a circle in the sand. Sitting, he refused to get up until water flowed to the surface.

Outside the circle, engaged in meditation around him, the other yogis steeled their minds for the battle to come. Eric periodically slipped into Father Agua's mind. At Father Agua's heart, a beautiful image of Jesus filled him with love for all those who suffered from lack of resources. Channeling that perfect being, Father Agua commanded the waters to rise.

In time, the image of water in his mind became linked with his image of the water underneath the ground. Both images depended on his consciousness to establish their existence—and thus were a part of him. Seeing this, he drew the images together. Closer... closer. Soon, the narrow stream moved toward him with considerable force, as if the water molecules were on a chain.

Water finally broke the surface, leaping as a small geyser before falling back to flow like a bath faucet. That was enough. Natural pressure from the earth would do the rest. Now that an opening had been created, the gush would grow.

Water coursed through Father Diego's circle, wetting his priestly robes. He gathered some water in his hands and offered it to heaven with ancient Indian hand gestures, *mudras*, for water to drink and water to bathe in. He said simply, "It is done."

Two days later, faithful farmers found a new stream

trickling into their aqueduct, channeling water to their fields.

At the same time, on an island an ocean away, the superyogis started their mission—to stop a mega-tsunami.

48. THE SEARCH FOR PHYSIQUE

Enthusiastic about the exotic adventure, the Unusuals aided Agent Rollins and Agent Kirby in a sweep of La Palma Island, looking for Physique. La Palma, known as "The Pretty Island," was the greenest of the Canaries with lush rainforests and unspoiled volcanic parks dominating the interior. Although the team had to cover an area as big as metropolitan New York with a population of over 86,000, most of the action confined them to coastline towns and resorts.

Unfortunately, the team had arrived in the Canaries at a difficult time to enlist much aid from local law enforcement. The chief of the *Policía Local* assured Agent Rollins that his men "would keep an eye out for your girl." But the truth was, local police already had their hands full keeping Carnival debauchery in balance, heavily intoxicated tourists from falling down on cobblestone streets, and the occasional local pickpocket from working the crowd.

Carnival did provide advantages though. Airspeed and Samsa worked crowds easily with Tina Tinsdale's picture without arousing suspicion. Amidst the good natured-revelry of costumes, music, dancing, and drinking on the Spanish streets, they asked, "*¿Has visto mi amiga?*" Meaning, "Have you seen my friend?" Among the more popular responses Samsa and Arial received from women was "she's probably just run off with a local boy" (as that kind of thing happened during Carnival). And from men, a mildly flirtatious compliment: "No, but I'd like to."

Making good use of his Spanish, Father Agua shortened the lilt of his accent to sound more local. In the costumed atmosphere of Carnival, a pair of rebellious women dressed as naughty nuns mistook him for a costumed reveler in priestly garb. Pointing to their fake bulging bellies, one girl said, "Wouldn't you like to pretend you did this… to both of us?" Embarrassed, Father Agua assured the normally good Catholic girls that he was in fact a priest—and they hadn't committed any major sins… yet.

Rollins and Kirby worked the hotels and resorts, interviewing staff. Kirby did most of the talking as Rollins preferred to lurk with a menacing scowl. Being much more charming, Diamond Mind (in plain-clothes) chatted up guests, particularly ones who looked like they might own a yoga mat.

One evening, Samsa, Airspeed, and Father Agua returned covered in talcum powder, after having joined a snowy battle in a town's square where neighbors tossed buckets of powder at one another in Carnival revelry. Seeing that, Rollins decided to move the search into the interior.

There, the team worked the nature preserves and *casas*

rurales, little houses for rent on banana farms and in the rainforest. Spirits were high until the actual trek up the volcanic ridge of *Cumbre Vieja* to see the threatening fault line.

High above the sea, the mountain was so massive that what had once seemed like a reasonable proposition in a conference room an ocean away—that Physique could use her supernatural abilities to bring the mountain down— now seemed ridiculous. After all, this mountain wasn't an airplane or a building: it was several trillion tons of rock spread over a substantial island. Even Agent Kirby willingly conceded, "If she came here, she probably concluded she couldn't take this mountain down and moved on."

The timing of Agent Kirby's conclusion was fortunate, because none of the team except Airspeed—who could fly—wanted to walk farther across a rickety old rope bridge, which swayed in the wind over a deep gorge.

Diamond Mind's hand clung to the first rope post for safety as he peered over the ledge. Far below, he could see a rocky beach. With two days of searching left before Physique's next attack—and possibly millions of people at risk—Diamond Mind didn't want to underestimate Physique. So he offered another angle. "You know, Milarepa once used a landslide to gain revenge for his family having been oppressed."

"I thought Milarepa was Tibet's favorite saint," Agent Rollins said. He'd been studying all he could about *mahasiddhas* gone wild to devise a plan for dealing with Physique.

Diamond Mind moved away from the gorge ledge. "He is. But before he reached enlightenment, in that same life, Milarepa got involved with black magic. He even killed people. Later he deeply regretted his actions." Indeed, the path to enlightenment wasn't always straight. Gross missteps that required dramatic correction did occur.

"So what are you suggesting?" Agent Rollins asked. He was tired from the many days of searching and grumpy as usual.

Diamond Mind looked toward the fault line high on La Palma Island. He said, "I don't think Physique is all bad. Over many lives, she clearly accumulated incredible merit to gain the abilities she has now. She just got twisted at the wrong time by the loss of someone important to her." Diamond Mind reflected on the tragic loss of her guru, apparently a man she was intimately involved with. "Is Physique really any different from people who call for or take up arms to revenge their family and protect their honor?"

Agent Rollins whipped off his sunglasses, snapping, "So you're ready to nominate Physique for sainthood? Is that what you're saying?"

Diamond Mind responded calmly, trying to help Rollins relax. "In her grief, she made a mistake. She drew a line." Diamond Mind scuffed his foot in the dirt. "She decided that people on one side have nothing to do with her and they deserve to be punished. And people on the other side are like her and they deserve to be protected."

"What are you getting at?" Rollins asked. The sun, the trek, and Diamond Mind's continuous teaching made his skin prickle.

"You've seen the people on this island," Diamond Mind answered. "Physique may try to use this mountain to strike at her perceived enemies in America, but I don't think she could bear being around the happy, helpful people of La Palma that she'd be hurting."

Agent Kirby understood this perspective. After all, even serial killers needed to dehumanize their victims. Joining the conversation, Kirby asked, "Where do you think she is?"

Finally, Diamond Mind made his point. "If I were her, in her state of mind, I think I would stay on another island before making my move to La Palma—only to attack."

Relieved that Eric actually had a point to his little sermon, Agent Rollins considered his reasoning. The other six islands were each only hours away by ferry. However, Diamond Mind's theory had even less evidence than Agent Kirby's elaborate speculation that had brought them to trek in the tropical Canary Islands in the first place. Still, after five days of intensive searching on La Palma—and only two days before their orders required them to return to the American capital—Rollins saw no harm in expanding the search.

Rollins put his sunglasses back on. "We'll split up tomorrow and search the nearby islands. You get two days."

49. DEVEREAUX DELIVERS

Meanwhile, in the deep waters between La Palma's neighboring islands, La Gomera and Tenerife, Physique rendezvoused aboard the luxury yacht for her promised tryst with international arms dealer, Max Devereaux.

"What exactly am I looking at?" Physique asked, unimpressed.

"What do you think it is?" Devereaux responded.

"It looks like a mortar shell from World War II."

"It is indeed."

The two sat at the dining room table where Physique had made her destructive request for something that could bring down a mountain. But this time there wasn't silverware or gourmet food. Instead, the only item on the table was a silver case about the length of Physique's arm. Inside rested a tarnished shell cradled by thin black foam.

Devereaux wore an Armani tuxedo suitable for the finest casino. Knowing his hand was strong, he played it slowly, choosing to draw out his words to excite Physique. "But there's more to this shell than meets the eye."

Max ran his fingers over the 203-millimeter shell, almost eight inches in width. When he reached the tip, he tapped at the seam. The shell looked as if it could be easily unscrewed. At the base, two wires entered from a modern digital timer that was unlocked by an unseen key.

"What's so special about this?" Physique asked, still unimpressed. She wore the low cut, backless red cocktail dress that Devereaux had laid out; her shade of lipstick even matched the dress. She needed to make sure that what Devereaux supplied was worth her exchange.

"This shell is enriched with plutonium," answered Devereaux coolly. He leaned back in his chair.

"Meaning... this antique is a nuclear bomb?" The small size and apparent age seemed impossible.

"Tactical nuclear ammunition to be precise. Made for a Soviet howitzer in the 1950s. Everyone had these shells for deterring invasion by conventional forces." Devereaux waved his hand as if shooing away a fly. He recalled how all kinds of tactical nuclear ammunition had been made in various shapes with yields ranging from 0.1 to 12 kilotons. "Nowadays, politicians worry about reducing the number of big warheads. But few want to account for all the nasty little stuff that was made during the Cold War."

Touching the shell for the first time, Physique's heart started to beat rapidly. They were alone in the middle of the ocean with a weapon of mass destruction. She asked, "Is it going to be big enough to take down a mountain?"

"You're looking at ten kilotons, equivalent to ten thousand tons of TNT. That's only a third less than the explosive power of the American bomb dropped on Hiroshima."

"And that's enough?" Physique tried to imagine the size of the explosion. She vaguely remembered something about nuclear bombs—that they were usually a thousand times more powerful than their atomic cousins—yet this weapon was so small.

"I believe you want the mountain to fall, not vaporize," answered Devereaux, reminding her of her request. As was necessary in his business, arms trader Devereaux remembered orders precisely. "Think World Trade Center. If you take out a floor, the mountain will topple."

Devereaux had personally researched classified data that the Bone Frightener had procured. The documents covered findings from over fifteen hundred underground tests performed by nearly a dozen nations—all in the development of nuclear weapons since 1952. At one point, over forty thousand nuclear weapons stocked the world's arsenals—enough to destroy the planet several times over. "My dear, this should produce a major earthquake," Devereaux said. "Maybe even a seven on the Richter scale."

Devereaux adjusted his onyx cufflinks; they were as dark as his eyes. "This is a very expensive weapon. A major purchase by the Bone Frightener on your behalf." It had been hard to procure and retrofit. Finally, ready to close, Devereaux called to see if Physique was in fact all in: "Are you sure you want it?"

Physique reached to unscrew the shell's tip, curious about the nuclear core inside. But Devereaux gently shooed her hands away. "If I were you, I wouldn't unscrew that without a radiation suit." Physique instantly understood. She withdrew her hands and put them on both sides of the metal case.

She leaned forward—enough for Devereaux to peek

at what was underneath the luxurious red fabric of her dress. "But where's the key?" she asked. "How do I start the timer?"

Devereaux loosened his black tie, then slowly unbuttoned his tuxedo shirt. His firm chest belonged to a yogi who had practiced one of the more physically demanding styles of yoga—*asthanga*. Around his neck, glistening on a silver chain, the key hung. "The key is for later, after you keep up your end of our agreement," Devereaux said. "Do you accept delivery?"

Physique touched the tactical nuclear device. It struck her that the small case could be lowered down the drilling shaft that ran almost a mile and a half inside the mountain. Everything was coming together perfectly. While the shaft may have been intended to allow the seismology team to better understand the mountain, now it would become the gateway for exploding the core. She found herself aroused by the bomb's power and by how close she was to furthering her revenge.

She reached for the key dangling around Devereaux's neck. Before kissing the devil, she answered, "Yes."

50. EL HIERRO

FATHER AGUA SAT IN THE BACK OF THE SPORT FISHING boat that Agent Rollins had rented, playing with a wave machine. Water, vinegar, and red food-coloring created a grade-schooler's science project that demonstrated wave motion. But instead of producing undulation by tilting the sealed glass bottle that had a tiny blue boat inside, Father Agua slowly drew his hand in the air to pull the liquid with his powers.

Diamond Mind cut the engines. Their boat drifted inside the prominent bay of El Hierro, the smallest of the volcanic Canary Islands. Water gently lapped at the boat's sides as Diamond Mind gazed at a craggy amphitheater-like coast, imagining what had happened.

About fifty thousand years ago, an earthquake had ripped away a third of the island and tossed it into the sea. This caused an early tsunami that had rolled through neighboring islands. Fortunately, this was long before nomadic *homo sapiens* had sailed their way to the Canaries. Still, the massive cleft on El Hierro's northern face warned of what could happen when earthquake meets island.

But Father Agua didn't look up to see the geological wonder. Still focused on the problem of how to stop a mega-tsuanmi, he said, "Since I'd be of little use defending the capital, maybe I should stay here a few weeks—in case something does happen."

"I thought you might feel that way," Diamond Mind answered. He sat on the stern of the ship.

Diamond Mind understood Father Agua's focus. "Actually, why don't you stay behind today? I can take a peek around." While Diamond Mind felt fairly indestructible, he didn't want Father Agua getting involved in a tussle with Physique, should he find her on El Hierro.

Diamond Mind was about to dive into the water to swim ashore when Father Agua looked up. "I'm glad we got to meet. There's not too many of us yet." Indeed, their particular mental dispositions were both rare and paradoxical. Transforming their consciousness had taken world-shifting effort—while making the final leap into the void took surrender.

"Though I'm curious about one thing," Father Agua said. "How did you find me?"

Stepping back from the boat's edge, Eric remembered one of Father Agua's essays.

"It was your brilliant reconciliation of the Trinity with non-duality,"

"Ah, yes. The Father is the pure void from which appearance comes. The Son is form appearing from the void. The mystery of the Holy Spirit is that any appearance is both Father and Son—both the absence of true existence and the illusion of form, always depending on each other." Father Agua saw that if people could understand this formula deeply, it would open whole new doors for Christianity and even provide a golden key for reconciling the world's religions.

Understanding the implication, Diamond Mind said, "So whatever you do unto the smallest, you do unto God in Heaven—for the divine is within everything."

"Yes," Father Agua responded, "the divine is inside each of us, reaching through every appearance like silence supports music. Perhaps that's why the only sensible reaction to any situation is love." Both yogis smiled, each knowing personally this truth. "But that still doesn't explain how you found me."

"Because you had so clearly gone beyond words, with Jesus as your guide, I suspected you would have similar powers to your guide."

"To calm stormy seas..." Father Agua nodded. "May that be so."

Diamond Mind made his way toward the center of El Hierro, the least-populated island of the Canaries. A nature lover's dream, El Hierro was an unspoiled, protected UNESCO biosphere with unique geography, animals, and plant life. While driving up the magnificent mountain rising five thousand feet above the sea, Diamond Mind saw windmills. With a thick accent, his electric-car taxi driver explained that this island was the first in the world to meet all power needs through self-sustaining solar, wind, and water. The cab driver asked if his passenger would like to go see El Hierro's giant lizards. "They're as big as cats."

Diamond Mind declined. Today, he was searching for something even more rare.

For days, Diamond Mind had tried to think like

Physique: a schizophrenic twist of benevolent intention mixed with cruel retribution. When he'd learned that a center specializing in yoga retreats sat at the top of El Hierro—on a mountain range unlikely to be hit by a La Palma mega-tsunami—Diamond Mind's intuition blazed. There, Physique could avoid people, TV, and the Internet, and keep her subtle body tuned for her biggest demonstration of supernatural power.

Eric arrived at the retreat center, a cluster of renovated stone farm buildings. A class had just broken up. Slender and graceful people milled in the grass around a table of fresh juices. Dressed in yoga clothes with his yoga mat slung via a Velcro strap around his shoulder, Eric easily blended into the group. He lingered long enough to see that none of the women could be Physique. However, in the distance, Eric spied another woman still practicing backbends on the outdoor yoga platform.

Investigating closer, Eric observed a tall, muscular blond women—obviously an accomplished yogi—balancing perfectly in Dancer's pose. She wore a white tank top over snug, black yoga shorts. Standing on one leg, she reached both arms over her head, arched back, and grabbed one ankle behind her. The circle formed by the deep curve of her spine and raised back leg made her look like an inspector's magnifying glass. *It could be her*, thought Eric. He had her picture memorized by now.

Eric didn't want to alert Agent Rollins and the other members of the team until he was certain. He'd hate to pull everyone from their searches to pounce on some poor spiritual retreat tourist who didn't turn out to be Physique. *But how to be certain?* At present, she was just an excellent yogi deeply focused on her personal practice.

Despite his uncertainty, Eric pressed twice on his tiny

earpiece. No bigger than a hearing aid, the beige earpiece was actually a mini transmitter receiver. It differed from a cell phone in that the whole team could now hear Eric and his surroundings, and differed from a walkie-talkie as Eric didn't have to hold a button each time he spoke.

"Heads up from El Hierro Island," Eric said softly. "I may have spotted Physique, but I need to move closer to be certain. Please keep radio silence. If you hear me say *diamond*, know that I've found her and please come help."

Unfortunately, at best, each member of the team was over an hour away. Agents Rollins and Kirby were both on La Gomera, the closest island to La Palma. Samsa and Airspeed had chosen bustling Tenerife after learning that Manolo Blahnik, the most famous shoe designer in the world, had been born there on a banana farm. They were hoping for a Manolo Blahnik museum or, at the least, a low-priced factory outlet.

Eric decided to engage this yogini enough to see what was going on in her mind. It was SEAL surveillance in a way, just a little closer up. Unrolling his mat beside her, Eric casually said, "Do you mind if I follow you?"

51. MALEFICENT

"I'M ALMOST DONE," THE BLOND YOGI ANSWERED WITHOUT losing her focus. She gazed toward the sky.

"That's OK," Eric replied, already rolling out his mat. "I might learn something from someone as advanced as you."

She didn't respond, just dove into a *vinyasa* before turning her back, ignoring his overly chummy intrusion on her personal practice. When she went into Half Moon pose, *ardha chandrasana*, Eric took the opportunity to scan her body. Again she balanced on one leg, but this time she touched the ground with one hand while extending the other arm straight up.

Mysteriously, the energies of her lower *chakras*—her *muladhara* and *svadhisthana*, near her secret place and tailbone—were wide open, but her upper *chakras* were as closed as oyster shells. Diamond Mind had read about this phenomenon before—but never actually seen it so clearly.

He recalled the eminent, recently-passed Swami Satyananda, the founder of the Bihar School of Yoga, warning people not to open the lower *chakras* without first opening the eye of wisdom because strange things could happen. Swami Satyananda, who had founded the Yoga Research Foundation to synchronize scientific research with yoga, wasn't prone to overstatement. It was his position that many of the yogic *siddhis* were actually the result of *kundalini (pranic* energy awakening in the central channel) getting stuck in one *chakra* instead of passing through quickly. He'd warned that the *svadhisthana*—the highest one unlocked by the yogini next to Eric—was the most dangerous. Apparently, the *chakra* inside the bulb of the tailbone was the seat of the unconscious. Unless it was unlocked under the careful guidance of a trusted guru, bizarre behavior could run wild. In his landmark book, *Kundalini Tantra*, Swami Satyananda made a point that Agent Kirby had used for his *Dangerous Yogi* report:

> It must be remembered that up to *svadhisthana*, the consciousness is not yet purified. Due to ignorance and confusion, the psychic powers awakened at this level are often accompanied by the maleficent mental attributes. What happens here when the aspirant tries to manifest or express himself through the psychic medium is that more often than not it becomes a vehicle for personal and lower tendencies rather than for the divine.

Maleficent was not a word with which Eric was familiar. Looking it up, he'd learned that maleficent was the polite way of saying, *capable of causing great harm or destruction especially by supernatural means.* Additionally, Swami Satyananda explained:

This is why the psychic powers that come to the *sadhaka* [student of spiritual practices] after having awakened and established the *kundalini* in the *manipura* [navel chakra and higher] are really benevolent and compassionate, whereas those which manifest in the *muladhara* and *svadhisthana* are still tinged by the dark aspect of the lower mind.

Looking at this yogini dressed in black and white, Diamond Mind saw an incredible example of incomplete *chakra* ripening. As if confronting a wild tiger in jungle grasslands, amazement and wonder came at first, but then a chill to the bone.

How did she get this way? Most yogis opened the *svadhisthana* by gaining true renunciation that realizes that desires can never be satisfied in one lifetime—or even in hundreds. But it was also taught in the yoga *tantras* that the *muladhara* and *svadhisthana* of a women or man could be opened through physical union with a master yogi or yogini who had already opened their own crucial points. Either was possible with Physique. Perhaps her guru, through their intimate relationship, had opened her lower *chakras*, no doubt believing that he was still going to be around to help her manage the unconscious upheaval occurring until the *kundalini* rose to the higher, benevolent points.

But Eric still couldn't say for certain whether the *yogini* in front of him was Physique or not. Her mind was completely focused on her breath, offering no other mental images. If this was indeed Physique, Eric still didn't understand her. After all, opening the lower *chakras* without accompanying wisdom of the higher crucial points didn't make one a supernatural killer—more likely just erratic. To go from meditating to throwing things at people was one thing; to bring mass destruction was another.

When they arched upside down into Wheel, Eric tried to prompt her with an unfortunately lame "So... what brings you to El Hierro?"

"Shhh," she hissed. Coming down from Wheel, she said, "That's it for me," clearly intending to get away from him.

Determined, Eric tried one last tactic. "You did such a beautiful practice. You should dedicate it to something... like ending war."

This caught her ear. Instead of getting up, she brought her legs together in meditation position and closed her eyes. They were alone on the wooden yoga platform, surrounded by stone cottages. Eric followed her deeper into her own mind, just in time to catch her thought, *I will bring an end to war, by breaking them....*

The yogini in front of him was definitely Physique.

Eric felt almost nauseous as he watched Physique's mind replay the missile explosion that buried her beloved guru. Then, surprisingly, he saw the image of her guru—dressed in bones on a ship—telling her: "Strike from afar with something they won't expect."

Next, Diamond Mind caught her imagining a mega-tsunami striking New York City.

Sitting in the presence of this murderous, deranged yogi, Eric felt like he was staring into the mouth of a snarling tiger.

Keeping cool, Diamond Mind drew upon the wisdom that the ultimate way to stop violence is to stop violence in your own heart. To manifest peace in his world, Eric had to first gain peace in his own mind. Unresolved anger motivated Physique's attacks. So if he was to help her, Diamond Mind would have to face his own unresolved resentments. Simply, she mirrored something twisted in him.

Diamond Mind understood the nuances of *karma*. He had no other choice. Otherwise, the cycle of unresolved anger and violence would continue to surface in another form… roaring at him, clawing at him, gnawing at his flesh. He must pass this test to love the unlovable or another tiger would appear to challenge him in a similar way.

This was something Physique had never learned—or had forgotten. As it said in *The Yoga Sutra*:

अहिंसाप्रतिष्ठायां तत्सन्निधौ वैरत्यागः ॥ ३५ ॥

ahinsa pratishthayam tat sannidau vaira tyagah

II.35 IF YOU MAKE IT A WAY OF LIFE
NEVER TO HURT OTHERS,
THEN IN YOUR PRESENCE
ALL CONFLICT COMES TO AN END.

One part of Diamond Mind wanted to strike a nasty blow to Physique while she wasn't expecting it. But what held him back was the wisdom blossoming in his mind: only peace can create peace, just as only apple seeds can sprout apple trees. As Jesus once said:

FOR OF THORNS MEN DO NOT GATHER FIGS,
NOR OF A BRAMBLE BUSH GATHER THEY GRAPES.
LUKE 6:44

In this moment, Diamond Mind found strength in Father Agua's words: "The only sensible reaction to any situation is love." Even in the twisted appearance before him, the divine reached through to Eric, challenging him to love.

I have to stop Physique with love.

While Physique's eyes were still closed, Diamond Mind pushed the white light of his own virtue into her heart. "I am you," he said gently. "There is no one to hurt without hurting yourself. Let go and forgive. Your powers don't make you super; caring for others first does."

Physique was about to rise from her evil dedication when she felt a release at her heart. She vaguely heard Eric's voice, but the feeling at her heart captured her... something akin to warmth and joy... almost like falling in love. She hadn't felt this beauty in so long. Without resisting, she lost herself in the feeling.

Focused on removing Physique's murderous rage by opening her heart, Eric didn't hear the sound of footsteps coming behind him. Stealthy at first, the footsteps quickened into a determined dash. In the next moment, a slap sounded like a thunderclap.

Blindside had struck Eric with his steel cane.

The smack sent a nasty bolt of fiery pain through Eric's lower vertebra. Blindside's hit damaged the same spot as Eric's paralyzing accident. Blindside shouted, "That's enough, Eric! The Bone Frightener has plans for her!"

Eric grimaced. For a moment, he couldn't feel his legs—only shooting pain from the bottom of his spine. Then a flash of terror spiked—trauma from deep within— reminding him of the loss of his physical abilities... and the loss of his fiancé.

Physique felt Eric's searing pain shut down the opening of her heart *chakra*. She snapped out of meditation, unsure of what had just happened. She saw a man cringing in front of her; then heard Blindside's aggressive voice, "Get out of here! He's been sent to take you down."

That voice, Diamond Mind thought, fighting through

the pain. *I know that voice.* Thinking of his missing student, he called out... "Marc Vincent?"

Blindside's cloudy eyes became visible first. Then his full form materialized. Eric saw a man in all black tapping a dragon-headed cane. "That's right, Eric. Only you can call me Blindside now."

Physique scrambled to her feet, disoriented.

Blindside spoke with anger and resentment. "I asked you repeatedly how to heal my blindness. All you offered were gradual techniques. But I found someone who gave me a short-cut." Again, Blindside turned invisible. Diamond Mind heard footsteps dashing toward him, but couldn't see the invisible fist that struck him on the side of the head so unexpectedly it knocked him down.

Watching Eric tumble, Physique laughed. She pressed her foot on Eric's chest as she slowly changed her weight to crush him. "You thought you could take me down?" she cackled. Her nails and hair shifted to black.

Some yogis from the retreat rushed over to break up whatever was happening on the yoga platform, but they were intercepted by Agnite, the dark-haired Asian woman in a black uniform and black domino mask. Stepping from the shadows, she shouted her name as a *mantra*, "Agnite!" Then she sparked a chain of fire from her hands before menacingly twirling a dangling ball of flame. Agnite shouted, "Get back!"

Trapped under Physique's rapidly increasing weight, Diamond Mind could feel his rib cage starting to crush like an egg carton under a child's foot. His mind raced forward to the being he would become in his next life. Exhaling a final breath, he uttered, "It's diamond time...."

52. DIAMOND TIME

FROM PRACTICE, ERIC PULLED HIS PRANIC WINDS INTO the central channel running near his spine. Quickly the winds gathered at his navel *chakra*, then shot past his open *chakras* to the tip of his head. Instantly, the mental image of his body shifted. As light cascaded down, he became transparent like a diamond.

Finding strength he hadn't possessed before, Diamond Mind tossed Physique. Crashing a tree-length away, she shattered the wooden yoga platform; beams broke like bones.

As Diamond Mind slowly got to his feet, his outline reflected the sun. Bright flashes of white light from his strong arms displayed his diamond body for all to see. Where not covered by yoga clothes, he looked like a crystal vase. And yet, he still moved organically. It was as if a diamond force field formed his body.

Physique scrambled as Blindside yelled, "He's ours. Get

out of here!" Unprepared for another battle with a strange, now alien-looking superyogi, Physique complied.

But before she raced off, Diamond Mind saw her grab a canvas yoga bag that obviously had something heavier than a yoga mat or costume inside. He wanted to chase her, but hesitated. His former student—invisible to the eye—circled around him.

Keeping his defenses up, ready for an attack from Blindside, Diamond Mind watched Physique leap from stone house to stone house with some difficulty—clearly trying to balance additional weight inside her bag. Finally, she glided off the mountain peak, making her escape.

There was nothing Eric could do about her now. Even if they had been alone, Diamond Mind wouldn't have been able to capture Physique once she'd taken to the air. Eric heard Blindside's sinister voice say, "Now I know more than you."

Diamond Mind remained cool, scanning the area around him… reaching for Blindside's next thought. He witnessed Blindside's mind preparing to swing his invisible cane. Just in time, he ducked as the air whooshed above his head.

Countering, Diamond Mind came up quickly and grabbed Blindside in a headlock, raising him off the ground. Much stronger than Blindside, Diamond Mind shook his catch until the man's silver cane dropped. Soon, Blindside became visible. Diamond Mind answered his former student's earlier taunt: "You know more than I do? Don't be so sure."

"Put him down, Eric." Agnite spoke with a familiarity that proved she was indeed Angie Kim, the other missing student of Eric's. "Or I'll start torching the island. It's a UNESCO biosphere for goodness sake."

Eric dropped Blindside hard. The man scrambled for

his cane before moving behind Agnite. Eric returned to his human flesh and blood appearance. "What happened to you two?" Eric asked, dismayed at what had become of his former students.

"We got powers," Agnite answered. "And the world got more fun."

"Don't you know they're just going to run out?" Eric asked, pleading with them to come to their senses.

Despite the fact that his life could have been ended moments ago in Eric's powerful clutches, Blindside answered, "Not for us. We found a more powerful master."

Growing impatient with this conversation, Agnite produced a ball of fire in her hands. The flame reflected in her wild eyes. "Look, I'm only going to say this once. You can join us, or we have to destroy you."

Eric answered defiantly: "You're already destroying yourselves. I won't join you."

Agnite's red lock of hair wagged like a taunting finger. "Marc always said you were a Boy Scout. Now we'll see how you'll look as a Brownie." With that, she hurled her ball of fire.

The fire ball exploded on Eric, engulfing him like a swarm of bees. In the explosion, his clothes burned to rags, but Eric had gotten good at quickly changing into his diamond body to avoid injury. Stripping off charred clothing, he stepped through the flames. "Diamonds don't burn." Agnite gasped.

Having felt Eric's strength, Blindside grabbed Agnite's arm. Due to their special connection, he made them both invisible for a covert escape.

At that moment, the sleek Airspeed swooped in like a diving hawk with a flying sidekick to the space where Agnite and Blindside were last standing. But she didn't make contact. Her thigh-high boots snapped and her red sash flapped in the wind. She'd flown as fast as a fighter jet to Diamond Mind's position using the locator built into her navigation glasses.

"You got here fast," Diamond Mind said. She floated above the platform in her full superyogi uniform, ignoring the rolling cameras of stunned witnesses.

"Not fast enough," Airspeed answered. She was impressed with her speed in crossing the islands, but now wasn't the time to brag. "Who were those two?"

"Former students," Diamond Mind answered, ashamed. He slowly returned to his human form. "I'm afraid they've been lured to the dark side."

"And Physique?" Airspeed asked, staying on task.

"Gone. If I'd had a few more minutes, I could have brought her in peacefully."

"You shouldn't have engaged without a wingman," Airspeed said.

Agent Rollins cursed in Diamond Mind's ear: "I don't care how super you think you are! That was an amateur move!"

Diamond Mind waited until Rollins' rant was complete— or at least until Rollins had to take a breath. Then Eric took responsibility. He knew he'd messed up. "You're both right. I'm sorry. I thought I had a window to end this peacefully."

"Which way did Physique go?" Airspeed asked, looking around. Eric pointed toward the bay. "She's either fleeing or making a desperate last strike on La Palma."

"I'm going to fly around to see if I can spot her."

Eric stood nearly naked. His charred clothes had already dropped away. Before flying off, Airspeed gave one last piece of advice: "I hope you brought your uniform. Before you fight Physique again, you're going to need some clothes."

53. TO THE ROPE BRIDGE

AIRSPEED SOARED LIKE A HAWK SEARCHING FOR A scurrying rodent. The more time she spent in the sky, the farther she could see. Conventionally, this seemed like building new muscles; but in truth, it was because her perception of herself had changed so dramatically. As the hard lines between space, her body, and her consciousness continued to dissolve, distance imposed fewer limitations.

After tense searching (while the rest of the earth-bound team bounced on waves toward La Palma Island), Airspeed finally located Physique. From her bird's eye view, Airspeed witnessed Physique demolish two police vehicles blocking her path. Now costumed in her full white and black body suit, she leapt from vehicle to vehicle, stomping squad cars like beer cans. The Canary Island cops quickly retreated. When Physique behaved like the biggest bull in the pasture, it was better to back away.

"She's headed for the Old Ridge!" shouted Airspeed, hovering far above Physique's tunnel vision.

Earlier, using his cell phone, Agent Kirby had scrambled local police to assist in locating Physique. Regrettably, Kirby felt his manhood diminish even more than usual: while most of the team displayed magnificent powers, the only thing he could do was dial for backup.

At the same time, Agent Rollins had placed a secure call to National Security Advisor Sujata Bansal in the White House. It was early morning in America. If Sujata was pleased they had found Physique, she hadn't expressed it. All she'd cared about were the next moves.

Following Diamond Mind's confrontation with Physique, a series of escalating strikes had been ordered, backed by presidential authority. First, the agents were to assist the superyogis in taking Physique down. If that failed, a heavily-armed team of Navy SEALs, already deployed to La Palma from a nearby battleship, would step in. And finally—as a last option—six missile-laden F-16s were scrambling from the U.S. airbase in Spain to blast Physique off the Old Ridge.

No one wanted to see American jets fire missiles on a vacation island nature preserve. But this was precisely what the White House intended to do, should all else fail. Vice President Lausunu had already made a phone call to the shocked Canary Islands' President to thank him for his "cooperation and support in coordinating land and air strikes on your soil." Not exactly the kind of event that made for an easy Canary Island re-election. The local President dearly hoped for superyogi success.

Each moment felt stretched like Professor's Jao's atomic clock. While the complete superyogi team struggled to get into physical proximity to Physique in the highlands of La Palma, both Kirby and Rollins fretted, wondering if Physique could succeed in taking the mountain down before they could get to her. For the first time, Agent Rollins wished things actually were like the comic books—so that in seconds, Samsa and Diamond Mind could come flying in. Instead, Diamond Mind piloted a fishing boat with Father Agua while Samsa, looking like another costumed reveler enjoying Carnival, rode in a water taxi.

Physique glided over treetops and large rocks like an angry raven, making her way to the mountaintop. She pressed her boots against branches with just enough force to keep her flitting.

When Airspeed reported Physique's position, Rollins briefly considered sending in Airspeed to disrupt Physique. Diving from ten thousand feet, she would have plenty of "smash." The attack was tantalizingly close. "I think I can take her," insisted Airspeed, radioing to Rollins.

Rollins had only to give the order….

Instead, Agent Rollins coolly answered, "Just hold your position until we all get into place." He didn't want to repeat Diamond Mind's solo mistake.

"But what about the mountain?" Airspeed asked, hovering over the tallest island peak in the world. This was the question on everyone's mind. No one believed the ridge could be toppled, but still, all were nervous.

Staying level-headed and firm, Rollins repeated, "Just hold your position."

As usual, Agent Kirby wasn't asked, but he agreed with Rollins' call.

Flying up by the clouds, keeping out of sight of Physique, Airspeed felt she was being treated like Tinkerbell. Still, a captain knew how to follow orders—even if she didn't like them. Occasionally, due to the verdant pine tree canopy and craggy mountain terrain, she lost sight of Physique. But Airspeed knew the general area she was in: the densest forest of the Old Ridge.

Airspeed spied a fast-moving black and red helicopter landing on the barren, brown soil of a nearby mountain ridge. Attention drawn away, Airspeed missed Physique emptying the contents of her yoga bag.

"I've got an unmarked helicopter on a nearby ridge. Is that one of ours?" Airspeed asked.

"Shouldn't be," Rollins answered as he made land on La Palma. Samsa and Diamond Mind were still moments away.

Airspeed moved closer to investigate; her nearly bionic vision discovered Blindside and Agnite setting up an escape for Physique. Blindside was easy to spot. After all, he was just a coat piloting a helicopter. Agnite was easy to identify too, in her now familiar black and red-trimmed body suit with black mask.

Like a good tactician, Airspeed scouted the terrain between the helicopter and Physique's last position on the Old Ridge. A long, scenic rope bridge spanning a rocky mountain gorge swayed gently in the breeze above a beach-lined cove. This was the same rope bridge that the team had discovered earlier: the one that no one had wanted to walk. Airspeed realized Physique would have to cross those rickety ropes to escape on the helicopter.

Airspeed's heart beat faster. There wasn't much time before Physique flew the coop again.

"Don't bother coming up the mountain," broadcasted Airspeed to the entire team. "I'll bring Physique to you. Get to the beach below the old rope bridge as fast as you can!"

54. SHOWDOWN

Airspeed landed gently in the center of the old rope ridge. Wind waved her red sash like an ancient battle flag. When Physique finally made her way to the bridge, she sauntered with an air of satisfaction. Overconfident and undeterred by the unknown lady in a mask and thigh-high boots blocking her way, Physique strolled to the center of the bridge to confront her adversary.

In this strange meeting, the two masked superyogis faced each other like gunslingers. The ropes looked like they belonged on a boxing ring. Physique studied this new woman from head-to-toe before asking, "Who are you supposed to be?"

"You'll find out," her adversary answered, cracking her knuckles, preparing for a fight.

Physique peered below into the deep gorge. She could barely see the bottom. She smashed her foot down, shattering one wooden plank between them, shaking the bridge. Arial grabbed the ropes, pretending to brace herself, as wood plummeted in pieces. Physique smirked, "You sure picked the wrong place to confront me."

Gripping the top ropes while spreading her legs to stand on the bottom lashes, Physique threw her head back laughing. As she increased her density, her flinging hair changed from sandy blond to midnight black. Instantly, her increased weight snapped the rope bridge as easily as snapping sewing thread.

The violent collapse sent Physique plummeting with her adversary, but Physique quickly became light as a feather—a trick she had mastered long before her plane downing. Gliding, she expected to see this other superyogi and her little red sash plummeting toward death—but she didn't spot her. Instead, glancing up, she saw Airspeed coming right at her.

Before connecting with outstretched fists, Airspeed shouted, "I picked exactly the right place!"

However, Physique increased her density just before Airspeed punched her to protect her feathery frame that certainly would have shattered. Still, Airspeed's powerful blow sent Physique spinning. Maneuvering swiftly as a falcon striking a kite, Airspeed kept coming. Physique kept increasing her weight, falling faster while trying to strike back—but Airspeed was too fast. In spite of all her flailing, Physique didn't touch Airspeed as she bobbed in and out. And worse, the ground was coming quickly.

Shouting, Airspeed pounded Physique. "I'm a jet. You're a glider!" Airspeed punched and kicked Physique all the way to the beach. She pulled up just before Physique hit the sand.

As if struck by a meteor, the ground exploded into a

geyser of sand with huge plumes filling the air. When the sand storm finally cleared, Airspeed hovered over the impact crater. Oddly, there was nothing to see.

Physique had disappeared beneath the sand.

Samsa and Diamond Mind, who'd just made it to the white sand beach, rushed to the edge of the crater. Samsa was clearly disappointed. "I was hoping you would leave something for me." Both she and Diamond Mind were in full costume and pumped with adrenalin.

Suddenly, Physique broke through the sand just outside the crater, gasping for air. As she freed herself, sand poured off of her. At first she looked like a sand-soaked zombie rising from the grave. But quickly she became a cornered tiger. When she saw that Physique had survived the fall, Airspeed realized that even with all her abilities, she wouldn't be enough to take Physique down.

It was time for Samsa.

"Remember me?" Samsa said, raising her fists to fight. Light radiated through her skin.

Physique snapped, "Well, look who got all glowy and bought new boots." She flicked sand away from her body.

Samsa boiled. This was the woman who had ended her human life… who'd made it so she couldn't even remember her mother… who'd brought her to such a confusing new existence.

"I can still go through you," Physique taunted, starting to increase her density for the fight. As she increased her weight, she immediately started sinking in the sand.

Samsa smiled, realizing the key benefit of Airspeed's brilliant strategy to confront Physique on the beach. "Not here." Physique couldn't go full heavy without turning the beach into quicksand.

No longer restraining herself, Samsa took advantage of

Physique's limited density. Hips squared, Samsa snapped a blazing two-punch combination, popping Physique's head back. Stunned, Physique clumsily swung back. Anticipating the counter attack, Samsa ducked before tossing Physique farther than a wrestling ring.

But instead of rumbling with Samsa further, Physique dashed toward the ocean. Lightening her weight, she hoped to escape by tip-toeing across crests of waves. However, Airspeed cut her off. Hovering in the air, Airspeed wagged her finger... signaling Physique not to come this way.

Desperate at the water's edge, Physique heard a whumping sound deeper than the blood pumping in her ears. The helicopter was coming to her rescue, or so she believed.

But seeing Physique trapped between three superyogis, Blindside called for a retreat. He'd have to leave Physique to fend for herself.

When the helicopter disappeared around the mountain, Physique felt fear for the first time.

Repulsed by this new feeling, she rushed toward Samsa, charging wildly. Prepared, Samsa spun a looping crescent kick that knocked Physique to the sand. Samsa was about to kick Physique again when Diamond Mind restrained her. Samsa was too focused on destroying Physique to notice how physically strong Diamond Mind had become.

"It doesn't matter..." Physique stammered. Spitting sand, she crawled like a shipwreck victim. "You're too late."

Diamond Mind heard her ominous words. "What do you mean, we're too late?"

Only slightly gaining her composure, Samsa's braceleted arms yanked Physique off the ground. Now held like a rag doll, Physique didn't try to resist. "You'll see," she said. "Everyone will see."

She was hiding something big, but that wouldn't stop Diamond Mind. Coming closer, the blue costumed superyogi rolled his eyes back toward his *ajna chakra*. He asked, "What have you done?"

Diamond Mind quickly entered her twisted thoughts. Mad with power, she had no concern for others. To Diamond Mind, it felt almost like blindness. Her tortured mind was consumed with revenge. But what Diamond Mind saw next sent shivers along his spine.

At the mountaintop, he saw Physique unzip her yoga bag. Inside was a long metal box. When she opened it, he saw her activate a bomb—a bomb she knew was a nuclear weapon! She set the timer for thirty minutes. Attaching the case to a silver cable on the drilling rig, she lowered the bomb down the shaft. Then, with a mighty tug, Physique ripped the cable off the rig. She even tossed the deactivation key somewhere in the woods!

Diamond Mind came back to his body on the beach. Numbly, he said the words, "There's a nuclear bomb.... It's going to take down the mountain."

Samsa spun Physique around. "You set a nuclear bomb?!"

Physique smirked before spitting on Samsa. "You're nothing to me."

"Oh, that's it," Samsa said. She decked Physique with a powerful right cross. Physique dropped into the sand, finally unconscious. Samsa stood over her like Muhammad Ali, wishing the fight could continue.

Seconds later, Agent Rollins walked up in his black suit and injected Physique with a tranquilizer strong enough for a winged horse. "That should keep her down," said Rollins, almost taking credit for the final blow.

"Where's the bomb?" Airspeed shouted.

Diamond Mind pointed toward the mountain. "It's along the fault line. There's a drilling rig. It's…." He'd seen pine trees and maybe some identifying rock formations, but he faltered, realizing he couldn't possibly describe it well enough to guide Airspeed. There were too many miles of terrain for her to stumble upon the site alone.

Airspeed's red sash flapped in the beach wind. She shouted, "How much time?"

Diamond Mind shook his head. "Not enough." The team looked at him, speechless. Two million people in the Canary Islands would die in minutes if he couldn't quickly get to a remote location that only he could see.

Airspeed tugged at her hair, looking panicked. Diamond Mind was too big for her to carry and fly—certainly not that far anyway.

But what to do? Diamond Mind reached into his *karmic* pockets to recall all the virtue he had collected in teaching Airspeed how to fly. He remembered the main principal of *karma*: anything you do *to* or *for* someone comes back to you. Further, he relied on one of the main teachings his lama had continually spoke around the world: "Whatever you want, you must give to someone else first."

Looking at Airspeed, Diamond Mind said, "There's a compelling need." He thought of saving others and the vast merit he had already generated. Then he leapt into the sky. For the first time, Diamond Mind flew.

55. BOMB SQUAD

DIAMOND MIND SOARED, SPEEDING TOWARD THE mountain location he held in his mind's eye. His body had turned slightly transparent and his skin sparkled as if only partially made of diamond. This was a new phenomenon— as was Diamond Mind flying. The blue racing stripes running down his arms tore through the wind. He felt as fast as a speeding bullet. Still, Airspeed easily caught him. Her voice cut through the wind: "You fly as slow as you drive."

Realizing he was barely faster than a softball, Diamond Mind asked, "How do I fly faster?"

"Grab my hand. Think supersonic."

Diamond Mind reached for her reassuring hand. Arial ramped up the speed like kicking in a jet fighter's afterburners, slinging them across the sky. "Whaaa..." uttered Diamond Mind. Airspeed nearly pulled his arm out of the socket.

The ground blurred. He almost blacked out. He couldn't believe they were traveling so fast.

When they approached the mountain peak, Diamond Mind let go of her gloved hand. He scanned the stony terrain, trying to imagine what he had seen from Physique's perspective. "There," he pointed. "I think she was between those two ridges."

Diamond Mind swooped down, quickly losing his sparkle. He landed as hard as a sack of tossed grain. While he tumbled across mossy dirt, Airspeed touched down like a ballerina on her tiptoes, scarcely making a sound. She said, "Landing is harder than it looks."

"You don't say." Diamond Mind shook off the fall while spitting out a mouth full of moss.

Rushing to the drilling rig along the fault line, he spotted the frayed end of a snapped cable. "This is the place," he concluded. There wasn't much cable left on the giant spool. Whatever Physique had lowered must be a long way down.

Standing nervously on the edge, Airspeed peered down the manhole-wide shaft that went dark immediately. A pocket of volcanic heat slowly rose from the vent, pressing against her cheeks. Flying in the bright sky was one thing, but she couldn't imagine plummeting underground. Airspeed backed away, looking for some sort of headlamp or other type of illumination, but Diamond Mind didn't hesitate. "Down the rabbit hole," he said. Then he leapt into the unknown—feet first.

Diamond Mind fell quickly. At first, his stomach rose worse than it had on any roller coaster. This had to be the strangest BASE jump ever performed. The volcanic heat increased steadily—five degrees every one hundred feet. Quickly, he pulled his *pranic* winds into his central channel to change into his diamond body. Descending, he occasionally glanced and scraped against rocky sides, but he was well protected now. Falling in the dark for what seemed like forever, he felt almost weightless... as if in space... or deep under the sea inside the belly of a whale. Bringing his mind to all the people he was trying to save, his heart started to glow white light. Soon, he was a shooting star crossing the night.

Over a mile down was a lake of dark water. The walls of this aquifer were the main concern of scientists. There wasn't consensus about what would happen if the water became superheated by volcanic lava flows. Would pressure escape through porous rock into the cooling sea? Or would pressure blast the top off the mountain?

Diamond Mind had just enough time to catch his breath before splashing hard into the underground lake. His momentum carried him deep under water, but he soon slowed. He pushed his hands against the rock sides to propel himself farther down the shaft. The water pressure at this depth was enough to crush an ordinary person's eardrums, but diamonds love pressure.

Fortunately, just a little farther down, the bomb case had turned sideways in the water and wedged between two rock outcroppings. Light from Diamond Mind's heart shimmered against the silver. It didn't look like much, almost like a case professional pool players might use for their favorite sticks. Diamond Mind grabbed the handle and unhooked the cable. Switching to flight mode, he raced toward the surface.

Moving through so much heat, his body steamed like a geyser when he shot out the top. Airspeed gasped.

After sticking the landing, Diamond Mind returned to his human form. Without even glancing at Airspeed, he popped open the metal case. Kneeling over the exposed bomb, Diamond Mind said, "When I woke up this morning, I didn't expect to be doing this."

Both he and Airspeed stared at the timer. There were only two minutes left on the clock. They'd just caught a live grenade, only millions of times more deadly.

"It needs a key," Diamond Mind said. But he knew their chances of locating the key Physique had tossed over the mountainside were next to impossible. "How do we stop it?"

Looking at the on/off switch, Airspeed said, "Maybe the key is only necessary to start it?"

"Are you sure?"

"No!" Her hands shook. The timer drifted past 1:45 seconds.

Diamond Mind closed his eyes and grabbed the switch. Airspeed clutched his arm. Boldly, he turned the switch....

After releasing their breath, they both realized they were still on the mountainside. Diamond Mind looked down at the timer: 1:30, and still counting down.

There were two wires connecting the timer to the body of the bomb. He asked Airspeed, "Red, black, or both?"

Airspeed pulled his hands away. "You can't just pull the wires. Once activated, it will still spark."

1:15 seconds. Neither had any idea how to stop the inevitable.

"Give it to me," she said. "I'll get it away from here."

Repeating her words in his mind, Diamond Mind understood what she was proposing. Airspeed could explode the bomb in the upper atmosphere—but it would certainly end her life.

"No," Diamond Mind replied, "I'll go. You still have things to learn here."

"I'll be faster," Airspeed countered.

Diamond Mind snapped the silver lid off in one strong gesture, so he could watch the timer. He tucked the bomb under his arm like a football. Leaping into the sky with the case, Diamond Mind called out: "I'll be fast enough."

As he sped away from the island, images of nuclear explosions filled Eric's mind. When a nuclear device detonates, it explodes with a force hotter than the center of the sun. Anything within the immediate blast range incinerates instantly. Diamond Mind tried to visualize his full diamond body, but he found he was unable to while flying. Instead, his skin remained only slightly transparent. It was just as well: diamonds may love heat and pressure, but no diamond could survive the center of the sun.

Even with his best track-star javelin toss, he wouldn't be far enough away to escape the blast wave of a nuclear bomb that would shatter and consume everything for miles.

In the final seconds of his life, Eric brought his mind to all he had learned. He had suffered from an early age, being abandoned in an orphanage. He had experienced success and love. But it was only when Eric had turned his mind to uncovering the causes of suffering and how to escape suffering that he truly began to learn.

Finally, on one momentous day, Eric had seen the deepest nature of reality directly. With that, he'd severed the root of suffering and achieved the highest purpose of a human life. When one pulls the plug, a bathtub can't fill with water; so too, Eric could no longer drown in suffering. All that he'd experienced since that day had been suffering draining out.

Since that time, Eric had spent every moment of his life trying to spare others from pain—willing to protect them as if they were himself. Because of this noble intention, his superyogic powers had emerged. Today, his unexpected abilities would allow him to protect millions. A worthy sacrifice, indeed.

Eric turned his mind to his next life; a life he had seen coming in meditation. He knew he would be even wiser and more powerful because he had proven repeatedly in this world that he was worthy of any power thrust on him.

Flying high in the sky somewhere over the Atlantic, Eric watched the last few seconds on the LCD tick away. *When I woke up this morning, I didn't know my life would end today.* But no one ever does.

With his final seconds, if Eric could teach the world one thing, he would say, "Give yourself away to others. Hold nothing back." But there weren't even birds at this altitude to hear his final words.

Three, two, one....

56. B00

INSTEAD OF BLINDING LIGHT FROM A NUCLEAR SUN, Diamond Mind found himself staring at a dim LCD timer. The frozen display read B00.

Floating in air, without thinking further, he tore both wires from the bomb. Nothing happened.

Looking at the timer again, he read it differently. Now he saw, "Boo."

What sick joke is this? This wasn't Physique's style.

Diamond Mind tried to remember Blindside's words. When the stealthy villain had violently interrupted Eric's attempt to bring Physique in peacefully, what was it that Blindside had said? *"The Bone Frightener has plans for her."*

Not wanting to bring anything dangerous back to the planet's surface, Eric unscrewed the tip to look inside—something he had not dared to do before. Inside, where the explosive radioactive core should be, he saw, of all things, a multicolored rubber-band ball. This didn't make sense. Physique believed she was detonating a nuclear weapon. Diamond Mind wondered, *How twisted is this Bone Frightener?*

As Diamond Mind flew back toward his team on the beach, he tried to comprehend the strange turn of events. He even felt oddly ambivalent about still being alive on this crazy planet.

Flying back took longer. While one could fly fast with a ticking time bomb, even a costumed superyogi felt silly carrying an elaborate case for a rubber band ball.

Diamond Mind landed on the beach in front of Airspeed who held her hands to her mouth in shock. Goggles removed, she had been crying. Airspeed punched Eric in the arm. "You didn't even say 'Goodbye.'"

"I'm sorry," Eric responded. "Too much on my mind."

Farther down the beach, Samsa and a team of black-clad Navy SEALs loaded an unconscious Physique into a Navy helicopter. Strapped into a stretcher, she looked like she'd be out for some time. At least that's what everyone hoped—except for Samsa.

Bringing the bomb to Rollins, Diamond Mind unscrewed the tip again; then shook the bomb. Rollins recoiled until he saw the rainbow ball of rubber bands fall into the sand.

"It's a fake," Diamond Mind said. "But why?" Agent Rollins shook his head. He had no idea either. But then a scary thought entered his mind. "A decoy? But for what?"

In the next instant, the team heard their answer. The sound of a huge, concussive, underground explosion thundered several miles north of their position. The ground rippled from the shockwave, knocking everyone to their knees.

Looking up, with the earth trembling and collapsing, Diamond Mind saw the unthinkable. The entire mountain range—at least a trillion tons of rock—was tipping slowly toward them and the sea.

Diving with others into the helicopter already taking off, Agent Rollins shouted, "Go, Go!"

Airspeed and Diamond Mind flew straight up, not believing their eyes. With their speed, they could clear the falling mountain range—but they were less certain about the helicopter.

What they saw looked like the entire world was being turned upside down. With the speed of a Mack truck, the mountain moved toward them. Nothing that big should move that fast. But lubricated by magma and liquefied sand and rock, the entire mountain seemed to be on wheels.

The helicopter pilot saw the top of the mountain filling his view. His instruments told him he was pulling straight up, but from his perspective it looked like he was diving into a cliff. In the co-pilot's seat, Agent Kirby squirmed. He was unable to suppress a squeal as the mountain bore down upon them.

Desperate, the pilot flicked off the governor switch and overspeeded the blades beyond all design limitations. The overload of g-forces damaged helicopter grip bearings, but the helicopter rocketed up. Stone struck landing wheels and even gashed the helicopter's bottom, but the daring pilot managed to keep the helicopter in the sky, clearing the bulk of the falling mountain by the narrowest distance.

From high up, Diamond Mind and Airspeed could now see six islands that in minutes would be waked by an enormous tsunami. Knocked out lights in the immediate area provided another telltale sign that an underground nuclear blast had just occurred.

When the mountain fell, the sound of thunder-slapped water was as if Zeus had just body-slammed Poseidon. After the earth disappeared, a mighty wave stood thousands of feet tall to strike the sky back.

Unable to stop the wave, Diamond Mind knew their only hope rested with an unlikely priest—who was in way over his head.

57. FATHER AGUA VS.
THE MEGA-TSUNAMI

AFTER DROPPING DIAMOND MIND OFF, FATHER AGUA had positioned the fishing boat in the deep sea between La Palma and highly populated Tenerife—just in case.

Even on the ocean, miles away, the terrible roar coming from underneath the Old Ridge of La Palma sounded like hell charging onto the planet's surface.

Father Agua stripped off his priestly garments, down to black trunks and a black T-shirt. He kissed the shining silver cross around his neck, and then he dove into dark water just as the mountain started to tumble. Father Agua saw the ominous fall and the giant splash. Bigger than any Goliath a shepherd could face, the mega-tsunami rolled his way three times faster than a bullet train.

Skeptical scientists had been right about many things: namely that La Palma couldn't fall under natural circumstances, and that a surface wave would dissipate before crossing the Atlantic. However, none of this would make a difference to the immediate coastal regions of the Canary Islands and even Morocco. Treading water, Father Agua had minutes before the terrifying wave—taller than a skyscraper—would overtake him.

Father Agua called on his vision of Jesus walking on water to rebuke the seas. Whatever happened now, he must not have fear, and he must not have doubt. His faith was as great as any who had walked the planet, because like Diamond Mind, Father Agua had seen the deepest nature of reality—an experience he labeled as meeting God. He saw that God was within everything. Thus, Father Agua could call on the divine nature within himself to demonstrate a miracle. Someone may have moved a mountain; but Father Agua would move an ocean.

Father Agua tasted the salty sea. *Think of water as firm. Increase the earth element.*

Concentrating, Father Agua worked to remove his mental image of water being wet. *Sometimes water can be hard like ice.* By first removing the mental connection that water could be only one way, he left space for a new image to arise.

Intensely focusing while still treading water, Father Agua felt the substance touching his skin become harder in quality. As it grew more and more dense, he began to rise. Soon his feet rested upon the surface. Father Agua boldly walked forward, confident in his command.

But Father Agua had to do more than walk on water. He had to raise it. Arms extended, Father Agua dragged water toward him. *Come to me.* He pulled as much as he possibly could. In some ways, this proved easier than drawing an underground stream through rock. But the volume was greater than anything he had ever directed before. Could he do the impossible? As he pulled, he stacked the height of the ocean around him, creating his own wave-like wall. Then, as if on a giant forklift, the priest rose on a cresting upswell.

He leaned the wall forward, starting his own wave to meet the approaching mega-tsunami. Quickly, he gained speed, moving as if he were standing on the back of a migrating whale. But his wave started to dissipate as he moved forward. *What's happening?* Father Agua realized he couldn't maintain two mental images: whatever he gained in speed, he lost in height.

He tried again with all his might to increase the height of his wave, but he started to falter.

Rolling toward him, the mega-tsunami blocked out the light of the sun. Dreadful, it looked like night coming to swallow him. If he couldn't get higher, his little wall would be little more than a speed bump.

Trembling, Father Agua raised his arms to the sky, calling on all that was divine to help him. There were so many lives to save. He begged, he implored. *By the power of whatever goodness I possess, please let me stop this wave!*

Just then, Diamond Mind and Airspeed each grabbed one of Father Agua's arms. Flying, they pulled Father Agua higher and faster toward the mega-tsunami. Teamwork freed Father Agua to concentrate on pulling water toward him. Now, the wave he generated grew exponentially, rising like a jutting volcano.

With only seconds left, all three superyogis realized they wouldn't clear the height of the mega-tsunami. But determined to create the biggest wave possible, they resolved to ride to the end. Airspeed stared into the dark wave's face and saw their shimmering reflection. They looked like colorful angels hoisting Father Agua off a cross.

When the waves crashed into each other, the three yogis disappeared into the foaming throat of the beast. Swallowing their wave in a thunderous collision, the jolted mega-tsunami convulsed and sputtered higher in the air. Then the mighty wave toppled over its cut foundation.

For minutes, the superyogis were gone from sight. Some large waves rocked the shores of nearby islands, but no more lives were lost.

Tumbling inside the foam, Father Agua pushed water away from them. They were like a beach ball dragged under the sea that eventually popped to the surface.

For nearly an hour they floated, exhausted on the exaggerated current that pushed them toward Tenerife, the nearest island. They were little more than limp leaves on the surface of a stream.

No one said a word. Instead, they marveled at the gorgeous blue sky, wondering how they were still alive.

Airspeed remembered that just before the final collision, Diamond Mind had pulled her and Father Agua to him, tucking behind their own wave—which took most the impact. His indestructible diamond body had taken the rest, but still the relentless pounding had felt to her like standing in front of a tornado.

After some time, a school of dolphins—curious about the commotion at the surface—swam up, squeaking and clicking, investigating the strange trio. For the moment, everything seemed peaceful and strangely perfect.

When land was in sight, Diamond Mind rose first from the ocean, flying up. Airspeed followed him. She felt relieved to be returning back to her element. They offered to carry Father Agua across the last stretch of water, but he declined. He simply said, "I prefer to walk."

58. EVERYONE

DIAMOND MIND, AIRSPEED, SAMSA, AND FATHER AGUA assisted with recovery efforts on La Palma. They also provided comfort to survivors who had witnessed their idyllic world split in two before tumbling into the sea.

Of the fortunate things that could be said, the southern nature preserve of La Palma, the Old Ridge that fell, was the least populated part of the island. And due to the superyogis' unusual efforts, millions were saved from the mega-tsunami. Still, there were deaths, particularly in one sprawling, self-contained resort complex that investigators identified as the site of the actual blast.

Like some disaster kaleidoscope, photos and video captured on cell phones and vacation cameras played around the clock on all the news channels. There was no end to the different angles people caught of the mountain's collapse and resulting tsunami. Even aerial views from remote-controlled drones with tiny cameras turned up, exposing the superyogis' efforts in creating a counter wave.

The official story was... well, authorities were still trying to compile an official story—one that could reassure the worldwide public that they were in control. This was as erroneous as eighth graders thinking that they ruled their school, but most preferred that conceit.

In short order, the superyogis felt overwhelmed by their newfound celebrity with grateful locals and the international press. There wasn't a newspaper, magazine, or television station that didn't lead with pictures and video of the superyogis in action. Whenever Samsa displayed her extraordinary strength or Airspeed pulled shipwrecked survivors from the water, vivid magazine covers followed. In one photo, Samsa lifted rubble with one hand while balancing a rescued child on her hip. The sunlight streaming behind her provided a halo worthy of the Madonna and Child.

Meanwhile, Diamond Mind added drama and urgency to search and rescues by hearing the thoughts of buried survivors in landslide areas. Each time another person was saved, hope and joy spread around the globe.

But there were also unanswered questions.

Already, powerful voices clamored on with an agenda to suppress superyogic activity. This contingent wasn't happy with new kinds of heroes surfacing. Understandably, these people feared powers beyond their own. They even openly ridiculed time-proven yogic and Buddhist philosophy that threatened their mundane views.

Diamond Mind could foresee a coming storm: a conflict in which an entrenched elite would do whatever they felt necessary to protect the status quo and materialist worldview that they believed best served them.

Meanwhile, supervillains Blindside and Agnite became the leading suspects in an operation that had planted the real nuclear charge deep under The Old Ridge. Mysteriously, contractors had drilled an additional irrigation tunnel during the recent construction of a notable resort hotel; this appeared to be ground zero for the blast. Agent Rollins was of course irate over the depth of the conspiracy and troubled over having to fight an invisible new enemy. His main question: *Who supplied the bomb?*

After people at the El Hierro yoga retreat described what they had seen to reporters, rumors regarding the mysterious pair of villains, both true and exaggerated, further increased people's fears.

As for Agent Kirby, he continued doing what he was best at: investigative research. Already, he had turned up several chilling references to the Bone Frightener in a terrible array of international crimes. Kirby sensed the Bone Frightener's activities might open doors to levels of complexity that few would be able to face—but he was still willing to travel into the unknown.

From further conversations with Agent Kirby, the Bone Frightener loomed in Vice President Lausunu's and Diamond Mind's thoughts like a dark shadow—though both men kept this figure from public discussion.

After two weeks of assistance and goodwill efforts in the Canary Islands, the Unusuals were finally called back to Washington. Exhausted, even Diamond Mind broke down, having his first shot of caffeine in years: two double espressos.

Waiting in Tenerife airport for their flight back to the States, the superyogis wore the least super outfits they could pull together in an attempt to go unrecognized.

Samsa lounged in an outfit that didn't suit her at all: a baggy, long floral dress with a floppy beach hat, Bono-style sunglasses, and white sneakers. She and Airspeed watched images on international TV of Samsa lifting heavy objects in what amounted to a bikini while Airspeed's bottom floated in the top frame. Shaking her head, Airspeed said to Eric, "When we get back, we're going to have a serious talk with the costume designers."

Samsa added, "And we both may have to be restrained."

Feeling grumpy today, Airspeed looked forward to watching an in-flight movie while someone else flew. She was wearing an outfit that could only be described as head-to-toe pink fleece. It gave her a distinctly Easter Bunny feel, but no one dared say anything.

Only Father Agua felt cheerful, doing his best to look like an amateur tennis player in tight white shorts, a yellow polo shirt, and white sweatbands on his forehead and wrists.

Sporting a La Palma baseball cap, jeans, and T-shirt that said "Canary Islands" over a leaping dolphin, Diamond Mind looked the most like a tourist. Certainly in these outfits, none of the yogis would be easily recognized as super.

Trying not to attract attention, they took turns doing some yoga stretches in the airport. Their bodies felt tight and sore after days of lifting debris. When Diamond Mind paused during a long hold *yin* stretch, the still grumpy Airspeed said, "You're not doing yoga. You're people watching."

Diamond Mind agreed. Feeling the buzzing effects of caffeine coursing through his body, he said, "I was just thinking how powerful each person is, but they don't even know it."

Airspeed looked at travelers nervously texting and chatting on smart phones while waiting for flights. She countered, "They're just ordinary people."

"Maybe," Diamond Mind said, "But I'm not so sure."

Sensing they were in for another teaching, Samsa suddenly felt the need to add push-ups to her sun salutations.

"Think about the eight traditional powers," Diamond Mind said. "If any of the ancient masters showed up in our world, they would think nearly everyone had yogic superpowers."

"Like sky walking?" Father Agua asked, enjoying the airport.

"Yeah," Diamond Mind answered. "To them, crossing continents through the sky in hours would have been miraculous. Now, we can fly while talking on a sky phone, sending messages around the world, and watching moving pictures at the same time. To yogis of old, everyone in this world would have powers."

Although there were many abilities, Eric's tired mind remembered a traditional list of eight yogic powers: the sword, the pill, the ointment, swift feet, taking the essence, sky walking, disappearing, and underground. Eric tried to imagine what a yogi from two hundred years ago would see if he or she were still walking the planet today as a *kaladanda*, someone who had overcome death itself.

Eric pointed at a television playing endless images from around the world and people on their computers surfing the Internet. "In ancient times, the sword power represented something that you held. It let you go wherever you wanted."

Airspeed got it. "So for us, it's a TV remote or computer." She was really looking forward to finally watching a movie.

"Exactly," Diamond Mind said. Stretching his neck, he checked out people wearing different types of clothes. He saw some Spanish women dressed to kill and others in tracksuits not unlike Arial's (well no one was in all pink like Arial). He couldn't say who held a more powerful job. "The pill is the ability to morph into different forms. In our culture we can change careers... change appearances. In ancient times, you were stuck to a caste and apprenticed to an occupation."

Father Agua—actually enjoying his ridiculous tennis clothes today—added, "Now it's not a big deal to be an accountant who teaches yoga on the side and goes from wearing a suit and tie to ashram clothes in one day."

Airspeed pointed to a teen-age girl strutting by in a tight T-shirt that read, "I heart Diamond Mind." Airspeed said, "From meditating hermit to international heartthrob... I bet you didn't see that coming."

Ignoring her, Eric pointed to a mother engaged in an overly loud video chat with her daughter on the latest smart phone—a device consolidating so much cutting-edge technology it practically bled magic. "The ointment is when you can see and hear what's occurring in another location."

Seeing the pattern, Father Agua shuffled his tennis shoes. He said, "Swift feet is traveling at fast speeds over land, like we can by car."

"But everyone has these abilities," chimed in Samsa, finally joining the conversation. "They aren't super."

Eric made his point again. "Wouldn't they be to someone who lived two hundred years ago?"

Eric thought about the unprecedented ripening of innovation. It took more than twenty thousand years for stone tools with handles to proliferate around the world, but only sixty-six years from the first powered flight over sand dunes to reach the moon.

Gazing at the wonder of it all, still hopped up on caffeine, Eric said, "I think this entire world is made up of people who have so much merit that they were born into a miraculous reality. And they just take it for granted."

Eric wished everyone would see for themselves how their experience of reality came from mental images—mere thought and label—projected from how they'd taken care of others in the past. Then, the biggest miracle could be revealed. All would realize that their world shouts, "You're close to full enlightenment! But only if you pursue some deeper wisdom, instead of just swiping your *karmic* credit card!" To Eric, it was an entire world of people with superpowers—but unfortunately, too many were just thinking about their own needs, instead of others'.

Adjusting his sweatbands, Father Agua asked, "What would the lineage masters warn about these superpowers if they saw us today?"

Diamond Mind thought before answering. "Mostly, that they can be a distraction from meditation and from achieving the highest purpose of a human life."

Samsa said, "So you want to teach people to put down their toys for a bit, take care of others, and meditate on ultimate reality."

"I'd like to," answered Diamond Mind wistfully. "Isn't life more important than endless emails and Internet surfing?" Then he shrugged, "Maybe everyone's so smart, they'll figure things out for themselves."

Diamond Mind closed his eyes briefly, sensing something deeper. Intuition was also a *karmic* ripening coming from helping others to make smarter choices. When he opened his eyes again, Airspeed asked, "What is it? What did you see?"

Eric felt connected to everyone in the world. And

this deepened his sense of responsibility. "If it's true that everything is a projection, maybe my whole world is a test. Maybe everyone else is perfect, just playing their role."

Even now, after all his studies and practice, Eric knew his heart could open more—that his wisdom could still grow. Eric knew he had further to travel to reach full enlightenment. Summing up his feeling, he said, "Maybe, it's all pieces of me and I'm the last to understand."

Diamond Mind saw a little blond boy with a red cape and rain boots pretending to fly. Eric saw him as an echo of his own mind. When the little boy swooshed to where Eric was doing yoga, Eric leaned forward and whispered, "Who are you saving?"

The little boy looked around, then whispered back, "I'm going to save everyone."

✧

SOURCES

The Superyogi Scenario is a work of fiction. However, this book relies on authentic scriptural and scholarly sources to explain the emergence of *siddhis,* meaning supernormal abilities.

Below, I've listed key scriptural and scholarly sources that support the narrative of this book in roughly the order they first appear.

I am grateful to the many teachers and scholars whose monumental translation efforts have made so many ancient texts publicly available for further study.

I encourage readers to come to their own conclusions about what types of transformation are possible for human consciousness.

Master Patanjali, *The Yoga Sutra.* Trans. Geshe Michael Roach for The Yoga Studies Institute, 2005.

Sri Swami Satchidanada, *The Yoga Sutras of Patanjali.* Buckingham, Virginia: Integral Yoga Publications, 2012.

Edwin Bryant, *The Yoga Sutras of Patanjali.* New York: North Point Press, 2009.

Yoga Journal 2012 Demographic Study.

Dean Radin, Ph.D., *Supernormal.* Deepak Chopra Books, 2013

Douglas Veenhof, *White Lama*. New York: Harmony Books, 2011.

Je Tsongkapa, *The Book of Three Beliefs*. Trans. Geshe Michael Roach. Arizona: Diamond Mountain University, 2008.

Arya Nagarjuna, *Root Text on Wisdom*. Trans. Lama Christie McNally. Bok Jinpa XII, IX, and XII. Arizona: Diamond Mountain University, 2006-2008.

Matthieu Ricard and Trinh Xuan Thuan, *The Quantum and the Lotus*. New York: Crown Publishers, 2001.

Sri Swami Sivananda, *Kundalini Yoga*. Tehri Garhwal, Uttar Pradesh, India: The Divine Life Society, tenth edition, 1994.

Bhagavad Gita. Trans. Geshe Michael Roach. New York: Yoga Studies Institute, 2007.

Master Shantideva, *Guide to the Bodhisattva's Way of Life*. Trans. Geshe Michael Roach. 3 Courses, Asian Classics Institute X, XI, and XII. New York: Asian Classics Institute.

Beatrice Bruteau, ed. *The Other Half of My Soul: Bede Griffiths and the Hindu-Christian Dialogue*. Wheaton, Illinois: Quest Books, 1996.

Je Tsongkapa, *Lamrim Chenmo: The Great Treatise on The Stages of The Path to Enlightenment*. Trans. Lamrim Chenmo Translation Committee; Joshua W. C. Cutler, editor-in-chief. 3 vols. Ithaca, New York: Snow Lion Publications, 2000, 2004, 2002.

The King James Bible. The Project Gutenberg eBook, 2004.

St. John of The Cross. *Dark Night of the Soul*. Trans. E. Allison Peers. New York: Doubleday, 1959.

Swami Satyananda Saraswati, *Kundalini Tantra*. Munger, Bihar, India: Bihar School of Yoga, 1984.

AUTHOR REQUEST

If you feel others would enjoy and benefit from reading this book, please post a review at Amazon.com, Goodreads, or with the bookseller you purchased this book from.

Honest reader reviews and word of mouth are the best ways to raise awareness of this book and get these ideas into our culture.

AUTHOR NOTE

Contributions from my author's royalties are donated to GoBeyond.org, a non-profit that teaches people how to meditate from scriptural sources in the Buddhist and yoga lineages. If you are interested in going deeper into the wisdom articulated in this book, I invite you to visit www.gobeyond.org for free guided audio meditations and further teachings.

ACKNOWLEDGEMENTS

For a book like this to succeed, with Eastern philosophy woven into the narrative, sizable shifts in the cultural landscape had to occur before a single word was written. I am grateful to the many scholars, yogis, and spiritual teachers in the world who keep the spirit of enlightenment alive through their work, example, and daily practice.

I had considerable help and guidance in bringing the final version of this novel to completion. Mostly, I want to thank Kristin Walsh who served as the front line developmental editor. She gave exceptional guidance and increased the vividness of characters, pacing, and sparkle of the book. Her cleverness can be best seen in her own remarkable work, *The Training of Kara Steele*.

Thank you to Bill McMichael, a yogi and former Air Force pilot, who also provided superb edits in addition to the background information and lingo necessary to bring Airspeed to life.

Thank you to Joyce Connor for helping as my research assistant.

Thank you to Bets Greer for her expert eye with the final copyedit.

I am particularly grateful to Jeff Chapman for his stunning work in creating the cover and character renderings to bring *The Superyogi Scenario* characters to life. Your talent is immense and you were wonderful to work with.

Thank you to Dennis Calero for the original illustration that provided guidance for the cover.

Thank you to Frank Vogt for posing as Diamond Mind and to photographer Teddy Sczudlo for his contribution to the cover.

Thank you to Rebecca Vinacour for taking the photo at the end of my three-year meditation retreat that is used as my author photo.

I feel mountains of gratitude toward the spiritual teachers who took so much time to teach me the Buddhist and yogic path. Thank you to Khen Rinpoche Lobsang Tharchin who first introduced me to such a deep path. Thank you to Lama Thupten Phuntsok for providing such an inspiring example of compassion and wisdom. Thank you to Geshe Michael Roach for so many remarkable years of teaching and gifting the world with extraordinary translations. Thank you to Lama Christie McNally for teaching me to meditate from authentic sources to learn how to experience the truth for myself.

I'm grateful as well to the yoga teachers who taught me personally enough *asana* so my body could sit comfortably in meditation. Particular thanks go to Jessica Kung and Stéphane Dreyfus, Mira Shani, Amy Mead, Tamara Standard, Earle Birney, and Kendra Rickert.

I am also grateful to the teachers at the Yoga Studies Institute and to Ben Kramer and Earle Birney for sharpening my understanding of yogic philosophy.

I'm grateful to my mom, Regina Connor, for providing such a good example in helping people daily as a social worker. And to my father, Michael Connor. Earlier in his life as a soldier he would often speak to me about military strategy. Now, as an engineer and inventor, he talks to me about how everything is light and love.

I'm grateful to Lisette Garcia for encouraging my fascination with superheroes and my drive to pursue this story from the beginning.

Thank you to the Raven Society who, during my undergraduate years at the University of Virginia, awarded me a grant in support of my creative writing. That early act of kindness gave me confidence in my writing ability.

The first drafts of this book were completed mostly on Sunday afternoons (my playtime) during a three-year meditation retreat in the high desert mountains of Arizona. I owe a further debt of gratitude to Rob Ruisinger, Nicole Davis, Scott Vacek, Orit Ben Besat, Chuck Vedova, Venerable Lobsang Chukyi, and the many anonymous caretakers who brought food to my cabin drop box. Thank you also to Doug Veenhof, John E. O., and Matt Gallup for their work building the cabin.

I am incredibly grateful to the thirty-four meditation superheroes who provided such a great example of continuous effort during three years of meditation retreat. You are a constant source of inspiration to me. I look forward to reading your books and watching all your great works.

Particular thanks go to Carmen Garcia, Liz DeJonge, and Joyce Connor for handling any special requests and even handling my finances while I was away in retreat.

I am grateful to Dennis and Sue Walsh for taking me into your home following retreat and giving me an opportunity to transition back into the busy world, finish this book, and get back on my feet.

Thank you to Jackie Lapin and Jeff Donovan at Conscious Media Relations for all your hard work and extra effort promoting this book. And much gratitude goes to Lilia Mead of Go Yoga for help with arranging the book tour launch.

I would also like to express my gratitude to my favorite writers of superhero stories: Mark Waid, Alan Moore, Christopher Nolan, Neil Gaiman, and Stan Lee. I am also particularly grateful to Andy and Lana Wachowski: *The Matrix* inspired me to start my own twelve-year journey to find "there is no spoon." These writers along with another of my favorites, C. S. Lewis, convinced me that I could combine fun with philosophy.

Finally, thank you to everyone who reads this book. I know you have many entertainment options. I'm grateful for the time you spent with me through this book. I hope this story entertained you and provided some inspiration for your own journey, in whatever form that takes. And finally, I hope you find spiritual guides that suit you to make all your dreams come true.

QUESTIONS
FOR DISCUSSION

1. At what point were you hooked by the story?

2. *The Superyogi Scenario* uses authentic quotes from scriptural sources like *The Yoga Sutra* to explain how supernatural abilities arise. What did you think of this device?

3. What was your favorite *Yoga Sutra* quote from the book?

4. Who's your favorite character and why?

5. Were you as surprised as Arial and Eric to learn that yoga was originally more a path of meditation than just physical poses?

6. How did you feel about Physique? What makes her a compelling villain?

7. How did you feel about Diamond Mind? What makes him a compelling hero?

8. If you could develop one superpower, what would it be?

9. How would you keep yourself from abusing your power?

10. What does *The Superyogi Scenario* say is the key to ending the cycle of violence?

11. According to ancient texts like *The Yoga Sutra*, all the supernormal abilities share one piece of wisdom: your experience of an outside world isn't separate from your mind and deeds. Do you think the wisdom revealed in this book will influence your actions in the world?

12. How has this novel changed you or broadened your perspective?

13. Did this book inspire you to want to meditate?

14. If you could ask the author one question, what would it be?

15. If you were to cast this as a movie, what actors would you choose for the lead roles?